I0585339

Crown of Fire

Awenmell Series : Book One

Lisa King

FELEN PRESS

Felen Press

Crown of Fire - Awenmell Series : Book One

Copyright © Lisa King 2018
Cover Art Copyright © Heather Musingo 2020

All rights reserved. No part of this publication may be reproduced, stored in a retrieval system, or transmitted in any form or by any means electronic, mechanical, photocopying, recording, or otherwise, without the prior written permission of the publisher.

ISBN 978-0-6483026-0-5 (eBook)
ISBN 978-0-6483026-1-2 (Print)

 A catalogue record for this book is available from the National Library of Australia

For You.

T hey won't hear me.

Even my footsteps are silent; drowned by the elders' ruckus that channels its way through the passageways, chasing me through the dark twists and turns, finally weakening as I scurry down a stairwell in search of a memory. The further I creep along the narrow hallway, the din above me muffles; barely discernable as I reach Eshnae's chamber. No longer gasping, I pause to listen at her door. Silence. The wooden door under my hand is warmer than the stone at my feet, and as I lean against it, it glides open and closes behind me as if I do not exist. There's space for me to breathe here; and my lungs suck at the air, over and over, as if they were prisoners desperately grasping for fading light.

They won't find me here.

My shoulders slump. Of course they will.

They always find me.

Eshnae! I've never seen her run before. She's twice my age. I hope she makes it.

Her room is smaller than it appeared in my childhood memories. Like me, she's lived surrounded by cold stone, yet she's been afforded a threadbare cloth that hangs over a small opening in the wall, allowing a soft light to play over her bed and chest. If I stretch as high as I can, my nose reaches the ledge of the window created by the missing stone. The brittle cloth holds firm under my gentle enquiry. On the other side lies the courtyard of Brennyn Hall.

As a child, I had no reason to wonder where her room was positioned within the Hall. One of her chamber walls meets the outer courtyard wall, and this window faces the main stable. The leather of my shoes pushes into the ridges in the stones as I strain to lift myself higher and catch a glimpse of the capping stones of the wall on the left. I hop down from my perch and try again; this time checking the right, where the gates that open the courtyard to the outside world stand tall. My toes sting, cramping at their unnatural hold on the tiny ledge of stone and beg for release. Shouts in the courtyard hold me still, breathless. My eyes dart around the walls, and the creak of the opening gates silences the pain in my toes and feet.

A small group of guards make their way across the courtyard towards the gate. Feeney follows them as they stumble along in a huddled formation and, once closer to the gate, struggle with the weight of their charge. They toss Eshnae's body outside the walls for her clan to collect. It rolls once or twice, settling next to the orange dots of some wild marigolds. The guards turn back to the Hall and I drop from my perch, uncertain of whether they noticed the cloth returning to cover the hole.

I have found my bearings.

Feeney flaps and squawks into my head as his talons scratch down the stone walls. The din inside my head causes me to tumble and my hands beat at my head in fury and grief. There is no way to stop his noise. Panic washes over me, toys with me, threatens

to consume me, then ebbs away. The last of my bravado from my
stand in the great hall drains through my feet as heaviness drags me
to the ground. My arms wrap around my body and for a moment I
believe if I just squeeze hard enough, tight enough, I will keep the
pain from spreading.

I am wrong.

Curled tightly into a ball, I squeeze and writhe, convinced I can
control and bear this moment. I'm practiced at remaining silent as
the pain works its way through my body, accusing and blaming,
ripping and tearing, searing and sealing. Eventually my heartbeat
slows, my breathing becomes steady and my mind clears.

"Get away from here!" I imagine Eshnae pulling on my arms,
pleading for me to stand, but I don't move. I remain curled on the
floor of her room and wonder if anyone would bother to collect
my body from the gates.

I nod a welcome to my sanity, grateful that I didn't wander into
the open fields in my panic to escape. My mind is partly back,
wandering and exhausted in a field of its own. The stone against
my cheek soothes me, drawing the heat from my face, and my eyes
close. Just as my eyelids settle, the coolness becomes sharp and
forms itself into icy fingers that grasp at me. They're still hunting
me. I push myself from the floor to escape the chill; my warm palm
bringing my cheek back to life. Distant voices in the hallway force
my brain and body to panic and reconnect before they are ready.

Strangely, nothing lives inside those seconds—just a paralyzing
void of indecision. Yet I emerge from their emptiness, opening
the modest chest at the foot of Eshnae's bed. The blanket inside
unfurls neatly onto the bed and leaves enough room for me to
squeeze into the chest. I make adjustments as I go, pulling at my
robe when it catches on a large splinter and twisting and turning

underneath its cover until my body takes up the least amount of space. My arm twists and contorts to pull the lid closed.

Confined now, I calm myself by concentrating on my breath. Next to my face, tiny seams of light show through cracks in the wood, but my mind finds more relief with closed eyes. Eshnae's straw doll is here somewhere with me; a hint of its comfort reaches my nose as hot, stale air squeezes my lungs and my body protests its contorted position. My heartbeat pounds in my ears and threatens to burst through my chest. I command my body to breathe slowly, to be calm, as my mind races with thoughts of suffocation and panic.

I should have run. This won't work.

They'll find me.

Get out!

I need air!

The door swings open with a bang and snaps my thoughts to silence. Determined footsteps and sharp voices enter the room. The men grunt and shuffle their feet as they move towards the bed. They would've already been to my chamber, seen the smashed in door and the shreds of my dress on the floor. But it's not what they think. It never is in this place.

A loud crack vibrates through the stones and the floor of the chest, and I imagine the bed flipped to its side.

"Waste of time," one of them mumbles.

"Isn't she the Lady of the Hall? She wouldn't be down here now, would she?"

"Feeney said to look everywhere."

The chest tips, and in a sudden thud, is kicked or shoved to its side. The light changes inside my cocoon as the lid flops open and my body tenses and rolls with the momentum. The rush of cool air is a relief; I hope the guards don't notice the exchange. Every muscle tense, I push harder, fighting against gravity and my inevitable discovery. A loud laugh outside the room distracts them and the men make their way through the doorway, shouting as they join the sport further down the passageway. I allow myself to gulp in the cool air around me as my muscles ache with fatigue. I won't move until the halls have remained silent for a while.

I creep around Eshnae's room in the shadows of dusk. An unearthly stillness intensifies the noise of the horses charging in and out of the courtyard. This constant contrast from peace to chaos, when I least expect it, infuriates me. I wish for the peace of darkness.

In the fading light, I examine the stonework of the ages. Brennyn Hall is ancient, and each generation has added to its history and size as time passed. According to the Council of Elders, it was bloodshed and battle that had kept the Hall from intruders during the last uprising. Those brutal years wiped many clans and families from our history and the elders claimed as long as the Hall stood, there was hope. I run my fingers along the rough-cut stone in this section of the Hall. Did the soul that laid these foundations ever mean for one of their descendants to prefer death rather than stay within its walls another night?

I sigh into the growing darkness. There was nothing unusual about this morn.

But the events that followed, that led me here. . .

And the words Eshnae said as she ran . . .

Patches of the day flicker in and out of my mind like candlelight trying to hold its own against a breeze. Snatched of light here and there. But understanding? I'm more confused than ever.

I gulp a breath as my chest constricts at memories. A wishing that events weren't so, but wondering what else they could possibly be.

I had woken dreaming about waterfalls again.

Eshnae had stopped describing anything outside the walls many summers ago, but her story about the waterfall had always been my favorite.

A stream has no choice but to follow the form of the earth.

My arm flopped over the side of the bed and wondered if waterfalls scrambled desperately against the forces that pushed them forwards. Or whether they simply abandoned themselves to the fall and caused delight just being what they are; powerful and uncontrollable. What would that look like? What would it feel like? My fingers slid down my neck. Sore throat. Not that anyone heard my screams in that part of the Hall, anyway.

The dark tapestry that hung precariously above my bed threatened me, just as it did every morning. *Come on then! Fall!* Suffocation might take too long for my comfort, but perhaps that's all I deserved.

The keys. They grated iron on iron like they usually did in the lock and rattled me from my challenge to the tapestry. My two maids, Eshnae and Bree, had entered as my feet touched the floorboards. They swept in a cloud of nervousness with them, the same cloud that arrived in the Hall every Council Day.

It was only a few silent steps across the chamber to my dressing stand, a carpeted circle raised a step above the floor and only a little wider than my body. Beside me, Eshnae held the copious amounts of fabric meant to transform me into the respectable "Lady of Brennyn Hall."

I widened my eyes and turned to stare into hers, mocking our morning ritual. Our noses almost touched, just like they've almost touched every single morning of my sixteen summers. Her eyes were soft and sad. Wisps of her dark brown hair escaped and fell around her weary face like they did every morning; no matter how she tied her hair. I used to imagine that if the flowers returned to her hair and the smile to her lips, she might have dared to sprout wings and fly around that miserable Hall scenting it with the marigolds from her forest clan. But today was like every other normal day. There were no smiles, no wings, and no marigolds. She nodded once, and I turned to face my reflection in the large mirror before me.

"You know he will want to check your eyes today," she reminded me.

My jaw tightened.

Of course he will.

Bree's expression was wooden, obeying the edict that only chosen servants could communicate with me—lest I fill them with evil, but her eyes contained her usual spark of youthful defiance. She gave a slight tilt of her head, wishing me a good morning, and with my eyes I wished her one in return. Then the pair gently guided me, removing my sleeping garments, and dressing me for the day ahead.

Bree bent to retrieve my clothing and a plait of her dark hair fell to the side of her neck. The pattern woven into her braid was only visible when touched by the gentlest light. It reminded me of the Trothsman who had arrived at the Hall the day before. Not the Trothsman himself; it's impossible to see under their dark clothing, but his horse—so sleek and powerful. The fastest horses in the land. Always black, forever energetically pawing at the ground or sweating with the heightened rush of an important message. Such majestic and fearful creatures. It's quite strange to admire something so dangerous, to swoon over their beauty and then earnestly hope their shining coats don't come calling for you. They seem to glow with an eerie light of their own, but the luster of Bree's hair reminded me that their glow is a mere reflection. An illusion.

I fingered some curls of my own hair hanging near my waist, hoping for a reminder of something as glorious as the color of a Trothsman's horse, but the only thing that came to mind was a dented copper pot I saw in the kitchen as a child. I flicked my hair away and squinted at my reflection, trying to imagine myself with elegant, long, dark hair, but all I saw was a fuzzy golden glow and I lost my balance on the stand.

Eshnae didn't even look up as she gently corrected my stance. Far away from my daydreams of horses and hairstyles, she stitched me into the day's dress. Her fingers moved with incredible skill and confidence over the green fabric, as if something had pre-destined them for that moment. My hands were useless in comparison.

What did they do?

What had they ever done?

Bree motioned for me to lift my arms to the side of my body, level with my shoulders.

Was that my life? To stand there like a tree, forced into a dress, my useless hands flopping at the ends of my branches?

They pulled the dress tight, and I frowned at the reflection in the mirror; I wondered what I did, or didn't do, to earn my particular fate. Surely our choices determine our fate. And if we alter our choices, we can alter our fate, so is anything really inescapable after all? My expression was as blank as when I had woken and didn't offer me any answers. Emotions only betray, giving the Hall an advantage—they're best kept hidden. I pursed my lips together and smiled in reprimand at the foolish girl in the mirror, the one who seemed to think choices fell from the sky, the one who wasted time thinking about choices when she had none of her own, and I squeezed the tears away before they did anything more than moisten my eyes.

Eshnae bound the soft leather shoes to my feet, then brushed at the unruly waves on one side of my head. Bree braided the other in our practiced routine to bring my hair under control. Confined within the dress, I too, was now under control. They joined me at the mirror and we honored their creation. An image so polished and perfect that it serves as my armor. Eshnae quietly took my hand, but there were no smiles, only concern.

Bang! I flinched, clenching Eshnae's hand as my chamber door smacked against the wall. Four guards charged in, shuffled, and created their formation before me. I relaxed my grip on her hand, grateful for support, and stepped from the stand with all the grace I could muster.

She led me to the center of the formation, two men at the front and two at the rear, that would deliver me down the stone passageways of Brennyn Hall. The guards never seemed proud to be in service, and every moment in their presence was as tense and unpredictable as their simmering anger.

Not that I would ever have preferred the Trothsmen to surround me. A strange cloud of emptiness follows those ones, as if the darkness of their clothes sucks in everything around them. Could I ever be like them, bound to the Hall, bound to nothing but duty? Dead inside, passionless. At least they know what they are, who they are. What would it be like to look one in the eye? What would their eyes say? What stories would their souls tell?

Around me, the guard's eyes were filled with wretched pain and an anger so fierce my eyes sought refuge from them on the floor. That walk was always the same. We followed ancient pathways, yet the steps we took lead us nowhere. Hidden in its sameness was my own routine of memory and emotions. They acted as glowing daggers on my heart, searing that moment into oblivion. Each stab and slice reminded me I tried to be obedient but somehow always failed, and that willful rebellion would result in much worse punishment. In time, the bruises and cuts healed, the tears ceased, and Brennyn Hall had won again. I was obedient only because they couldn't punish me if they couldn't fault me. By the time we reached the lord's chamber, my light was closed to the world, and my heart as sealed, constrained, and protective as the costume I wore.

The guards peeled off as they made their delivery, and left me exposed to the lord seated at the far end of the chamber. Dull light from a nearby window made a half-hearted attempt to illuminate his seat but was beaten back by the dust and darkness before it even entered the room. My stomach wrung and pinched at the sight of Feeney by his side. A wiry, dark-haired man, Feeney always reminded me of a raven sitting on the lord's shoulder squawking and making judgments. His black eyes bored into me and a smirk crept its way across his beak.

Breathe.

The mere sight of the man caused actual pain in my body, as if his presence contained some strange vice or torturous rack that squeezed my stomach and chest so tightly I had to use all my energy and concentration simply to breathe, leaving nothing for me.

Breathe.

A guard's fingers clamped around my upper arm and pushed me forward. "Kneel!"

I clenched my teeth and complied, grateful for the skins between my knees and the stone floor.

The lord forced his gluttonous body from the chair and lurched towards me. My focus stayed on his chair until his belt and the plush fabric of his tunic swallowed my vision. His hand latched onto my chin, squeezed and jolted it towards him. Pain shot along my jawline, but I refused to show him any acknowledgment. He stared into my eyes but didn't see me—his eyes darted, searched, and scanned. Then he had grunted, unfulfilled, released my chin and signaled for me to stand. I obeyed and quickly dismissed the tingling urge to rub my chin. The lord turned and mumbled something about today's council as Feeney moved to interrupt him with a nod in my direction.

The lord turned to face me again. "Smile!" he barked.

And I obeyed. I was his show, his achievement.

Yet, I know to keep quiet about the waterfalls that fall softly upon my head, as smooth as a jug of warm oil that fills my body with knowing and vibrant visions. Even if I could speak freely, I'd never tell him I feel the unexpressed intentions of others, that I am sure of secrets never acknowledged. The decree that demands I remain silent keeps me safe. My thoughts and understandings, however evil they might be, are the only things left to wrench from me. They are mine.

He turned his back on me, but rather than take his seat, the lord had looked through the window and leaned into the wall as if he begged it to hold him up, and sighed so deeply I wondered if he might be ill. I only wondered. I didn't care. He sighed again and watched the only road that leads from the forest, crosses the fields and continues to the gates of the Hall.

Without turning he announced to the room, "The elders are arriving, Ashling. The guards will escort you to the great hall."

I bowed my head.

"Yes, Father."

<hr/>

Two guards held the heavy arched doors open for my arrival and channeled me towards my seat. Icy air cut through the odor of stale wood smoke and goose bumps rose under my clothing. My feet stepped silently onto the raised platform that contained my solitary chair; the carved balustrade was designed to ensure I would always be on display while it sectioned me away from the remaining floor. The elders were yet to enter, and apart from the guards who remained at the door, I was alone to ponder the vast room. It was a space large enough to hold endless possibilities, but at each full moon remained as dark and lifeless as if the moon had not graced us with her wisdom at all.

Narrow windows created slices of light that beamed along the long wall. Their glass panels bent the light and looked like a crone's fingers trying to scratch a message into the waxed heavy tables. The elders would slam their fists on those slabs of timber by the day's end, ensuring enough noise to scare away the silence. Any message left there wouldn't be seen. Nor would they would see it along the walls, nor on the doors at each end of the great hall; there was nowhere to leave a message there. No truth was welcome.

My chest stung, and no matter how I shifted in my seat, the dress wouldn't let me catch my breath. My heart boomed in my ears and nausea rose and fell within me. Just another council day.

Remain calm.

Breathe.

My hands rested dutifully in my lap, but underneath, I pinched my fingers with such force that my mind stayed occupied on the pain. To survive today, that's all I needed to do.

Survive.

Life's easier if I focus on one thing. It seems there are many ways to die before you're fully dead. Lots of steps, like a staircase. Each step takes you further down until you've forgotten how far you've descended. You don't even notice the darkness; you become part of it. And nothing much matters down there, anyway.

The elder's shouts invaded the great hall before their bodies, and even with the warning, their presence buffeted me when they arrived. Tension followed the elders like a strong wind that then settled and clamped around my body. The danger didn't lie in their daggers or their swords. Their leathered armor was always imposing with its studded metal and thick belts, as were the strongmen who attend council by their side. The danger lurked inside them, as unpredictable and savage as a wounded dog.

M ost of the elders acted as representatives of the lord's holdings and were men I saw at every council. They ignored me
and my jagged breath and continued to argue, back slap, posture
and preen, and only formed a loose order of respect when the lord
arrived and took his seat. Feeney trailed behind him, shiny, dark
and smooth, the jeweled book of law under his arm. I concentrated
on the invisible dagger that twisted inside my stomach. I pinched
at my hands again and forced its blade to turn to mist.

There was nothing unusual in council either. Reports from each
holding brought the elders to order; cheers and thumped tables for
the Hall's successes, shouted promises of retribution for anything
less. There was more tension this moon though; as if they all feared
to address something. The coming unrest; maybe it all started with
Ronell. Maybe it was him that sent this day awry.

Elder Ronell stood. Of course he did; his province was in the
East. The others saw his holding as a barrier to protect them. They

needn't worry about the unrest—surely it must destroy Ronell before it comes to them, and he has good men.

"News comes from the East," he began. Ronell stood firm, coughed away the tremble in his voice, and tugged at the sleeves that covered his scarred arms. I've watched his scars appear and change in shape and color with each full moon council. He might be an elder, but at least he fought alongside his men in battles worthy of his strength. "Unsettling rumors of lights—of noble houses and cities falling. None are like they once were."

Silence.

My chest ached, and the pain spread through my body. *Breathe.*

"Death to the invaders!" a voice shouted, followed by loud agreement from the others.

"It travels this way, my Lord." Ronell raised his voice and covered the rumble of the elders. He faced them now, extending his hands to calm them before dropping them to his side. "And all should know: there are no invaders—this unrest... it comes from within."

The elders erupted and shouted curses of death at the unrest, yet searched each other's eyes for solidarity, checked for stability in their alliances, and questioned who could best withstand this fresh assault moving in from the East. Even now, I don't understand why no one mentioned the Eariss.

Feeney squawked into the lord's ear and stood, positioning his hands under the book he held as it effortlessly fell open and revealed its laws and consequences. He straddled the words, riding them with unquestionable authority; drawing from the pages a host of brutal examples to bolster the men and remind them of his power.

"Only the strictest of our laws," he said, holding the book aloft, "Will keep your holdings safe from any ruthless uprising. Those who foster this unrest are lawbreakers, and we will treat them as such!"

The men raised their arms, cheered, and thumped on the tables for good measure.

Why didn't he tell them all he knows about the Eariss? My eyes strained and I corrected my frown before Feeney noticed. Surely it would have comforted the elders if Feeney told them the things he regularly spat at me? How the Eariss was behind the uprising and was coming to feed on my evilness and spare everyone else? Then they'll all be safe. He could even tell them about how he's going to banish the Eariss forever after it destroys me. Surely that would have calmed them. I've seen how the thought of the Eariss brings terror even to Feeney's eyes. Yet the bedlam continued.

It comes from within.

Elder Ronell's words stirred inside me as a strange concoction of excitement and dread. The last unrest had been so brutal, the Hall had created new laws to end the murderous rioting as people fought for power and houses fell. It wasn't just the invaders who slaughtered entire families; ambitious, mid-born families took advantage of the bloody chaos with their own sense of justice. Now any suspicious or untimely high-born death results in the rewriting of the family's succession. But Ronell said this is *inside* the kingdom. What level of brutality would they need to defeat unrest from within? Invaders were surely easier to deal with.

It was then that Feeney developed a small twitch. He seemed oblivious. My teeth pinched at the lining of my mouth so I didn't smile. Whenever someone mentioned the unrest, it was as if they had stuck him with a pin. Each pin spread him open like a raven in a butterfly collection. Could simple pins hold his menace? Would there ever be enough pins in the world? The elders continued to question him, urging him to clarify his stance, and he became flustered, stumbling over his words. His hand wiped at the leathered scar on his cheek as if he was trying to wipe it away; at other times, he swatted at it. He eyed me and talked to the elders, agitated. The pressure within him swelled; I tasted blood in my mouth.

My humor had fled. Comply. I needed to stay blameless.

Thoughts are forceful things though, barging in without asking and ransacking my mind. Memories don't understand boundaries and they gently seduced me before they twisted and turned with such savagery, they made me catch my breath. I pinched my hands to remain stoic under his gaze while the images flashed before me. Memories sent by Feeney himself to terrorize me.

A fingernail pierced my skin.

I refused to break.

❧❧❧

C ouncil moved on, its business unfinished and unsecured. Feeney looked at me, his eyebrows raised in challenge as he announced the first trial.

Did he know?

He must have.

He knew my heart ripped open with every untruth. That watching their bullying sport caused me physical pain, that holding my silence and being party to their trials terrorized every part of my body.

Two guards walked a bent man to the center of the gathered elders, who closed in around him. Feeney strutted around the man and made accusations of treachery and poisoning, his wings wide and flapping to stir up the elders. The accused looked at the floor, bewildered and resigned. He wore peasant's clothes, his dirty shirt hung from his body as forlornly as his head. Dried blood matted strands of his hair and in my mind's eye I saw him in the sun, working the fields. His two children. His home. His life. His innocence.

Then blood.

The knife I thought had faded to mist turned violently in my chest. My breath came in tiny gasps, bile crept up my throat. Outwardly, I sat with my hands perfectly poised in my lap, but inside I crawled along the floor of the great hall, heaving and weak, clutching at my heart. Pain bound me and allowed no escape, and still the peasant wiped his hands.

By the Stars man, would you stop wiping your hands!

My palms were hot. Red from rubbing them on my skirt. I hadn't even noticed. Feeney watched me and chuckled.

Enough!

My legs pushed me to stand as if I was some kind of offering on their behalf.

I cleared my throat, more in horror at my action than to actually speak, while my fingers fumbled along the oak balustrade before me, half grasping and half sensing. Slack-jawed elders who had momentarily turned to stone stared up from the floor before me.

"She speaks," one said.

It did not surprise me they were astonished or had no idea how to behave. Neither did I. What was the protocol? I'd never spoken in Council.

Feeney's dark eyes flashed from the other side of the gathering, and he strode towards me. I'm familiar with the blows impudence brings. I had to speak before he got any closer. My hands fidgeted along the rail as I tried to find the right words.

"Traitors should be punished!" I called to the men, and they replied with cheers and curses.

Feeney's sharp attention switched between the men and my face and he slowed his stride, standing cautiously with the men on the floor.

"This man carted hay for Feeney this morning; at Feeney's direction."

My voice was squeaky, unsure, and a quake shuddered its way from deep inside me to my skin. At that moment, retreat was still possible. I could apologize. Perhaps I'd only receive a simple beating. But in the center of the elders was the face of a man torn from his family, blood streaks in his hair and eyes wider than I had ever seen. I also saw in vivid detail the events of that morning, as smooth and clear as the water I imagine tumbling over my head.

I pointed to the peasant, who dropped his gaze to the ground. "Another poisoned the lord's horses—for this very sport. And for treachery. Feeney is your traitor!" My voice was now strong and sure and surprising.

The elder's shouts dissolved into a confused argument, and I grasped the balustrade as the quake threatened to overtake my body completely.

A guard touched Feeney's shoulder, and he flung the guard to the ground and stood on his throat. "Don't touch me!" he screeched with a force well above the elder's din.

It was as he always said. I had spoken and the entire world was falling apart.

Lord Brennyn's voice bellowed, "Ashling! You will sit down!"

Feeney lunged at me then, flapping his wings and squawking, and the elders yelled and fought among each other; unsure if I'd gone mad or told them the truth. Perhaps I was mad, because I smiled at the chaos. The peasant escaped through the far door and I waved to him. If they had killed me then, I would have died happy. A life saved on my account. A worthy swap, the lightness of his joy to justify the weight of my existence.

Feeney jumped the balustrade and pulled the hair at the back of my head. Pain shot through my scalp and my back arched as he pulled my head towards him. "How dare you—filth!" Droplets of spittle landed on my cheek, along with his insults.

Amusement faded from my heart, sucked into that strange viciousness in his eyes, but I wasn't scared. I conjured up a small smile and a quiet proclamation. "Liar." How I wish my eyes could have transformed to daggers, dig his eyes out and finally end the rage that lives in them. It wouldn't strangle my bravado, force me to cower in the corner and await my punishment. I would not behave.

"Earissssssss!" he squawked for all to hear and threw me to the ground. Was it just to confuse the room?

The Eariss was here? Where? It's come for me?

I rubbed at my eyes and the room was in such an uproar it was as if another hundred men had entered the hall. The sound of so many swords released from their sheaths at once sounded familiar—it was the magnified rasp of the iron lock. The elders shouted against evil and drew their weapons, unsure where any of their alliances now lay. The room swirled with fear. Fear of being overtaken, fear of losing, fear of nothingness. I knew little of the Eariss, only that its evil presence would destroy our world.

"Feeney, explain yourself!" The elders surrounded him; weapons drawn. Feeney jumped back with his arms wide to control the crowd and calmed them, assuring them justice would be done, while the lord continued to shout across the hall for me to sit down.

I scrambled to my feet and within seconds, Eshnae appeared beside me and pulled me from the fringe. My eyes widened to absorb the turmoil around me as she dragged me back through the doors of the great hall.

I created something, even if it was only chaos.

We raced through the hallways; Eshnae in the lead. My dress, ever my captor, threatened to trip me as often as Eshane's robe tangled her feet. The shouts of the elders and the horror on Feeney's face acted like strong ale on my mind. Drunk with pleasure, I smiled, almost laughed, with the joy of it all.

Feeney—explain yourself!

Excitement bubbled through my chest, erupted into laughter and sapped the energy from my legs. The flames of the torches flickered with the rush of our passing. It always saddened me that these walls needed torches on a midsummer's day, but today I laughed at their weakness.

"Hurry along, girl." Eshnae pulled my arms, her voice fighting its way above the shouting elders. She babbled about clans and legends as we headed towards my chamber. It was easy to dismiss her voice when there was more joy in conjuring images of their shocked faces. I giggled and leaned against the door frame.

"Did you see his face, Eshnae? Did you see it?"

Her muttering dissolved to whispers as she concentrated on the lock. I opened my mouth, but she held up her hand, pushed me through the door and locked it behind us.

E shnae's face was red, she panted and puffed out words that made no sense.

"Eshnae, I wish you'd stop your mumbling. I just saved a man's life. What on earth have the forest folk got to do with this?"

Eshnae's voice was laced with sorrow. "I was told to keep you safe and I've failed." She extended her hand toward me. "Look what they've done to you. Look what I've done to you. Just look!"

Green skirts billowed over my legs, but I couldn't see anything that showed what she was talking about. I was still searching when I caught Eshnae's movement from the corner of my eye. She charged towards me; her eyes filled with rage. I backed away but not in time as she ripped the dress from the front of my body, tearing the fine fabric from the stitches she had so deftly worked a short time before.

I covered myself with my arms. "Eshnae, have you lost your mind?"

She tugged at the emerald sleeves and when they wouldn't rip; she peeled them down my arms, jerking my limbs when the sleeves refused to obey. With a single-minded determination, she removed every thread of my costume, my image and my restraint, and left me standing in my undergarments, surrounded by a sea of green. She stepped back from me panting; her face a curious mix of loyalty and pain.

"You must be free. Get away from here! Now! Before you...." Her voice quieted to a mumble.

My teeth didn't clench at her command; Eshnae had never ordered me to do anything. She removed the traveling robe from around her shoulders and hid it beneath the pillows of my bed. She offered her hand, and I stepped out of the remnants towards her. Still holding my hand, she took a breath, stepped closer and bowed her head.

"My confession, dear Ashling."

My hand wanted to recoil. Confessions are for the dying. A life without Eshnae? What have I done? She would end like the others. But I couldn't pull my hand away. I wouldn't cause her more pain. I took her other hand in mine, bowed my head so it leaned against hers, and closed my eyes to accept her last statement of peace.

"My dear, you must know this truth—my ambition placed you in danger. This fool is to blame. Grand halls and fine clothes...." She squeezed my hands to her chest and sobbed. "They told me to keep you safe in the forest, keep you hidden. I–I didn't believe. You have to go now. Go! Find what hides in plain sight."

I opened my eyes, staring into hers as they had done so many times before. This time her eyes were so sorrowful they poured her heartbreak into my own heart that was threatening to burst with pain.

Sudden shouts in the hallways. Our heads snapped towards sound.

"They'll be here soon," she whispered, and I chased her to the door and held it ajar.

"What's hidden, Eshnae? Where do I look?"

She squeezed halfway through the gap, stopped, and leaned back to kiss me on the forehead.

"It's you, don't you see?" Her lips moved within the crack of the door. "The truth is hidden right in front of you. Use your eyes. The world waits for you to see. This world needs you to see."

The click of the lock vibrated in my chest, and she was gone. My focus stayed on the lock while I tried to absorb what was happening. My heart pounded in my ears. Its steady rhythm set the pace of the spinning room. Heavy footfall and shouts outside my door caused me to retreat. My eyes stayed on the door as I stepped backwards, finally aware of the true danger on the other side. I don't care for my *own* life, and he knew that way before I dared admit it to myself.

The chamber door burst open and a cloud of splintered wood delivered the door to the far side of the room. I watched it slide by, determined to not be shaken by his latest tactic. The guards charged, then halted at the sight of me in my underwear. Feeney's anger blinded him as he stormed in and grabbed my shoulders, shook me violently and screeched, "Where is your maid?"

My contempt surprised me. Teeth clenched, I stared deep into his black eyes, daring him to something I knew nothing of, but feeling unafraid. His claws dug into my shoulders and he shoved me to the ground with such force he had to stride after me before he could slam his boot onto my chest. Above me, he collected mucous and saliva as I tried in vain to wrench his foot from my body, and turned my head as he aimed, splattering his disdain over my cheek and neck. He released his boot, clipping my chin in promise, and shook his taloned finger.

"Look what you've made me do. You will watch them die, and this time you *will* weep!"

The shout in my mind couldn't make its way to my lips. He stepped over me and rallied his guards in search of Eshnae. I scrambled after them, wanting to shut them out only to discover the locks I had despised all my life have abandoned me, leaving me frail and unprotected.

An unscathed fragment of green cloth made a welcome rag to remove every trace of him from my skin. Torn cloth and splintered timber lay everywhere about me, and unsettled dust formed bars of light across the room. My focus drifted to the pillows. Eshnae's command returned and sparked life into my trembling legs. Each step I took towards the bed charged them with strength and resolve.

As I pulled the robe from its hiding place, a tiny straw doll fell to the floor. Its gentle thud softened my heart. My fingers curled around it, and the familiar faded straw crinkled in my hand as I instinctively brought the doll to my nose. Not half the size of my hand, it contained the most kindness I'd ever received. I closed my eyes and breathed in once more, the hint of horse hair just discernible now. With a smile, I remembered Eshnae telling me that hair from Mardu's mane filled the little doll. I remembered long nights when I would rely on its scent to remember him and beg him to return and rescue me. I thought about the horses that donated pieces of their mane over the years for Eshnae to continue her gift, providing secret comfort to a frightened little girl. I remembered to open my eyes before my memories show me the blood seeping around the cobblestones. Eshnae's latest gift to me was time. I dropped the doll onto the bed, secured the robe around me, and moved towards the shattered door.

The continuing shouts and thumps from the great hall were louder at the doorway. The lord's voice boomed in the lulls, then the snaps and snarls of the elder pack took it down. I imagined them watching, circling, as they demanded Feeney die for his treason. Some shouted a reminder it was the prisoner on trial, a louder voice interjected for the death of the accuser. I rushed to the bed, grabbed the straw doll, and ran through the doorway at speed.

The moon rises through the small window in Eshnae's chamber and shares her wisdom with me. The hallways are quiet enough for me to hear her.

"But that's the difference you see," I whisper to her, "I will make it this time. I've no idea what Eshnae was talking about, but the answer is out there. And she said I must go."

Do the people outside the walls, the ones Eshnae told me about in secret; the ones who live in villages and forests, and farm the land and swim in streams of water, does the Hall silence them too, or will they provide the answers for me? I bite my lower lip. What if they don't exist? What if every story she told was untrue?

The moon is round and bold and takes up most of the window space. My breath catches in my throat. If I can fit through there, I'll avoid having to navigate the hallways. The chest rasps across the stones and I squeeze my eyes shut, wishing I had thought of moving it while horses were in the courtyard. Laying the robe underneath the chest dulls the sound a little, but it takes longer than I'd hoped to position it under the window.

From atop the chest, I lean up and forward, not knowing what I should hope for. My arms reach through the thick wall as the stone edges of the hole scrape the skin on my shoulders, but I'm sure I can make it through. I rock side to side and wiggle backwards. My feet find the chest again and I jump down, wrap the robe around me and stand on the chest again, but the hole is too snug on my shoulders. I won't fit if I take the robe with me.

The hallway is not an option. I consider my plan again.

What plan?

There is no plan, only a desperate longing to move forward.

The robe falls to the floor with a soft thud. I shuffle into the window space, my arms pulling me through until my head is clear of the wall. Dark clouds now stifle the moon's light, but I notice the shadow of the courtyard wall on my left, the vile cobblestones below me, and there's occasional foot traffic in the distance. The courtyard wall is out of reach. Even if I was standing, I couldn't leap that distance. Squinting, I spot an irregular placement of stones above me. Turning over in a confined space tests my patience, but I move in small increments and am soon on my back with my shoulders free of the wall, my arms and hands stretching above me. The ledge that the odd placement has created is not as wide as I'd hoped, but it's a solid beginning. This has to be my way out.

Eshnae's room is humble and quiet when I re-enter to prepare myself. The robe comforts me with her presence as I wind it around my leg and place the doll between my teeth. Hoisting myself up to the window, I ease my way through the thick hole on my belly. My chest is soon free and I struggle to suppress my grunts as I turn around to face the night sky. A bold moon hides behind a cloud and shares the moment of suspension with me; we are both neither here nor there.

My finger grip slides along the gritty ledge as I pull my lower body through the window. More ledges reveal themselves as my arms reach higher. The drop to the courtyard below isn't life threatening, but being discovered there surely is. I pull and push and stand on the outside of the window space, hanging onto the overlap of stones above me with my hands. The stones scrape my face as I look across to the wall. It's only a short distance away. The other side of the wall slopes into the fields and is higher, but I'll half-climb, half-fall it if I have to.

I take a breath and support myself from the ledge. My fingers and hands sting and scream as I ask them to support my bodyweight. They tremble, threatening to dump me onto the cobblestones, as I desperately try to placate them by shuffling to find a firmer hold. A better handhold soon relieves my hands and my feet find a slightly wider ledge. A slinking sensation runs down my left leg. The robe! The stone's surface has loosened it and I point my toes up to create a hook to stop its fall. As I turn my head to see how close I am to dropping the robe, I notice red spots in the distance.

There are approaching torches on the road.

Trothsmen!

Fear shocks me into action and mutes every muscle in my body as I scramble towards the wall. One more large stone across and I grunt as I stretch my right foot and it encounters the top of the courtyard wall. My right hand, then my arm, hugs at the corner of the Hall. I'm almost there. I place as much weight as I can on the stable capping of the courtyard wall. My left hand releases its grip on the stone as I pivot and lean down towards the courtyard to collect the robe dangling from my foot and I lose my balance.

No! No! Not the courtyard!

My arms flail around and tangle in the now-loose robe. I flap blindly and swing and sway in panic, then over-correct my balance, falling backwards from the top of the courtyard wall into the darkness.

P ain unlike anything I have experienced before is radiating
from my chest. I can't move, I can't do anything, I can't even
breathe. Anger rises. I've made it outside the wall only to die flat
on my back on the ground! I imagine the guards finding me in the
morning and console myself that they will at least report that they
found me *outside* the walls.

My breath returns, small timid gasps at first, then huge gulps
as the pain eases. I look up at the shadow of the wall and clench
the earth around me; cool blades of grass interlock my fingers in
welcome. I hesitate before I let them go, then cautiously check
my limbs for damage. I wince at my own touch but am thankful
nothing appears broken.

The moon shares enough of her light for me to see the shadow of
the robe, and after a short search, I find the doll nearby. I stand and
take in the dark fields while a cool breeze draws goosebumps on my
skin. The forest waits for me at the end of the sloping fields, yet I
can't resist looking behind to the stones towering above me. Their

darkness reaches into the night sky and tries to cover the stars, but the further I move away from them, the more light I see. My arms swing the robe over me in a flourish, and I invite the walls to watch as I pull the hood close to my face and head to the woods.

The edge of the forest beckons me inside just as the moon takes her place to brighten the fields behind me. The trees, sparse at first, have closed around me, blocking the light and making the way more difficult than I imagined. A gap in the canopy allows me to stand in the moonlight and adjust the robe, thread the doll to my belt and choose which direction to travel. All I see is darkness.

I push the hood from my head and stumble into the dark bramble, tripping and grasping blindly at everything. My mind tries reasoning with me, but I ignore it, focusing only on my need to keep moving. With each step, my ability to distinguish between real and imagined threats blurs. My hands and feet land on things that slush and move and wiggle. A scream tightens my throat and battles the belief that I should remain silent and unseen, but loses before it gains any strength. My eyes do their best to adjust to the darkness, ignoring my quiet pleas that I much prefer ignorance. Patches of dappled moonlight highlight shapes and branches that appear familiar and solid—until they move unexpectedly. I can't trust my own senses. Panic rises with each step that leads me away from everything I've known. I don't know where I'm going or what I'm doing. My shoes slip in the mud and I tumble and become further disorientated. Nauseous, I vomit as I move, my hands scratched and bruised from clinging to things I'm not sure even existed.

My feet are heavy as I come across a low bush and shake it, only half prepared for whatever might emerge. After a few more shakes, I crawl in under its fanning branches. Stray twigs pull at my hair and scratch at my forearms, but I ignore their protests, curl into a ball and cover myself as much as I can with the robe. The earth is soft under me. My body releases its tension and pain as it melts into the heaviness of exhaustion.

As I rest into the earth, my body disappears. There is nothing in the world but my thoughts, but my eyes remain open in the darkness. When I close them, faces appear. Flashes of scenes and shouts. Blood and cobblestones. I try to keep my eyes open, but before long the scenes play again and I can't make them stop. They march across my open eyes, leaving me unsure if I am dreaming or if they have invaded my mind.

Eshnae is speaking, but a bird squawks so loudly I can't hear.
The chest screeches across the courtyard and shatters.
Bree's body is dressed in green and thrown into my chamber.
Elders shout and scream.
Eshnae's sorrowful eyes.
Feeney's laughter.
Squawking.
Trothsmen.
Blood.

My body jolts and I lift my hands to my eyes to be sure they are open. My hands touch the branches of the bush surrounding me.

I am awake.

Alive. Under a bush in the forest in the dead of night.

I am free of the Hall.

And I don't feel anything. I am numb.

⁑

I awake with a start and squint at the morning light. I lay still, safe within the leafy hollow, and listen and watch with wide eyes. Birds converse in songs and calls both loud and soft while other life buzzes and whirs by. A certain crispness, a strange and refreshing newness, scents the air. One bird calls; I listen for the reply of another and smile when I hear it answer.

My mind tries to convince me I am dreaming. I'm not interested in arguing, and I roll to my side to enjoy the song. I'm sore but rested. My heart feels as heavy as an iron lock, but as I close my eyes to listen to the forest's song, it stops seeking my attention. Perhaps it is listening too. There are no stones here, so maybe it will feel safe. Is this what safety feels like? Sweet songs and rest, color, and not a stone in sight? The crescendo plays and dances with the silence, and little by little the forest noises settle into a soft music of their own, creating tunes and melodies only heard by the quiet and attentive.

I crawl from my hiding place and stand to brush stray leaves and twigs from my clothes and hair, squinting as my eyes adjust to the dappled sunlight coming through the trees. It's not as bad as I thought. Once free of its shadows and my imagination, the forest is warm and accepting. Greens turn to yellows when the sun hides behind them, and as much as I'd like to explore, reminders of the Hall creep into my mind and the urgency to move tugs at me. It leads me towards sloping land where a small stream in the gully quenches my thirst. The sound of cart wheels and horses' hooves wind their way through the trees and tell me where I will find the forest road.

On my way out of the gully, I listen for more horses, straining, hoping for a clue, and I slip on a rock and tumble halfway back into the gully. Wet leaves cling to my lower legs and slide off as I wipe them away, leaving streaks of light mud on my skin. The fall hurt more than it should have, and I sit and catch my breath, rubbing at my body where bruises upon bruises are likely to appear.

The forest road first appears as a clearing in the trees. I peer at it from behind thick trunks, crouching in the underbrush as I move closer. The road is quiet now. It's only a serene dirt path through the middle of the woods, yet it could fill with charging Trothsmen at any time. I pull the robe tighter and walk alongside the road, hidden by the trees and ready to draw on the forest's protection in an instant. The simple strip of dirt that travels beside me is an enemy waiting to attack, and I eye it with suspicion at every opportunity. Pain chants at me with each low bough I pull myself over. Every sting in my muscles reminds me that as I squeeze between bushes and vines, I move further from the Hall.

My hands pull me over a log and I notice their strength for the first time. It hurts to make a fist, and my fingers wiggle with the joy of release. Although untrained and weak, I feel ridiculously brave. Thoughts of intimidation fire me to a challenge rather than fear. I smile at the thought and my skin pulls at the bruise on my chin. My hand moves to calm it, and I see Feeney's boots and his wild eyes. I don't tremble. My body keeps moving forward. A branch snags my hair and I raise my hand to untangle it. The bumps of the plaits under my fingers remind me of Eshnae.

Those sorrowful eyes.

What did she say? *Hiding? Waiting?*

My muscles tense with each question I have no answers for. Thoughts travel down paths that lead nowhere. No matter how hard I try, I don't know the answers—I don't even know the questions. My mind feels as bound as these vines I'm trying to fight my way through. Tangled and woven, tighter and thicker, until they strangle my thoughts and stop me from moving.

The vines on the other side of the road don't tangle around the trees as badly. In my mind, I make a path through them before I creep my way towards the road. My shoes snap twigs on the forest floor, and the sound echoes through my body as I hide behind a tree on the roadside. Up ahead, the bend in the road looks peaceful enough. I focus on the thick trunk that will hide me once I have sprinted across and am safely on the other side.

Go! The moment my feet touch the road, an agitated horse appears at the bend. Nostrils flaring, he charges towards me, his terrified eyes blind to anything but his foe. The momentum of my second step places me directly in his path and into his fear. I raise my hands as he rears, and his panic flies like feathered wings from his body and dissipates into the forest. He bounces on his forefeet as he calms and I rub his belly to assure him all is well, grateful he is not injured. Big brown eyes watch me gather the long reins that trail behind him, freeing them of the thin branches and weeds he has collected along the way. A playful neck scratch releases dust between my fingers and he swings his neck around in delight as we laugh silently together at our chance meeting.

A man runs from the bend towards us, and I leap to the other side of the horse. Checking my robe is secure, I lower my gaze and wait. He stops, places his hand on the horse's flank and, in between great heaves of breath, beams a thankful smile. The horse stands steady.

"Oh, thank the Stars he stopped!"

The young man leans over, his large hands resting on his knees, and concentrates on his breath, that is now less gasping and more puffing. I step around the horse's head, scratching his jaw, but more interested in the man's work clothes. His shirt drapes over the muscles of his back and I tilt my head as I try to guess his guild and position. He looks dirty, and then I remember I rolled down a gully this morning and smile. He looks up and I wipe it from my face with a question I direct to the ground.

"How far along the road have you run?"

"Oh, about one marker," he says, then stands with a final puff for flourish. "Took a few tumbles in my eagerness, I'm afraid." He rubs at his elbow and spots of blood seep through the coarse weave of his shirt. He takes the reins and wipes a comforting hand over his horse, then gently shakes the loosely wrapped reins in my direction. "And thank you. Most would have let the horse be on its way or taken it as their own."

"We met in the middle of the road. Quite suddenly, in fact."

"Well, I'm glad he had the sense to bump into you." He offers his hand. "Galen."

I take his hand and shake it gently, "Ash... ling." *By the Stars! How could I be so stupid?* "Ashling of Lewtshire," I correct. "An idle traveler."

My mouth is dry, and my eyes couldn't be wider if I held them open with my own fingers. I pull the hood of the robe closer around me. Not exactly a lie, but not exactly the truth, either. I haven't thought of who I will be. I am turned inside out, my feet suddenly aware they stand on open ground. Galen's forehead pinches into a quick frown, then smooths to an odd look I've not seen before. Unsure? Suspicious?

"Well met. I'm Galen of the farm down the next lane and I wish to thank you, Ashling of Lewtshire, for stopping my crazy horse." He bows in mock reverence, smiles and motions with his head towards the road. "Shall we walk together?"

And I obey.

We retrace his run at a calmer pace. The horse walks between us, and my eyes are constantly on the woods. Galen leans forward and uses his free hand to ruffle the dust and leaves from his brown hair.

"No, seriously, how did you stop my horse? He bolted when the cog on the old cart broke. Just look at how calm he is with you."

I shrug. Strange question. Surely Galen listens to his own horse?

What a relief to discover that Galen is a talker. He tells me about Maeve, his wife, and his daughter, and how they were on their way home from the markets at Smoutlea when their cart broke.

"I think it's the cog pin, but I didn't have time to look. See, you trust a Tallefix and this happens—the whole thing came down with such a crash—even scared my little Joss, and she's a tough one."

"You've met a Tallefix?" I forget to hide my excitement, or my lack of knowledge. Eshnae always told me that the Tallefix could heal or fix anything; they always sounded like heroes. Galen's story disappoints me, but I'm excited to find that Tallefixes are real people. Eshnae *was* truthful about the strange people that traveled the land with a horse and cart, relaxing people with mystical tales before they performed their magic. Or, in Galen's case, their lack of it.

"Yep, but to be honest, I don't know whether I'd be happy to hear the sound of those tinkling bells again. I might just run in the other direction now."

He shakes his head and sighs at the memory. The briefest amount of time passes before he seems to forget about the Tallefix and goes back to his stories about his family with such animation and love I feel like I know them already. I hear all about the purchases they made at Smoutlea and his plans for the upcoming season on his farm.

"Just a couple more bends now," he announces.

A shriek fills the air. Galen doesn't look back as he hands me the reins and runs. I trot with the horse after him. A few bends in the road later, we come upon a cart limped on its side and missing a wheel. A young lady leans forward against the cart with Galen already by her side. It must be Maeve. A little girl with blond ringlets bouncing on her shoulders is performing a jumping dance at their feet. Maeve is distressed. I can hear her sobbing as I approach with the horse. Galen steps away from her and I see she is heavily pregnant and laboring. Galen looks at me bewildered, pleading with his eyes for help. I spy a tunic in the cart.

"May I?"

Galen steps away from the cart, confused.

I remove my robe in one motion and discard it at my feet. The sight of my undergarments stuns Galen, and he turns circles, not knowing where to look. Joss shrieks with laughter at the crazy lady in her underwear and Maeve's eyes widen while she concentrates on her pain. There's no time to explain. The tunic slips over my head and I scan the surrounding forest for somewhere comfortable. A tree with a low bough stands down an embankment from the road. Maeve nods as we leave her leaning on the cart and head down the embankment, armed with sacks from the cart. Galen drapes a large sack over the low bough and I gather stones to hold it open. Another sack laid on the moss and leaves under the tree creates as much privacy and comfort as we can afford.

We lead Maeve slowly down the embankment with Joss's little head bobbing along behind while she sings, "Ba-by, Ba-by."

Once Maeve is comfortable, Galen and Joss go to wait by the cart.

I don't question how it is I know what to do. The labor is quick and powerful, and the child is almost born when the sound of horses arriving at the cart distracts me. Voices discuss the cart and our small shelter. A lump forms in my throat; they're not Galen's fellow farmers, but guards. It's odd to see the guards on horses, as usually only Trothsmen have that luxury. My hand reaches to pull my hood closer to my face, and then I remember it's on the road. I grab at a loose sack and fashion a new hood to cover my exposed hair.

What did I tell Galen?

Did I mention I was hiding?

What if he tells them I'm here?

I can't leave Maeve like this and run—or can I?

My eyes dart from under the sack and sneak a glance at the road. Galen kicks my robe under the cart, and Maeve's sudden cry brings me back to reality. The guards move on, their commotion fading into the distance as I welcome Galen and Maeve's son into my arms. He's so new and perfect.

I call out to Galen, "You have a son!"

Galen whoops as Maeve asks gently and hopefully, "Have you checked yet?"

"Checked what?"

Like waking from a dream, I look at the newborn I'm holding in my hands despite the fact that I know nothing of birth. I'd been so caught up in doing what they needed that there was no time to think of what I did or didn't know.

"Have you checked?" Galen calls from the bank.

I sit back on my feet, still holding their precious child.

What if I have done something wrong?

Who do I think I am? I don't even know what I'm doing.

Panic stirs within me, its claws rising in my throat. I subdue it with a deep breath. Silence has always been my refuge and my jaw sets like stone. I will my mouth to open.

Open.

Work!

"I'm sorry," I begin, addressing Galen as loudly as I dare, with a baby in my arms. "I don't know what you're asking me to check for."

"Check for the Eariss, of course," he calls back. Maeve nods, a small smile on her lips.

The Eariss? Have you all gone mad? But I obey. "How do I do that?" I whisper to her.

"Hold the baby's eyes open and tell us if you see lots of colors—like in a rainbow."

I suddenly feel like Eshnae. Is that what they were doing each morning? Looking for evil? The sacks create a milder light inside the little tent. Their baby boy is alert and doesn't struggle against me trying to see into his eyes. I blink my tears away in order to see clearly.

"No, there are no colors," I say, loud enough for Galen to hear, and I wrap the child. Is this news a blessing or a disappointment to their family? Maeve holds her arms out for her son. I leave her to rest, reminding her I'll be at the road if she needs me. Galen runs down the bank with Joss in one arm and squeezes me with excitement.

"A son!" he says, beaming, then bounds towards his love.

My robe lies bunched under the cart and, once shaken to shape, it secures me again. The cart wheels aren't badly damaged, and I busy myself removing the family's goods from the cart to ready it for repair.

As I remove the goods, I see the accident happen as clearly as if I had been standing by. I watch the cog pin splinter, the wheel turn and tilt, breaking the shaft and setting the frightened horse free. I see the answer too. A piece of hardwood that lies beneath a birch tree in the forest, and a length suitable for a new shaft nearby.

Galen returns to the cart and we discuss how best to fix the cog pin and shaft, then head into the surrounding forest in search of hardwood the right size. We scan the forest floor as I gently direct Galen towards the birch tree I have seen, so he alone finds the answer for his family.

"Be Star struck Tallefix!" Galen kicks up the dead leaves on the forest floor and takes a small branch with them, sending it further into the forest. "They always sound like a good idea, don't they? Making promises they can't keep."

"But they work most of the time, don't they?"

"If you believe their tales, I suppose, lulling you into a dream state, then *bam!* They set your bone or pull your tooth." Galen reaches down to collect a stick that breaks easily in his hand. "Not sure about their expertise with carts, though. Cog pins don't care so much for mystical tales."

There's my birch tree. I move towards it, pulling Galen along as if there is an invisible cord between us.

The leaves shuffle under feet and I make conversation as I step further away from him. "I heard some men by the cart while we were in the tent. There wasn't any trouble?"

Galen continues his earnest scanning. "No, they were just Brennyn guards looking for someone. They asked who was in the tent."

Galen looks up from his search and considers me. I know he heard my gasp. I can see him from the corner of my eye as I pretend I have found something interesting among some roots.

"I told them it was my wife who was confined and my sister who was helping her," he calls across to me. "But they don't believe anyone, those guards. They were about to head down when Maeve cried out and I think it scared them a little. I know it scared me!"

I look over to see him beaming again, no doubt remembering he had a son he would take home once we found the right piece of wood to act as a pin.

"It's a shame they didn't offer to help you with the cart."

"Those bullies wouldn't be helping anyone! Can't wait for this promised unrest to set everything right."

"Unrest?" I say to the ground.

"I don't know what they've been telling you across the river in Lewtshire, but it's not far away. I can feel it in my bones. Tell me, Ashling, what is the word in Lewtshire of the coming unrest?"

Galen raises an eyebrow, and I pretend to have my attention caught by a branch.

"Well," I begin, wondering if people outside the Hall sense another's panic the way I do. "Some believe it will set everything aright, while others say it will destroy all we have known."

"And that's the point—to destroy it all. We need a new way!" Galen throws a rejected branch and it smashes against a tree.

"Yes. Yes, of course," I murmur.

The invisible cord leads Galen to the hardwood and we return to the cart triumphant. I climb in under the tilted cart and hold the wheel in position while he secures it as best he can for now.

"You," he says, watching me behind the wheel. "You must be a talented idler, well sought after." Galen grunts as he forces the hardwood through the hub. "You calmed our horse, birthed our baby and fixed a wheel—and all in one afternoon!"

My chest squeezes. I force the words out: "Glad to be of service."

He stops his work, looks down to me and smiles. "So what's your secret?"

The pressure of his attention crushes me. My nerves flutter and jump. Is it even possible to have a secret if you don't know you have one?

Eshnae said she was hiding me; what did I do?

My free hand rubs at the tunic until my palm burns. He chooses to ignore my wide-eyed silence and returns his attention to the wheel.

"You know, the first time I saw your smile was when the baby was born. Your face lit up!" He lets out a small chuckle at the memory, but doesn't look at me as he continues. "Life will always give us reasons not to smile, it's just the way it is. But you still get to decide whether you'll search for the good that's out there and choose to smile, choose to be happy." Galen steps back and gives the cartwheel a solid spin. With his hands on his hips, he nods at his handiwork.

I crawl out from under the cart, wipe some dirt and leaves from my tunic and make my way towards him. We watch as the wheel slows down.

"Don't you get punished for smiling?" I ask, my eyes fixed on the wheel.

"Whoever heard of such a thing?"

We regard each other, and I mirror his frown. How can we be speaking a different language over something as simple as a smile?

"You can tell me all about it over some ale when we get home. What do you say? Will you join us for a meal?"

Kindness.

It pours over my head and runs through my empty body. I lower my chin. "Thank you."

We right the cart and carefully hitch the horse. Galen collects Maeve, Joss and the baby from the tent and escorts his family to the cart. I load the last of the goods onto the cart and we head to their home. Galen and I walk on either side of the horse and Maeve and Joss ride in the cart, with Joss solely focused on the baby, talking to him and touching his face. She will be such an attentive big sister. A discussion about baby names leads them to choose Glyn.

"A fine, strong name," Galen says.

As we travel back along the road towards Brennyn Hall, dread
sludges into my stomach with each step—could this be an elaborate trap? Galen was speaking to the guards earlier...

Surely not.

Further down the road, we turn off to a lane that leads to their
farmhouse, and I welcome the relief like an old friend as it floods
my body. We emerge from the forest into larger clearings dotted
with trees.

"Home sweet home," Galen says as he points into the distance.
A tiny stone hut squats on the horizon. Wisps of smoke from a
tired fire rise from its chimney, the dull brown of a thatched roof
like a sewn patch on the green hills behind it.

"It looks wonderful," I say. "All your own work?"

As dark gray clouds swirl in the sky, Galen talks about rain and
mud and mice and threshing, and I nod in the appropriate places
and feel myself relax the further we travel from the forest road.

D istances can be deceiving, and the storm is almost upon us as we arrive at the farm. Galen and I usher Maeve and the children inside and coax the fire to life before we shelter the stock. Galen unhitches the cart and brings the horse in while I round up their small flock of sheep. I herd them towards the safety of the separate stone room attached to the side of their hut. It's snug and dark, but they are safe.

"You got these sheep in quickly," Galen says as he wades through his flock, touching each one as if bestowing a blessing. The sheep concentrate on the hay I have spread on the dirt floor.

"I think they were just glad to be heading somewhere dry."

"Ah, no. There's something about you, something mysterious."

My shoulders tense as I turn my back to Galen. I retrieve the hay from the floor to scatter it again, sprinkling it here and there. "There is?"

He must have heard the squeak in my voice, but he doesn't react. Why is my body betraying me now?

"Hmm," he continues. "The animals are calm around you. Yet you're a stranger to them. I've never seen it before."

"Sometimes I think animals know us better than we know ourselves," I say and glance towards him, not to search his face but to plan an escape route. He stands between me and the door.

"True enough," he agrees, and flips one of his sheep onto her back and checks her hoof. "I'd have to agree with that. They might not speak with their mouths, but they do sense things, don't they? Like who they can trust." He pats the sheep and let her rise. She trots to her flock as if having her entire world flipped upside down has no more consequence than a mouth full of clover.

The horse nudges me, rescuing me from deeper thoughts about the utter lunacy of trust. I rest my head on his neck and take in his heady scent. Scenes of daggers and blood-soaked cobblestones parade in front of my eyes and I squeeze them shut, forcing the images away, but not before the ground falls away and there's nowhere to stand. Galen's cheerful banter calls to me from his earthy den, the musty hay, the steady horse and the murmuring sheep, before I am completely lost.

"I can tell you've had horses; there's no mistaking the way you relate to him. But I can't imagine you to be farming lass. A trotting pony, was it then?"

Not a farming lass.

Too close to the Hall.

Eye on the door.

Say something!

"Yes, I love to ride."

Galen makes his way over to the horse. My shoulders slump as he draws closer. I smooth the horse's neck, shushing him even though he makes no sound.

"See those hands?" he begins. "Those fine hands are not the hands of a farming family—or an idler."

My hands rest on reddish horse hair, the rough coat caressing between my fingers. I stare at them, willing them to be dirty and calloused. They are not.

"And yet you are strong, thoughtful and a problem solver . . . not really a highborn type, either. Yes, lass, you are a mystery to me."

Galen scratches his horse's ears and smiles, as if we share a secret. I cannot imagine him ever turning me into the Trothsmen. He's waiting for me to say something, to trust him, but I can't. Feigning interest in the horse's legs, I hide my face.

"May I ask you a question?" I say. I glance up and watch him nod as he walks towards the door. "When the guards came by the side of the road today, you kicked my robe under the cart." He nods again in acknowledgment. "Why did you do that?"

"I don't rightly know." He folds his arms and leans back against the door. "And even that I told them you were my sister. It just kind of fell out of my mouth as if they weren't supposed to know you and that little tent existed. They were surely agitated and frustrated; all this talk of unrest has made people nervy. Oh, did you want them to see you—?"

"No! No, not at all," I correct him with a bit too much enthusiasm. In the silence, Galen considers me for a moment, the corner of his mouth pinched in, before his body softens as he exhales. He looks to the ground and gently shakes his head. "The animals are secure and that pot should be ready now. Let's move inside."

And I don't think, I just follow.

⚬⚬⚬

T he day's waning has a way of preparing hearts and minds for stillness. The black pot that hangs over the fire creates aromas that cause my mouth to water, releasing a scent so deliciously thick that the air itself seems edible. A few chairs surround the table that takes up half of their home, and candlelight flickers, stretching shadows down to the furs and skins on the floor pallet where we will sleep. This is all they need. What a perfect arrangement. Their whole home is smaller than my chamber, but there is more kindness and compassion in one corner than you could scratch out of the whole of Brennyn Hall.

Food tastes so much nicer in pleasant company; peacefulness is the most powerful of seasonings. The wooden bowls on the table contain the finest pottage I've ever tasted. Maeve's chestnut bread sops up the dregs of liquid resting in the base of my bowl and I battle to keep my appetite somewhere between savoring each bite and delightful gluttony. I don't even waste the drip that runs on my chin, wiping it with my finger and then licking it clean.

Amidst the gentle thunder and flickering candles, I hear how Galen and Maeve met, came to their little farm and what their plans are for the future. Galen impresses me with exciting and new thoughts. I don't pretend to understand the workings of a farm or his ideas about a new society, but I know Maeve certainly has her hands full. Galen's grand ideas can be dangerous and often end with hilarious results. Not your regular kind of shepherd, that's for sure. My cheeks sting with the joy of laughter and in my exuberance I knock over a cup. The ale floods across the table and the whole world slows down. Voices deepen and slow.

All I see is spilled ale on other tables, the clatter of cooking implements. Terror shreds inside me, looking for an escape.

Fists smash onto tables. Onto me.

Can't you do anything right?

My arms cover my head in protection. In my panic to get away from the table, I stumble backwards, fall over my chair and land on the floor, leaning against the wall. Galen and Maeve watch wide-eyed and Joss stares with a puzzled half-smile, unsure whether to laugh at my antics. I scramble to my feet and pretend to wipe invisible dust from the tunic I wear.

"I'm sorry. I'll take some air," I say, and flee to the door.

The rain is still solid. I halt just outside the door and close it behind me. My breath jumps and shudders as if it's climbing a slippery and icy staircase, puffing a wisp of white at each tread. The thatched eaves cover and protect me from a stream of water coming from the roof. In the yard, divots made by the horse's hooves fill with water and create ordered puddles. I look to the gray sky and fold my arms against all that is cold.

I ruin everything.

Look at how ungrateful I am.

I've made more work for Maeve.

Stupid child!

Should I put my head to the door and thank them for the meal before I go? I look out through the rain; perhaps it's safer to move on without a word.

Maeve appears at the door and closes it behind her, and I attempt to shoo her back inside. "No, no, please go back inside, Maeve, you need not be getting ill on my account."

But she stands firm and I look at the puddles at my feet. They fill and overflow and join to form larger puddles.

"You know, spilled drinks are a part of life," she begins softly. "A big part of my life, at the moment, what with Joss *and* Galen."

I look up and see her smile. Maeve rubs her hand on my arm. I flinch, and another wave of shame crashes over me.

"Spilled ale will always be cleaned up, there's nothing to it, but shattered spirits—." She takes a breath and exhales. "They do not so easily recover; they need time to become whole."

Shattered. Yes, that's how I feel. Like there are little pieces of me everywhere. Tears sting at my eyes, but I won't allow them to fall. "Perhaps I should just go back where I came from and forget this—this idling."

The rain fills the larger puddles that join up to flow across the yard, and we stand in silence watching the rain wash the idea of puddles away.

"Have you ever considered that there's a flow to life?" Maeve crosses her arms and turns towards me as she asks the question. I shake my head in reply. "It flows just like a river." She tilts her head to the stream gathering strength in her yard. "And you can choose to jump into it and see where it takes you, or you can choose to fight it and waste a lot of energy, but there's one thing you can never do with your life, or with a river."

"What's that?"

"Go backwards."

I nod.

"Your life is waiting to teach you all you need to know," she says. "Some lessons stare straight at us, others we need to search for. Answers can appear in the strangest places and sometimes they only arrive when we're brave enough to step away from all we've ever known, and sometimes they are hidden within us." Maeve touches my face gently with the back of her hand. "I can see the flush has gone from your cheeks. Come inside where it's warm and help me settle Joss for bed."

The heaviness of my shame has disappeared, melted into the puddles at my feet, diluted and banished. I nod, slowly at first, then a small smile appears as I relax. There's a bubble of excitement in my belly. It dances and twirls every time I think about making my own decisions and never going backwards. Maeve returns my smile, her eyes lit with a calmness that intrigues me. She takes my hand and leads me back through the door.

Our entrance surprises Galen and Joss; they've been busy making animal noises and faces at each other. We all laugh at a particularly noisy rendition of a piglet and enjoy more ale. Maeve prepares Joss for sleep while Galen and I move the table a little further away from the skins on the floor that will become our bed for the night. Our hearts are still light when I remember my earlier question for Galen. My elbows lean on the table and I hold my face.

"So much laughter pains my cheeks, yet it feels too good to be truly evil. Tell me, why don't you punish happiness and laughter?"

"Punish happiness?" Galen's smile fades as he remembers our conversation at the cart. He shakes his head sadly at me from across the table. "Living this life already takes so much from us.

Happiness is like a wellspring that gives us strength to continue through the dry times. It comes in many forms, but always makes us light and strong. To punish laughter and happiness? Seems to me that kind of person wants to stop people drinking from the well." Galen considers the cup of ale in his hand and then looks about his home. "You only need to keep your heart focused on one good thing, just one, and it will grow like a little seedling into joy. If we can find one good thing to be grateful for, we can enjoy happiness. You, my dear lass, should make an effort to enjoy every bit of happiness that comes your way."

I tuck my hands under my chin and make a promise. "I will."

Joss interrupts with a request for a story and lies down on the pallet.

"But of course," Galen says. He turns his chair towards her, leans forward and rests his hands on his knees before taking a breath to begin. Glyn stirs in his little basket and Maeve moves to attend to him.

"No," Joss protests. "I wanna hear tale from Ashling."

Joss's sweet eyes peer at me from the floor and Galen half turns in his chair. My heart beats so hard I'm sure they can hear it outside my chest and my mind is occupied with puddles, flowing streams and rivers. Maeve looks up with a smile.

I am safe and capable of making a choice.

My own choice.

I decide I will jump, and I tell myself to be brave. A strange noise escapes as I clear my throat. "Tell me, Joss, what would you like to hear a story about?"

My mind is screaming at me. It reminds me I know nothing of life outside the Hall, then accuses me—wondering what kind of stupid tale I plan to tell and how badly I will tell it.

"I wanna hear 'bout a baby!"

"Oh, of course you do!" we all agree with smiles and rolling eyes.

Galen makes himself comfortable at the table while Maeve sits nearby, nursing baby Glyn and I make my way beside the pallet.

Playing dramatic, I stand and hold my finger to my chin, copying the bards I had seen occasionally at Council. I think back to a simple tale Eshnae often told me when I was very young. If I remember the important parts of the story, I might save myself from being a fool, and maybe even learn one of the lessons Maeve spoke of.

"Hmm, a story about a baby. . . oh, I know! This was a tale that my friend Eshnae told me. Are you ready?"

Joss wiggles under her blanket and nods.

"**A** long time ago, in the land of sacred mist, there was a beautiful queen who was adored by her people. She so wanted a baby of her own, but for some reason, her babies didn't live long. Oh! Unlike your beautiful strong brother Glyn." I glance over at Glyn and Maeve. "He's so beautiful." I sigh.

Joss sighs loudly. "He so boodiful."

"But guess what?"

"What?" Joss giggles.

"The queen was going to have another baby, and she was so happy!" I clap my hands together excitedly, and little Joss claps along. "The queen knew the baby would come soon and wanted to make the castle perfect for when the baby arrived. She wanted to pick some pretty flowers and make it a surprise for the king. So the queen secretly took her horse and rode and rode all day until she came to the top of a hill. Spread out before her was a large valley that had the most beautiful flowers! There were red ones and yellow ones—"

"And boo ones? Boo is my favorite."

"Oh, yes! There were blue ones and orange ones and even some stripy ones, too. It was so hard to choose which flowers to pick because they were all so beautiful. The queen was gathering flowers when—Oh dear! The baby was coming!" I clutch at my stomach and Joss laughs.

"Like mama!" she giggles.

"Down from the other side of the valley, the forest people came. They took the queen into the forest and made her as comfortable as they could. One of their clansmen rode the queen's horse back to the castle to let the king know the baby was coming. The queen was very sad when she heard the clansman had gone to the castle; remember, the queen didn't want the king to know until all the beautiful flowers were in place. Now her surprise would be ruined!" Joss and I pull the sides of our mouths into sad faces. Maeve smiles at our silly faces as she places Glyn in his basket. "Of course, it was the next day by the time the clansman arrived at the castle and the king was so relieved to know where the queen was! He had been running around the castle, stamping his feet, saying, 'Where is my queen! Where is my queen!' Now that he knew the baby had been born, he got even more upset.

'I MUST see my baby, take me to my beautiful baby!'

Then from out of nowhere came a tremendous storm, the biggest storm anyone had ever seen, and even though it was springtime, the storm brought so much rain it flooded the whole valley! The king was told he had to wait until the storm had passed and the floods were all gone before he could see his beautiful baby. He cried and cried because he wanted so much to see his baby."

'Boo! Hoo! Hoo!'"

Joss and I rub at our eyes, pretending to cry. "The day came when the king's army could finally cross the valley. The king was very sad when he arrived and was told the queen had died, but his heart was bright and happy because now he had a baby who would grow up and look after his kingdom. A kind lady from the forest clan brought lots of flowers with her when she traveled back to the castle to care for the baby, just as the queen had asked. By now, word had spread and everyone knew he was bringing his beautiful baby back to the castle and there were celebrations throughout the land. People came from everywhere to congratulate him and the king felt very proud. Because, as we know, there's nothing more divine than to have a baby in your household. The end. Well, it's not actually the end."

I kneel beside Joss. "Here, give me your hands. This is how it always ended." I clasp my hands around Joss's and chant Eshnae's little rhyme. "Open flowers, crown of fire, taught by stars and fueled by pyre."

Maeve and Galen smile at each other and then at me.

I shrug.

"I've no idea what it means. Eshnae always made me recite it with her, so it must be part of the story."

Memories of Eshnae lay heavy on me, but still I smile and tuck Joss into her blanket.

"Let's pick some flowers in the morning," I whisper.

She nods and turns over to sleep. Glyn's basket is only a few steps away from me. I can't resist gently stroking his sleeping head. His presence lifts the sadness from my heart.

"Divine," I whisper to myself and spend a luxurious moment adoring those little ears and pure hands, the downy skin of an untarnished life.

A peculiar sensation swirls in my mind. A knowing, but it's not as clear as a waterfall. Fog and searing sunshine, brightness and heaviness, reality and dream. I hold on to the walls as I move away from Glyn's basket, unsure of where I place my feet, of anything. As if I'd just heard Eshnae's tale for the very first time and made connections that were never there before.

A kind lady from the forest clan . . . brought flowers with her . . . to care for the baby, just as the queen had asked.

I bring a hand to my mouth and turn to Galen and Maeve. They both watch me as I step further along the wall. My mouth won't form words. I'm not even sure what I'm thinking. Galen speaks to no one in particular. "I remember that storm. I was only a child, but no one had seen anything like it before."

I rub at my forehead, but the fog won't lift. "But it was in the land of sacred mists," I say, trailing off, my thoughts trapped somewhere between legend and reality. I shake my head to rattle them loose. "How long ago was the storm?" I ask.

"About fifteen summers, I'd say. You can ask at the village of Sirban. They record everything there, they'd know for sure."

Their expressions don't waver, watching over me as I frown and shudder through my thoughts. Only when my hand reaches out and finds the stability of the table, do I dare release the wall. I find my chair and lean forward to speak, cringing with how pompous the question feels on my tongue, but compelled to utter the words.

"That was me? That story was me?"

M aeve shifts in her seat, flicks a look at Galen and lowers her gaze. "We believe so... Lady Ashling."

"You know who I am?" My face flops into my folded arms and I try to recall the horse, the wheel, anything I might have said or done that exposed me. How far do I honestly expect to travel if I'm discovered by a simple farmer on the first day?

Pathetic.

"Everyone knows about you." I'm sure Galen meant for his words to cheer me, but as I raise my head, he reacts to the horror on my face and moves his hands to cover mine. "But please don't fear, most wish you well."

"Most?"

Maeve rises and pours more ale for us, the contents of my cup trembling into ripples as I sip. Questions spill from my mind faster than I can form them into words, and my mouth shuts down in confused defeat.

Galen swallows his ale and chases a refill. "It's been said you were a gift of connection, but the lord shunned you for grief. Others say he crushed you as he would an enemy, fearful of your power and gifts."

I frown at him and shake my head. Connected to what? What gifts?

"You can't see it, can you—how different you are?" he says.

This morning I was an accuser escaping from the Hall. Now I'm some kind of strange gift, according to this deluded farmer.

Maybe it's the ale he's drinking.

I shrug.

Galen lifts his hand up to count on his fingers. "The horse stopped for you. The animals respond to you, you know the answers to things. You helped with Glyn's birth. You fixed the cart—how did you know what to do?"

"I don't know, I just did."

"And that's my point. People just don't know these things, Ashling, there's something good about you."

"Oh no, no, that's not me, that can't be me." The ale sways in the cup as I lean back in the chair. I steady it with both hands. "Ha! I'm not good. I do nothing right, can't be trusted and I must only rely on others because I am really quite a dolt." My hands should be out counting on their fingers too. "The real truth is, I know nothing. I'm always in the way. I make people do bad things. I'm a bad person." Words are the strongest ale, secure, familiar and warm.

Galen pats the table and shakes his head. "I don't believe that for a minute."

I defend myself from his lies with anger. "How can you be sure? You've known me less than one day. I could be the most evil person to walk this land. And you've just invited me into your home." The force of my words shudders through my body. I look into the ripples of my ale to see if my reflection might be there. The door remains a few strides away, but I am fixed on the settling of the ale, not noticing I have drawn my feet onto the chair until my knees tuck between my arms.

Maeve strokes my hair as she passes me to sit down. "When we believe what others tell us to, rather than what we see with our own eyes or know with our own senses, we blind ourselves. We hand them our entire lives and become an extension of them, a weakened version of who we are." She leans towards me and holds my chin in her hand, tilting it to be sure our eyes meet. "Let no one tell you what your heart contains. You say you need the truth? Well, first you must choose to release the lie."

My knees tremble inside my arms, the pressure of my forehead on them dulls their quake only a little, and the whole world falls away from my chair. Maeve pats my shoulder and takes the jittering cup from my hands. It's true what she says. I don't know how it's true, but it is.

You can't search for truth without discovering lies. They're like the markers on the forest road that remind us where we are. What we do when we come across them is up to us; they're our lies, after all. They only ask us to choose between the same path or dare us to forge an unknown one.

The fog in my head lifts. Nothing has changed in my world other than my thoughts, and they are now clear. My feet find the floor, and I pull my chair closer to the table.

"Those records you spoke of . . . is it far to the village of Sirban? I need to know who I am."

Smiles, I discover, have a language of their own.

⁂

Later, Maeve and Galen listen as I tell them about Feeney and my escape. "Plans?" I say, "Ah no, it was rather a quick exit."

They gasp when I explain how I reached the wall, but fell, anyway.

"Maybe there's more about me at Sirban. Eshnae mentioned strange things to me about trusting no one... and finding hidden things, or things being hidden that aren't. Would the people at Sirban help me?"

"Don't see why not," Galen says. "They're supposed to know everything. I mean, *everything*. It'll take you a few good days of travel to get there, though. Some strange man covered in embroidered cloth settled the village on top of a mountain ages ago." He shakes his head. "Dumbest thing I've ever heard of, but what would I know?" He taps my hand. "So, how are we going to get you there safely?"

Maeve slides the candle to the center of the table. "I like the idler idea, lowly and non-remarkable."

I drum my fingers on the table. "It seems perfect, but right now the Hall is reacting to a loss of control in the East. An elder said that people have lost faith in the Hall; that they're looking for something new. So the other elders are making plans to confuse them."

"What kinds of plans?"

"They said things like; 'Make 'em fear and blame each other. Start rumors, then have them rely on us for their truth. Blame the idlers. Those lowborn jugglers won't complain.'"

"If everyone will soon blame idlers for this mess, we'd better get you on and off the road as quickly as we can."

We nod, the shadows bouncing on our features. Maeve places both hands on the table. "Right, tomorrow I'll find some old clothes. Not befitting a lady at all, but you must stay safe. The roads are dangerous enough, just be sure to find lodgings before nightfall." She wags her finger at me. "If anyone meets you on the road, you are an idler." Then she grins. "You could always tell them a story."

Galen jumps in his seat. "My brother and his family live about fifteen road markers from here—you could make it by nightfall if you keep up a good pace. They won't ask questions of you." He chuckles at some distant thought. "My family's not that good at obeying the lord — my brother Rand in particular."

Our conversation continues through to the stub of the candle. Though we were tense and fearful at first, we relax into chatter as plans become real and possible. Galen reminds me of common traveling customs and prepares me for what I might find along the way. I appreciate their effort to balance all their warnings with cheerful stories of providence and friendship.

Later that night, I pull the shared blankets to my chin to rest. Old aches from my limbs fade and new tender bruises hint at their arrival, even against the softness of the sheepskins beneath us. My mind occupies itself with worry about where this plan might lead. I force myself to only consider the next step—finding my way to Rand's home. Galen blows out the last of the candle and my eyes adjust, barely making out the shapes of the furniture in the room. I could lay here forever and never want for another thing. A sigh escapes my lips and Joss stirs in her sleep next to me. They didn't check her sweet little eyes. Maybe they'll do it in the morning, like my routine at the Hall.

My routines at the Hall. I pull the blanket closer to me. Feeney always said my mind was bewitched, and that my screams showed people how much evil was inside me, fighting to get out. What if I start screaming in my sleep? Who knows what I might do.

I tap Maeve's shoulder in the dark. "Shouldn't you lock me up?" I whisper.

She turns and strokes my hair. "We'll be fine. I promise."

D espite my protests, the next morning the whole family in-
sists on walking with me through the woods to the forest
road. They have shared what little they had, versed me in the
expected behavior of idlers and given me a small cloth sack of
provisions.

Maeve gently lifts the edges of my hood. "Those pins still holding your hair in place?"

The touch of her hands reminds me of Eshnae. "They're fine,
really," I say, and lift my arms. "Look at the size of this robe."
'Ladylike' is certainly not how the old sackcloth robe appears, but
it is the perfect disguise to keep me safe. The tunic I took from
the cart yesterday is a welcome barrier between my skin and the
itchiness of the robe, and a pair of Galen's old pants have been cut
and sewn into trousers for me.

Maeve hugs me warmly with her free arm, holding Glyn between
us. Joss sobs, pushes between our legs and finds her way inside the
robe to hug my thigh.

I kneel and straighten her crown of large blue flowers. The thin stems of the wildflowers woven among them have begun to dry and make it sturdy. "Thank you for coming to the stream with me this morning," I say. "Wasn't it lovely?"

"Mmm-hmm," she says, and I wipe a tiny tear from the edge of her eye. Her curls wrap themselves around my fingers and I tuck them behind her ears, passing their silky embrace to the wayward white daisies trailing from her crown. This morning those blue flowers stood tall and strong on the bank, their straps of green bending to just skim the water, then bouncing as the waves created by Joss's steps invited them to dance. Joss bent to their faces and stuck out her tongue, as she imagined they were doing to her, then laughed and fell back into the stream with a plop. Her little legs took her all about the stream, investigating each cranny, studying every bug. Her tender feet slipped on pebbles and she kicked the cool water of still pools, giggling at her airborne creations.

From my seat on the bank, she was the whole world at play with itself. Cool pebbles slid under my feet, rubbed life into my soles, and sent ripples of water to the gentle flow of the stream. There they disappeared, gathered into a bigger purpose. A sudden nervousness rolled in my stomach. Tiny leaves, blown free from the surrounding trees, fluttered down. Once settled on the water, they bobbed and floated, hesitated, then bounced around the larger pebbles to be on their way. At that moment, Joss' tower of stones splashed into the water and she squealed with such delight I thought she might burst open like a ripe fruit. We laughed and clapped together.

"Try it again," I encouraged, completely taken with the fullness of her joy. I was still smiling when I spotted the small blackbird spreading his wings on a willow branch above us. I wished him a good morning as silently as I would to anyone at the Hall.

Would you like to join me here on the bank?

He cocked his head and bounced up and down on the branch, then spread his wings and dropped to the rock beside me. Each note of his song warbled and hopped joyfully over the pebbles.

"What about you, blackbird? Do you think I'm as different as Galen says?"

Joss looked up from her pebbles and pointed at the bird, droplets of water making it to her elbows before they dripped back into the stream. She shook the water from her hands, rearranged the larger pebbles to distort the flow of the stream and sent daisy heads down the new paths she created for them. When I looked back to the rock, the blackbird had gone.

The flowers in her hair are wilted now. Their insolent tongues fold quietly, only daring to flutter when they catch the breeze. Joss falls towards me and squeezes my neck in goodbye. My arms wrap around her little body and lift her from the ground, hoping that a sliver of her joy might join me.

"Come now, you two," Galen interrupts us, nudging Joss to her mother and helping me to my feet. Mere steps away, the forest road cuts across the end of the lane, sweeping it into oblivion. Rushing water sounds in my ears, my heart beats in my throat. The treetops form an arch overhead, a darkened doorway that illuminates the forest road as it rushes past. Galen cups my hands in his and bends close to me. "It's been an honor to meet you," he says.

I nod, but what he says is ridiculous. Visions of water droplets bouncing off polished leather play in the back of my mind before transforming themselves to road markers and ripples.

"And you," I say.

There can be no hiding from the road now. No running among the vines and hiding behind trees. I wave over my shoulder, conscious that the smile I wear for Joss is not part of me. My shoes step onto the road and I don't look back as I walk, plunging all my thoughts into Rand, his family and Galen's instructions from last night.

"Towards the end of your travel, watch for a wooden bridge that crosses a small dale covered with flowers," he said.

"It's very pretty—," Maeve added. "Rand's home sits at the top of the next ridge. Look for a stone hut, larger than mine and shaded by a large oak. Tell them you come with news of Galen and they'll welcome you heartily."

Bearers of good news are always well received, and I'll be the one to bring news of Glyn's birth to their home. The road is damp from the recent rain, and I easily avoid the few remaining muddy patches. Horse's hooves thud into the packed earth and sound their approach, giving me ample warning to move. As they near, I bend my back and lean heavily on the long stick I collected from the roadside. The robe covers me completely and my confidence grows as people pass and nod their greeting to the old idler. Much time passes between each greeting of fellow travelers, yet the road is busier than I had expected. Most travelers and idlers appear to move together in groups for safety, just as Maeve told me. When a group of seven travelers pass by, I hurry to follow close to them, with Galen's warning echoing in my mind.

"They'll wish you well, the ones you meet. You'll fascinate them, I bet. But mind who you trust. No one is ready to lay down their life for a fanciful myth or story—but they may lay yours down for some silver."

S afe, unsafe.

   Truth, lie.

How strange that this experience of freedom is both exhilarating and terrifying. I alternate between relaxing into my performance as the idler and feeling that my robe is somehow invisible and everyone can see through my deception. Little prickles of itchiness distract me, a reminder that my life is about being safe, not comfortable. Even though the clothing I wear is rough, it allows for more freedom of movement than I am used to. Simple thoughts are easy to delight in. My body moves as it chooses to, and my mind soon follows. I let it wander, hoping it will find something to fixate on other than my swirling emotions.

The road provides me with endless possibilities for wonder. My mind soaks in the colors of the forest. The sun blinds me as it blinks through the treetops, and I welcome the musty and earthy smell of the forest floor after rain. There is something refreshing about the forest, as if it has taken a large drink from the passing storm and transfers its new zest for life to anyone who passes by. Thoughts fly into my mind, clear and light, and an invisible heaviness lifts from my shoulders. When no one is looking my way, I smile for no reason at all. Tiny dents on the softer parts of the road are the only evidence I have passed this way. One step after the other. One at a time. That's all I need to do. That's all I need to know.

The group stops for their morning meal at a small clearing beside the road. They pull food from their sacks and rest on the grass, chatting among themselves. Thankfully, no one is preparing a fire so, we'll be on our way again soon. Along the roadside, a fallen tree hides a bed of small ferns behind it. This part of the forest is quite open, but the little ferns continue to the base of a nearby tree, the perfect place for me to rest and still be watchful.

My stomach growls. The knot on the cloth sack unties easily and the four corners open to reveal not only some food, but my little straw doll, re-stuffed with mane hair and a little lavender. I smile at the doll, and at Maeve's kindness, and set it on the mossy log as my dinner companion. Chestnut bread, a little cheese and some root vegetables make for a feast lay out on the ferns. The straw doll isn't my only dining companion—Maeve, Galen, Joss and Glyn are here with me too, if only in spirit.

People continue to travel the road on foot, horseback and carts, and I busy myself creating stories about where people are going and their reason for traveling. A group of four Trothsmen charge along the road, scattering everyone in their path. My back slides down the tree until the log hides me and even though I'm confident I didn't attract their attention, it still feels like the whole world is holding its breath. My little group soon resumes talking and an occasional laugh escapes their murmuring circle. Does the strange little 'man' who watches them from the forest bother them at all?

The day is warm, but a cool breeze winds its way around the scattered tree trunks. At first, I pull the robe closer, irritated, but the wind is my ally. Without it, I might look suspicious in such a heavy robe and I wiggle and position myself to be more comfortable. Grateful for the meal, I relax, lean back against the tree and curl up to block the wind.

⁂

My body jolts awake in fear. The group has gone. The clearing where they sat to eat their meal was empty. Above the trees, the sun sits reasonably high. They can't be too far ahead. I snatch the doll from the log, threading it onto the tie of my robe and tying it off as I leap to the road, my legs picking up pace.

Then I halt.

My walking stick is still against the tree. Do I really need it? Yes. I charge to the tree, slap the stick into my hand and run on my way.

Idiot! Fool!

By the Stars,—YOU FOOL!

Little bits of bark dig into my palm from the stick, but I don't care. Let it bleed! And my feet can stop complaining too! The familiar thud of horses moving on the road hunches me into the posture of an idler, and I can catch my breath and think. I nod a greeting to the passing rider. It's too dangerous to run on this road. There is safety in the pace of a brisk walk, and it will allow me to transform into an idler in an instant. One foot after the other, my shoes dent the roadway. With each curve in the road, I tell myself I'll see them just around the next corner, or perhaps the next. But

I don't see them. A fork in the road appears ahead. I know I am to take the left. What I don't know is if any other traveler takes it with me.

Thoughts of traveling groups, bandits and bounty hunters fade as I slow my walk and consider where I am headed. A stone hut on the ridge. I imagine it as a warm little house with a small window that will glow its light out into the dusk. The oak tree will be a silhouette, its giant caring arms stretched around it, keeping it safe until morning. It promises to be as welcoming and as happy as Galen's home. Sweet baby Glyn fills my mind and I'm honored to be his messenger, trusted to tell his arrival story. Before I can catch it, a laugh escapes my mouth and I can't wait to tell them how Maeve's scream scared off not only the guards but Galen as well! I'm sure they'll chuckle at that.

I can't believe I forgot to ask them what the checking was about.

"Check his eyes, check his eyes," I mutter as I walk, excited that I'll understand this wretched eyes thing by the end of this night. Why would they want to check for the Eariss? Why would they actually search for evil—and in their own children?

Every morning, they checked my eyes for evil. Did they see it? All those iron locks... they must have. I don't feel evil. How do you feel if you're evil, anyway? Wouldn't Eshnae have told me? Her words run through my head. What was it again? Trust... no, it was *don't* trust, get away... something about finding the truth? What if the truth is something I don't want to know? Will it be worth finding? Worth my life?

I stop in the middle of the road. Ahead of me the road continues, and it will continue whether I travel it or not.

Behind me, every dent my feet have made will be for nothing if I choose to return to Maeve and Galen. What is my life worth, and why does everyone seem more interested in it than I am? The questions speak to my feet, which are swallowed up by the forest road and moving forward.

The sun lowers, drawing all color and warmth from the day, and I pull the hood closer to my face. Each time my heavy feet cause me to stumble, I attempt to walk with renewed purpose... until the next stumble. The road is now a soft ribbon that follows a series of hills and dales, and the forest has given way to scattered groves of trees surrounded by fields.

It can't be much further now.

What began as a statement is now a wish. At the next rise, I pause. The road trails towards a small stream in the distance. Beyond the stream, the road rises again, a dark strip through lighter fields. Tiny flecks of light gray dot the field near the stream. This must be Maeve's flower field. There are no beautiful colors to greet me at this hour, but I imagine how lovely it would be during the day. If their home is not too far from the field, I could come and appreciate it before heading on my way in the morning.

On my way to where?

I shrug at no one in particular and step out again.

A flicker of light catches my eye. Within the large grove of trees to my right, travelers have made camp for the night. The loud voices around the campfire are not *my* travelers. They have camped a reasonable distance from the road and I sneak by as quietly as I can. Their fire is going well and bursts of raucous laughter tell me the ale is flowing as freely as the stories. Watching the darkened road, I choose where to put my feet and grab glances at the camp as I make my way forward. It's not long until I need to look far over my shoulder to place the campfire and I can breathe freely.

"Well, what do we have here?" a gruff voice booms.

A hulk of a man stands before me on the road. He must be more than twice my size. He steps towards me, holding a torch.

My stomach falls to my feet, and I instinctively lower my gaze. "An idler on the way to my lodgings, sir." I lower my voice as best I can while still sounding natural, or at least convincing. Annoyed with the waver in my voice, I bow in respect and continue to walk past him. *One step, two steps . . .*

He grabs my shoulder and roars with laughter. The stench of heavy ale is thick on his breath.

"No, dear idler, you must camp with us for the night! Come, treat us to your entertainment."

I gently lunge away and bow once more. "Thank you for your kindness, but my companions are waiting for me just over the rise."

He laughs again, the same uproarious sound as before. "And they'll be there in the morning!"

In one swoop, he grabs my arm and drags me towards the camp. My legs are no match for his large stride and I leap and twist to avoid tripping on branches as we make our way through the grove. Oblivious to my lack of footing, he continues his march through the trees, dragging me backwards behind him by the shoulder.

"Please sir, I really should—" I plead quietly with him to release me, terrified of any further attention, but he ignores me. In my twisting efforts to get away, I catch glimpses of the campfire getting closer with each of his steps.

"It can't be said we're not generous to our fellow travelers," he shouts within earshot of the camp. "Grab another bowl, men. We've got idler entertainment this fine evening!"

He thrusts me into the clearing with a dramatic twirl, the final spinning action breaking the tie on my robe and sending it to the ground. In the firelight, I see the men surrounding the fire and hovering over their bowls like hungry dogs.

They wear the uniforms of Brennyn Hall.

❦

S hock wipes any expression from the faces around the campfire.

"Ha! What great fortune," a guard says. "We didn't have to hunt her, she came to us."

Several men stand, their bowls forgotten as their eyes dart and exchange looks. The air feels so thick I can barely draw breath. All this time, I thought it was the Hall that made the guards angry, but it was me all along. When you don't care whether you live or die, it's easy to shrug danger off as an inconvenience; this time foreign sensations smolder behind my panic. A gap between the men widens and I charge three paces towards it before I am wrenched back into the fire-lit circle. Being shackled by their grip somehow imprisons my mind. Garbled speech and mutinous laughter echo inside my head, clashing with the panic that rises from my chest and scatters into my limbs.

I had somewhere to go! I had people to see!

For once, for once, I actually mattered!

They laugh, and while they're caught up in their revelry, I attempt another useless break.

"You're not going anywhere."

"Thomas! Thomas! Bring more ale, boy!"

Thomas appears from the darkness, lugging two corked jugs of ale. He's older than I expected for their unholy page. I imagine they must keep him busy, heaving things from one place to another when they're so drunk they're incapable of doing anything for themselves. It's not until he is almost fireside that he sees me in their clutches. Behind the scraggly waves of hair that partly cover his face, a large scar on his jaw flashes white with light from the campfire. His wide eyes consider my predicament before he drops the jugs at his feet and runs off into the dark. Some yell obscenities after him and laugh more. The guards close in. My wits seem to have left along with Thomas, running for their lives through the dark.

Hands tear at my tunic and clothing, appearing everywhere. It seems pushing them from me and swatting at them only makes them multiply. Their power and roughness petrifies me and I am compensated with slaps and punches for my resistance, but I have been beaten before.

The terror of ownership plays in my head.

I am here! I am here! Do you not see me?

Look at me!

See me!

Vomit forces its way from my stomach. Strange emotions take control of my body, and I scream and shout. One guard who holds my arms laughs and I spit at him, only to receive a blow to the head.

⁘⁘⁘⁘⁘

Roused by shouting, I don't understand time or place. The pain in my head outweighs the aches of my body. My eyelids are heavy and unresponsive. Panicked voices, near and distant, shout and whine.

"What magic is this?"

"Kill her, kill it!"

"Eariss! Ark of Eariss!"

"I didn't touch her."

"Yes, you did."

"It'll burn us, set us on fire!"

"I want nothing to do with it."

"She's so ruined, she won't be causing him any more trouble."

"She's as good as dead in these parts, anyway."

"The lord can hunt and kill her himself."

"And Feeney can watch!" Such loud laughter. Blended with screams of terror.

Puzzling statements ride in and out of my mind on a ribbon. Sometimes the words curl around the ribbon and create new phrases of nonsense and leave me dreaming. One phrase never changes. ". . . hunt and kill . . .." The logs on the fire crack and shatter my nerves. I don't even fight the darkness when it calls again.

⁂

C lammy skin shivers under my hands and I dare not move. My fingers lightly press the skin and I wait. Several presses later, I confirm it as mine. The fire burns too low for me to feel any warmth from where I was discarded. A brutish man sits on a log and prods the fire with a stick, sending sparks upwards. He waves his wand, encouraging them to flee. They dance free against the night, some twirling high with energy, others floating softly. The sparks only make their escape a little distance before they are extinguished. Shadows of bodies snore around the fire in a mishmash of contortions.

Move!

Burning pain surges through my body as I force myself to sit. I cry out and the man at the fire spins and glares at me for disturbing his magic-making. His head wobbles as he tries to focus, then the stirs and grunts of the snorers distract him. In the low firelight, I see my robe and garments scattered around the campfire. I know I will need clothing. A drum beats loudly in my head and my ears buzz, and I casually notice my limbs work. I watch myself gather my garments from the mud and dirt. Occasionally, I disturb the snorers as I crawl by and they sneer and growl at me for momentarily blocking their warmth. My body welcomes the protection clothes give from the chill of the night air. But that's barely acknowledged somewhere in the back of my mind, in a place I can't reach right now.

Across the fire sits the magic man and his wand. He chuckles and a sadistic grin spreads across his inebriated face. I only have eyes for the straw doll he holds in his hands. He flips it this way and that, pretending to drop it into the fire and catching it, eager for a reaction. It's not that I don't understand the game we are playing, I just don't wish to play. Stepping over bodies, I slowly make my way to him, being careful to stay out of lunging distance lest I end up in the fire instead. There is no reason for discussion. Neither of us is capable of one, anyway. I hold out my hand and a flicker of emotion crosses his eyes. Is it sadness, pity? . . guilt? He gently leans forward and extends the doll to me. In the firelight I see some hair through a gap in the straw and desperation for comfort hollows my body. As I lean to collect my treasure, he tosses it into the fire, laughs and slaps his thigh. I'm unable to move. The doll smokes and then quickly catches alight. The faint smell of burning hair hangs among the smoke, leaving less for me to draw strength from. My head nods, but I don't understand.

The voices sound distant but are inside my head.

Are you waiting for permission to leave?

Why are you still standing here?

Without acknowledging their presence, I turn and walk.

The gray of dawn exposes a tree that has fallen in the forest. Drawn to it like kin, we share our devastation. The robe covers me as I curl up under the shelf of roots that form its brokenness.

The light mustn't find me.

S ensations of being stung and fiery heat rouse me from my sleep. Dazzling sunshine pierces the treetops and heats the robe against my skin. Even with my hand protecting me from the bright light, it takes a while to absorb my surroundings. The root well is musty with odors of rotting wood, and I pull a hard lump of dirt from behind my back. Pain strikes me the moment I sit up, and it puzzles me.

Oh, that's right, I'm walking from Brennyn Hall.

Am I going to the town market? No, I'm leaving the Hall forever.

Good! I congratulate myself; that was something I always wanted to do.

Light shimmers in the distance through the trees. The thought of water sparks my thirst and as I prepare to move, my clothing comes into focus.

Dirty clothes.

There's something strange about me wearing pants and a tunic, but it doesn't seem to be of consequence.

Odd that my mouth tastes of blood.

Tiny lumps of dried earth pinch my hands and knees as I crawl out of the hollow in the ground. Some stay with me, dropping to my feet and bouncing away as I brush them from the little dents they've made in my palms. Standing above the hollow, the shimmer expands to a lake, its brightness broken by the stripes of the casually spaced trees.

The forest tumbles towards the lake, leaving itself behind as it goes. Ferns and grasses give way to gravel that diminishes in size the closer it gets to the water's edge until only coarse sand forms the shore. Tall trees oversee the entire lake and above them is a cloudless sky with the sun high and proud. Gentle breezes rustle at the water and a fallen tree lies with half its body dipped into the water. Stripped by decay, it resembles a sun-hardened shell of what it once was, yet its essence remains. It is still 'tree.'

My skin sighs into the cool air as I remove the robe and clothes from my body. They land as a bundle on the water before spreading themselves out to bob lightly on the waves. I wade in after them, stopping to drink from my hands and chase the robe before it sinks. The clothes join me, floating nearby, and I grab each in turn, scrubbing them with sand, then setting them on the log to dry.

From the shore I admire the clothes lying in the sun like wares for sale. A cooler breeze strikes at my wet skin. My hands attempt to warm me but only smear dirt onto my skin. Skin in need of washing.

Little waves lap at my thighs as I position myself on the shore. With no activity to busy me, my aches return. Cuts and bruises show on my legs as they stretch out into the coolness, and I discover that if I disturb the surface of the water, it makes them shimmer away. Instead of washing, I play with the water, disguising, reflecting and distorting. Big waves and small waves, always in motion. Always busy. I scoop the silky water towards my face. Gently, the water washes over it and I wince.

How can the barest of touches rip and tear?

Eyes wide and without breath, I try to comprehend. A tear slides down my cheek and stings the cuts of my swollen lip.

Birds take flight around the lake, and I search for the cause of their disturbance. My arms are in the way, flailing wildly, and I try to make them stop to place where this awful noise is coming from, this angry wail, the terrified roar of some wounded animal. It is me.

The screams demand to be heard, with more power than my lungs can handle. Fistfuls of coarse wet sand scrub at my skin. Numb to the grit of the sand, I lunge at gravel in deeper water to clean the horror away, each slash and tear of my skin an unfeeling road marker to the pain I am digging inside myself to eradicate.

Small sobs still arrive unbidden and I regain control of myself. In a distant part of my mind, I recall stories of great beasts, lake-dwelling creatures that eat men by the dozens. This is where I will go. This is how I will end.

The water splashes at my thighs as I walk into the lake—surely there is peace in nothingness. The tall trees that surround the lake can't hide the turrets of the Hall in the distance. A last glimpse for me to acknowledge its victory, and my dutiful sacrifice at its feet.

Thoughts stab mercilessly at my heart and steal my breath as I force myself through the water.

Grown men scared.

The Eariss.

Diseased.

Evil.

So stupid to believe I could be anything else.

Deep water envelops me and its coolness washes over my hot, swollen eyes. Under the water, nothing exists. Swallowed water sears my throat and washes away the familiar taste of my blood. Still, the voices of the Hall boom in my aching head.

You caused this!

Look what you made me do!

It's always your fault!

As I surface, the wind blows across my ears, the only sound in the center of the lake. Pathetic sobs jab at my body while my chest crushes with a desolate sorrow so heavy I wonder how it's possible I'm not plunged to the depths. Leaning back, I float and wait for the monsters to take me, to rip me to pieces.

❦

D eath doesn't even want me.

And I don't know if I care anymore.

Floating.

Floating.

Breathe in.

Breathe out.

Warm sun on my face.

I move my arms and the gentle tinkle of moving water creates a melody against the steady heartbeat in my ears.

Breathe in.

Breathe out.

There is nothing. The whole world is warm and red behind my eyelids, and the beat continues in my ears.

Breathe in.

Breathe out.

My breath sounds like winds in a cavern. The water acts like a cradle, supporting me. I have no weight; I have no body.

Breathe in.

Breathe out.

All is well.

A strange voice speaks to my entire body, as if it rose up inside me and flooded every piece of me.

All is well, it says again, soothing and calm, solid and powerful. Trustworthy.

Perhaps I've gone mad, as fragmented as the glass panes in the great hall, each view changing depending on which pane you look through. But if this is madness, then I welcome the peace it brings. Amid the sounds of my breath and the steady beating of my heart, the heaviness in my chest somehow becomes bearable.

Have no fear, the voice soothes. *I've got you.*

My vigilance lies in ruin, and I don't bother to raise its walls. I am not alone. I am seen. By something powerful and mysterious. Gratitude swallows me, and for a time, is all that exists.

I formulate a question for this Mystery with my mind.

Why aren't I dead?

There is work to do.

Me? I think you have the wrong person.

I don't.

But I have nothing. No name, no strength, no class and no reputation. I fear there's nothing left of me to be useful for anything.

Those things have no value, but you do.

But I'm broken, useless.

I want you to trust me.

But I have nothing.

You have me. You have you.

My body bends as I sink into the water to cool my warmed face, and a burst of red greets my eyelids as I resurface. What a strange place to find myself, floating naked in a lake and possessing nothing that my society would use to categorize me. Yet I feel I have everything I need. This Mystery is cradling and caring for me. Columns of hope slide the heaviness from my chest and I relax into the sensation of weightlessness.

I don't care if I've gone mad.

I can breathe.

I lose track of the days as I share them with the Mystery. Strength returns to my body as I explore the forest, and I heal. My lips don't split and bleed if I smile, and the healthy ache of well-used muscles rises to conquer the physical pain, a kind gesture to sweep away memory. The leaf litter and ferns at the base of trees provide comfortable bedding, and the roots shield me from the winds that smooth across the surface of the lake. Berries and fruit are in ample supply, and even though my voice rests, my mind fills with an extraordinary amount of knowledge and understanding. Concepts that at first seemed strange and unsettling now feel perfectly commonplace and I no longer fear for my mind.

I have no inclination to leave the forest. Sometimes I wonder if it's possible to stay here forever and imagine myself as a gray-haired crone living in the forest, perpetuating the old tales that scare village children into staying close to their homes. Apart from the plume of smoke over the mountain, I am entirely alone.

A fawn emerges from the forest to drink, exposed. My mouth dries, the boom of my heartbeat drowns out my mind's plea for it to run as if its vulnerability somehow asks for it to be hunted. The wisp of its tail disappears into the undergrowth before I breathe again and allow myself to settle. No one is here to see me being kind to myself, or to judge me for being patient with my nerves. I can take all the time I need.

The Mystery is here too. While I explore the forest, it stays close at hand, always available to guide and explain. Our conversations often circle back to the gully, a small ravine near the tree where I sleep. Ferns and grasses line its steep sides and a small rocky stream splashes its way along the base. A fallen tree creates a bridge from one side to the other as clear a pathway as a cobbled road. Every morning I look across the gully to the raspberries on the other side, and every morning the Mystery offers me the opportunity to cross the gully on the log provided. And every morning, I acknowledge the bridge, but still make my way down the gully and back up to the other side.

Perhaps you might like to cross the log on the way back? The Mystery suggests one day as I pluck the berries.

"Perhaps," I reply and eye the bridge as I eat the plump raspberries cupped in my hand.

One morning, I walked right up to the log and placed my foot upon it. It was strong and sure. Another morning I actually stood on the log and inched my way forward, but when I raised my arms to balance, the flashes of cobblestones in my mind made me ill.

Today, the last berry squishes between my teeth, and I wipe my hands on my tunic. "Tomorrow." I tell myself, and I make my way back through the ferns and grasses into the gully.

The clumps of grass that grow on the other side of the gully are perfect grip-holds for my hands as I pull myself up the steepest parts. My knees cup into the soft earth, help with my scramble, and take some weight from my arms as I catch my breath.

Why didn't I just cross the log?

That log looks as solid and safe as the Mystery itself, the place I hide when my memories are painful, when I'm trying to make sense of my tale. But I'm not that brave. It takes a courage I don't have yet to step there.

There's freedom in the forest's wide-open spaces, yet its constant exposure terrifies me. It depends on which I concentrate on. My mind seems eager to remind me of the Hall. Instead, I use it to imagine the Hall as an old heavy robe on my tired shoulders; they sting and hunch under its weight and push my feet into the ground. My back tenses and straightens as I fight against it, squirming for the best stance to force it from me. I twist and push it back from me, amazed I don't float away as I discard it. It looks pathetic lying crumpled on the ground, lifeless even. I can't help myself. I prod it with a stick. Was I the one that kept it alive? I try to understand it, make sense of it, as if things I can bundle and package neatly will lose their sharp corners.

Who was I at the Hall?

Even the words I spoke were not my own.

Who am I in this vast space with no restrictions?

Why were they so scared of me?

Memories of the Hall rise in a seething, tangled mess inside, and I cringe in shame. The trees bend to cover me, protect me, as images flash and tear at my heart. Here, my body is free to respond how it chooses. I won't demand its silence or force it to deny anything. When I land on my knees, crawl and wretch, the Mystery kneels beside me and holds me in its presence. At the shore I slide into the lake and the water rushes in and fills the empty spaces, trickling through me and finding gaps inside me I didn't even know existed. Each time I return, the water fills and heals, and slowly I feel whole. The smoke from behind the mountain continues. I swat at it as I would a troublesome fly.

The trees are teaching me—how could this be true? Their hum is unmistakable, comforting and wise. My hands stroke their bark and I wander through the forest, seeing lessons everywhere, as clear as if someone had just opened a window. The strength of the tree is in its roots, unseen and powerful. My roots need to be in the Mystery, not in my body or my mind. I can't believe I couldn't see it before, as if their message was hidden in plain view.

Hidden. Eyes to see. *Is this what Eshnae was talking about?*

The back of my hand pushes branches from the path, my breath catches in my throat and I stop.

How did I end up here?

The fallen log doesn't look as terrifying now, the gully not as deep. Small steps. The Mystery is here with me. The trees around me hold their breath as I prepare to step up onto the log.

Will you trust?

The question beats in my heart and radiates to my fingertips. I provide my answer by stepping onto the log but my knees shudder and barely hold me up.

Will you trust?

I take a step along the log—my feet now level with where the gully drops away.

Will you trust?

I step out and wobble, my arms raise to my sides for balance. Among the flashes of cobblestones, green dresses, swords, screeching anger and shame, the Mystery breaks through the noise and calls,

Will you trust?

My hands waver, sending a tremor down my arms into my body, and my knees shake. A sob escapes my lips, tears sting my eyes, my breath trembles. The gully below is a blur that threatens to swirl. I spy the green of the slippery moss between my feet and the log through my tears. I blink them away and lift my chin.

And I take another step.

The forest exhales with joy.

I breathe and regain my balance before I take my time crossing the log, small measured steps that cleanse with each footfall, wobble and slip. I know I'm different when I step from the log to the other side. The world is different. The forest is greener, the raspberries sweeter and my heart that bit lighter. My knowing that bit deeper.

Lessons fill some days, others I relax and blend into the surrounding life. Physically, I'm strong, and my emotions are recovering, but my nerves are slow to heal, and they battle with my latest thoughts. However much I would like to stay here, I won't be safe until I understand my threat to the Hall—to everyone. An overwhelming wiggle is under my skin, made worse each time I notice the smoke in the distance. Like an itch, it irritates but promises something magnificent is waiting, if I will only find it for myself.

For days I have passed a stick on the forest floor. It's my new walking stick, but I'm not ready to pick it up yet. Just like the smoke, it reminds me that the forest is not my home. The Mystery is a gentleman, and even though I'm braver than before, I still act like a frightened fawn. I turn my face away from the stick whenever I see it, sometimes turning on my heels and walking in the opposite direction. This game we play is still about trust, or rather, my lack of it.

I wake to see smoke again on the other side of the mountain. As I watch it, the voice is unmistakable and firm.

Today.

Resignation escapes from my chest in a flustered sigh. "I know . . . but . . . there will be people."

That is true.

The mountain looks like a merchant's hat, its gray feather streaky and blowing in the wind. The lake below shimmers like it always does in the morning sun. With my eyes closed, I concentrate on every color and reflection, forcing it into my memory. I wander into the forest touching my favorite trees in goodbye, trying so hard to force everything, every tiny sensation, into my mind—the way the moss smells, the bumpy bark of the tree that watches over the gully. Halfway across the log I sit and watch the water tumble over the rounded rocks, then close my eyes and listen to it as a background to the birdsong. The sun glows red behind my eyelids and smooths across my cheeks. I hold my arms out and I think about balance and I think about trust.

Curiosity bubbles within me as I head to where my walking stick is waiting. I hesitate, then pick it up and wipe the rough bark from where I will place my hand. I'm not surprised that it's a perfect fit, yet I'm agitated that the Mystery knows me so well.

"But I don't want to walk on the road. Please don't ask me to walk on the road."

Where is the smoke?

"Over the mountain."

Well, go over the mountain.

The thing about walking is it clears your mind. Each step a connection, sometimes backward, sometimes forward, but always making connection and setting things aright. The view from the opposite side of the lake is just as incredible as the one I'd looked at each day. From this side, the trees still look like they hover over the lake and tend it. The forest floor rises and falls making its way up the mountain, the grasses thicken and I follow the tracks that animals have made on their way to the higher pasture lands. A small stream winds its way down to the lake. The path splits into two, snaking its way through the grass, and indecision arrives in the familiar form of fear.

Am I even capable of making a decision? What if I make the wrong one?

Fear sneers at me and holds out a robe that promises to make me comfortable. But I know that robe will be heavy and hard to remove. It's clear I travel with two companions at hand. The Mystery and fear.

Do I trust myself?

If I met myself walking on the road, would I trust my own advice? I close my eyes, take a deep breath and try to exhale the nerves from my body. I imagine my feet growing strong roots down into the ground. In my mind, I push the robe away and ask after the Mystery.

Sunlight bounces from the stream in front of me. I can forge my own path alongside it. The light forest and grassland make way to mossy rocks dotting the landscape as I trek higher following the stream's course. By the time the sun is high in the sky only windswept boulders surround me, and I find a shady perch on one beside the stream. Trees and rolling hills spread out in front of me and I wonder where Galen's home sits among all those pockets of green, and whether someone made it to Rand's. Surely they have. Would I be in their thoughts? Would they wonder why I didn't make it? My eyes water against the wind that patters at the ridge above me and I lower my face to the stream that bounces its way through the boulders.

Puddles.

Rivers.

"Gifts," I mumble, repeating the word Galen used to describe me and tumble it over in my mind. Yes. I believe others have gifts. I've seen them. Perhaps I could believe I have gifts myself. The thought seizes me, crushes my stomach and fear offers me another robe. The wind seems colder. I imagine myself reaching for the robe but choose instead to keep moving.

A t the ridge, the stream continues to the higher peaks and I step to the other side, moving my way down over the large stones. Grateful relief floods my muscles. Who would have thought a change in direction would be so welcome? The tree line grows higher on this side of the mountain and the source of the smoke appears through the tops of the trees. It's a village cut into the base of the next mountain, as if someone had carved a hunk out of roasted meat. Smoutlea.

Trees surround it entirely, except for where thatched roofs butt up against the cut in the mountain, and the road creates a thin line of shadow leading in and out. Pasture land flattens beyond the mountain in different shades of greens and browns dotted with pockets of forest. I scoot down the larger stones, slipping occasionally on the moss, and jump from one to another as they tumble down in size the lower I travel. Back inside the cover of the forest the winds stop their constant battering and I pull back my hood to enjoy the silky stillness.

The energy of the village comes through the trees. First it's a hum, then a song of different noises. The breeze carries smells, faint at first then stronger as I get closer. I jump when I hear shouts and laughter, then smile and use the trees as my cover, moving from one to another, each one closer to the village than the one before.

The forest ends—at a wall. A fence of timbers higher than my head. The smell of food had already removed any doubt about entering the village and my stomach growls in disappointment. The timber slats don't budge when I push them, even the ones further along the wall hidden behind bushes. I clamber up a nearby tree, moving high into its branches until I see over the wall. Between the leaves and gaps in the branches fragments of a new world appear. So many people fill Smoutlea's walls. Carts and animals, buying and selling, laughing, shouting, noise and smell. The protective wall, although in disrepair, circles this side of the village, and the steep mountainside provides a natural wall on the other. People gather at the gates. They're tipping the hoods of robes off travelers as they enter the village.

Guards.

Disappointment silences my stomach and I rest my head against the branch.

Below me, thick brush runs along the length of the wall. I raise my head and tip it to each side and confirm that some of the boards in the wall are askew. Beyond the gap, a large crowd mills about on its way to the main square. I wind my way to the ground.

My hands lay on either side of the gap in the wall as the brush pushes me gently against it and my senses urge me onward. This wood under my hands separates me from the village and while it's no longer alive, it still contains its purpose, hopefully leading me to mine.

I step inside and look around, convinced the whole village can hear the thumping of my heart. My knuckles are white on my stick and I concentrate on forcing them to relax as I shuffle towards the square as the old idler. The sensations and energy of the village choke and overwhelm me, and I weaken and search for somewhere to rest from the bustle. A passing nurse takes pity on the old idler and breaks a small piece of bread from a loaf and waves it under my nose to get my attention. The bread is still warm in my hand. The crust dissolves in my mouth as I nibble at the bread and defy the urge to swallow it whole. A small patch of ground in the corner of the busy marketplace provides me with a place to settle and savor each small bite until the bread is gone. With a calmer heart I watch the procession of buyers and sellers, absorb the sights and smells, and as I relax further, hear the hidden stories of those around me.

A red-faced and rigid man haggles over the price of a goat. His actions have nothing to do with the goat or its price. He boasts to the trader about his knowledge but I know that hidden beneath that story is one where his wife recently told him he is incapable of making a sound decision. He will win his argument and prove the trader wrong—how proud he will be—but will take home a defective goat to his wife. The truth of some stories hide and they live in the village of Smoutlea just as they live within the walls of the Hall.

The baker's apprentice sorts and places the best bread on a plat-ter and offers it to the guards at the gate. The guards laugh at his timidity as he trembles in fear at their unpredictable nature. They are unaware he also shakes with an inability to contain his rage, a strength that makes me fear for the future safety of the guards. The unrest is brewing in the village as much as it was in the Hall.

Children play and sing, weaving among the traveling nurses who offer hope and smiles with their satchels of herbs and ointments. How sweet to hear something familiar. . . . *saved by blood, crown of fire, taught by stars, fueled by pyre* . . . Flower sellers do nothing more than brighten the scene with dots of color and welcome perfume. Blue flowers bounce past, their tongues poking out from the side of a basket, and the melody of Joss's voice plays in my head.

The village is a magical dance of people, their hopes and dreams, their anguish and fears, and it plays out before me. Each of them knows the steps of their dance well; it's the only dance they've been taught. Any change of step upsets the whole dance and theirs is one of safety and predictability. The unrest hasn't arrived yet. A sense of dread and compassion clamps around my heart and I hope that the village of Smoutlea will find its courage and knows to be brave.

The uneasiness won't lift. I force my thoughts to return to the flower sellers and look about for something encouraging and uplifting to take this sensation from me.

But it won't move.

Nervous energy crackles through my body and screams *danger* but I don't know where the danger lies.

Let your guard down and this is what happens! You fool!

Fear hands me a robe and I wrap myself snugly. The hairs on my arms stand on end. Unknown eyes watch me and my mouth dries in panic. My legs wobble as I stand but I lean heavily on the walking stick and I don't fall. I step away from the square slowly, hoping to dissuade any suspicions with my disguise. Houses line the streets around the square like soldiers in a row, watchful, eying my every move.

In the narrower side street I increase my pace as much as my costume will allow, desperate to put some distance between me and the eyes I feel as keenly as a dagger held at my back. The heavy hood covers most of my face and when I turn to look behind me all I catch is a glimpse of a passing building and the inside of the hood. The street softens under my shoes, and soggy patches of household waste make their way into the open ditch in the center of the street. My fingers pinch my chin as I pull the hood tightly around my head and turn to see a robed figure following my route.

Think! Think! My brain repeats the words but offers nothing, silenced by the panic rising in my chest and still crackling through my limbs. The stick digs into the softer earth as I sidestep dogs playing in the path. I remember to nod to everyone as I pass, not sure whether it would help or damn me if they could see the terror in my eyes. My legs are at a trot while the careful strides of my follower thud into the earth behind me.

Could this be a misunderstanding? My imagination?

I turn at a lane that runs between two houses. If the dark robe follows me back towards the square on another street, I will know if I am truly in danger. As I round the corner, throngs of people appear ahead of me in the square at the end of the street. The square offers multiple places to hide, but only if I can get there in time. I don't bother to hide my face as I check back for the last time to see the dark robe turning and heading towards me at speed.

I charge into the crowd then slow myself. I am within arm's reach of anyone who would choose to grab me. Fear grips my heart, squeezing it within an inch of its life, and I forget to breathe. The slush on the road makes me slip. A farmer parades a young horse for sale across my path followed by interested buyers who surround him. I push my way past the horse admirers and make my way down a narrow lane where I hope to disappear among the debris of village life. The taller houses close in together and hover as I gasp my way along the lane. Away from the noise of the crowd I can hear the blood rushing in my ears and feel cloudy, nauseous. Fear wraps itself around any thought and contorts it and it's not until I catch my breath that my mind starts to analyze.

Aren't I just mindlessly reacting?

What do I truly need to do right now?

Get away from the dark robe.

But I need to know why they follow me.

The thud of steps closes in behind me. Curiosity grows. Everything closes in, the houses, the sounds, the smell, the robe—everything closes in with no escape. Every fiber of every muscle tenses and I force myself to turn and face my attacker. The dark robe is upon me in one stride.

T he robe halts before me, raises its head and I seethe.
That jagged scar! "Thomas?" The word hisses through my
teeth.

Thomas breaks into a senseless grin. "You know my name!"

A raging fury overwhelms any remaining fear and charges it
away. My fists and teeth clench, and I step closer to him to avoid
any attention from the villagers. My teeth don't unclench even as
I speak. "You scared me to death! Why are you following me?"

His ridiculous smile droops when he realizes I'm not as ecstatic
about our meeting as he is. "I knew it. I just knew I'd find you."

I'm not sure whether he is addressing me or himself, and his
answer does nothing to soothe me. I shake my head in frustration
and anger. It is completely beyond me why he would think our
meeting a happy occasion. This lad must be simple. That's why he
ran that night. And now he stands before me, smiling like we're
old friends. I pinch his robe and lead him to walk with me towards
the noise of the market, heads down in our robes. I hope no one

has noticed our awkward scene. I tug hard on his robe, which is still pinched between my fingers.

"What were you thinking?" I tug again for good measure. "What makes you think I would ever want to meet you again? You do remember that night, don't you? Stop. Following. Me!" People cross in front of us at the edge of the square and my anger and fright wanes a little, then fear swoops into its place. "Wait. Why were you following me? To do me harm?" My eyes scan for any exit as fear takes hold again.

"I could never harm you," he whispers, head down. The joy has left his words. He is serious now. "Don't run. I must speak with you."

Did he mean to remind me of my disguise when he placed his hand on my walking stick? I bring my head low and take the old idler's stance again and breathe and calm myself as we watch people pass us by. Thomas looks ahead over the crowd, pulls back his hood and makes checks in all directions. The determination on his face wipes away the simpleton I imagined and I notice that he is older and seemingly wiser than I had given him credit for. His dark hair falls in waves at his shoulders but doesn't hide the battle scar along his jawline. Unlike my sackcloth disguise, his dark robe is woven with fine wool and gives him a regal air. I nod. Now it is his turn to pinch at my robe. He leads me towards an alehouse at the side of the square.

My emotions have shaken the Mystery from me and I claw for anything that might calm me. I could read the people in the marketplace but now I can't read Thomas. Dodging people and animals, we cross the square unnoticed. Thomas pulls on my robe, not urgently but to lead me around puddles and loose animals. My body follows but inside I grasp at any sensation that resembles the Mystery. I find nothing. We stop in a short lane that separates the alehouse and its stables. Ahead of us, the gray wall of the mountain towers into the sky.

Thomas stands next to a large pile of tied and loose hay stored between the holding stalls. He releases my robe and watches the crowd as it mills around in the square and the people spill in and out of the alehouse. He watches intently, scans, then watches again. His concentration is so intense I stand still, unsure of whether he has forgotten I am here. Without taking his eyes from the crowd he moves a large sack with his foot. What I thought was a large sack of grain is actually stuffed with something light, probably hay. Behind the sack is a small hole in the hay. He flicks his head sideways towards the hay.

"Get in."

My feet pace up and down.

I try to think, but my mind is a jumble.

I obey.

Straw scrapes and scratches at my robe as I crawl through the hole. A short tunnel leads to a larger opening hidden inside the hay. Tall enough for me to sit up in, the space is surrounded by hay but supported by a framework that stops it from caving in. The only entrance and exit is behind me now. Straw flicks up from the ground as I twist and scoot my back to the wall opposite the tunnel and clutch my knees to my chest. *Fool!*

Without speaking, Thomas crawls into the small space and digs around at the bottom of one of the hay walls. If I stretched out my legs, I could touch him; maybe I could kick him, but he is still between me and escape. A thinner wall of hay on one side allows the sunlight to gather a yellow hue before entering the room. Thomas pulls out a large lump of bread and uses a great deal of strength to break a piece from it. Once torn, he tears the piece in half again and offers it to me.

It tastes like straw.

We chew in silence. He reclines on one elbow, looks down at the floor of padded hay and ignores me. My breathing calms and the muscles of my legs soften, then my back and my arms. Air rushes about my head and ears as I push my hood away. Sounds from the

busy square muffle their way through the straw but this moment
is silence to me. A dry mouth and dry bread makes chewing hard,
but at least I don't have to talk. Thomas still stares at the ground,
sometimes lifting his eyes to check on me.

You fool! You're trapped!

But he's only shown me kindness.

*You're still trapped. You're still a fool, and an ungrateful one at
that!*

Thomas already trusts me enough to show me the hiding place
for his food, and all I have shown him is anger. Any lessons I
thought I'd learned at the lake and my trek across the mountains
were obliterated by my reactions and fears. And where is the Mystery? Not even a full day has passed, and I have ruined my peace and
accused Thomas of wishing to harm me. I've messed everything up
again.

I moan loudly at my stupidity.

"Are you unwell?" His words shock me from my thoughts.

My jaw stops half chew and my eyes threaten to leap from my
head. "Mmm, bread's good," I lie.

He raises his eyebrows. We both know the bread is terrible.

"I've been eating lots of berries." I say, and now I'm the one who
sounds simple.

❧❦☙

T homas finishes his bread and fidgets, leaning this way and
that, never quite comfortable with his position. He finally
settles with his back leaning on the wall, his legs stretched out like
brown-clothed barriers that cover my escape tunnel. His shoulders
jostle against the wall as he speaks.

"I've been waiting to talk to you since I first saw you, and now I
don't know where to start." He offers a light-hearted chuckle, but
I feel little like smiling.

Footsteps and conversation outside the hay halt his laugh and we sit in silence and listen as the voices attend to their horses and discuss their day. The quiet rumble of the square continues; an occasional shout or laugh reaches through the hay and I hear the strum of a minstrel as he passes by the alehouse. The footsteps move away from the stalls as the last of the bread slides down my throat. Thomas waits until I make eye contact.

"What do you know about yourself?"

The question is jarring. I know I've just been shoved in a hole and eaten gravel disguised as bread. My heart beats with remnants of fear; everything has turned upside down. In one afternoon, judgment and irrational thoughts have replaced the peace I thought I understood. I don't want to answer his stupid question. I don't even want to think about it. I shake my head. "Myself? You said you wanted to speak with me, not me with you!"

The words tumble out of my mouth like daggers, such a contrast to his gentle enquiry. Does he sense I'm not proud of my response? I can't bring myself to look at his face, or to apologize for my reaction either. His hand collects a single piece of straw from the floor, one that the threshers have left some grain in, and he picks at the wheat, eating the seeds as the husk releases them.

"Perhaps I can offer you some kindness, some help." He crunches a grain with his teeth. "You're obviously traveling. I've been crossing the holdings for a while. I might know of things unfamiliar to you. Ask away."

His focus returns to the grain and I consider his offer. Does he know anything about the Eariss? I force myself to think about travel. "I came to this village from the mountains." I look up to see I have his full attention. "There were guards at the gate. Do all villages have them?"

"Most do. They're a recent thing. The elders demanded them for the safety of the villagers." He shakes his head. "But now they're used to collect silver and control our movements. If you're a want-

ed man, they'll find you, or else someone will talk. They always
do."

The lump in my throat chokes me when he mentions 'wanted,'
and I cough to settle my throat. "I see. Who mans them? Who
supplies the men?"

"The landholder. We're still in the holdings of Brennyn Hall
here, so that's where the men would be picked from."

"So they're guards of the Hall?"

"No, not guards, just men that are rounded up for service for a
short time. Then they get to go back to their families."

Thomas continues to answer my questions and not once does
he make me feel stupid. More and more questions spill from my
mouth as I begin to understand the world outside the walls.

"Have you heard of Sirban? How far is it? What other villages
are around here? Are they far away?"

Thomas smiles gently and spreads the straw away to reveal the
dirt underneath. He takes a thick piece of straw and begins to
draw.

"This is where we are now, in Smoutlea village." He draws a
circle in the center of his 'map' then scratches a larger circle off to
the left. "This is the forest, and these..." he says, drawing a zigzag
line above the forest, "are the mountains you crossed."

"Where is Brennyn Hall?"

"Here." He draws another circle, this time on the other side of
the mountains to where we are.

I must get further away.

The straw stylus buckles under his fingers and he stops to select
another before continuing with lines and circles. "On this side
of Smoutlea, if you take the road that follows the base of the
mountain there are only a couple of villages before the next range.
The village of Sirban is on top but I've never been there myself."

I move to my knees for a closer look. "Are all these villages under
the jurisdiction of Brennyn Hall?"

He nods and keeps his eyes on the map. "The Hall's power reaches all the way to Sirban. So tell me, Ashling, what's so important about Sirban?"

My breath catches in my throat, but I'm not angry anymore, just curious. "How do you know my name?"

"Everyone knows who you are."

"I've heard that. How?"

"Everyone knows the story of the lovely Lady Ashling, kept prisoner in the Hall." He pushes himself up and sits cross-legged in front of me. "Her presence is a gift to the world, but the Hall condemns her, and us, to silence."

Straw slides under my hands as I push myself back into the wall. Thomas moves away from me and blocks the exit as he continues. "The villagers aren't stupid, Ashling. The lord and his guards might tell us one thing, but we all have hearts to listen, if only you will tell us."

"Me tell you? Tell you what? I have nothing to say. I just want to get away from Brennyn Hall." He stares at me accusingly. "What? I don't know anything. I don't even know where villages are or understand this world. How can I tell you anything?"

"The children sing of you in the streets." Thomas ignores my frown. "Ashling, what do you know about the Eariss?"

Oh, thank the Stars, he's changing the subject. "The Eariss. Yes. I've heard a little. But I'm not sure if it's good or bad, helpful or evil. What's it about, do you know?"

"You know nothing at all of the Eariss?"

"Not really." I shake my head, partly to shed images of Feeney from it. "Do you?"

A smile stretches across his face and I expect him to pick up another piece of straw and explain everything, but something pounds three times on the hay pile and dusty straw rains onto us. Thomas raises his finger to his lips and I obey.

"Thomas! With all your talk of magic you haven't made the firewood chop itself yet."

"On my way, Winnie, you luscious creature!" he yells to the straw above him and Winnie's voice mutters into the distance. He lets out a small chuckle and looks to me. A change settles over him, and all joy fades from his face and pulls the smile from mine.

"Please stay," he says. "I'll understand if you're gone. But whatever you do..." Thomas reaches for my hand and I pull it away, "...you must stay safe." He offers me a half-smile and enters the tunnel. His shoulders drag more straw from above him as he crawls, and little pieces sparkle and cascade down his back and over his thighs like a curtain. The light inside his straw home blinks brighter as he exits then dulls as he replaces the sack at the entrance.

Layers of straw under my hands bend like soft moss when I put my weight on them. The tunnel is an arm length away but my mind floods with the comforting sensation of the padding under my hands and knees. I surrender and stretch out into the softness. After all my nights spent at the base of trees, I'm floating on a cloud. Even on my back or side, there's no way to be uncomfortable. The ceiling is out of reach when I'm on my back and I stretch my arms far back above my head and point my toes but still can't feel the confines of the walls. My arms flop to my sides and I close my eyes.

Thomas didn't demand I stay.

He demanded nothing of me.

R ustling.
Straw.
Dull light.

The fog in my head clears as my limbs scramble and move me back to my familiar place in the straw room. My fingers rub at my eyes and rake hay from my hair. While I slept the room has grown creamier, the light less urgent for attention. Thomas crawls into the room on his elbows. In one hand he holds two spoons upright, and the other guides a wooden bowl through the tunnel. The rich aroma of a mixed stew reaches me and my mouth waters before he has even placed the bowl down. He crawls out again and returns with a jug of ale. By the time he positions himself and hands me a spoon I'm sure I'd do almost anything for that stew, even apologize for being rude, but still he makes no demands.

We sit cross-legged in the little straw house, our spoons resting in the bowl that sits between us. The stew's not hot enough to burn, but just the right kind of hot that warms your stomach and spreads through the rest of your body. How will I pay for this happiness, this moment in time? I can be sure it will catch me, but for now, I hope Thomas knows I appreciate his kindness, even if my behavior says otherwise. "Thank you. It's delicious."

"She's not a bad cook, the old ale-keep, though she clips me around the ear enough." He grins and adds, "Poor Winnie. But she's always up for a bit of cheek."

He dips his spoon into the bowl and chuckles when the spoon reaches his mouth, no doubt remembering some jest at Winnie's expense. I can understand her wanting to keep him around; he can even make *me* smile. How satisfying it must be for her to smack at his cheekiness.

The bread tears in jagged strips, perfect for soaking up the last of the stew. They become tough straps of flavor and put our jaws to work to finish our meal, leaving us alone with our thoughts.

Thomas finishes first. "I'm glad you stayed," he says.

I nod.

The ale is warm and not at all strong. We pass the jug between us and try to guess the spices and flavors in this mix. Thomas makes me laugh with his tales of the different tastes he has experienced and the places he has traveled.

"Well, that's it," he says as he tips the jug upside down and looks into the empty bowl. He gathers them up and moves towards the exit. "No point inviting any more rats. There's enough in this village already." He scurries out through the tunnel.

I breathe in slow and deep, the scent of straw, stew and ale all about me and now within me. My body relaxes when I exhale. I am content. Yes, this is what contentment must feel like. Safety, food and laughter. Like Galen's farm. If only I could let them know I'm laughing again. I imagine them smiling and shaking their heads at me as I sit curled here in a house of straw.

Thomas returns and crawls to another section of the straw wall, pulls out a leather satchel and sits cross-legged with the satchel on his lap. His hands grip the leather side gussets, his thumbs massage its clasp and a serious air hovers about him. The yellow straw wall fades to creamy gray in the dying light. "If you won't tell me your story, I will tell you mine," he says. "My father was a carpenter in Feldston. Ever been to Feldston?"

I raise my eyebrows. No, I haven't. My chains didn't reach that far.

Thomas lowers his gaze and picks at the odd-shaped clasp on the satchel. He rubs at his cheek and his fingertips settle on massaging his temple before he sighs and returns his hand to the clasp. "I have a great interest in the Eariss." Thomas squares his shoulders, but parts of him disappear, fading behind his words. "It's a fascinating topic. I've traveled the holdings, asking questions, listening to folklore and making observations. I'm recording it all in a book." He taps the satchel.

I nod. "Can you tell me what you know?"

Thomas ignores my question. "This book will be truth, not hatred. Not vile accusations that...." His body trembles just like the baker's apprentice did at the gates. His eyes scan the room and recognize me. He remembers I am here. "...and you can help me."

"No, I can't. I can't even write."

"I don't need you to write, I need you to talk."

Not this again. "I already told you I don't know anything."

"I know you don't. That's why you're in danger."

"I'm always in danger!"

"Ashling. Listen to me. You're the Eariss."

"What? I don't even know what the Eariss is. How can I be something I don't know anything about?" I shuffle in the straw trying to get to my knees, with flashes of Feeney's accusing eyes boring into my mind. *The Eariss is evil. Sent to destroy us all.* "You're mad! At first I thought you were just simple but you're really just completely mad, aren't you? Let me out of here. Now!"

Thomas won't move, and I stand, hit my head on the ceiling and fall to the ground. The shame of being face first in the straw pales against the stupidity of having felt secure in the presence of a madman. My only way out is past Thomas, and I dive for the opening to the tunnel. Thomas grabs me mid-dive, flips me onto my back and pins me down by holding my wrists on either side of my head. My legs are free and I swing them around trying to make contact with his head, or failing that, any part of his body. He slams his thigh over my legs and lies beside me.

"I'll scream," I hiss at him.

"You scream and you'll be dead by dawn, and not at my hand."

We puff and pant in tense silence, our bodies as hard and unforgiving as our minds. His hands push my wrists into the straw. I push back with equal force, my muscles charged and ready to fight, waiting for any opportunity, but none arrives.

Daisies?

Why do daisies come to mind?

Now of all times?

Their heads bobbing down Joss's stream as she moves the rocks and directs their course. Droplets of water tip them slightly, but they continue on their way. My mind follows them down the stream, my hands and wrists softening against his force.

Thomas loosens his grip on my wrists and I wriggle them out from under his hands.

"Sorry," he says. "But you need to be safe."

"And you're the one to decide how that happens?"

Thomas shakes his head and slides his leg from mine, sits up and gestures to the tunnel. I sit and brush straw from my arms, picking at the last pieces with my fingers.

"You're just going to get covered again going out the tunnel," he says. He wears one of his half-smiles and the tunnel that once held the promise of hope and freedom looks decidedly sinister. "You scared?" he asks as I stare at the exit.

My head trembles into a nod.

"You don't need to be scared, you just need to listen. Will you listen?"

17

"The Eariss isn't evil—at least I don't think it is," he says.

Oh Stars, this will be a long night. If Thomas isn't sure of anything about the Eariss what hope do *I* have of understanding it? Weight presses on my shoulders; its heaviness floods into my body and courses its way to my fingers and toes. Immovable. Heavy. Thomas strokes the satchel again, his fingers tracing its cut leather edges as he prepares to speak.

I'll leave when he sleeps.

"It's always been around, this hatred of the Eariss, and the stories always come from the Hall. They're the ones that brought in the laws that all newborns should be checked and then tried to pass it off as a quaint tradition. It's the Hall that's at war with the Eariss, but I'm not exactly sure why."

"That's the colors in a babe's eyes?"

Thomas nods. "Any child born with the sign of the Eariss shall be put to death." All color fades from his face and he adds, "According to Feeney's book."

"You know about Feeney's book?"

Thomas grasps at the satchel again. "I want this to put an end to Feeney's book. People believe his tales of destruction and the horror of the Eariss. They work themselves up over rumors and lies. I need to find the truth about the Eariss." His hands are now fists, his eyes distant.

"Tell me about the colors," I say.

His eyes connect with mine again and I wait a few seconds for him to respond.

"Legend says they're only in a newborn's eyes for a few days. After that it becomes difficult to prove, but the Hall still accuses when it needs to."

I understand the power of accusation. There were no rainbows in Glyn's eyes. What if there were? Surely Galen and Maeve would not have killed their own child. Would they? Murder for fear? I remember the moment in the square when I grabbed at the robe offered by fear and the incessant noise that came along with it. I close my eyes and imagine myself removing the fear robe and my shoulders feel lighter as I discard it.

Straw rustles and Thomas sits up straighter, eager to pour out the information that flows from his brain, as if secret thoughts are only valid once spoken aloud.

"Tales of the Eariss fascinate people, but they hate it at the same time. People gossip about it, but mostly in rumor and half-truths. Here's one: the young child killed by guards in Feldston. They say flames of rainbows decimated the village. Flames of rainbows, can you imagine it? Burned the accuser's face in retaliation. It's natural then that people fear and more and more half-truths and lies pile into Feeney's book."

That book always filled me with dread. Its jeweled cover promised delight and safety, but it only contained pain and sorrow.

It seems to be given as much weight out here as it does in the Hall, and I don't know how any of us can ever escape its hold, particularly if what Thomas says is true and it's filling with even more lies. I remember Feeney's fingers scratching into those words, how his whole body seemed to vibrate with hatred. The Eariss. He hates the Eariss. How can I be the Eariss? Me? *I'm* the one who will destroy humankind?

I shake my head. "Well, I'm not a newborn. What makes you so sure I am the Eariss?"

"I saw those flaming rainbows, oh, by the Stars, they were incredible... the night in the forest." He looks off above my head as if he still sees them then lowers his chin to his chest.

The steady thump of my heart beats in every part of my body, a dull ache in my extremities that moves in time with the sharper pain in my chest. I draw a deep breath. "Please continue," I whisper. "I need to know."

Thomas shuffles in an effort to get comfortable but it's not possible. His heart beats in the same pain rhythm as mine. "When I was instructed to bring the ale that night and saw you there, I...I can't explain it. I knew. I mean, I knew *who* you were but I also knew *what* you were and I couldn't—," Pain continues its rhythmic boom. Thomas stares at the straw at his feet for the longest time. "When I stopped running, the campfire was just a dot through the trees. I sat in the dark and wondered how to talk to you without putting your life in more danger. Then there was this huge burst of rainbow light." Thomas arcs his arms through the air and I jump. Little pieces of straw rain down and settle on his shoulders. "It swirled around the campfire, so bright against the night sky, so magnificent . . . I thought they'd killed you. There were shouts and screams and when I returned at dawn, they said you were gone."

Lost in the shouts and screams, my mind follows those silky ribbons again, hearing their voices and accusations. They still stab, but they cause less pain this time. Thomas takes my silence for disbelief and furthers his point. Perhaps he senses I'll leave if he can't persuade me.

"There are other signs too. In the deep forests and far villages they treasure their folklore and I've learned a lot there. They say the Eariss knows things. Connects. Heals. And the animals—" He moves his hands in tumbling circles, trying to gather his thoughts. "The animals. They know you. And your hands—and you translate a different story than the one you are told. You saw things in the village today, didn't you?"

"You forgot the talking trees." I say the words to the straw on the ground in front of me and hear Thomas catch his breath. When I look to his face and offer him a small smile, he exhales and relief pours over his face. But I still don't understand. "So what does it mean if I'm the Eariss?" The words sound ridiculous coming from my mouth. How can I be the thing that terrorizes Feeney and the rest of the world? Thomas doesn't look scared of me at all.

"I don't know, exactly. But it's obvious the Hall does."

The straw home feels safe, yet constrictive at the same time. I should hide, but I need to seek. "The only thing I was told was to look for what is hidden within sight, and even that makes no sense. I'm hoping there might be some answers at Sirban."

He shrugs. "Could be, and you won't know until you get there." He reaches for the satchel and then turns back to me, "We could aim for Sirban, but it's always possible the answers might lie somewhere else."

"We?"

"I decree we travel together. I'll record what we learn." He taps the satchel. "And I'll keep you safe. Don't try to do this alone."

He is an eager traveling companion, one that knows more of the Eariss than I do. He knows more about the roads and customs and is physically stronger. I don't think I could figure this out alone. I straighten my back and jut my chin towards him.

"May I be honest and say you haven't really proven yourself reliable?"

He flicks me a quick smile. "May I be honest and say you don't really have a choice?" The room grows dark and Thomas flattens his robe out on the straw, lies on one half and pulls the other half over to cover him. On my side of the room I try to copy him but I lie on too much of my robe so there's not enough left to cover me. I need to wriggle and pull at the robe to get comfortable. I should have just lay down while wearing the robe, but the softness of the straw draws out my irritability and I settle.

"We'll leave in the morning," Thomas says. "The general busyness of the place should give us enough cover. I have no silver. You?"

I shake my head.

"The checkpoint guards will want payment, so we'll go through the woods; there are gaps on the other side of the square."

"That's where I came in from the mountains."

"Yep. So we'll follow the stream round to the bridge near the road then be on the road as legitimate idlers."

"Sounds like you've done this before."

"Possibly."

"How long to the next village?"

"Two days at most, and your hair—it's too obvious. You must stay hooded."

I gather my hair by my neck. "Why don't I just cut it all off?"

"It'll only make things worse. Harlots have their hair cut off to shame them. If you're discovered, you'll be even more vulnerable."

I twist my hair into a thick rope and I continue turning it until it coils around itself and snakes towards my scalp. I thought I understood, but I don't. This world absolves people of shame by publicly increasing their shame and charges a man more silver because he doesn't have enough in the first place. Is it the Hall that keeps everyone in place, or do people find their own comfort in punishing others?

Thomas interrupts my thoughts. "Rest well, Lady Ashling."

"Yes. Thank you. Rest well, Thomas." I turn to my side and consider how permission to be ungracious can strike out compassion in a single blow. And I wonder if compassion can recover after so many repeated blows.

Winnie screams and Thomas leaps awake among a flurry of straw and disappears into the tunnel. More shouts and screams crack open the morning and force their way through the straw walls. Thomas reappears moments later.

"Move!"

He grabs at the wall for his satchel with one hand while throwing his robe on with the other. I follow his lead and hurriedly tie my robe.

"Trothsmen and guards," he says, "They're turning the village upside down in search of an outlaw." He pulls my hood further over my face and tucks away some hair that is falling loose at my shoulder. "Wait for my signal that it is clear." Thomas crawls into the tunnel first. It's darker inside the short tunnel, the scent of straw diluted with the closeness of fresh air. We wait. My breath pants louder than the Trothsmen who shout orders in the square and the people who cry and call to each other in the marketplace. The soles of Thomas's boots sit between my hands as we wait ominously like livestock heading to —Light shines into the tunnel interrupts my thoughts and his feet flick straw up to my face as he sprints across the lane towards the side of the alehouse. In his stride he loses his grip on the satchel and turns to save it. Pages flutter loose escaping their case as the satchel lands in the center of the laneway. I leave the tunnel and wave him on and stop to collect the spilled parchment in my sprint towards him. My fingers fumble on the dirt of the road as I stuff the papers back into the satchel and I stumble forward. A cloud settles on my thoughts, but it's not until I hand the satchel to Thomas and stand next to him, our backs against the alehouse wall, that they clear.

There is nothing on the parchment.

His so-called 'book of truth' is blank.

T rothsmen sit atop their black beasts pointing and shouting orders at the guards. The alehouse lodgers scurry out of the building straight into their grip, straight into judgment. Some men shout their innocence while others are silent, yet both are ignored and released into the crush that moves towards the gates. The hunters have not found their prey. Thomas watches them and his chest rises and falls in a pant as desperate as my own thoughts. He feels along the wall for my hand. I don't move it away. The line of guards that stretches from the alehouse doors to the baker across the square doesn't act as the border relief it should. Tension wrings into the air on both sides. The unchecked await their chance to be mishandled and falsely accused, their faces as pale as sheep towards their slaughter. On the other side of the line of guards those already cleared squirm in the crush, desperate to be free of entrapment but delayed by the collections at the checkpoint.

Thomas squeezes my hand and releases it. He slides his back over me and moves along the contour of the alehouse wall towards the mountain. There is no need for him to tug at my robe. I follow. Smoothly. Silently amid the din. The stables at the rear of the alehouse butt up against the gray wall of the mountain, so close you might not see the gap if you weren't looking for it. It's only wide enough for the manure channel that flows behind and for wild bracken to grow undisturbed.

Thomas shuffles his feet sideways along the narrow ledge of bricks that jut out under the stable wall. He pushes the bracken away as he teeters his way behind the stables. The rough daub of the stable wall scratches the inside of my ankles and the edges of the bricks barely support half the width of my feet. It must be worse for Thomas. The daub on the back of the stables offers nothing but stray pieces of straw and animal hair as handholds. Even though the bracken feels like a hovering hand behind me, if I fall backwards it won't be strong enough to keep me from the channel. Thomas releases branches as he passes and they flick back and scratch at my face and tug on my robe. I turn to protect myself, trying not to dwell on the stench and ingredients of the daub that rubs on my face. Instead I concentrate on my balance and on sliding my feet along the edge of the bricks that now feels like a knife edge. Behind me, guards talk in the laneway. Thomas pulls me through the last of the bracken as the guards slash at the other side and my face must look just like his—pale and unsmiling.

The fringe of the gathering of checked villagers provides decent enough cover. Our robes blend with the others, but we still need to cross the square to enter the woods. Thomas stands tall, looking for a way across the crowd. The agitated crush of people has a life of its own and it slides its way towards the checkpoint, sweeping us with it. People, carts and animals vie for space and add to the chaos in the narrow streets. Girls call out to Thomas from the loft of a home as we pass.

"Thomas, Thomas!" They wave their kerchiefs at him and giggle. "When will you return?" Thomas waves back, lifts his palms and shrugs his shoulders. Brightly colored ribbons adorn their dark hair. Why aren't they in the throng with us? I'm about to ask when Thomas grabs my hand and ducks under the crowd.

We surface a short distance away and within sight of the checkpoint. Thomas lifts a sack of grain from the cart in front of us and pushes me onto the cart.

"Curl up," he instructs and I take my place among the sacks, which are the same color as my robe.

People stop talking among themselves at the checkpoint. They let the guards do the talking and the laughing as they take the last of people's silver. The world inside my robe is brown and musty and filled with held breath and desperate control.

Stay still.

Very, very still.

The cart driver pays his due and the cart moves on a little then stops, and I hear Thomas' voice. "Yes, I have my silver. Let me find it."

I imagine him fiddling with the purse attached to his belt. People behind grumble their impatience. The guard raises his voice. *Thump!* A heavy weight crushes me. It's dark and I struggle to breathe. The cart driver shouts but I can't make out what he says... my leg is cold. My leg is exposed!

Thump! Something crushes my leg. It has a strange warmth to it. By the Stars! Someone is sitting on my leg. A guard?

The cart begins it lopsided gait along the path. Each bump in the road pushes the weight into me and threatens to snap my leg. But I'm too terrified to move in case it will give us away.

Are we being taken away by the guards?

Where is Thomas?

Why can't I hear Thomas?

Bumps and rattles move the crushing weight from my leg, but I still don't dare move as the original load lifts from my body and my world changes from black to brown again and the cart continues on. Hands grab at me.

Do they think I'm grain? Do they know I'm here?

Light sneaks through my hood before the hands pull it back and flood my face with brightness. I squint into the daylight that surrounds Thomas's beaming face.

"Are you well?" he asks, and as I nod he adds, "Told you I'd keep you safe. Sit up, but keep your hood on. People talk."

The back of the cart bumps and sways as Thomas introduces me to Philip, our bulbous-nosed cart driver. His portly frame, along with the way his white hair escapes at the bottom of his wool cap, reminds me of a forest mushroom. Thomas sits sideways on the bench seat and faces both me and Philip as they tell me their story while I rub at my bruises and stretch my limbs.

"I got you through without a problem," Philip says and then flicks his head at Thomas. "It was his bumbling that nearly had us undone."

"I was trying to delay the guards."

"Delay them? You captured the attention of the one who loves to spear my sacks of grain!"

"True," Thomas concedes. "But at least I saved the lady from a spearing by throwing the sack of grain on top of her."

"But you left her leg hanging there for the world to see!" Philip turns to the back of the cart. "Quite a nice leg, I must say."

Thomas smacks him on the side of the head and Philip laughs so hard the whole cart sways with his merriment. Between laughs he gasps, "It didn't even take too much explaining for them to believe he was a dolt I should have just left on the farm! I pushed him onto your leg and told him to 'Stay! Good boy!'—at least he got that part right."

I smile at Thomas and grin along with Philip. Yes, at least he got that part right. We are safe. A few more dog jokes and we say goodbye to Philip at the next fork in the road.

"I will remember you, Philip," I say.

"And I'll remember you." He lifts his wool cap and his hair puffs out like a dandelion. "We'll light a fire in the center of our village tonight, and I'll tell my wife this story while we wait for the youngsters to return. I wondered why I did well this market. Seems it was for Thomas's travel fee and a new story for the wife." He laughs and the cart wobbles with him. "Travel well, you two."

Thomas reaches up to shake his hand. "Travel well, Philip, and thank you."

The road out of Smoutlea is very much like the forest road and we walk it carefully. We travel alongside it, taking refuge from horseback riders behind trees and transforming into idlers when anyone passes on foot. For a long time we don't talk. So many things fill my mind, each one vying for attention—things that are too hard to think about. I need something light to occupy my mind.

"Philip seemed nice," I say.

"He'll talk, everyone talks, and the next thing you know you're alone with your throat cut open."

"But he helped us. I don't think he had to, did he?"

Thomas stops short and faces me. His face is stern. I move my weight away from him. Could I outrun him if I had to?

"Friends betray you," he says in a measured tone that makes me believe every word he speaks. "Just don't trust anyone. Anyone. Did you hear me?"

I nod and my palms find their comfort on the rough surface of my robe.

There's nothing missing in silence.
It's perfect.
Complete.

The leaves rustle above, the birds still sing and Thomas's feet thud into the ground in front of me, ordered and measured, rhythmic. But inside there is silence, stillness and surety. The Mystery waits there and greets me like an old friend. There are no answers because my heart holds no questions. The Mystery takes me, cradles and strengthens me. The feet I follow are true, this path I walk is right and that is all I need to know for now. This is enough. Enthusiasm springs into my legs and I trot to catch up to Thomas and bump him with my shoulder as I come level with him.

"Tell me your plans," I say.

He turns his head and frowns. "Plans?"

I tap the satchel. "Your book."

He keeps the same determined pace. "I'll record what you tell me. What's different about you and what it's like to be the Eariss."

"But I'm not entirely sure I am the Eariss . . . and how am I meant to know what's different?"

"Do you feel different?"

"How?"

"Because you're the Eariss."

"How would I know? It's the only body I've had."

Oh Stars! Perhaps the Mystery is only playing in jest. These feet can't be true. How will I ever learn anything? The sound of horses approaching sends us into the woods to wait for their passing, and once clear we step back onto the road. Thomas resumes his pace and clears his throat.

"Do you have questions, then? That could also work."

I trot to catch up to him again. "The guards said something about an Ark of Eariss. Have you heard anything about an ark on your travels?"

"What's an ark?"

My hands move around, shaping something in the air in front of me. "A container, a box or a trunk. Usually holds things like jewels or treasure."

Thomas shakes his head, "That's a new one. Intriguing though . . ." he walks lost in his thoughts. "Wonder what it does."

"Maybe it's magic and can take the Eariss away from me."

Thomas doesn't seem to hear me or notice when I slow and fall in step behind him.

⁕⁓✦⁓⁕

T he forest gives way to fields that stretch to the surrounding mountains in a valley of yellows, limes and the deeper green of tree groves. Like splashes of dark moss on the landscape the groves offer protection for animals and travelers alike. The sun is high and heats through the robe to my scalp and shoulders. I look forward to passing through the shade of the scattered groves and feeling the coolness pull the heat from the robe before the road snakes back into the fields. Thomas walks ahead of me in the groove made by summers of passing cart wheels, as lost in his thoughts as I am in the Mystery.

My mouth waters the moment I smell it. Thomas's head moves around, searching. A thin column of smoke rises from the next grove and the breeze taunts us with the aroma of a traveler's pot. Once in the shade of the grove, Thomas holds my elbow as I hobble through as the old idler. I clench my teeth, angry that I flinched at his touch. I know he means me no harm, but my body seems to have a memory of its own, reacting to stupid things and racing out of control. Even so, his presence convinces my mind I won't meet any brutes on the road today. We receive nothing more than the expected customary nod as we pass. Feeding idlers is for the nurses and almshouses and not for those wealthy enough to be traveling with a cart and nourishing food, and with the added luxury of time enough to stop for a meal. The groves thicken again and the fields in between them grow smaller as we walk our way out of the valley.

Thomas clutches at his stomach. "Wish I'd grabbed the bread."

As much as his bread was unpalatable, it was still food and the thought of straw bread makes my stomach twist with hunger.

"We can just ask for something to eat," I suggest.

Thomas stops and looks around at the patchy groves. "Just ask? Ask who?"

"The Mys...tery," As the word falls from my mouth I know there can be no return. I've spoken it aloud.

"Is this some kind of Eariss thing?"

"Possibly . . .probably . . . ."

Thomas tugs at my robe and draws me level with him as we turn to walk again. "Talk," he says.

"The Mystery is everywhere. Look at the birds. It provides all that they need, their shelter, their food. We get in the way of what the Mystery would like to give us because we make demands and tell it what it should be. As if we know better."

"So this Mystery can make a bowl of pottage appear now, in the middle of this road?"

"If it wanted to, I suppose—"

"Can you make it do that then? Now? I'm hungry."

A laugh bursts from my lips. "I can't make it do anything. It's much too big for that."

Thomas sighs and shakes his head. "What's the point of it then? If it won't do what it's told?"

"Its point?" It feels disrespectful to ask something as vast as the Mystery to prove its worth. "It doesn't need a point, it just is. And you're either working with it or working against it." I point ahead to a small grove, tilt my head and smile at him. Thomas looks to the grove and then to me, his features caught somewhere between a frown and a smile, before he hurries ahead of me towards the trees.

He has found the berries and filled his mouth and hands by the time I reach the shade. Thomas runs past and with a child's joy he dumps berries into my hands and heads back to the bush to refill. He mumbles something in the exchange, but there is no way I can understand him.

"Thanks," I call after him and recline against one of the shady trees. I eat the berries straight from one hand and massage my feet with the other.

The fervor of his berry collecting slows and with less food in his mouth his mumbles start to make sense. His fingers are more selective now, choosing only the plumpest fruit.

"So when you were in the forest...." He throws three more berries into his mouth. "And like just now, you say, 'Oh, I'm hungry' and a berry bush appears?"

"No, not quite like that. I'm thankful for what I come across, what I can use, and I don't seem to lack anything."

"Ha!" he laughs, and a berry falls out of his mouth. He tries to catch it but misses. "You don't lack anything? You have no home, clothes, silver or food." He leans over the bush towards me and whispers, "If you don't mind me saying, you don't even have a *name* anyone would want right now. So tell me again, what *do* you have that's actually worth having?"

I study the berries in my hand. They blur as I fight the sting and threat of my tears.

What do I have that's worth having?

The Mystery swirls in my chest and reminds me of its lesson.

Me. I have me. I mouth the words but my voice won't work. I straighten my back, clear my throat and stare at Thomas.

"Me. I have me."

Thomas stares into my eyes and challenges me. I hold my stare, convinced more in the Mystery than myself. Does he see me?

A smile slowly spreads across his face and he winks.

Thomas piles more berries into the bowl he creates with the front of his shirt and makes his way to me. He offers his lower arm for me to lift myself onto my feet and hands me an old idler's walking stick he found by the bush. "So tell me, is having 'just me' a good thing or a bad thing?"

I help myself to his berries as we step back on to the road. "Good."

"Why?"

"Because there's nothing to tell me who I am."

"So who are you then?"

The sky is wide and blue, and anything is possible. "I don't know."

"So you're not Lady Ashling of Brennyn Hall?"

"No. I mean yes—but that's just what everyone tells me I am. I'm someone different."

"Someone different like the Eariss perhaps?"

I have no answer for him. I don't even have one for myself. I point into the thickening groves and try to explain something I don't even understand. "My life feels like a forest where every tree has been cut down and there's nothing, and I'm devastated at the destruction because all those trees were the things I was or had, but because it's now so open I'm filled with possibility at the same time—like the space can be filled with anything."

"Anything? So what's filling that space now?"

"The Mystery, but it feels like that space is growing so more of the Mystery can fit in."

"Less of you, more of the Mystery, got it. So how does you being the Eariss fit into this?"

I shrug. "They have to tie together some way, don't you think? Otherwise, why would the Mystery be the only thing I have?"

"Other than 'just you,'" he corrects.

I accept his correction with a sigh. "Other than just me."

⁂

T he trees are thicker now, and although I miss the expanse of the sky, the way they hover and fuss as we pass by grounds me to the moment. My brain seems clearer, as if their stability anchors my soul and I hear them whisper their encouragement to keep moving. Thomas walks beside me with a slower stride. Along with the drop in pace I notice his questions become more thoughtful.

"So if this Mystery thing is tied to the Eariss . . . and the Mystery is everywhere, right?" I nod and he continues. "Then there could be more than one Eariss!" He walks backwards in front of me and ignores his occasional trips, more focused on where his mind is taking him than on his feet. "Could people learn to be the Eariss, or is something *in* you—like with you?"

I reach out to catch him as he trips again. "You make it sound like I have worms." My hand misses his arm and grabs the side of the satchel instead, but he rights himself and walks beside me. The satchel sways with the movement of his stride. "All these questions," I say. "You should write them down."

He flicks his head to me and glares, and my feet lose their rhythm. "I mean, don't ruin the book. Maybe you could make notes in the margins so you don't forget your thoughts."

Thud!

A man drops from the trees to the ground in front of us, crouched and menacing.

Thud!

Another man lands behind us. Thomas wrests the stick from my hands and pushes me to the side of the road as the men circle about him. The men are larger than Thomas and move with strength. They might wear the ill-fitting and ragged clothes of the poor, but I'm sure these bandits are in costume. Their agility and intentions are not humble. One carries a hammer he tosses from hand to hand as they circle Thomas, and the shorter man menaces him with a dagger held out at chest height. Thomas moves constantly to keep an eye on both.

"We are idlers," he calls to them. "We have nothing you want."

"We'll decide on that." The one with the dagger waves the weapon towards me. "That one might have the silver."

T homas's robe falls to the ground and he swings the walking stick towards the dagger and gets the thief's attention, "Leave the old man alone."

"Hey, look at this! It's the kid from Feldston." The taller man stops tossing the hammer and stands straight.

"This'll be easy then," the man with the dagger says, and lunges at Thomas. The other man raises the hammer and I find myself in the middle of the fray, unsure of how I might help. Sticks and knives and hammers flash in front of me and my eyes hurt. Where is that light coming from? It can't be from the blade, the sun's not bright enough. My eyes! It's like someone has thrown dirt into my face. The bandits' faces melt from anger to fear, and compassion swells inside me as I feel their stories, even as they drop their weapons and run. Thomas retrieves his robe and pulls at mine and we run in the other direction.

"Don't you ever do that again!" He shouts with such force it reverberates through my chest and bounces back at him.

"Would you have preferred to be hacked and beaten?"

"Do you have any idea what you did back there?"

"Saved you from certain injury? 'Thank you', I believe, is the common response!"

"Cursed Stars, Ashling! Colors, all different colors were in your eyes! You seemed to wipe it away. Those men were terrified, did you not see their faces? They'll talk—everyone talks!" He runs behind me, urging me to move faster. "We're dead now. Not only you, Rainbow Girl, but me for being with you!"

"Don't curse the Stars on my account!" I stop but he pushes into me and forces me to keep moving. I trip over my feet, unable to make a stand. "I'll just stay here and wait for them—you get on your way."

"You'll do no such thing." He pushes me off the road and into the forest. "Move! We need to put as much distance between us and those bandits that we can."

When I slow my pace, Thomas pushes me on farther over roots around trees and through vines, over small treed hills and dales. If he's so anxious why doesn't he take the lead? I answer my own question when I acknowledge I'm so angry I wouldn't follow him anywhere.

I shouldn't speak so I make sure to hold branches as I pass by and release them to smack into his face.

I shouldn't speak so I'm sure to loosen dirt and rocks onto him as he follows on steep dales.

I shouldn't speak.

Why *shouldn't* I speak? I turn on him in a small clearing of dried grasses and tall, thin, white-trunked trees.

"You, Thomas of Feldston, are an ignorant dolt." He stops and considers me, his mood no better than mine, and tries to walk past me. My hand pushes on his chest and he steps back to hear me. My words rush out in a hateful torrent. "Don't blame me for this! How am I not meant to give us away when I don't even know when I'm doing it? What *am* I supposed to be doing? You're the Eariss expert. Get your Star-riddled book out and tell me what's going on!"

"I don't know what's going on!" he shouts back.

I grab at the satchel, but he pulls it from me. I can't believe I'm grasping for answers that don't even exist. "Tell me how to make it go away. Then you'll get to live, then you'll be safe."

"My safety is of no matter. I'm not scared!" His words boom into my ears.

"You can say you just met me on the road, nothing to do with me. You're not a servant, you're not a maid, you don't need to be scared of what they'll do to you!"

He grabs my arms and shakes me. "You can't be in danger. You need to stay safe. Anything could have happened!" His voice rages louder than any I had heard before. "Stop telling me I am scared! You might be afraid, but I am not scared of anything, do you understand?"

My legs disappear and a ball of swirling energy in my chest draws in everything around it. I drop to the ground and curl into the tightest ball I can imagine, tense and waiting. A familiar scenario plays in my mind. If I squeeze tight enough I can fold in on myself, folding and folding until I disappear altogether. When the blows do not arrive I open my eyes to dry grasses that bounce in my panting breath. Insects crawl among the dirt and rotting leaves and a tender green shoot fights its way through debris. I breathe the scent of dirt and feel the soothing that only comes from contact with the earth. I unclench a little and look to Thomas. He steps back, his hands raised by his sides. He moves towards me then changes his mind. Confusion hangs in the air. I offer no explanation for my atrocious behavior; I simply stand, dust myself off and walk away. If I pretend it didn't happen, then perhaps it didn't—maybe that's the only place my 'magic' really lies.

It's much later when my breath returns to a steady rhythm and I move among the small saplings and undergrowth. I hear the crunch of Thomas's feet further behind me and feel no aggravation this time. I'm grateful he is here.

"Hey Ashling, you know that vast forest of destruction you talked about?"

I keep walking and direct my answer to the trees in front of me. "Yes."

"Seems to me there's things creeping out from under those fallen logs."

I don't answer.

"Awful crawling things," he continues. "Do you know what I mean?"

I know what he means. There are no chains and locks here, but I am still a prisoner.

"You're not invincible, Rainbow Girl. You need to remember that."

And I wish he was closer behind me so this large branch I hold back would knock him off his feet.

Light-gray clouds creep over the blue and give the forest a somber stillness. Even the birds seem to sing with less enthusiasm. Small rain droplets tap at leaves here and there as if the sky is still deciding whether to bother raining at all. Each drop that slides down a leaf leaves a brighter shade of green, washing it anew one gentle stroke at a time. The air is as heavy as my feet, yet the forest continues with its work, growing, freshening and busying itself with provisions and cycles. Everywhere creatures move, prepare and signal to each other and the trees hum.

Thomas puffs and thuds behind me and curses the roots that have tripped him once again. We haven't spoken other than to discuss directions. I stop and rest my hands on an ancient trunk and absorb its stillness.

"I had no idea about all of this," I say.

"All of what?" Thomas wipes his hands on his trousers as he walks towards me.

"This. I mean, when you grow up around stone you don't get to see this kind of magic...." I look up to the far branches, "... all this wisdom."

"Wisdom from a plant? Surely you jest?"

I frown and turn my back to rest on the tree. "No, I'm not. What if it's an Eariss thing?"

"Plants that are full of wisdom and help the Eariss to wield swords to calm the unrest?" He shakes his head and walks past me.

"No. Yes. I don't know." I follow after him. "Maybe it's just a part of it." I walk forward, but my head and my heart look back at the tree and heaviness drops into my heart. Like I've missed something. Like I wasn't listening properly.

The day closes in a dreary fashion, as if it's lost all momentum, as if the greyness and damp will weigh it down until it stops forever. Thomas gestures to an odd patch of greenery in the forest and heads towards it. There's something different about it, but I can't think of what it is. Vines still grow and climb, but with less abandon, and the trees hover in an ordered, almost purposeful, way. It's not until we are almost upon it that my mind registers the shape beyond the foliage and the ruins of a stone cottage.

Time has beaten one of the stone walls to the ground and vines now cover and reclaim the tumbled rocks, curling their fingers around them and returning them to the soil. Thick trees surround the other dark walls and nudge at them with their roots while their overhanging branches replace the threshed roof. The lichen and moss are cold to touch, but still bring life to the stones.

"Quiet determination," I murmur.

"Did you say something?" Thomas's voice is flat and tired. He drops to the floor, leans his back against a wall and releases a long sigh. Something about his sigh draws my body to the hardened floor and I copy his stance, leaning into the next wall, legs apart, and rest my arms by my side. Our feet almost touch in the center of the room. I'm sure I have never felt more comfortable in my life. I could sleep like this. It takes a ridiculous amount of effort to answer his question.

"I was just thinking about how quiet and continuous determination always wins over force."

Thomas rolls his head on the wall to look at me. "I can't believe you just said 'quiet and continuous determination.' Does your mouth never get tired?"

I smile and rest my head on the stone wall like Thomas does. Being this tired is like drinking strong ale. "So it's *not* good to be precise? To choose exactly the right word?"

"You'll find it doesn't matter to most people." He turns his face back to the center of the room. "Why does it matter to you?"

"So people outside the Hall aren't afraid of punishment?"

"Punishment for a wrong word?"

"Or look, or movement, or breath . . ."

Thomas doesn't say anything. Perhaps I've said the wrong thing again. Spoken out of turn. I slide sideways from the wall, lie on my side and pull my robe around me. Thomas's boots are in my line of sight, and beyond that, the open wall and the darkness of the forest. "It's important I be precise—blameless. Everyone is safer that way," I mumble.

"Safer? How?"

Thomas waits while I organize my thoughts. This started in jest about the words I spoke, but the humor has left me and I don't understand the heaviness that grows in my chest. It forces the words from me.

"When I make a mistake, I die."

The truth takes my breath away. But it was never my death, it was always the others. Perhaps it's just a different way to die. Torture, a slow death from the inside out. Silent. Without witnesses, without the label of 'crime' other than my own layered guilt of betrayal. If only I'd done better, I could have saved them. My heart feels like it is slashed open with a dagger and the whole world is still and silent. Thomas's feet tap to a tune only he can hear. For the longest time I watch them move, focused on their silhouette. Thomas doesn't need to know everyone around me dies. Does he? Eventually he moves his legs to lie along the side of his wall and reaches for my hand to stop it rubbing on the robe.

"That's quite a burden for a child to carry," he says.

I can't see him, so I speak to the darkness. "It was true for me in the Hall."

"And now? Is it true now?"

I pull my hand away from his and tuck it close to me. "We shall see."

He shuffles in the darkness, making himself comfortable, then sighs gently and whispers, "Know that I am glad you're here."

No one's ever been glad I'm anywhere.

I'm grateful for the darkness, and that he can't see my face or even that I heard his words. And I'm strangely grateful for the exhaustion that keeps me from running far away from him and his delusion that I deserve to be alive.

The morning light shimmers on the forest outside the broken cottage. There's movement. There, in the underbrush. I spring up and Thomas's robe falls from my shoulders. At the bottom of the dale, Thomas uses his elbows to push aside saplings, his hands holding the hem of his shirt that reminds my stomach of yesterday's raspberries—it growls on cue. He smiles when he sees I'm awake and waits until he's closer before describing our meal.

"The berries weren't very ripe, but I found some wild apples. Oh, and I think these are nuts."

With his robe spread on the floor, we separate his collection into two and eat. The crabapples are as ripe as the berries he left on the bush, but we crunch through them and leave the few ripe berries for last. "Thanks." I almost gurgle the word as the last berry dissolves in my mouth and I manage to catch wayward drips with my finger.

Thomas looks back down into the dale. "There's a small stream down there. First stop before we move on."

"Do you know where we are?"

"Almost. If we keep the sun behind us, Muscone should only be a couple of hills away— maybe a day?"

I nod, but have no idea what he's talking about. Thomas shakes the robe off and ties it before he secures the satchel. Memories of those blank pages flutter in my mind and I push my curiosity aside. Best to wait and ask questions when we are within sight of Muscone.

The soil has a sweet, spongy feel and we slip occasionally on our way down to the stream. My walking stick doesn't help too much, but it's a familiar prop to seize when the soil gives way. The evening's gentle rain has encouraged new insects to emerge and the birds are singing about where to find the best catches. After I drink, a richer song becomes clearer and I hear it everywhere; whichever way I turn my head it is still there.

"There's a song." I turn my head in all directions as I sit on a large stone. "It's everywhere."

Thomas splashes water on his face. "They're called birds, Ashling."

"No, this is different to birdsong. It's old, it wants us to learn the song." I listen a bit longer. "We try to tell it how to sing a different song. No matter how loudly we sing, it will sing its own ancient song. It's the only one it knows."

"Singing trees again?" Thomas stands and wipes his mouth with the back of his hand. "And where do they hide their swords?"

My shoulders slump. I don't know how to explain any of this, but it's as real as Thomas standing in front of me.

"Come along," Thomas says. "Muscone awaits."

I shake my head. "I'm not sure about what we're doing."

"Going to Muscone, remember? Come along then."

"I mean about the Eariss, your book..." I look up to him and he exhales.

"Look, I don't think talking trees and ancient songs have much to do with the Eariss, that's all."

"Why not?"

"Because the Eariss is strong and powerful and is meant to end all this madness around us, overturn kingdoms and right wrongs; it's not about singing trees."

"How can you be sure? Are you sure?"

He purses his lips, studies me for a while and looks into the trees above me. "No, no, I'm not *absolutely* sure that trees won't come to our rescue. Happy now?"

"Feeney said the Eariss is evil and bent on destruction. You're saying it's wondrous."

"I know what it's *meant* to do," he says, pointing to his chest. "And so do the legends. We just don't know *how*, that's all."

"Well, why don't we leave the *how* to the Eariss? Stop telling it what it should be and just let it be what it is?"

Thomas nods thoughtfully. "Fair enough. You talk... and I'll listen." He extends his hand. "Muscone?"

From the top of a lightly treed hill the road in the distance channels its way towards Muscone. We track it like hunters, checking on its whereabouts whenever we get a chance as we move through the groves and clearings. The groves are open now; there are just large trees with tufts of grasses and leaves underfoot. I stop to flex my ankles and rest against a tree.

"Feet all right?" Thomas asks.

I offer him a quick nod. "Much better than yesterday."

"I'm surprised at your endurance."

"You are?"

Thomas shrugs. "I thought ladies of the Hall were meant to whine and complain, but you don't do much of that, do you?" He tips his head sideways to take in the idler's costume. "But I suppose you're not much of a lady."

I finish flexing my ankles and walk away from him. "It wasn't much of a Hall."

Thomas catches up and walks beside me. "Everyone talks about how terrifying the place is. But it always looks so impressive, like it has an air of grandeur or something."

"What's easier to believe, your eyes or your heart?"

"Bit of both, I suppose. You need to remember the world outside the Hall is terrifying too. It's easy for people to believe there's safety behind those massive walls. But you weren't safe, were you?"

"Never."

"I hope you feel safer now." He inhales and stands taller.

"You mean while I'm being hunted by the Hall and attacked by bandits?"

Thomas deflates and kicks at a loose stone. "You should learn to defend yourself. What if there's a time I'm not around?"

I almost mention the bandits again but clasp my hand over my mouth and pretend I'm in deep concentration. "I've not thought about it. What about a dagger? I could attach it to my belt and—"

"No, they'll just overpower you, take it and use it against you."

"Thanks for the vote of confidence." I want to prove him wrong ... but I know he's right.

"Use your walking stick."

My stick is solid, and my fingers and thumb almost touch around its head. It tapers towards the ground but wouldn't do much damage if I were to stab it at someone. I suppose I could use it to strike an attacker, but it seems pretty absurd. "Only if they stand still long enough for me to hit them on the head." I stop and talk to a mossy rock. "Pardon me, sir, put your head a little to the left . . ."

"Here, I'll show you." Thomas pushes past me and pulls the stick from my grasp. He swings it around, flipping and spinning it. It travels from behind his back to the front, under his arm and out to the front again, wiping out imaginary assailants with every sweep.

"Amazing. How did you learn to do that? Why didn't you tell me you could?"

Thomas continues swinging and twirling and finishes with a solid thump upon the ground. "Well, I would have been able to *show* you if you hadn't jumped in and done the whole sparkly eyes thing, remember?"

He stabs the stick into the ground in front of him and leans on it with one hand, the other on his hip, and awaits my answer. I fold my arms. He has a point, but I'm not about to concede it.

※

I'm quite capable of following directions. Does he really have to stand behind me to show me how to hold a stick? At first it seemed strange when he untied my robe, but I can understand how it's easier to teach without the extra cloth on our bodies, and besides, we're so deep in the forest we don't have to worry about discovery. What's strange is that I actually don't mind him standing so close while he murmurs his instructions. Thomas breathes onto my neck and the outside world disappears. Funny sensations thread their way through my body and tingle in an interesting response. Thomas talks, but I can't hear. For a moment I'm someplace else. Before long he is standing in front of me.

"Got it?"

"Huh?"

"Got it?" he says again, showing me the grip.

"Yes, yes I've got it." What just happened to me?

Thomas smiles from the corner of his mouth. I smile back, but I'm not even sure what we're smiling about. Did he notice how confused I am?

His hands hold a large branch he found nearby. I hold my idler's stick, and we circle, watching for opportunities to sweep each other's feet or practice skull-cracking blows. Thomas coaches me and explains where he has left himself open and congratulates me when I spot an advantage without his prompt. He swings and jabs slowly to remind me where I'm exposed, and as I gain more confidence, he speeds his movements. His branch swings towards me at head height. He is expecting me to duck, but I attempt a jab to his belly instead and the branch cracks into my skull. He drops the branch to come to my aid and I take him out with a blow to the backs of his knees.

I shake my head as I hover over him. "You've got to hit me a lot harder than that to get a response."

Thomas scrambles to his feet and checks the side of my head. "You sure you're all right?"

"I'm fine. Stop fussing about me."

"I need to keep you safe."

That's right, I'm meant to be the Eariss, aren't I? "Maybe you're like a Trothsman for the Eariss."

"A Trothsman?"

"You know, like a guardian or protector." I lift my stick high in the air like a sword. "Protector of the Eariss!"

"Cursed Stars, Ashling!" he shouts into my face and storms off.

All right.

Not a Trothsman then . . .

⚜

B y the time we spot the apple tree Thomas has long since calmed down and I've given up trying to understand why he was upset. Deer and other animals have cleared the lower branches of fruit, and Thomas reaches to pull a high branch laden with its red and yellow apples and plucks two of the largest ones from its offering. The long grasses at the base of the tree, once flattened down, become a comfortable place to rest.

He slaps an apple into my hand and clasps his hands around the other one and twists. A loud snap and crunch and the apple splits into two. I try to copy him, but my apple holds firm. Thomas offers to twist mine but I persevere and it gives way with a satisfying crunch. The first bite of an apple is always the nicest. It breaks into your mouth with just the right amount of sweetness and powerful tartness. I rest back against the trunk and Thomas lies beside me, as lost in his own thoughts as I am in mine. He rolls to his belly and takes the half apple from my hand in my lap, stares at the apple and looks at me.

"Now you're staring at apple seeds? And I expect they're talking to you too? Tell me what they're saying." I snatch my apple back and he continues. "Well, are they?"

"No. I mean... yes, kind of." My hand drops to my lap and I sigh. "What if I'm mad? I mean, really truly mad?"

"It must be an Eariss thing."

I hold the half apple in front of his face. "So when you look at this apple, it doesn't teach you something? You don't get knowledge and lessons taught to you?"

"It's an apple . . . ." He rolls onto his back and looks up into the branches above. "What's it telling you, then?"

"That we're apple seeds."

"Apple seeds? I was hoping for something more mysterious and frightful than apple seeds."

"Things are only mysterious and frightful when we don't understand them."

It's easy to talk to Thomas about the strange things that arise in my mind. I'd never spoken to anyone about them before, and if he believes I'm the Eariss, then he might be even madder than I am.

He continues to study the branches then taps at the half apple in my hand. "So what's this about the apple seeds?"

"It's the seed that holds all the power. We pay attention to the outside, the flesh—but we're missing the important bit, the life and the power that's contained in the seed. Think of us as seeds, you as a scribe, me as a . . . whatever I am . . . . When we ignore the seed, or don't acknowledge it, we cover up its power.

"If we're expected to produce pears, but can't help but produce apples, we're ridiculed and maybe even chopped down. So we try desperately to not produce apples and exhaust ourselves to create a low-quality pear. Can you imagine how perfect those apples would be if we could produce what we were meant to produce? If that power wasn't covered up?"

I remove one of the apple seeds and drop it into his hand. "There's always more than what's on the surface, just like this little seed. Inside it are the instructions to grow tall and wide, to produce fruit for people, animals and birds. To provide homes for birds and insects and be a shelter for them and us. To offer protection in a storm, shade on a hot day and hold the soil together...all in that tiny seed in your hand. The most amazing things are hidden; you just have to look with eyes that can see."

"But I know this is an apple seed. I know it will produce apples; it can't do anything else."

"Exactly, but that's only because you know what the seed is. Unknown seeds could be anything. When you plant an unknown seed in the ground, you don't get to tell it what it should be. It has to grow into what it already is within itself. All its potential hides inside it just waiting for the right moment. Perhaps your potential was waiting for our meeting, perhaps your book would never be written if you'd done what was expected and stayed a carpenter's son. Can you see how we are all unknown seeds and what is inside us can be different from what is expected?"

Thomas studies the seed, turning it over with his finger. I add a few more seeds to his palm and spread them out. "If we nurtured those unknown seeds instead of dismissing them, I wonder what would grow. I imagine it would be something powerful, wouldn't it?"

Thomas brushes the seeds from his hand, rises to his feet and holds out his hand for me to stand. "As powerful as an apple being an apple, I suppose."

"Or a scribe being a scribe?"

Thomas pulls me to my feet and considers my statement. I wait with him while he dwells on how powerful he would be if only he would produce what he is meant to produce, be what he is meant to be, and do what he is meant to do. He looks to me, nods thoughtfully and rubs his chin.

"Or," he says, "the Eariss being the Eariss?"

D irt laneways crisscross the fields that lay outside Muscone.
We weave our way along them, sometimes finding ourselves
back at the main road and having to double back. Apart from the
occasional loose stones or rocks, the lanes are smooth, but the day
has been long. Cramps hint in my feet; little spasms that I try to
stretch out with each step as I attempt to keep pace with Thomas.
I stop and find relief on my tiptoes, then rock back to my heels
and onto my toes again. My plan is to give my feet some rest and a
stretch and then catch up to Thomas, but he stops a distance ahead
and watches me with his head tilted.

"I thought it'd help." I clearly have no idea what I'm doing, but
the motion is making my feet feel better, if only for seconds at a
time. My soles feel like they are being stabbed with each step. "Is
there somewhere we can rest?"

Thomas considers my feet, releases a heavy sigh and gazes over
the fields. "There." He points a short way down the lane. "Can you
make it to that field?"

I nod. I'd walk over brambles in my bare feet to get anywhere that promised rest.

The green stalks of the field tower over our heads. Thomas parts the reeds carefully with his arm and beckons me to follow inside.

"Don't step on the stalks. Be as gentle as you can."

My feet find their place on the earth in between each plant and for the most part I follow each step Thomas takes. He stops occasionally and watches as the stalks close in behind us like a curtain. Then, apparently satisfied with our position, he kneels, flattens the plants around him and rocks from side to side to create a space for himself in the field. I copy him, leaving a thin wall of reeds between us.

Flat on my back, I take the deepest breath I possibly can, and release it slowly. The heaviness of relaxation fills my arms and legs. The sting in my feet still distracts me, but it is fading as I concentrate on the blissful weight of my resting limbs. The bugs we disturbed as we entered the field return to flit about and continue their work around us. With my eyes closed, the warmth of the sun reminds of the lake and I can be anywhere I choose to be. A shadow crosses my face as clouds form along my horizon, which is made of the tops of grassy reeds. My hands slide across the reeds and I play them gently like a harp.

I jump when Thomas lists all the places we need to get to and how best to get there. It sounds way too far ahead. The last thing I want to think about is how much further we need to walk, but at the same time I'm thankful for his planning and knowledge. He repeats himself and corrects himself. He's not really talking to me, just running through his list, and I think of all the other things he might be doing with his life than lying in a grass field with aching feet. I wait for him to settle before I speak.

"I'm sorry I put you in danger." I say it to the sky and turn my face in his direction. His shirt appears as little flashes of colored light through the stalks. The reeds rustle under him as he moves and then sighs.

"So you're just following this Mystery thing—its orders."

"Well, I wouldn't call them orders."

"Aren't you worried it'll ask you to do something you don't want to do? Something bad?"

"I can't imagine it turning on itself. So far it seems all about helping, not pain."

"Have we known it to do anything evil so far?'

I think about the bandits and the fear that showed on their faces. "Its power...sometimes I can feel it and it scares me."

"Ah, that's because things are only mysterious and frightful when we don't understand them, remember?"

I roll my eyes, breathe deeply and watch the sheets of gray clouds meet and overlap as if weaving a blanket over the entire sky. The Eariss and the little we know about it causes more confusion than it solves. I can't wait to get to Sirban and find some answers.

Thomas changes position and the stalks that surround him sway and bounce. He moves again and complains then settles. I catch his eye through the gaps in the reeds, but he quickly turns away and speaks. "Anything else scare you?"

"I was just thinking about Sirban—"

"You're scared of a village?"

"Not the village, but what we might find there. Perhaps what we might *not* find there. What if they can't help? What if I'm nothing?"

"Sirban is famed for its knowledge, and I would stake my life that you are *not* nothing."

"You're always so certain. My fears turn up and offer me heavy robes and tell me to stay safe and not search for answers."

Thomas shuffles again. "Fear robes? You must tell me this one."

I take a deep breath and talk to the sky. "There are two kinds of fear. A real fear that keeps us safe, like running when a wolf chases you or fear of falling that makes you grasp on to a tree branch. And a deceitful fear that holds us still like a carved statue and then criticizes us for not moving."

"You said they were robes."

"They arrive like magic robes. The first one slips over you the moment a wolf shows interest in you; it gives you power to try to outrun the wolf. The second one wraps itself around you and paralyzes you."

"Ah, the robe that keeps you safe by not doing anything."

I nod even though he can't see me and continue talking to the gray sky. "I decided I need to know why I fear, why I find comfort in those heavy robes. I'm not about to stop and ask the wolf why he chases me, but once I understand the Eariss, and anything else that causes me fear, I'll be able to choose how I behave, not blindly react to the robe that smothers me of my own thought." I roll to my side and face the grass wall that separates us. "You?"

"Huh?"

"Are you going to suggest you have no challenges?"

He's quiet again, and I don't feel like talking just to fill the silence. It was easy for me to explain the fear robes without having to look at his face—it's easier to say difficult things this way. Stupid doltish things.

He blurts the words out so quickly it takes a moment for me to understand. "I don't know how to write."

Vision of parchment and dirt and satchels flash through my mind and delay my response even further.

"Did you hear me? You think your call is strange? I'm a bird that has rocks for wings. I'm an idiot traveling from village to village with this satchel of nothingness. I've tried to forsake it, but I can't."

"Like it has a life of its own inside you?"

"Eating me alive," he replies.

"It's exciting."

"Exciting? More like excruciating."

"You have the satchel, right? How did you come about it?"

"A hire offered it in place of wages."

"So the things you need for your quest are slowly coming your way."

His hands thump into the ground beside him. "There's no point having it if I can't write a word on it!"

"Trust."

"What?"

"You don't have to chase anything. Do everything you can, but don't force it—let it make its way to you. You have your satchel and your parchment, that's a start. Prepare for the rest to come to you."

"Prepare?"

"Make room for it, as if you're waiting for it to come along and you're ready to welcome it. Like if you were expecting a guest, you'd make up a bed and perhaps put extra in the pot."

"Surely I'm not meant to sit around and do nothing."

"Of course not. We have to head towards what we want, but trust makes it easy to believe we'll be met along the way. A vine doesn't wait for its support. It stretches and searches and the Mystery meets it. The vine trusts it will find its support; it doesn't sit and wait, it searches with expectation."

"What if it doesn't find anything?"

"Have you ever known a vine not to find anything? Even if it's just trailing the ground, it doesn't give up. It always ends up where it's meant to go. Consider every possibility, not just the ones you're expecting. The Mystery has a delightful sense of timing and finds its way quicker to a grateful smile than a demanding scowl."

"And do you ever take your own advice?"

I sigh. "I try to."

"This is absurd!" I laugh and push the grass barrier down. Thomas looks at me with the strangest expression; somewhere between pity and exhaustion and concern. "You do understand," I say, "that I'm searching for something I know nothing about, and you're intending to do something you don't even know how to do." I must sound simple, yet I smile and offer Thomas my hand. "Anything is possible, right?"

Thomas considers my hand for a moment and then grins and takes it in a firm shake. "I don't even know what I'm agreeing to."

"Neither do I."

❦

S o there's Muscone. The little village we've fought through the forest to, sits in the valley below us, its dusk-filled streets so lit with torches you can make out the intersections that lead to the center of the village.

"Look how it shines," I say, forgetting that Thomas has seen this sight before.

"Shine is exactly what Muscone does. Here..." Thomas looks around at the large trees that surround us on the ridge. "Let's camp here and enter the village fresh in the morning."

Once settled among the roots, our robes wrapped closely to ward off the light breeze, I position myself so I can see the lights of Muscone. Cloud still covers the sky and I'm glad I don't have to make the choice of which I prefer—the stars or the beauty of the village below me. Nights at the Hall were never this pretty, but they were still wonderful, even in their blackness. "Nighttime is always magical," I say.

"Magical?" Thomas shuffles next to me. "Nighttime is quiet and lonely."

"Exactly."

Is it the dark or the quiet that expands everything? Your fears huge, your dreams wild ... and what exactly is it about the morning that washes them away?

But maybe I have it wrong, maybe the morning is the magical one.

❦

Orderly plumes of smoke rise from the breakfast chimneys of Muscone. Even in the early dawn the village seems lighter, perhaps brighter than the fields around it. Thomas said Muscone shines, but I'm surprised and a little confused about how it lights up the day. Thomas murmurs in the final stages of his sleep and I resist the temptation to wipe fallen leaves from his robe in case he wakes.

The satchel lies in the gap between us and I lift it onto my chest to examine the clasp. It's definitely metal and acts like a kind of button with a thin loop of leather that seals the flap shut. Dark-gray spikes run out from its center, but they don't appear to have any order. My fingers lift the loop and it releases the clasp without a sound. Inside, a collection of paper, parchment and small pieces of vellum are neatly placed and waiting for Thomas to begin his work. A sensation of trespass presses on my shoulders and I close and re-loop the satchel, my fingers tracing the gusset and its stitching before returning to the clasp again. This time the disorderly spikes seem to make sense, and my finger follows them in and out of its center.

"It's molten metal." Thomas's voice squeezes out from the midst of his morning stretch.

My fingers continue to trace. "Looks a bit like a tree, see here?"

Thomas turns his head this way and that, more involved in the stretching than trying to see the tree in the clasp. He shrugs and I think back to the blank pages.

"Why write it down? Why not just commit it to memory and spread it around like everyone else?"

Thomas stretches his arms above his head. "Feeney has a book. Everyone can read it or have it read to them. Oral traditions get mixed up. This is truth, and I don't want anyone to mess it up."

As if taken by a sudden idea, he gets to his feet and paces, and I push myself up to sit. What has him so agitated? He approaches me and snatches the satchel from my hands. "That's what I used to think, but I've changed my mind. I don't want to write anymore."

"But you said—"

"Forget what I said. I shouldn't have told you anything."

"Am I the first person you told?"

"Told what?"

"About this challenge of yours?"

He alternates between staring down at me and looking around for a distraction. Fear and panic surrounds him like a cloud. "I'm not doing it anymore!"

I make my way past him to some old fruit that has dropped on the ground. As surely as I knew to lead Galen to the birch tree, I know the Mystery wants me to lead Thomas to a particular place inside him. I don't know the way there, but the Mystery does. *You're a dolt!* my mind yells, but I drown its voice with total concentration on what the Mystery says to my heart.

"It's perfectly fine, you know," I say.

"What is?"

"To be fearful."

"I'm not—"

"You see, the moment you told me, the moment you were honest, you became vulnerable. It's only now you're realizing how open to attack you are. Do you trust that I won't attack you?"

"It's not about that."

"Do you trust I won't attack you?"

Thomas stops pacing and stands still. "Yes, I trust you,"

"So you're safe?"

Thomas nods and I circle around him. "Inside, you're now like a wolf that has exposed their belly and yet you say you're safe. What are you basing that decision on?"

"Trust."

"Doesn't this feel better than the panic you were in just before?"

"But I'm still exposed. You might not attack, but others will."

"The only way forward is through the fear. See how quickly it made you retreat?" I twist the old apple I collected open with a slide more than a crunch. "Don't let the fear make you run from who you are; it only comes to teach you."

Thomas peers into the spongy half apple in my hand and his upper lips curls into a sneer. "It's rotten."

"What about the seeds?"

"They're unchanged."

"Even with all that rot around them? They'll still grow into what they're meant to be?"

Thomas shrugs. "As long as they're planted, I suppose, and tended."

"As long as they don't run from their call?"

Thomas looks from the rotten fruit to me; his defenses are down, his eyes soft. "How do you do it?"

"Do what?"

"Not fear your call."

In the valley, Muscone shines brighter as the sun's rays stretch to it from behind the mountain. It's impossible to deny its boldness. "What makes you think I'm not terrified of it? I don't even know what it is."

"So you're scared too?"

I close my eyes and let his words sit in the air. When I open them, he is beside me and we watch Muscone glow like a coal in the valley, each passing cloud dulling it a little before the sun dazzles us again. I place my palm on his chest. "What does your call feel like?"

He looks puzzled so I grab his arm and turn him towards me. "Close your eyes," I say, and he opens his mouth to protest but obeys and lowers his head. He places his hand over mine and I slide mine away.

"I want you to imagine there is no call, no quest, and you're working as a carpenter."

Thomas shuffles his feet, lifts his head and pulls a few faces. "All right."

"How does it feel?"

"All right."

"Just all right?"

"Bit boring. Bland. Dead."

"Now take a moment to imagine your quest." He repositions his feet and stands a little stronger.

"How does your quest feel?"

"Petrifying."

"Anything else?"

"It feels right. True. A bit . . . exciting." He opens his eyes and they wrinkle with his grin.

"You're smiling," I say

"I am."

"But you're petrified, remember?"

"That I am."

"Still want to give up?"

He shakes his head, picks up the satchel and strides towards the path that leads to Muscone.

"The gate . . .." I'm aware the words are coming from my mouth, but my mind can't think of anything beyond the elaborately carved gates of Muscone.

"Yes, the gate." Thomas grabs my upper arm as a cart passes by and he pushes me into the bushes that line the road into the town. I peer over his shoulder to catch another glimpse of them.

Smoutlea's gates may as well have been loose planks, and the fortified gates at the Hall were impressive, but nothing I've ever seen matches the workmanship that glows a short distance away. The carved patterns look like they're inlaid with a fine metal that even catches the light dulled by a passing cloud and reflects it all around.

Thomas darts across the road, pulling me off balance, and my feet trip on themselves as he charges after the cart. He bends low and walks beside the solid wheel at the front and I copy him with my hand hovering over the one at the rear. Items clang and tinkle under the cart's covering blanket as it bumps its way towards Muscone. The closer we get to the gates, the more my stomach sinks with a strange dread of insignificance. The skin at the back of my neck pinches as I try to take in the gates' height. The shadow they cast upon the road envelops the entire cart and its coolness strikes me like judgment. Yet still the gate glows.

"The gate...it's beautiful," I whisper to Thomas and point.

Thomas nods. "They put effort into things here ... you'll see."

"Whoa." The horse's hooves fall silent along with our sound cover of turning wheels and rattling wares. Positioned behind the solid wheels, we watch underneath for movement from the two guards on the other side. Their legs saunter to the cart and the cart rocks as the driver moves and grumbles incomprehensibly.

A guard taps the side of the cart. "You're entering to trade in Muscone?"

"Of course I am, you uniformed dolt!"

My eyes stretch open. *Is this driver mad? He's going to get himself killed.*

The guard steps closer and the cart sways with the movement of the driver.

"Stay away from my wares," the driver calls. "You two wouldn't have enough silver to even view them."

The guards' feet shuffle and they murmur amongst themselves.

"Well, are you going to open the gate or not? They're waiting for me."

Two knocks thud into the gate and it opens. A thin strip of luster appears between the gates and soon the glowing space is wide enough for the cart to pass. We trail alongside the wheels and I follow Thomas's lead and stand tall after we clear the gate. The driver and his cart rumble ahead of us and I turn to watch the gates close. It disappoints me to see that the back of those beautiful gates is plain and unkempt, but the last view of the antics of the guards mimicking the driver stretches a smile across my lips.

"Potseller!" My body jumps at the sudden squeal, my muscles ready to take me anywhere safe. But it's a squeal of delight.

People come from everywhere, shouting and scrambling, and heading towards the cart ahead of us. They run to and fro in a delightful dance of panic, blind to anything but the potseller; even newcomers dressed as idlers don't seem to exist. The driver hasn't yet made it to the market square and seems torn between taking the silver that is being thrust in his face and delightedly telling them there are plenty of pots for everyone. Thomas offers me his hand and leads me along the frenzied procession.

In the short amount of time from the driver's entry to arrival at the square, the prices he shouts have increased. He leads his horse through the crowd to the center of the square and holds a shiny pot decorated with an ornate metal braid above his head, a beacon for everyone who hasn't heard of his arrival—the deaf, perhaps. Someone forces their silver among the reins he holds in one hand and grabs at the pot held high in the other. The crowd erupts in cheers and jeers, and the new owner holds the shiny pot aloft. "I have the first pot! The first pot. I'm the first in the village!"

Many stop to admire this lady's new purchase, and others run to share the exciting news as the potseller lines the pots up in a row and readies his cart for sales.

"Eadie just bought the first shiny pot in the village," someone says as they rush past and disappear into the crowd. They remind me of a gaggle of birds when you throw bread to them; they squawk and fight and make a lot of noise.

I shake my head and giggle. "This is insanity."

Thomas leans close to me so I can hear him above the crowd. "Told you they're a bit extreme."

We leave the frenzy of the square and make our way through the paved streets of Muscone. The streets are tidy, the homes so neatly stacked against each other that they create order, a channel for people to flow in and out without thought. The further we travel, the larger the windows of the buildings grow.

"There are a lot of pot vendors here, Thomas. The people of Muscone must cook a lot of stews."

Thomas laughs. "I've never asked them. Perhaps you should." He snorts and adds, "I'd love to see the look on their faces."

The streets continue in their neatness, branching off in the perfect crisscross pattern I'd noticed from the ridge. Displays of shiny pots fill each window we pass. Some of the smaller homes are so full I wonder how the people inside can move. But it seems that rather than remove some pots, they create a larger place to store them. The next place has better windows, and they set to work filling up the available space with their wares. Inside the homes, people polish and dust and admire their pots and look at me with narrowed eyes if they see me watching. In the streets, people carry pots close to their bodies and puff up ready to attack if anyone gets too close.

This must be Eadie's home. The new shiny pot with the metal braid has pride of place in her front window, complete with an adoring crowd outside. Her neighbors have also put new braided pots in their windows. It soon becomes obvious which neighbors don't have the new shiny pots in their window yet.

Perhaps they don't have the silver?

Whether they have silver is not any concern of mine, yet I've just made an assumption about someone I've never met based on the ridiculous notion that your value increases and is dependent on the *placement of a pot.* I try shaking the disbelief from my mind.

A group of villagers cross the path in front of us, and I imagine they're off to buy new polishing cloths. They move as a gaggle, watching and pecking at anyone who comes too close and flapping their wings and screeching if anyone touches their pots. The last of the group catches my eye and I smile only for them to hug their pot closer to their chest and watch over their shoulder as they hasten away. I must be trapped in some strange dream.

"I'm yet to see a friendly face," I say to Thomas.

"I think they save those for the pots."

The street rises in front of us, but before we reach the climb we pass a line of women, all facing the street without a smile, arranged just as neatly and organized as the pots on the edge of the potseller's cart. I can't see their price tags, but I know someone will pay far less than their value. The order I admired isn't pretty anymore, it's stifling. There is nothing humorous about the pots of Muscone.

How stupid of me. I snicker at myself and my earlier question about stews. The shiny pots don't get used for anything other than polishing and comparing. I stop to admire the view from this raised section of the village, the ordered houses all in rows and the glow that comes from everything so highly polished that the only things seen are reflections. Illusions.

"Is this all there is to Muscone? This is their entire life?" I turn to Thomas. "Do you think anyone's happy here?"

He points to the square, the cart just visible among the people still gathered there. "Only the potsellers, I expect."

My muscles suddenly feel weak and I sigh. "They're all so flighty, unpredictable—did you notice how scared they are?"

A voice behind us catches us by surprise.

"It's only natural they're scared."

Thomas leaps between me and the voice, his feet in a ready stance, hands clenched around his raised walking stick. My mouth dries in an instant and the sides of my hood drop to cover my face as I lean my head into Thomas's back. I draw the sides across my face before I peer around his shoulder.

The man's hair is dark and falls over his face as he leans forward with his work. The knife he uses to whittle is small, and I'm confident Thomas could handle any outburst that might arise. Tiny stripes of gray trace through the waves of the man's hair, yet his stance is strong, almost youthful. He wears clothes that are decidedly plainer than any we have seen the villagers wearing. There are no pots nearby and he seems unperturbed that Thomas hovers above him.

"Of course they're scared," he repeats to the whittled stick. "They are their pots."

Thomas doesn't change his stance. "Are your old eyes foggy? They're people, not pots!"

The man lays aside his whittle and gently folds his light-brown hands together, leans his forearms on his knees and looks up to Thomas. "Ah, but they don't believe that. Take away their pots, you take away their identity. They're all terrified of who they are without them."

Thomas maintains his stance but removes one hand from his stick to reach behind, making sure I am close to him. His body softens as he lowers his stick. "Surely they know how stupid they look to outsiders, putting all this energy into polishing and securing pots?"

"They don't, I'm afraid, and the Hall keeps supplying bigger and shinier pots." The man rises and extends his hand to Thomas. "I am Besnik."

Thomas stiffens, but I nod close to his shoulder, a calmness spreading through my veins. This man sees the things we see. He extends his hand. "Thomas."

"Well met," they say in unison, but Thomas doesn't relax.

"And now," Besnik says as he leans around Thomas, who is quick to raise his arms and step between us. "We must get her to safety, no?"

My eyes widen. Thomas tenses to shield me, preparing to land a blow, when Besnik smiles and slaps Thomas on the back. "We have been waiting for you." Thomas tries to form words and Besnik answers him with a wink. "People talk, Thomas, you know how it works."

Who's been waiting? Why?

Shouts reach us from the square. There's some kind of disturbance down there but at first I can't see what—Trothsmen!

Thomas latches onto my hand. "Looks like your bandits have their wits about them."

"*My* bandits? Seemed to me they were more acquainted with the 'kid from Feldston.'"

Besnik pushes us down a side street and as we run I try to decipher the pain that appeared in Thomas's eyes. Like I'd betrayed him or punched him in the stomach. I promise myself to never mention Feldston again.

M y mouth is still dry as Besnik leads us through Muscone's
lanes, slowing as we zigzag further away from the square.
The smaller paths are just as ordered and lead to cozy houses that
line the village walls. We stop outside a home with a colorful flower
box that hides its small window. There are no pots in sight. Besnik
raps on the door twice, turns his head to us and beckons. "Come,"
he says as he turns the handle and leads us inside.

Inside it is dark but warm and my eyes adjust quickly, taking
in the small room with sparse furniture and a small fire. Besnik
closes the door behind us and makes his way to the side of an older
woman kneading dough on a table.

His hands gently hold her shoulders. "How goes your day?"

"I am well, young Bez." She gazes into his face with soft eyes and
looks to us then back to Bez. "Yours goes well too, I see."

"Yes, very well."

Thomas thumps his walking stick into the rammed-earth floor
and pushes me back towards the door. "Besnick! Explain yourself!"

Bez dips his chin and holds his palms up in surrender. "Thomas," he says calmly. "We are here to help. I couldn't explain earlier."

Thomas readies his grip to defend us. "Why should I trust you?" he demands.

"Would you prefer to take your chances with the Trothsmen?"

Thomas shuffles his weight from side to side but doesn't answer the other man's question.

Bez directs his statement to me. "Word is spreading about your escape from the Hall." The woman beside him nods, and her hands stop their work and disappear inside the soft dough.

My voice is croaky, yet I find it. "But doesn't that put me in more danger?"

Bez offers a slow, tilted nod. "It also gives people the chance to help, to join with you. You see, the word is not only about your escape, but the purpose of your escape."

The pit of my stomach is heavy, as if a rock has landed there.

Bez steps towards Thomas and holds his shoulders as he speaks. "You have done well, young man. She is safe. Let's work together to keep it that way."

Bez collects a candle and ushers us into a second room. Even though I duck, my hood scrapes on the low lintel of the door and any warmth disappears as if a curtain has been drawn across its threshold. Once standing, we press our backs into the rough shelving that surrounds a large hole in the floor. Bez nods and we follow him down the damp ladder that leads to a cold store that seems too sodden to be any good for storage.

Thomas stands between me and Bez and juts his chin towards the rough narrow tunnel ahead of us. "What's this?"

"Nearly there." Bez lights a torch and drops the candle to the wet floor. His boots slush into the tunnel entrance. Thomas turns to me and I shrug. What other choice do we have?

The light from Bez's torch outlines the jagged walls of the tunnel. Wet rock and clay bustle for attention, flashing the reflections from the flames from wall to wall. A curved shape passes above me and doesn't reflect the light like the showy rocks. Another one appears in the rocks ahead and my hand slides along its rough surface as I pass. Roots. We are being held by the trees, even under the earth and in the dark. My hands stroke each root in thanks as we pass, and I don't notice the tunnel growing lighter until the smoke from the extinguished torch makes me cough.

I am the last one to climb out of the shrinking tunnel. Bez's hand appears in front of me, but Thomas knocks it out of the way and helps me to my feet. My eyes squint in the dappled sunlight of the forest, and I thank him for steadying me.

Thomas looks back to the hidden entrance of the tunnel and to the village wall that rises in the distance. "Well, that's one way to save on travel silver, I suppose."

Bez walks into the forest and beckons us to follow along his path. "I've been in and out of Muscone for many summers. They've stopped fearing me now; they know I'm not interested in their pots."

"Why keep going back then?" Thomas asks, following Bez along the path with me behind him.

"Because every so often, one of them will look around, I mean really look around, and put down their polishing cloth and come looking for me."

"They know to look for you?"

The back of Bez's head bounces in a nod. "I used to be one of them. They gossip that I went mad because I don't care about their pots." He chuckles a little. "I don't mind the gossip; at least they know who to look for when they stop panicking and the fog in their mind clears."

I think back to the frenzied scene in the market, the women standing in line. "How did the craziness start?"

Bez shrugs. "Someone had two pots and decided he was better than the people with one pot. Who knows the reason why? If everyone laughed at their absurd idea, it would have stopped there, but this lie took hold of Muscone and here we are, generations later, believing a person's value lies in the shine of a pot and not in themselves."

He stops and points back in the direction of the wall. "Did you know they give the poor a black pot for cooking?"

We shake our heads.

"Then they shame the poor for not being able to make their pot shine; a constant reminder they are unsalvageable."

"There are so many shiny things in the village that aren't used," I say. "Could they share a little? Wouldn't they feel less threatened, calmer, perhaps?"

Bez moves his head from side to side. "Maybe, but it's not about the actual pots themselves, it's their thoughts about the pots that are the problem. Sharing pots would make others equal with them. If there were no rungs on Muscone's ladder they wouldn't know how much more superior to feel." He raises his hands in the air as he walks. "How would they know who to put in the stocks for being found near the windowed houses?"

Bez walks and talks, twisting back to us for emphasis and even walking backwards on occasion. Just when we think he's going to walk into a tree, he sidesteps with the precision of one who knows his trail.

The waves of hair at his shoulders shimmy as he shakes his head. "They have food and health, yet if you asked any poor man what they want more than anything, it would be a shiny pot and a window for everyone to see it. Muscone's lie is so insidious even some among my family have begun to polish their black pots, hesitate in generosity and cling to their pot in fear."

Thomas scratches his head. "And I thought *your* eyes were foggy. What a strange form of blindness."

"Strange it is," Bez says. "It affects everything but the eyes. Want to know what's even more fascinating about this blindness? Those in the center of the village are blind to their own pots. The only pots they see are the ones other people have and obsess over making them their own." He points ahead. "We're almost there."

"Where?" Thomas asks.

Small bushes not much higher than our heads conceal the clearing; we don't even know it's there until we step into it. Brightly covered wagons surround campfires, people mill about and children run across our path giggling.

Bez extends his arm to the clearing. "My home."

Thomas holds my wrist as people approach us with smiles of welcome. Some women take my hand to lead me with them and when he pulls me back, they release their hold. His face holds the same distrust I hold in my heart. In time he relaxes and involves himself with the other men but whenever I look for him he is there, watchful. The circle of wagons surround all manner of activities and loose livestock. Thomas is being vigilant enough for both of us, so I rest against a bale of hay and end up sharing it with a hungry sheep. A woman with soft eyes and that same wavy dark hair shoos the sheep away. "Away with you," she says. "Go find some fresh grass."

The sheep protests as she pushes, but it quickly finds interest elsewhere and trots away. I hadn't noticed the blankets the lady carried until she opens them. She places them over me and I sit up, embarrassed that I'm resting while others about me work.

"No," she soothes. "You rest here. You've a long journey ahead of you."

Thomas must have mentioned our travels—how much has he told them? Will she question me? She doesn't ask anything of me, but she watches Bez, Thomas and the other men prepare wood for chopping and splitting.

"You admire Bez, don't you?" I say, and she nods and smiles but doesn't take her eyes from him.

"I admire anyone who can see hearts and not pots," she says. "Particularly those like Bez who were born into households filled with shining pots. Those beaten and shamed who still stay true to their hearts."

"Bez said *this* was his home."

"It is now. We are his family."

"Why doesn't he just move on? Why return to the village?"

"He says it's his purpose. He doesn't go to upset or challenge them, but to be some kind of signpost, to help the same people who hurt him so badly. He says no one can solve a problem if they don't first acknowledge it's there, and he feels he can help them do both."

"How does he do that?"

"By staying true. By being himself."

We watch them together in silence for a while. Then she turns and smiles and goes about her business. The men chop into the logs and I drift off to the rhythmic sound of their axe blades.

❦

T he last light of day makes itself known; voices call to each other, pots simmer and people gather around the large fire that Bez and Thomas oversee. The camp's activity fascinates me. Everyone is busy, yet no hearts are harsh, no one barks orders, no one threatens punishment. Thomas finishes with the fire and settles next to me.

Before we eat, Besnik speaks to his family, giving thanks for the food and welcoming us as visitors to their family.

He extends his arm towards us. "Tonight, we celebrate your freedom. We have waited patiently, and now change is on its way."

I force a smile and gulp so loud I'm sure everyone within five road markers can hear it.

Thomas leans in to me. "Are you all right?"

"All these people *do* believe I'm an idler, don't they?" I keep my smile and speak through my teeth.

Thomas looks to Bez and they smile at each other before he nudges me. "Trust me, you're safe. These people believe the legends; every one of them would rather *die* than let any harm come to you. They're honored you're here, and honored to be part of your story."

"You want me to trust them?"

"I want you to trust me."

I want you to trust me. The words of the Mystery speak louder into my heart than Thomas's words ever could.

I nod at all the smiling faces and exhale through my teeth when Bez speaks and their faces turn back to him. He speaks about the unrest that he can feel coming. And come it must, he says. He describes the world as a growing child that must break free from its parents to operate in a better way. Will the pots stop shining, he wonders? The very Stars have blessed this village with a man who loves them and waits for them to see they don't need their pots after all. But my heart aches for the people of Muscone. The unrest promises to tip their world upside down and no amount of polishing and rearranging will keep the coming chaos at bay.

T homas nudges me from my thoughts. "What do you think the people in the village would do if they found their seed? Polish it to compare it with others, or polish it till it no longer existed?"

I smile. "I don't think they know they have a seed. While they focus on the pots, they can't see anything else." The puzzle of how to make a seed visible weighs me down, but I remember the villagers have Bez and his family and I trust the Mystery that answers will arrive when needed. Just like berry bushes.

Servers bring bowls of steaming food to us then move quickly between the pot and the hungry bodies that surround the camp-fire. Strange scents hover about me and I can barely wait for my bowl to cool before eating. The vegetables are cut so thick and chunky we pick them up with our fingers. What a strange mix of flavors and textures; some vegetables have been roasted in the fire, others boiled in the pot. The herbs and spices the people gather taste like we eat the essence of the forest itself. The family's campfire circle is large, and even at this distance from the fire, the occasional breeze wraps its warmth around us like a blanket. The sound of instruments being plucked and tuned grabs my attention and wonder.

I've never held an instrument. The players are generous and let me play or strike theirs before they gather together. Pipes and drums, a timbrel, lute and a small harp play separately and strike odd individual melodies before settling together and creating a pleasing and happy tune. The servers bring jugs of ale to the circle and Bez and his family begin to dance. Surrounded by such gladness, my fingers hold on to the grass beside me; I'm so light I feel I might float away.

Bez approaches me, jumping and twirling in some delightful jig. "Come and dance," he shouts above the music.

My hands raise in a shrug. "I don't know your dances—in fact, I've never danced."

"Never danced? Ha!" he says as he bends towards me. "Then now is the time to learn."

Bez takes my hands and pulls me to my feet. He signals to the minstrels to slow their tune and walks me in and out of the gathered dancers and takes my shoulders to turn me in the right direction when I get confused. I copy his bows and jigs at the appointed times and join in with the surrounding laughter. No matter how much I concentrate there's too much to remember yet I have no fear of appearing foolish or being punished. Another challenge, another river to leap into.

The dance begins in a loose circle around the campfire. We weave in and out and under arms and spin. I giggle when I get it wrong and the others correct me, spinning me the right way and crashing into me when I misstep. Each time we travel around the circle I'm happiest when I come across Thomas's face again, and with each passing we welcome each other with a laugh. At the dance's end, he takes my waist with a mix of strength and tenderness and for the first time, perhaps in my entire life, my body forgets to flinch.

We retire to the outer circle to catch our breath and enjoy more ale. Eventually the minstrels play slower pieces and a woman sings a melody that enthralls me. Her hair is dark, like the others, with the same waves that reach to her waist. The kerchief that covers her hair keeps her face clear so she has no need for braids. I try to stop staring but am always drawn back to her face and delightful voice. I whisper to Thomas without moving my eyes from her, "She looks like she's singing that song to me. She keeps looking at me, and I can't stop watching her."

Thomas pours himself another ale. "It's a song of blessing. If she's singing it to you, it's a good sign."

"What should I do?"

"With a blessing? Accept it, of course."

Immersed in the melody, I'm enchanted by her words of courage and peace, even if I don't understand them, and I'm saddened when the song comes to an end. The minstrels play another jig and people rise to be part of the dance. My mysterious singer is almost upon me when I see her through the dancing bodies. Without a word, she kneels and sits on her feet in front of me and presents me with a flower. The same kind of blue flower I wove into Joss's hair. I reach out to accept it and she rises on her knees, her hands rest gently on my shoulder and she kisses my forehead. A sense of strength travels from her kiss and courses its way through my entire body.

Occasional sounds from drunken instruments and joyous but tired bodies signal the end of the evening. Thomas and I lie on the grass, relaxed and ready for sleep. He rolls to his side and places his arm over me, our knees fitting together like pieces of a puzzle.

"I'm glad you're here," he mumbles into my back in such a way it is easy to ignore. A blanket drapes over us, perfecting our cocoon, and as I drift off, somewhere in the back of my mind a warning stirs. If these people are our friends, does Thomas's warning about trust still apply to them? Is it truly impossible to be betrayed by a stranger?

⚜

A fine blanket of early mist hangs over Bez's camp and waits cheekily for the sun to chase it away. Thomas faces me as he sleeps. I pull our blanket closer to my neck, trying to conserve the pocket of warmth between us. His eyelids flutter in his dreams and he tilts his head to find a more comfortable position. The scar on his face follows his jawline from his chin to his ear. It's paler than the skin around it, shiny and white, as if the parts we use to heal ourselves are somehow purer for being touched by the Mystery in the midst of our pain. Many of my scars are on the inside, and I wonder if they'll shine with the same vibrancy when they heal. I sneak my warm hand to the side of his face and touch his scar. Thomas opens his eyes, grabs my hand and pushes it away from his face.

"Don't!"

"Sorry, I—it tells a beautiful story."

"Well, I don't want to hear it." He tosses the blanket open and the cold rushes in before I can close it around me. As he storms off through the low mist, Bez catches him, places a hand on his shoulder and leads him towards the morning fire. I want to feel angry, but I can't. I react the same way when my scars are touched without permission.

⚜

We spend the early morning separately but in the company of others, as we prepare meals and offer service in thanks to the family. By the time we come together ready to travel, it's easier to pretend his scar doesn't exist. We are both stronger now, powered by full bellies, a warm sleep and a night of laughter and protection. We leave camp with their blessings in our ears and a small sack of food that Thomas loops onto the belt of his tunic.

A short distance out of the forest we find the roads on this side of Muscone mirror the other, crisscrossing the fields. Our idler costumes have lost some their safety; it can't only be Bez who's heard we travel as idlers. As soon as the fields fade into grazing land, we search out forest to trek through. It's slower but it provides respite from our constant vigilance.

Light forest thickens and welcomes me. Thomas isn't as talkative today, leaving me to commune with the Mystery and try to learn more of the ancient song. It flits in and out of my consciousness, as if focusing on it with my mind causes it to float away. This game is more playful than frustrating, and I have all the time in the world to hear. My hands press into the rough bark of an old trunk.

If only they could talk...

I correct myself: *if only I would listen.* I won't chase the song but be quiet and observant and let its wisdom come to me.

So many places here remind me of the forest by the lake. Gullies and trunks, ferns and moss. I find a small sapling growing and can't resist touching it and wishing it well.

"You have a long way to go, little one," I whisper.

Thomas and I are both saplings, learning and growing, and I understand we have a long way to go too, although I'm not sure what that means. The forest darkens. Vines, ferns and trees block our way. It's easy to fear when you can't see ahead, when every direction confuses and paths that lead nowhere offer up hopeful distractions. Standing still is fruitless. Stepping out and backtracking takes time, but is the only way for us to test our confusion and find our path. Thomas grumbles and puffs every time we make no progress, but I make no comment. His arms sweep aside a group of branches and reveal a wide and long gully filled with bramble.

Climbing up and down the sides is not an option, and no logs have fallen to provide us with a bridge. The edge of the gully is firm, and we work our way along it, under and around trees searching for a way across. Thomas grabs a thick vine that droops from a tall tree and launches himself across the gully only for it to snap under his weight, dumping him in almost the same place where his feet left the ground. My breath catches in my throat waiting for his reaction and a tirade of curses. His landing grunt breaks into chuckles and our laughter rolls up and down the length of the gully.

The bracken looks dry and sharp, and the snapped vine lies alongside his body. He picks it up, considers it for a moment then drops it to the ground. "I'll be sure to test the next one."

Every vine we pass he tugs, swings on and inspects before he decides on a twisted vine trailing from a branch that overhangs the bracken. He leaps towards the gully and swings across in one clean pass.

"Ready?" he calls. The vine swings back to me before I have a chance to answer. Fine dimples cover the bark on the vine and scratch my hands when I catch it. Thomas beckons from the other side and my body leaps towards the gully before my mind has a chance to talk me out of it. The bark digs into my palms and pinches at my skin, but I have no intention of letting go. Thomas grabs at me as I swing to the other side and my momentum pulls him off balance as the vine twists to return. Visions of me hanging forlornly above the gully with nowhere to go but into the bracken smash out of my mind as his arms latch on to me and pull me back to solid ground. I cling to him and gasp for air. "Stars! Thank you!"

He stands taller, nods and rearranges my robe. "Let's keep moving."

B etween the thinning canopy, mottled gray clouds move across
the sky.

"Should we find shelter?" I call to Thomas as he creates our path
through the clearing undergrowth.

"We've got a bit of time yet."

The clouds shuffle around, changing from light gray to gray
blue. "I've always wondered about people who say they didn't see
a storm coming; surely everyone can see the sky?"

"Lots of people watch things, but they don't necessarily see.
There's always time for preparation if you know what you're
watching for."

"So what are we watching for?"

Thomas checks the color of the sky as he walks, turning around
in a full circle to gauge what surrounds us. "Keep an eye out for
some kind of shelter for now, but our time'll be up when the
birds disappear. If we're without shelter when the wind arrives we
might have to sit it out in the wet." He continues forging our path.

"Another fact of life for you. You can't stop the wind, and you won't stop the storm."

Why had I never noticed how observant he was? Maybe watching for signs was a part of village life taught to all children. "Thomas?"

He turns back to look at me. "Yeah?"

"The birds have gone."

The forest is eerily silent, but I'm sure I can hear a river somewhere far off. Yet now it seems closer...

A wall of wind punches into me and knocks me off balance. Leaves fly from the ground and swirl around us while the branches above us roar with the storm's arrival. Large splashes of rain seem to scout ahead, followed by an army of noise. We run from tree to tree and I'm amazed at how much rain makes it through them. An old oak with a trunk deformity comes into view. Part of its trunk appears hollow and a low branch has grown above it, creating a protected area almost like a cave. There's only enough room for us to crawl in and sit bent over with our knees pulled up against our chests, our feet slotting in between each other. Drips come in, but nothing like what's outside of this little space.

We catch our breath as the noise continues. My hand rests on the edge of the oak opening and sheets of white rain drive past us. "I love storms. So much power and strength. How can we ever compete with that?"

"Cursed inconvenience," he mutters and reacts to my frown with one of his own. "What? This is bad. Now it's just going to take us longer to get to the next village."

"Bad for you maybe, but good for the farmer who's been waiting for rain. Labeling it as 'bad' or complaining about it isn't going to change what it is. Just enjoy it."

A drip lands on the side of his face and he wipes it with the back of his hand. "How am I meant to enjoy this?"

A crack of thunder makes me jump and he snorts. "Enjoying it?"

I smile at him as the thunder rolls away. "It surprised me, it didn't scare me."

Another deep rumble begins in the sky and rattles its way to the earth. I put my hand to my chest. "Feel that?"

He looks up at the drips. "Did you get one? I keep getting them on my face."

"No, the thunder. You can feel the sound inside you as if just for a moment the thunder puts its heart into yours and they beat together."

Thomas dutifully puts his hand to his chest and we wait for the next rumble, listening through the spray and hisses of the rain as it rushes through and pushes everything before it aside by force. The forest flashes like a sunny day before the boom of another thunderclap makes us both jump.

"And what about the lightning? You're not going to ask me to feel that, are you? We'd end up like Bez's charred vegetables,"

"There's rocks further up this mountainside." Some time has passed, and now Thomas's voice brings me back to the moment. When the rain softened, I'd leaned my head outside the trunk and let it sprinkle through the leaves above and onto my face. Some trickled down over my smile and some were so light they sat like mist on my face.

Thomas stares at me and our hiding space feels more cramped than before. "There might be caves," he explains.

I turn my face back to the rain outside.

"Will we have to walk in this tomorrow?"

"Afternoon storms. Fast at the front, steady at the back. Should be clear by morning."

My hands squeeze my calves and rub at my knees. "I think my legs are numb."

Thomas untangles his legs from mine and grunts as he wriggles his body out of the trunk and feels the light rain land on his face. "We should keep moving."

When you're damp, cold and tired, even the thought of a simple cave feels like a warm inn. We find no caves, but a ledge with its rocky overhang is large enough for us to stretch out and it feels like a palace. The last of the light is dying as Thomas unwraps the cloth of food from Bez and assesses our situation.

"If it wasn't for Bez we'd have aching bellies from hunger right about now. When you farm you get to think ahead, but this? While we travel like this, we can no more plan a meal than fly in the sky."

He separates the vegetables into two piles and we each eat from a corner of the cloth. The food is cold, but the flavors from last night linger. I point a piece of parsnip at him thoughtfully, "But we've been provided for. I think it depends on where your stability and certainty comes from, and mine doesn't come from outside myself."

"You sure about that?"

I nod. There's nothing outside myself anyway.

"Well, that'll be the first thing you've ever been sure of." He picks up his last few chunks of vegetables and leans back against the stone. "So you're not worried about what tomorrow might bring?"

"Worrying about it won't change what it is. Today is enough for me." I finish my meal, fold the cloth and pass it to Thomas before wiggling my body back as far into the overhang as I can. The stone is cold, but at least it's not wet.

Thomas joins me, as far back from the wind as possible. "Don't you ever wonder about your future? Where you'll end up, what you'll do?"

I'd never considered it before. I shake my head and the cold seeps into me. You can't dream of a future when you believe you have no right to be in the present. "Maybe one day I will," I tell him. "But for now, the farthest future I can see is Sirban."

Thomas slides next to me and places his robe over both of us. "Tomorrow, Ferce Point, and the day after that, Sirban."

"You make it sound easy."

"One foot in front of the other. How hard can it be?"

T he morning is warm and everything is new. Storms do that. Without a storm, things don't get washed away. Another reminder it's all as it should be.

My feet are steady and strong. I sidestep small puddles and keep in mind that each step along this forest track takes me closer to Sirban. Closer to some answers.

"Are you well?" The track has widened enough for Thomas to walk beside me as a companion, but he's yet to give up his role of concerned guide.

I nod slowly. "Did you hear the talk in Muscone about how they believe the Eariss is evil and it will take all their pots away? No wonder they hate the Eariss. Will that go in your book too?"

"A tale that's only full of goodness is just as bad as one only full of darkness, I suppose."

"True," I say.

Thomas moves the satchel from one shoulder to the other so it sits between us. "So what do we actually know?"

"*You* think I'm the Eariss."

"I *know* you're the Eariss, and so does everyone else. Their hopes are on you to bring about change."

"But what if I don't want to be the Eariss? I don't even know what it's meant to do."

"The original legends say the Eariss will come to set things right. Bring peace. Word spreads quickly, and that's why the bravest are so happy to see you—they know change is coming."

"But the unrest ... surely that will bring more change than I ever could? And peace? How am I meant to stop the unrest? May as well try to stop a storm from coming."

Thomas sighs deeply and we walk in silence for a while.

The satchel bounces with Thomas's shrug. "How about we try again with the things we *do* know?"

"Like what?"

"The lights from your eyes."

It's my turn to shrug. "I don't know anything about it. I don't know why it happens sometimes and not others. It must have something to do with the newborn's eyes, right? And why they constantly checked my eyes at the Hall."

"They did what?"

"Every morning, for as long as I can remember, they checked my eyes. It was usually left to Eshnae, but on important dates the lord would check himself. They didn't tell me what they were looking for, but I was always terrified they would find whatever it was."

"And you didn't think it was unusual, all that checking?"

"Forsaken Stars, Thomas! It was my *normal*. How was I to know it wasn't a part of everyone else's daily life?" My blood feels cold and heavy, as if it has pooled at my feet. Eyes flash before me, all those eyes peering into mine ... waiting, watching ... for what? "They_knew!"

My hands grasp at the next tree and I suck in air but feel none in my lungs. Over and over I gasp, but I feel no relief. Thomas puts his hand on my shoulder and I push it away, concerned that his hovering is stopping the air from reaching me. Tiny flashes of light dance in my eyes and I drop to the base of the tree lightheaded, but at least I can feel my lungs expanding now. Thomas slides his back down the tree and sits next to me, drawing me to him and guiding my head to his shoulder.

"Feeney," I croak from my dry mouth. I sit stunned while images parade across my mind, too brutal to ever put into words. The pain rises and falls and I retch and tremble. "Why didn't he just kill me like the others?"

Thomas makes no sound, and no answer rises within me.

"He needs you," Thomas finally says. "He needs your story—or rather, the one he created for you."

"For what, though?" I whisper, too drained to clear my throat.

Thomas strokes my head. "It is said the Eariss creates a weapon against which no army can stand."

A weapon?

I sit up and move away from Thomas, remembering Bez's words about keeping me safe. Everyone seems to know more about my life than I do. "The only thing I know about weapons is what you taught me."

Thomas nods a little. "I know."

"Can't see how I'm meant to defeat an army with a stick."

Thomas stands and offers me his hand. "Neither can I."

Once back on the track, another memory clears in my mind. "Eshnae said it was my fault."

"What was?"

"Everything, I expect. Feeney always found a way to make things my fault, but it was the first time Eshnae had blamed me."

"What did she say?"

"She said, 'It's *you*'—and that I had to go. That I should look for things that were hidden right in front of me."

"Hmm." Thomas walks and rubs his chin and I alternate between watching the road and his face, hoping he might have some answers or at least some new ideas. He pulls his hood back to make an announcement. "Makes about as much sense as your stick army, if you ask me."

The weight of my shoulders pushes my face to the sky, and what I thought was a sigh becomes a groan. Thomas laughs and nudges at my shoulder and pushes me off balance. I smile along with him. There's nothing to be gained in forcing an understanding from something so obscure.

"Come now," he says. "Enough puzzles. Tell me about the lessons, like the apple seeds. How does that work?"

I snort and shrug. I'd never thought about how any of it *worked*, it just was. "Sometimes I'll understand straight away, other times I have to be quiet to understand."

"Like standing still?"

"No, more like still inside." My hands find their way to the place where Feeney's knives would twist and turn. "You can be rushed on the outside and be quite still on the inside." Sweet air fills my lungs and I release it gently. Even the thought of the Mystery's stillness makes me smile. "When my mind spins or my body reacts it's hard to slow down and be still. It takes practice. But it's like finding the right road. The more often you travel down it, the easier it is to find, and it becomes familiar."

"And then the explanations just appear in your head,"

I feel them throughout my body but it's too hard to explain. I look to Thomas and nod.

"How does it get in there?"

"I think it's the Mystery."

"So the Mystery gives you the lesson?"

"I think so. Where else could it come from? ... I expect that sounds strange."

"Not any stranger than me trying to explain the rainbows and lights I've seen. So tell me about the second story, where you hear a different story than the one someone is telling you."

"Well, it's kind of like a waterfall—." I leap in front of him and hold his arms. "Have you ever *seen* a waterfall?"

He stops and straightens his back, raises an eyebrow . . . and nods.

"They're real then?"

A broad smile erupts from his face and he chuckles. "Yes, they are."

A truth. One simple truth and the world feels like it has expanded and goes on forever. Thomas follows me, leaving me to my happiness as we pass over small streams and rolling hills dotted with white-trunked trees before he enquires about the waterfalls again. "So the second story is like a waterfall?"

"It just pours over me," I explain. "And I know."

"What sorts of things do you know?"

"Oh, things like what the elders were planning, their motivations and fears. Sometimes my head fills with information—knowing what caused a situation and how to solve it. Sometimes it's as if I'm sharing someone else's memory, other times it might be a hint, an uneasy feeling and other times . . .." I stop on top of a small hill and squint through the trees.

"Yes?"

I throw my hands in the air. "Other times I have no idea at all."

Thomas catches up and walks down the other side of the hill. "Come along then," he says, and I follow.

"So you don't know *everything* then?" he says.

"No, of course not, but I have this strange sense of having access to everything—but not knowing anything. Like there's too much to know, but I know it anyway."

"So you're saying you know nothing and everything at the same time?"

It takes me awhile to process his question, and I consider whether to be truthful in my answer. "Oh Stars, that's exactly what I'm saying. Are you sure you have the right person? It sounds too strange now, saying it out loud. I promise I'm not trying to frustrate you."

"That just happens naturally."

"Bit like a storm."

"Shh." Thomas places his arm in front of me and we stop. The familiar rhythm of a galloping horse weaves its way through the grove of trees in front of us and we spy the white legs of the charger make its way along the road high on the next rise.

Once it has passed, Thomas turns to me. "Ferce Point. You ready?"

I nod even though I can't swallow. We move through the grove, only taking cover when someone passes on the road.

"What I'd like to know," I say as we crawl behind some fallen trunks, "is if I'm meant to be searching for the hidden ... how come they do the searching and I do all the hiding?"

"Tell me about certainty," Thomas says.

I frown at him.

"I'm serious, pretend we're talking about certainty."

"Why?"

"Look, I'll start ... nothing is certain." He lifts his eyebrows and stares at me before rising and sneaking over to a large tree a short distance away.

I follow shortly after and ask, "Does anything *need* to be certain?"

"Tell me, if you don't know what's ahead of you, why would you bother going?"

"Why should that stop you from going?" I counter as we move between the trees. "You could miss out on something spectacular based on what it *could* be, not on what it *is*."

"Well, you can prepare when you know what is ahead."

"I think it's an adventure if you don't know."

Thomas stops and faces me. He's no longer smiling. "You're certain of the Mystery?"

"Yes."

"So how does uncertainty work with that?"

I don't even have to stop to think of an answer. "I'm as certain of the Mystery as you are certain of the ground beneath your feet. It's the kind of certainty that isn't made by our minds—it just is."

He leans his face close to mine. "This is Ferce Point, Ashling. Hold the Mystery close."

S mall leaves from the white-trunked trees litter the grove, creating a spectacular tapestry of colors on the floor. Greens
and reds dot the ground, calling for attention among the varying
shades of yellows and browns. I shuffle my shoes through them,
disturbing the tapestry's shining exterior, my tracks revealing the
dark and rotting leaves underneath. Somehow the darkness feels
more real, its bitter and sweet richness of decay filling my nostrils.
Ahead, small flashes appear among the trees. Curious, I leave my
dark trail of steps and move towards them.

Ornate hand mirrors hang from the tree branches at measured
intervals. Gossamer ribbons with hints of color tie them to the
lowest branches, and even the finished bow is light and delicate,
making the mirrors appear as if they float in the air by themselves.
My fingers trace the floral carvings surrounding the looking glass
and move their way up and down the handle. The mirror swings
lightly from my touch. Thomas watches as I move from mirror to

mirror and proclaim each one more elaborate and beautiful than the one before.

I stop to check my senses. Everywhere I look is incredible beauty. Light floral scents drift on the air with hints of a harpist's melody. I turn in a full circle and soak it all in.

"Why didn't we get here earlier?" I call to Thomas as I spin. "It's beautiful." I scramble up the final rise to the road. A headland appears between the gaps of the trees ahead. Waves caress its cliffs as if they are just as desperate as us to reach the white walls of Ferce Point. The walls follow the cliff line, broken only by a gate that shines in the sunlight, and my mouth hangs open in wonder. Thomas arrives at my side and I point at its beauty, but no words come. He pulls at my arm, turning me towards him, but my face swings back to the gate. I'm curious about why he scrunches at the hem of his robe, but it's not enough to draw my eyes from the gate. He holds my chin and wipes my face with its damp edges, before turning me to wipe my own robe free of leaves and forest debris.

"Here." He thrusts a mirror into my hand and keeps one for himself. The crunch of gravel under his feet as he walks forward doesn't cover his labored sigh.

Thomas doesn't seem as tense about Ferce Point as the other villages, yet it's the only one he felt I needed a warning about.

Hold the Mystery close, he said.

I try to remember his words, but the shimmer from the polished pearl gates ahead of us sucks them from my head, leaving me dumbfounded in such a way that I don't mind the sensation at all. We approach the gates as idlers and Thomas motions for me to hold the mirror up to my face, but he corrects me by turning my mirror around so the glass is facing away from me. I follow his directions with a frown. We pass through the gates holding the mirrors at our faces. The guards nod at their reflections in our mirrors and let us through.

The world inside the walls expands as if it is all that exists. Flawless people wander the streets carrying mirrors and the glass sheets embedded in the walls reflect upon themselves. Beauty reflects and multiplies in a confusion of loveliness that warps my senses, but I smile and I don't mind at all.

I peek from behind my mirror. Water fountains and clipped hedges fill the village square, flower boxes line avenues made only for admiration. The only other village squares I'd seen were made of mud and grass. The sun kisses my face. Is it possible for rain to ever fall from their perfect blue sky? People pass by almost floating in their elegance while admiring themselves in their reflections. They all wear white flowing robes that serve only as frames for their beauty. The women wear fresh flowers in their hair and their skin is soft and sensual. I try to hide my scratched and dirty hands and my mirror lowers. The sea of white-draped people are so absorbed they don't even know we are here. Thomas nudges my shoulder, waves his mirror at me and tilts his head at a lady who moves towards me. I raise my mirror and duck behind it. If she noticed me, she quickly forgets and stops to adjust her hair, smile and murmur to my mirror before moving along.

We follow the manicured street through the town and pass merchants selling their wares. Thomas stops to admire the works of a parchment seller. His fingers caress a particularly beautiful sample.

"I bet Feeney's book is covered in jewels and gilt with the finest gold," he whispers.

"It is," I say, moving further along the stand. "But it's filled with the vilest mold and slime."

Thomas continues stroking the parchment and I'm not sure he heard me. I return to his side, close enough to hold our mirrors together. "Your book may look humble on the outside, but remember, it will be filled with the greatest of truths. Once we know what they are, of course."

Thomas huffs a smile, which gains the attention of the merchant.

"Sir," he announces. "May I help you with your selection? I can tell you are a man of discernment, only accepting of the finest quality."

While the merchant focuses on Thomas, I take the opportunity to focus on the merchant. His shirt must be silk, or perhaps fine cotton. It drapes over the firmness of his back as he reaches forward to interest Thomas in another piece. His strong, tanned forearms shuffle parchment pieces loose and the action moves his shirt further up his body. His trousers are snug, and his thigh muscles move underneath them with every change in his balance. At the top of his thighs, the fabric shapes his...

Thomas grabs the mirror in my hand and raises it in front of my face while he continues to speak to the merchant. I close my mouth again.

Thomas's stance changes as he speaks with the merchant. He puffs his chest like a pigeon and announces himself as a scribe with an important task. The merchant engages him in conversation and Thomas mumbles and deflects the questions he has no answer for before he bids the merchant a hasty farewell and leads me away by the elbow. As we walk, he leans in close to my ear. "Did you notice he called me a *man of discernment*?"

"I did," I respond sounding impressed, "but did you notice he was speaking to your mirror when he said it?"

Thomas halts for a second and I pull my hood down and push my smile away.

My shoes may as well be walking on glass. The stones inlaid in the path are perfect too, smooth and even without so much as a bump along the entire road. People continue to mill about in the streets, their beauty glowing and reflecting as they brush past us. Thomas stares beyond his mirror as he walks, always watching—and all at once I see his scar as the only perfect object before my eyes.

"Do you believe in your work?" I ask him. My mirror faces the upcoming street and I turn to watch his reaction.

His eyes meet mine, then flicker to the satchel before returning. "Of course I do."

"Then why should it matter what the cover is like or what anyone else thinks?"

He stares ahead and doesn't respond.

"And particularly these people," I continue. "They're so confused they believe falsehood is reality and they can't see beyond themselves. Where do the mirrors come from, anyway?" I drop my mirror down and let out an exasperated sigh. "The Hall, I expect."

Thomas nods at me. "But why would the Hall care about a place like Ferce Point? It's not like a showpiece of their power, is it?"

"If the Hall can keep them fixed on their mirrors, they won't notice what's going on around them, let alone complain about it."

The sea of white stops its flow, confused. It seems an ugly truth dares to exist in their midst. An awful noise of bitterness hisses from behind their perfect teeth. I flash my mirror in different directions, but it seems a lost cause; they have spotted imperfection within their walls. Intolerable! Thomas grabs my hand and we sprint towards the exit gate, dodging items thrown from behind us.

"Out!" they scream, a terror in their voice I've never heard before. "Out! Lies!"

I duck and call to Thomas, "Are they accusing *us* of being false?"

"It seems that way—Ugh!" an apple bounces delightfully off the top of Thomas's head. I catch it and giggle.

"Even their fruit is perfect," I say, holding it aloft.

We stop just outside the gates and collect some fruit that was thrown past us. A wipe and a polish tidy them for our imperfect meal, and we laugh as we walk away from the closing gate.

"Look there." Thomas points through the trees to the Ferce Point headland. Waves relentlessly crash up against its cliffs. The air smells different here. Thomas says it's salt from the ocean. My eyes close and the wind pats my hood. All I feel is the wind, all I hear are the waves. "If you'd told me that the ocean's roar is the same as the wind's through the trees I would never have believed you," I say.

"It seems some things you can only learn by experiencing them."

I agree but I don't respond for a while. "I would never have believed many things if it wasn't for you." I open my eyes to see his reaction but he's already further down the road waiting, and I move to catch up to him.

He shakes his head slowly as I approach. "Those damn Fercies."

"Fercies?"

"The people of Ferce Point. They'd never harm anyone, you know."

"Do they know about the unrest?"

"They might've been told." He shrugs. "But even if they had, it wouldn't fit in their acceptable mold."

"But if they're not prepared—"

"They'd be more upset about the appearance of worry lines than the actual unrest."

"All of those mirrors reflecting everywhere, and if their seed isn't in the mirror, how will they find it?"

"The seed must be there somewhere, hidden under all those muscles and those soft flowing robes." Thomas's eyes seem to glaze over.

The talk of muscles makes me think about the merchant again, and all those beautiful women floating past; when they murmured they may as well have been singing. I remember wanting to reach out and touch them, stroke their skin. I imagine it would feel like silk. I'm sure I could have stared at them all day, they were... perfect. Surely Thomas noticed them too, how could he not? My feet slip on a rock on the road and I'm aware of my dirty shoes, my coarse robe and an awful feeling in the pit of my stomach.

"Do you think I'm beautiful?" As soon as I blurt the words out I wish I could take them back, but I have a desperate need to know the answer.

Thomas readjusts the strap on his shoulder and stands taller. "Yes, you are."

"Really?" A warm sensation spreads across my chest. I want to hear him say the words again and again.

I pick some flowers as we walk and string them into a garland and wind them through my hair like the girls at Ferce Point. But he doesn't notice my behavior and doesn't say anything. Perhaps I need more flowers. I reach for some bluebells that are growing along the road. Thomas drops his satchel and grabs my arm, pulls the hood from my head and rakes the flowers from my hair, dumping them onto the ground.

"You're only adorning yourself with flowers because of Ferce Point. True?"

Heat flushes my cheeks. I fold my arms across my chest and nod gently.

"You had no concerns about beauty and comparisons before that, did you?"

I shake my head and a flush of embarrassment heats my cheeks. I'd been so overwhelmed with the lives of the Fercies and their beauty I'd forgotten his words. *Hold the Mystery close.* I open my mouth to speak, but as he turns to collect the satchel he speaks first.

"This Mystery of yours is doing a better job of telling you who you are than those Fercies ever could. Keep it close to your heart and don't fall for any of their nonsense."

He adjusts the satchel onto his shoulder, glances my way and lifts an eyebrow. My mouth is open again, this time stunned that Thomas has recited the same words I was about to speak.

The connections I experience with trees and animals are deeper than anything I have known with another person. Could the Mystery be a bridge between me and Thomas? It was only a simple observation, but we both shared the same moment with the same information as if we were the only two people alive. Happiness bubbles through my body and I feel more certain of this journey and finding answers at Sirban.

Thomas walks in the other cart track a few paces ahead of me. Even though fields and trees surround us, he's confident this road is less traveled so we take advantage of the smooth passage it offers. The back of his robe sways as he walks, tapping at the grasses that grow between the tracks. I wonder what he is thinking. My mind fills with all the road markers I've passed looking at the back of that robe, the times I have run ahead, and the times we walked side by side. I remember ale, apples and berries, and nights of safe sleep, and I choose not to think about how far from Sirban I'd be if we hadn't met.

Thomas turns to check on me and stops when he notices I've fallen back. "Anything wrong?"

"Nothing's ever wrong," I reply.

He turns and walks again. "Now you sound like a delusional Fercie."

"Ha!" I trot to catch up to him. "Fercies label all sorts of things as wrong. Almost everything, in fact." I trip on loose rocks as I get to him and he catches my arm. "They hiss and get upset about things they *decide* are wrong, even if they're not."

"Like the wind and stopping a storm."

"If they gave up the need to label things and just let them be, they'd hiss a lot less."

"And I guess the Eariss doesn't hiss?"

"I imagine the Eariss would try not to."

✦✦✦

The road rises along the side of a ridge and Thomas stops and watches a grove in the valley below. He beckons me to come closer.

"See that field below us?"

I scan the length of his arm past the steep slope that separates us from the overgrown field below.

"Just inside the forest where it meets the field...can you see that different shade of green?"

Sure enough, a brighter patch appears in the treetops.

"It might be a pear tree." He drops his arm. "In fact, I'm sure it is. Come along."

Thoughts of juicy pears make my mouth water. I rub at my arms, convinced I can feel the drips of juice running down them. Thomas heads towards the edge and I grab at his robe. "You can't jump down there—you'll break your neck."

He pushes my hand away and scans the side of the slope. "The road will take too long. We'll cut across. He squats on one foot, stretches the other leg out in front of him and pats the ground next to him. "Here," he says. "This is how you get down without injury." He scoots off the edge and uses his arms for balance, steering with his extended leg and arriving safely into the field moments later.

"Come along. Your turn," he calls and points to the strip of crushed grasses on the slope. "I've made a path for you."

He mumbles encouragement as I ready myself in the position he showed me before launching myself onto his path. Exhilaration and speed overcome me and I lose control and roll sideways down the last part of the hill, slowing only once I tumble into the field of grasses. Thomas hovers above me and once he is sure I am not harmed bursts into a peal of laughter that seems to bounce around the whole valley. His chuckling face blocks the sun from my eyes as he helps me to my feet.

Lumps of dried earth tumble around the uneven ground of the field, and I walk it just like the old idler I pretend to be. My hands brush the tops of the grasses, ready to correct my balance. Thomas is ahead of me and doesn't fare any better, cursing occasionally at the terrain.

"It's like they just plowed it and left it," he grunts.

My foot rolls into a small ditch and I pull back my hood for a clearer view. The wind slices cold through the perspiration on my scalp and I tip my head to the sun. I close my eyes and imagine the wind's fingers caressing the heat from my hair. The scent of grass and earth fills my lungs. Such a brief moment of respite over too soon. I open my eyes to see Thomas smiling at me. As I smile in return, his fades and his face grows pale. He focuses beyond my shoulder and the sound of horse's hooves makes its way to me on the breeze. I pull my hood close, but it is already too late. They have seen us from the ridge.

Trothsman's horses are brave but not stupid, and they baulk at charging down the steep slope. Their riders urge them back to the road where they charge towards the forest. Our only hope is to get there before them.

❦

M y body is drained yet surges with energy at the same time. All at once, I feel hot and cold, fast and so painfully, incredibly, slow. We slip and trip and scramble through the grasses to the edge of the forest. I gasp for air, desperate for the safety of the trees.

Scattered thick trunks support the canopy that hangs above us like a roof. I didn't hear any hounds with them; perhaps we can hide. Where? It may as well be an open field in here, there are only patches of undergrowth. We can't outrun horses. Thomas runs faster than I do, and I follow his path to keep up. My feet, already twisted by the field, weaken. I trip on a root, slip in the leaf litter and squeal as my foot twists unnaturally. Thomas turns to see me flail and fall. He rushes towards me while I stand and urge him away. I have no breath to speak. I step toward him and pain shoots through my leg and I yelp like a dog. Thomas arrives just as my lungs receive enough air to apologize. He ignores me and pushes me back to the closest trunk, drops the satchel and removes his robe. He rips mine from me and hands me his in a bundle.

"Get above the leaf line," he grunts as he hoists me into the tree and then tosses his satchel into my hands. He kicks the leaf litter around to cover the disturbance and makes an obvious path for the Trothsmen to follow before racing away. I climb higher and am still panting as the horses bolt into the forest. Five of the Hall's Trothsmen pass under the tree. They charge off in the direction that Thomas has led them. My throat is so dry I can't swallow.

❦

The birds recover from the disruption to their day and flit around the forest once more. My body is taut along a thick bough and I strain to hear or see anything of Thomas. The forest falls silent again as a cheery conversation grows louder as it approaches.

I count the horses.

Five.

No one is bound and walking behind them—perhaps Thomas is safe. Soon they are near enough to hear without strain.

"No one could have survived that fall."

"Ha! Who leaps off a cliff like that?"

"Impressive splash for a little wench."

The air feels heavy as if it presses on me. So heavy I don't breathe. They pass beneath me, chuckling, and discuss how many markers to the nearest tavern and the food they'll enjoy.

I wait until they are well away. I tell myself I'm being strategic, but I'm really just a coward. Another life wasted because of my frivolity and disobedience.

Thomas.

My mouth wants to speak his name but my heart fills with rocks.

See what you've made me do? Feeney's words nestle back into the hidden place of my heart where they belong. How foolish to think they could be anywhere else.

The lowest branch isn't that high from the ground, but I struggle to decide how to get down without injuring myself further. Should I jump and favor my good foot and risk damaging it, or leap and hope for the best? The wretched dread returns. Thomas has just leapt from a cliff to his death and I can't even jump out of a tree. I'm so ashamed at my lack of bravery that I jump in a fit of self-disgust and pain shoots through my injured foot. I welcome the pain as worthy penance for my thoughts. Everywhere I look the forest is open, but I am closed. I stand for the longest time trying to decide which direction to travel, but no ideas come. My teeth clench in preparation and I walk, pain stabbing into my lower leg with each step I take. I need to see the cliff. I need to see what I have done.

❧✿❧

A grassy verge appears outside the tree line, and beyond it is a gorge. The grass at the edge of the ravine is churned up where the horses have protested moving any closer. I hobble nearer to the edge and wince as my foot rolls in the divots. The wind carries my cry away; it pummels my face from the depths of the gorge, and I squint to see over the edge. There is no way he could have survived that fall. The tension from my clenched fists radiates up my arms and into my body.

I hate the Trothsmen. I hate that they were right.

I fall to the grass and rest my head at the edge of the cliff. At the bottom of the gorge, the sodden robe clings to the rocks. Its tail dangles in the water, toyed by the ripples as they pass by. Occasionally it flickers and comes to life in the passing water, but the mat of cold sackcloth holds firm, despondent, not going anywhere. Maeve said that rivers always move forwards, but she forgot to tell me they're not always kind. Maybe they get blocked by things like Joss's rocks and go stagnant and have all life choked out of them. Then they turn to quicksand and when they die, take everything with them.

The grass at my face is cool, soft and earthy. The breeze is gentler now, and I lay in silence and close my eyes. I listen to the wind as it climbs the valley and imagine just for a moment that it strokes my hair like Thomas did when he thought I was asleep.

There is still beauty in the silence.

The Mystery waits for an invitation to join me.

But I send it away.

The strength of the wind hasn't changed. It still cools my tears and batters my ears when I move my head. That strange noise can't be from the wind. I roll to my stomach and look into the gorge.

The water moves slowly then speeds up as it approaches the rocks and tumbles over them, shushing everything as if it has a secret. The trees behind me hiss in the breeze, and then... that murmuring sound.

I look over and under the edge of the cliff to a small ledge underneath. A boot. It moves.

"Thomas?" I shout, but my voice is taken by the wind and the dryness of my throat.

I wiggle my stomach alongside the ledge to see his position in the little alcove. "Thomas!"

He rubs the back of his head and frowns at me. "I tried to jump under here and the rocks gave way, must've hit my head." The strangest sounds escape my body as I scream and cry and laugh all at once. I nod at the dark patch of earth near his feet where a boulder must have dropped into the gorge, taking my robe with it.

He groans and appears to collect his thoughts. "You!" he shouts then grabs at his head, "You're safe?"

"Yes!" I motion for him to make his way towards me and hold out my arms to support him as he swings a leg onto the ledge. We work awkwardly, groaning, pulling and wincing until Thomas lies safely next to me.

We stare at each other and our hands run over each other's face and hair. I'm dreaming. I must be. My wishes never come true. I pull his face to me and I kiss him. His lips are dry and taste like dirt and are the most delicious thing I have ever tasted. Thomas returns my kiss. The moment melts us into nothing, it melts us deep into the Mystery, and we stay there together until the moon is high in the sky.

❦

In the morning light, the area around the ledge is simple and open through the trees. Under the canopy, Thomas smiles towards the morning sky. "I loved the Eariss."

"Is it allowed?"

"I hope so."

"Can't I just be me and not the Eariss for once?"

"You're one and the same. You can't be any less of the Eariss than you can be any less of yourself."

Thomas props himself up on one arm and squeezes an eye shut against the pain.

I stroke the side of his face. "Still hurts?"

"Only if I move quickly. You?"

I raise my swollen foot up for observation. "A little."

Thomas lies next to me and moves my head to rest on his shoulder. "We should stay here and recover. We've got time. Sirban's not too far away."

I turn my head into his shoulder and rest. The deep heavy kind of rest that I now understand only comes with safety.

The day is almost over when a gentle tinkling comes through the trees. We push ourselves to sitting, scan the forest, and see nothing.

Thomas jumps to his feet. "Tallefix! It's a Tallefix." He runs in search of the sound.

"Are you sure we *need* a Tallefix?" I call after him.

"He'll help us if we can catch him."

Nervousness rolls in my stomach and Galen's words about the Tallefix come to mind. *"It's up to you whether to trust them or not. I don't know whether to run or hide when I hear their bells now."*

I wave to Thomas as he returns.

"I found him," he calls. "Said we can camp with him for the night. It'll be warmer there." Thomas pulls a wad of chewed leaves from his mouth. "Gave me this for my head, can hardly feel it now." He deposits the wad into his mouth and giggles. "Can hardly feel anything, if I'm honest." He points at my foot. "He'll help you with that too."

The nervousness rolls again as Thomas helps me to my feet. "Are you sure about this? Can we trust him?"

"Well, he said he'd help, and besides, Tallefixes aren't known for their loyalty to the Hall." Thomas grins at me. I'd feel ungrateful if I turned down his eagerness to help. After I've been hobbling for a distance, he suggests I climb onto his back to travel the rest of the way to the camp.

"They're good at setting bones. It's how they got their name," Thomas explains.

"Tallefix? How?"

"It's all about how they put you to sleep. They have this way of telling a story. It makes you go to sleep."

"Then they fix you while you sleep?"

"Tale. Fix. Get it?"

"But we're not being put to sleep, are we?"

"They use herbs and tools and things too. They're quite clever, like magic, you'll see . . . .." When I don't answer, Thomas has another question. "You don't trust anyone, do you? What about me?"

The nervousness rolls again and again. "I don't even trust myself."

A decorated wagon with a rounded cover stands in a clearing, a circle of stones laid out in front with the promise of a fire. The Tallefix bends over and all we see is an ample backside in brown pants and an embroidered tunic. When he stands we see he has been attending to his dark horse's fetlock. He holds a jar and a brush in his hand, and as he pushes his black, shoulder-length hair away, he swipes some of the black stuff across his face and into his mouth.

He spits it out. "Ugh! Good for healing sore legs, not good for tasting." He holds the jar up to Thomas as if toasting him. "Ah, you've returned with the injured one, just as you said you would. A man of honor."

I slide from Thomas's back and take a seat on the logs that surround the fire pit. I feel useless not helping prepare for the evening as they go about collecting kindling and starting the fire. The wagon looks cozy, and as Thomas said, at least we will have a good rest and warmth for the night. I just wish this nervousness would go away and I could enjoy the evening as much as Thomas. Maybe I need some of those leaves he keeps chewing. The Tallefix slips him more as they place meat and vegetables into a pot that rests on the ailing fire.

"We're on our way to Sirban," Thomas announces.

Thomas! What? What is in those leaves?

"What a coincidence," the Tallefix says, "I've just come down from Sirban. Not very friendly people up there, but I did hear of some lucrative offers."

Tension rides across my shoulders. The Tallefix knows our plans. Time feels shorter, as if I can't catch my breath, and for the first time, I'm fearful of the coming night.

The Tallefix looks to me from across the fire. "This meal is twice cooked. We need only heat it." He wipes a large knife on the thigh of his pants. "Thomas, collect more firewood. I will splint the lady's foot and prepare her herbs."

Thomas doesn't even glance back at me. Could the Tallefix have already told Thomas one of his stories?

The Tallefix moves about the camp gathering items, and I try to read his intentions, but I feel all scattered inside and I don't immediately connect to the Mystery. My priority is to appear pleasant, to not startle him, but I fear I will be taken before Thomas returns. This man can't tell my fortune. His heart is full of trickery. Besides, he missed a patch when he colored the chestnut horse with his paint.

The Tallefix appears frustrated when Thomas returns with the wood so quickly and he slops the food into our bowls and tosses the wood harshly onto the fire. I lean back from the heat. His fire burns so hot that the sparks don't have a chance.

The Tallefix chuckles to himself. "Such a profitable and prosperous evening."

He watches me even when he talks to Thomas. He doesn't look at me in the way the lord or Feeney did, as an annoyance in need of correction, or in the way that Thomas gazes at me, but with a measure of greed, like I'm cooked poultry. No, it's not poultry he sees when he looks at me, it's a bag of silver. No matter how smooth his talk or how kind his words, he does not see *me*.

Thomas is taken by the Tallefix's constant offers of ale and herbs and has been dulled by campfire camaraderie. I remain pleasant, pretending to be unaware of his plans as I invite Thomas to stare at me and tap my feet against his to get his attention. In our excitement of discovering who we are to each other, I'm afraid we have forgotten who we are to the rest of the world.

The Tallefix collects our bowls and entertains us with tricks as the fire dulls. He juggles and plays with colorful scarves and even pretends to pull them from Thomas's ears, always watching for my reaction. I clap and laugh at the appropriate places. He tugs on his embroidered tunic and talks about a wondrous trick he performs in only the biggest villages and produces shackles. "Oh, but you wouldn't want to see that one, would you?"

Thomas claps his hands. "Of course we would."

"Perhaps it's best we retire now?" I say, but I'm not heard. A cool breeze blows through the camp and the sparks from the fire extinguish themselves in fear of facing the night alone.

The clunk of the shackles around his wrists shudder through my heart, and Thomas still wears an expectant smile as the Tallefix and I rise to face each other—he armed with a pole and me with the branch I made sure to keep within reach.

In one swift move the Tallefix kicks Thomas backwards from the log and pushes a heavy branch across his belly. Thomas growls and curses and calls my name. The Tallefix's pole smashes into the branch I hold and reverberates into my hands. His next hit sends the branch flying from my grasp before he swings a blow that will surely send me to the ground. I land with it, catch Thomas's eye and don't move.

"Cursed Stars! You've killed her!" Thomas shouts.

"I'll still get the same reward." The Tallefix sighs and saunters to the back of his wagon.

"Get us out of this!" Thomas hisses through his teeth.

I lift my head from the ground and hiss back at him, "I don't know how to!"

"Yes you do! You always know, you just never shut up about how you don't."

"Don't tell me what I do and do not know!"

"Would you just trust yourself, for both our sakes?"

"You can't become something just because someone *tells* you what you are, it's not as simple as that!"

"Didn't you just do that at the Hall for your whole life? And you're not *becoming* anything—you already are!"

I stand and look to Thomas. "But I don't know what to do."

"You're the Eariss. Ask!"

I draw a deep breath into my belly and silently call to the Mystery in more desperation than I've ever known. The world steps away and changes form before my eyes. It's still there, but changed, soft and supple and flowing like sheer silk.

I speak to the shackles and ask them to release Thomas.

They bend, open and release.

The Tallefix charges into the space and his anger dissolves into the pliable force that surrounds us. It exposes him and his deeds, but doesn't accuse him; rather I sense that it waits for his response. He stands stunned, as still as one of the statues in the great hall. I take the paint jar from his hands and turn to leave.

Thomas, wide eyed, moves away from me.

Was he right to be scared of me?

I was scared of me.

※

We don't say a word as we move away from the camp into the night without direction or plan.

Thomas is the first to speak.

"Come along." He motions to his back and bends lower for me to jump up.

Again, we don't speak for the longest time. No words seem to make sense, and I can only guess at what Thomas might be thinking of me. Eventually he asks gently, "How did you do that?"

"I don't know," I whisper close to his ear. "Everything blended. I just asked the shackles to release you and they were happy to."

"Happy to?"

I smile at how ridiculous that sounds, but I also want to cry.

Thomas speaks louder now. "Did you see how he stood still like that? Did you hurt him?"

"I don't think so. I hope not. I don't ever want to do that again. Things wove together."

"Wove?"

"Like a weaving loom. I knew things about him, his future and his past. I'm afraid I've addled his brain. Poor man, I *did* hurt him. He's scared and confused."

"Well, if he didn't want to be addled he shouldn't have tried to capture us. I'd say he got what he deserved." Thomas laughs out loud and his shoulders soften. "Ha! Did you see his eyes? They looked like they belonged on a bug."

I smile but it's not a smile of satisfaction.

What on earth am I?

The midday sun flashes into my eyes so I keep them closed. The rock Thomas suggested I lay on is jagged and uncomfortable; not that I can expect to relax while he tugs at my hair and fans it out behind me. He walked most of the night with me on his back, and after sleeping the morning away its time to change our plan.

"If they're looking for the lady with the crown of fire, they won't find her here," he says as he opens the Tallefix's jar. "Ugh! Bleah!" He gags and I leap to my feet and clamp my hand over my nose and mouth.

Thomas squints his eyes and squeezes his lips together. "You sure about this?"

I nod. What other choice do we have? I mumble through my fingers, "Maybe it won't be as strong over time."

"Yes. I'm sure you're right," he holds the jar at arm's length and squeezes one eye shut. He circles around the rock. "Here, lie this way. Downwind."

He concentrates on raking the horse paint through my hair and I close my eyes to the sun.

"Doesn't stink so bad now," he says.

"It might be we're used to its … aroma."

"Aroma!" He laughs, then rakes my hair harder. "Ugh, that cursed Tallefix."

"It wasn't fair, you know."

"What wasn't?"

"My encounter with him."

"Your 'encounter.' Is that what you're calling it? He was going to kill you."

"But I had a huge advantage. He was like an ant; his power was in his chains and his silver reward. My power came from within me. It completely dwindled his. That's not a fair battle. Poor man."

"Poor man? He had me in shackles and clubbed you. How does that make him a poor man?"

"He might've just met the Eariss—and it wasn't pleasant for him."

Thomas twists my hair like a rope and pushes my shoulders for me to stand. "He should never have met you in the first place. Here, cover your hair until we find a stream."

I take the robe he offers and screw my nose against the wafts of odor as I wrap my hair.

❦

Even though he says it's no bother to carry me, Thomas stretches his back when I slide from it to the road. Crushed cream rocks form the path that lead to Sirban. It seems to glow brighter in the afternoon sun. The sun also heats the robe on top of my head and fills the air with the pungent odor of my unwashed hair. My jaw is sore from clenching my teeth with each step and the road grows rockier the further we travel up the mountain. Why would someone ever want to build a village at the top of a rocky hill? Dry scrubby trees and shrubs line the road and offer no shade at all.

Thomas spends more time sighing and quietly complaining. He slips on a rock and nearly tumbles in the center of the road.

"Are you well? You're not hurt?" I ask.

He grunts in reply and throws a rock into the bushes beside us. He slips again and curses, then walks steadily ahead of me. While waiting for me at a bend ahead, he throws stones and rocks into the trees along the road. Rocks bigger than his hands bounce back at him from the thick mass of branches of the trees as he curses, grunts and throws them again. I hobble to his side and watch. Sweat drips down his temples and leaves fine lines of creamy dust on either side of their tracks. There's no point asking him to explain; whatever troubles him will find its way to the surface soon enough. His hands rest on his knees as he gathers his thoughts. He wipes his brow, coughs and takes a deep breath. A calmer Thomas is making his way back to me. He opens his mouth to speak and a voice calls from around the bend.

"Oh good, I'm in need of some doltish lowers."

A thin face with a short white beard appears around the bushes, sizing us up like market wares. The man steps onto the road, his tunic and pants blending into the colors of the road so that at a quick glance he resembles a shepherd with only a head. We're unsure whether to laugh or be insulted.

"Come. Along. Then," he beckons with exaggerated gestures and speaks slowly. "I. Have. Fooood."

Fooood. We forget to be insulted and dutifully follow our shepherd.

Around the corner, clear sky rises above the large tree at the end of the clearing. Sirban must be nearby. The ground slopes up towards the tree but not too steep for this strange man, his donkey and his cart to be almost to the top.

At the roadside the shepherd pushes his hands towards us. "Stay," he commands before making his way to the odd wooden contraption sitting beside the cart. I tilt my head. It's not a catapult—perhaps it's a plow, but it has notches and markings on its thin arches and beams. The shepherd and his exaggerated movements distract me from the contraption.

"I. Need. You," he says, pointing at us with both hands. "To. Pick. This. Up ... " more dramatic gesturing, "and put it on the cart."

My eyebrows rise as high as Thomas's and we laugh. The kind of laugh that cleanses as it rises from deep inside and washes away worry and tension.

The shepherd puts his hands on his hips and huffs at us. "Stop this lower nonsense," he says, but we only laugh harder, too tired for politeness.

Thomas pulls the satchel strap over his head and hands it to me. "Stay here." His eyes are soft again.

"Not that way! Higher! Tilt it here!" I don't know how Thomas stays so patient as the shepherd barks his instructions as they load the contraption onto the cart. My eyes wander to the large tree on the far side of the clearing. A path? A beacon? I don't understand what I'm feeling.

"Look out!" Thomas calls, and I step aside to allow the boisterous donkey onto the road.

The shepherd inclines his head to me. "So what's wrong with this one?" he asks Thomas.

Thomas shakes his head. "Too many things to list, I'm afraid, but it's a foot injury that's causing the most trouble." He lifts me onto the cart next to the contraption and I dangle my legs from the back and watch the cream-colored rocks pass underneath me. Thomas and the shepherd walk on either side of the donkey, ready to encourage and coerce him when larger rocks on the path trap the thick, solid wheels.

The contraption is made of wood and glass and is unlike anything I have seen before. The notches I saw from the roadside are very specific, with finer markings etched into dials and thin beams.

My fingers trace a dial before a bump on the road makes me fearful of touching it, as if by even sitting beside it I might ruin its delicacy and precision. My foot aches with each bump but it's nothing like the sting of walking.

Over the scraping and knocking of the cart wheels I hear the shepherd mention Sirban and I twist and see its gates come into view. The gates are similar to the contraption, very precise and adorned with symbols and intricate writings. My eyes dart all over the detail on the gates, only half grasping an idea before moving to the next. I fidget and wish I could leap from the cart. If Sirban's gate is this precise, imagine how they keep their records.

The people we pass inside the gates wear the same cream-colored clothes and nod their heads in deference to our shepherd. "Greetings, Guthrie," they call and he lifts a hand in acknowledgment.

"Who's this you have with you, Guthrie?" someone chuckles.

"I have acquired some lackeys for manual labor," he says as he sweeps his arm towards the cart. I turn each way to find Thomas, but only see the back of his head beside the donkey as it pulls its way through the cream pathways of Sirban. A cliff marks the edge of the village before it drops into a deep valley and the cart stops at a house built on its edge. Thomas comes to the back of the cart to help me down.

"Lackeys?" I question him.

"I'm to repair his fences and labor, and he'll feed us and help your foot. He's a very clever man, Ashling. We should be thankful."

For a moment my shoulders slump. Then I kiss his cheek. Thomas is right. Shelter, food, healing, and we've made it to Sirban. Let the villagers believe we are slaves; it will be good for my pride. I hobble to the front of the cart and look down onto the treetops in the valley below.

"Your home is so high, Guthrie. What a wonderful view."

"View? Yes, the higher you are, the crisper the air. Crisper air allows for greater knowledge, you see. Not that lowers would understand." He shakes his head and looks me over before waving his hand to clear the air around his face. I raise my hands and try to better secure the robe to my head before he turns towards his house and sighs, "Follow me."

Guthrie's little rock home oversees the whole village on one side and the valley on the other. A small yard and a stable for the donkey are at the far end of his home. I follow Guthrie inside while Thomas obeys his instructions to unload the cart and house the donkey. His home is filled with intricate things. Shelves filled with herbs line the walls and where there are no shelves, charts with scribbles, lines and dots cover the walls. A huge table covered with drawings and diagrams takes up most of the space inside his home, and he pushes some aside and motions for me to sit before pulling up a chair to examine my foot.

"So what are you two lowers doing here?"

"We're not lowers."

"Of course you are, now answer the question, or is it too difficult for you?"

I sigh. "We're looking for something."

"Looking for something? And without a plan, I bet." The look on my face makes him snort. "See, this is why lowers aren't allowed in Sirban. You just waste our time with your nonsense. You need a plan for everything if you want to succeed. You need to follow the steps, do you see?"

Guthrie moves to the other side of the room, muttering about herbs and the benefits of different splint sizes. His head must be so full of information it simply falls out of his mouth. Thomas was right. Guthrie is a very clever man.

He hands me a cup of cool tea. "For the pain," he says, before he fashions the splint for my foot from thin pieces of wood. He settles back into his chair and gently taps the orderly supply of cloth and wood lying beside him. "Yes," he begins. "Predictable outcomes, order, knowledge, this is all you need for a successful life."

I finish my tea. "Really, Guthrie? Is that what you believe?"

He pats my leg and stretches it to the chair in preparation. "Believe? It's what I know. You lowers with your silly beliefs hold us back from seeking more knowledge. You either know something, or you don't."

I watch Thomas fighting with the donkey through the open doorway. "But what about love?"

Guthrie watches me then grabs at strips of cloth to bind around the splint. "Love is just the word for an agreement between two people to work together to solve problems."

I shake my head. "No ... I mean, yes." I rub my forehead. "Yes that people work together to solve problems, but I believe it's also a feeling, an emotion that lifts the spirit. It makes us scared, but also secure and brave; it lives outside of us as well as in us."

"Do you hear yourself? How can something be one thing and then another? It doesn't make sense." He taps his temple so hard I can hear the thuds. "No. It can't be. We will only advance through knowledge. Feelings change, they can't be measured, can't be trusted and it's better for all concerned not to have any. Do you hear my words, lower girl?" Guthrie digs his fingers into my foot and stares at me to ensure I understand his statement. I gasp, more from surprise than the pain he inflicts. I'm saddened he made a choice to hurt me, but then I think back to the Tallefix. Am I not the same as him anyway?

He finishes binding the splint and moves back to the other side of the room. "Listen here, my inner workings are none of your business, understand?"

Safely away from his hands, I mumble, "Your inner workings, as you call them, are who you are."

He faces me. "I am Guthrie. The wisest man in this village. And that's all you need to know."

He doesn't remove his eyes from mine even as Thomas bursts through the door rubbing his hands together. "So, about that food ...."

Guthrie nods at Thomas and directs him to gather bowls and utensils in preparation. I'm surprised when he resurrects our dead conversation. It must be for Thomas's benefit.

"Within, without, doesn't matter. What matters is that I know more than you. Look at your position in life, an idler. You might be very good at entertaining, but really, look at yourself—you're born an idler and you'll die an idler."

Thomas raises an eyebrow and places the bowls in an orderly line on the table. "My travels have made me weary of assumptions, Guthrie. Surely it's best to witness an outcome than decide it ahead of time?"

"Assumptions? I don't make assumptions. I know the truth. I observe conditions around me, not what my 'feelings' tell me. My brain tells me so." He picks up a bowl and taps his temples again. "And I trust it implicitly." Guthrie walks over to stir at the pot in the corner of the room. The smell of something like gruel escapes in soft wafts and makes its way to us at the table. Thomas turns my splint this way and that, admiring Guthrie's handiwork until he arrives beside us, filled bowls in hand. Thomas's meal lands before him and he wastes no time in latching onto a spoon and digging it into the thick porridge. My mouth waters and I reach for a spoon in the center of the table. Guthrie taps it out of my reach and holds my bowl closer to his chest, his nose wrinkled in disgust. "There's water in the donkey's trough. Don't get the splint wet."

"Need help?" Thomas asks between mouthfuls of gruel.

"I'll be fine," I say, sure that Guthrie's tea has lessened my shame along with my pain.

❧⳾⳾❧

Thomas and Guthrie emerge from his house and head to the stable as I limp towards them dragging my fingers through my hair. Thomas stops and lifts my hair on either side of my head.

"What's it like?" I ask.

He leans forward to sniff it. "Well, it's not as bad as before."

I bring my hair over my shoulder to show him. "The color is not at all like the Tallefix's horse." The streaky mess of blacks and browns look more like rotting reeds in a stream. They smell like them too. Thomas struggles to find something to say, so I answer for him. "At least the hounds won't be able to find me."

Guthrie leads the donkey from the stable and Thomas lifts me under my arms and onto its back. "Up you get. Guthrie's decided to show us the village."

We soon tire of Guthrie's commentary about the spectacular brilliance of Sirban and its people. The villagers pass us along the village streets, they nod at Guthrie, and frown at our presence in their beautiful creamy existence, as if they can't quite understand the oddities before them. After hearing about their architecture, village planning and fascinating history, I try to frame a question that will entice Guthrie into boasting about their records, but he doesn't offer us much opportunity to speak. Thomas steals looks back at me and rolls his eyes, desperate now for any other topic than the virtues of Sirban.

"What are your thoughts of the unrest, Guthrie?" His question dives into the smallest gap as Guthrie takes a breath.

"Ah yes, the lord controlling by force what he could easily control by intellect. If he had intellect, or at least a member of the Sirbahn to advise him, there'd be no need for this bloodshed and the destruction of our parchments." He rubs at his whiskered chin.

"If the Hall applied itself to knowledge and removed the lowers, we could create a peaceful, logical world."

"Remove the lowers? How would you decide who is lower?" I ask.

"Easy enough, your place of birth determines that."

Even the donkey halts at his statement.

Guthrie sighs. "Let me explain it slowly. Sirban is brilliant, am I not right?" He sweeps his hand in a circle and waits until we grumble an agreement. "And we know that in other villages, the people are inept and can't further our knowledge."

"But," Thomas says, "How do you know someone born in a lower village can't have the knowledge of the Sirbahn?"

"Like one of those silly pot people at Muscone? Impossible!" Guthrie shakes his head and laughs.

The mention of Muscone brings Bez's compassion to mind, and his hope that people might see beyond the Hall's influence. "People are so much more than where they were born and what they are told to do, Guthrie," I say.

"Is that what you believe, lower girl?"

"Thomas does the work of a carpenter, but he stands before you as a man. So what would you say he is?"

Guthrie sizes Thomas up. "A carpenter."

"You believe no one can alter the station of their birth?"

"No, I don't *believe* it—I know it—we have already spoken of this." He raises his voice and moves closer to the splint. "It is a known fact. Do not presume to argue with facts, lower girl!" People stare and Thomas moves to stand between me and Guthrie. If Guthrie only knew Thomas moves for his safety, not mine.

Guthrie looks about him and snorts. "Fine. As it turns out, your presence is conducive to studies of a scientific nature." He leans in closer to us, his face reddening, and stabs a finger at Thomas's chest. "I shall attempt to teach this idiot to read and write while you recover. We will see if he is capable of being more than his station."

Guthrie turns and trots through the village and waves to the watching crowd as he continues to prattle on. Thomas and I stare at each other wide eyed and I wonder if I might have transformed into one of those bewildered villagers, looking upon something new, an oddity that I can't quite believe I am witnessing.

❦

T he straw in the stable is warm and dry, and the donkey doesn't seem to mind sharing his space. He's a likable fellow, not particularly fond of the tabby cat that comes and goes, but happy that it controls some of the mice that rustle under the straw. He's even stopped biting Thomas in his sleep now. Thomas works with his hands in the early part of the day and with his mind in the other. I hobble around the stall and the house, tidying where Guthrie will allow, and preparing evening meals. Thomas is excited about the tasks Guthrie sets for him and spends most of his time in deep concentration, even into the night. How consuming it must be to have all you've wanted, right within reach.

One evening I find him sitting on the pathway by the house with the stub of a candle and a selection of parchment pieces.

"Nearly done?" I stroke his head and he doesn't reply. His fingers gently follow the lines on the parchment, his lips move in silent conversation. I'm yet to learn how to do anything gracefully with this splint and I murmur an apology as I sit with a thud beside him. He reads a little longer, then looks straight ahead into the darkness. His eyelids droop a little and I reach for the candle stub and puff it out. "I'll take the parchment to Guthrie... into the stable for you."

Thomas rises to his feet and pulls me to mine. I look at the parchment in my hand. "Has Guthrie spoken about the records yet?"

"Only to say lowers have no need of them." He looks at the ground. "Trothsmen recently burned their parchments and threatened worse. The Sirbahn are protective of everything now."

"Oh," is all I can manage. I'm disappointed, but I understand why they would hold their beloved works closer. Talk of Troths-men reminds me that Guthrie takes a huge chance on having us in his house, or rather we put him in danger by being here. I'm grateful, but is this situation fair to him?

"I'll find them," Thomas says. "By the time I've read all their parchments they might consider me worthy."

"Yes, of course they will." I nod in encouragement.

I can't imagine the villagers of Sirban finding anyone worthy. They are not just the villagers here, they are *The Sirbahn*. They come to the top of the cliff at Guthrie's house and take readings from a spinning machine, but they don't notice how the glass reflects colored patterns across the wall of Guthrie's house, and they constantly polish dust from the glass they carry with them for the readings but stay blind to the view in front of them. On warm days I offer them water from the barrel, but they refuse, preferring their dryness to admitting a lower has anything of value to offer them.

At the edge of the cliff I close my eyes and feel the wind from the valley whip up and around my body. The sun warms my skin, the wind rushes past my ears and scents that have been diluted and carried on breezes from far away reach my nostrils. Each time I open my eyes the view greets me with treetops that huddle together and close over the valley like a carpet of moss-covered pebbles. My fingers pinch in front of me and I pretend I can touch them, stroking my hand along their bumps and trying desperately to remember the touch and smell of the forest. A gust of wind blows dust into my face and forces my eyes closed. This is where Guthrie and Thomas learn to find me when I am not busy with my work. Eyes closed and face to the wind, desperate for a place I cannot reach.

One late afternoon the insistent braying of the donkey breaks me from my spell. I pass through the empty house to the pathway and find Thomas attempting to hitch the donkey to the cart. I take one look at their clash of wills and then step in to calm them both before it becomes anything more severe.

"Any problems?" Guthrie calls from the stable.

"Only that the two souls closest to me are both asses," I reply.

Thomas tightens the last of the donkey's straps and helps Guthrie carry the contraption from the stable to the cart. He stops to whisper to the donkey just as Guthrie startles everyone with his call to me and a tap on the back of the cart. "Come, girl," he says. "You've got some learning to do."

It's almost dark as the cart travels past those heading to their homes from the main library in the center of the village. I catch snippets of their whispers and their talk of what horrors we must be putting Guthrie through. Horrors? They should be made to endure meals while he reads documents that almost bore us to our deaths. Passages as dry as the rocks and dust around his home. The stars twinkle slightly against the changing color of the sky. Will we miss out on his reading tonight?

The gates look as impressive as they did when we first entered Sirban. Every empty space on them is filled with intricacies of knowledge, so filled that there's no room left for a valid response. I smile to myself; they're filled as much as Guthrie's brain, but at least these gates are open. The cart rolls through the gates and down the creamy rock road to the clearing where we first met our shepherd. Guthrie urges the donkey up the grassed slope close to where he will position his contraption, orders us from the cart and seats himself on the back. He pulls a parchment from beneath his tunic. He sure knows how to ruin a nice evening.

"I thought you'd enjoy something different—a version of comedy, if you will," he says as he unrolls the parchment. Guthrie's version of comedy would be a missing bead on his companion's abacus. We resign ourselves to his lesson and lie on the grass watching the sky as he imparts his knowledge in his usual monotone voice. I try hard to concentrate, just like I do when he reads over our evening meal when I'm usually so tired I fail. I've taken to lis-

tening intently to one section, so when he is finished I can politely
tell him things like "I liked the part about the mountain best,"
or "How interesting that the bridge collapsed . . .." But really, I
prefer the wanderings of my own mind, chasing down my own
interesting thoughts rather than letting my mind be filled with
his. This night is far too beautiful to have his voice ruin it. I take
Thomas's hand, interlocking our fingers, and watch the sky turn
from pink to orange to purple. Are there special names for all the
colors in between? Each increment must be special enough in its
own right to have a name.

"I'm glad you're here," Thomas whispers, just loud enough for
me to hear. I need to tell him to stop saying it, that even though
I'm perfectly still on the outside, his words make me panic on the
inside. I don't know why I want to run from his words; I just need
him to stop. How do I find the words to describe something like
that?

Thomas pumps my hand so hard it hurts.

"Ow!"

He springs to his knees and faces the cart as Guthrie's voice
moves from a drone in my ears back to clarity, "Saved blood, the
crown of fire . . . ."

"Stop!" Thomas shouts and Guthrie almost falls out of the cart.
"Where's this from?"

"Wha—Well, I—" Guthrie twists and holds the scroll close to
his chest as Thomas stands to his feet.

I pull Thomas's arm back to give Guthrie some space. "Do you
have the whole verse there, Guthrie?" I say gently. "Please read it
to us." I watch Guthrie's face as he processes my request, knowing
he has the power to lock this parchment away with the records if
he chooses.

Have I displeased him in previous days?

Would he wish to harm me?

He *has* recently stopped calling me names. . . .

The color returns to Guthrie's face. "Questions, questions, although I am happy for your enthusiasm." He unfurls the scroll again in preparation but drops it to his lap to make a point. "The mark of a great teacher is the enthusiasm of his students."

We nod in gracious understanding. Thomas points to something on the parchment and Guthrie slaps his hand away. We stand around the cart and watch over his shoulder as he reads,

From darkness an escape to light,
Hope armed across the land,
To run through all that stand before,
The change hid in our hand.
Slashed hearts and willing stretch of arms,
To fight a holy war,
Of stomping feet and chargers led,
Leave all unlike before.
"Anew!" hearts cry, for they are spent,
Sparks die for dusty ashen,
The alchemy of all to one,
Destruction for its passion.
The forest yearns to hold its own,
Saved blood, the crown of fire,
Yon bridge will rise despite itself,
With stars that lead to pyre.
A waiting oak at Awenmell,
Kind shelter through the mist,
Life of all lives scratched into stone,
The iris forms a fist.
The courage borne of sweetness charred,
Seized wheels that bear no turn.
The Acamar doth shine as guide,
On paths lit with concern.
Life from the ashes, burning flesh,
Stones weighed before their cast,
Of naked armies wailing deep,

The final storm has passed.
So far apart, yet just the same,
Hands hope into the past,
Betrayal and cinders fall like rain,
Till peace arrives at last.

G uthrie sighs and rolls the parchment, watching the last of the light leave the sky. "Fortuitous timing, just as the light dies."

Thomas and I concentrated hard on the parts we hadn't heard, but it still doesn't make a lot of sense.

"You know this work? What does it mean, Guthrie?" I ask.

"I don't think it means anything really—whimsy."

Thomas winks at me as he helps Guthrie down from the cart. "We've heard parts of this work sung in the valleys below. I imagine you know everything there is to know about it, yet no one sings it here."

"Why would we waste time with this nonsense?" Guthrie peels the scroll open and lifts it to our faces in the twilight. "These stanzas don't even make sense; why would people wail that a storm was over? It's not a serious work. The lines aren't even set out properly as they should be. I brought it here to have some lighthearted fun, but if you two can't see the frivolity of it, I wonder why I even bother." Guthrie taps the contraption as an order for Thomas to lift it from the cart and walks away to look at the night sky.

If the song is supposed to be about the Eariss, I don't understand it. It doesn't tell us anything. "Do you remember any of it?" I whisper to Thomas.

He shakes his head. "Not all. I'll make a copy of it somehow."

My mouth is so dry it's hard to swallow, and he looks as pale as I feel. He must have noticed all those lines about slashing and burning too. "Perhaps it's as Guthrie says . . . all just whimsy."

Thomas lifts the contraption from the cart and stops in front of me. "You can feel your heart thumping, can't you? We both know this is not whimsy."

He carries the contraption past me to where Guthrie waits in the clearing. My teeth clench. I hate it when he's right.

Guthrie directs Thomas on the exact placement of the contraption and uses the light of small candle to alter the settings on the dial and notches. The night is still, the moon new, and the stars vibrant. Guthrie appears beside me and looks into the sky.

"That one there," he says, as I follow his finger into the night sky, "is Meissa."

"They have names?"

He smiles that condescending smile of his and continues naming them. "And this one is Acamar."

"Acamar," I mouth. It sounds familiar.

Thomas interrupts us. "Is this the same Acamar that was mentioned in the scroll?"

We all stare into the night sky.

"I know of no other," Guthrie replies.

Our heads tilt back into another world, explorers of nothing but vastness. Guthrie tells us that the stars are always there whether you can see them or not. "It's a fact," he reminds me before I can say anything. "It's the darkness that reveals them."

I agree. Does darkness exist for any other reason than to show light?

"Come now." Guthrie taps our arms and leads us to the contraption, makes a few adjustments and looks into the wooden tube. "Perfect," he whispers, and he calls me closer. "This will help you see the stars."

I lean over the wooden tube and see clouds of light and darkness.

"Close one eye," he suggests.

It's as if the stars have come to visit us and we can reach out and touch them. Guthrie explains it's the crystal he's studying that allows us to see the stars closer than ever before.

Thomas is just as impressed, "It's like magi—, I mean, you're a genius among the Sirbahn, Guthrie."

Guthrie's face beams in the candlelight as he adjusts the dials again and swings the entire contraption around to a different direction.

"And that," he says, almost bursting with pride, "that is the Always Star. And from it, every other deduction can be made. It's always there. It's still there whether you see it or not."

Guthrie's theory of the Always Star is beautiful, although I would never dare tell him that. He explains that like a flame on a bright day, we don't witness its power unless it is in darkness. Its power is still there, but unseen until needed. It takes a certain measure of faith to believe that something is there when it can't be seen, whether it's love, the Eariss or stars. Darkness is where we learn about ourselves and about others. Too many things hide in the light. Tomorrow, I'll remind myself to look to the sky and know the stars shine quietly for me. I decide they are our teachers too, patiently waiting for us to see the lesson. Just like every other mystery, they are hidden in plain view.

Thomas and I admire the sky while Guthrie confirms his star is safe and records a few more movements. It's an honor that he has trusted us with his star, his knowledge and himself. Loaded safely onto the cart next to the contraption, I touch Guthrie's arm as he passes me on his way to lead the donkey. "Our thoughts have much in common, Guthrie."

He pats my shoulder. "Don't be silly, lower girl."

B y the time the cooler winds blow up from the valley we have settled into life in Sirban. We are by no means considered Sirbahn, but at least the traders tolerate me in the marketplace. The traders themselves aren't Sirbahn—it would be beneath anyone in the village to till the soil— instead they are carefully vetted and classified as appropriate visitors, but somehow that badge infiltrates their behavior.

"Here's Guthrie's girl." One trader nudges another as I approach their stand. They've cleaned their clothes to appear lighter, trying to match the cream rocks. They might look down on me, but they're only here because their vegetables meet the Sirbahn's exacting standards.

"These. Are. Beets."

I nod, offer them a small smile in greeting and reach toward a basket where a particularly healthy-looking bundle has caught my eye.

One trader whisks the basket from under my hand. "Not those. Not for you," he says, waving his finger from side to side.

The other trader holds a bunch of warm and wilted leaves. The beets must be somewhere underneath them. "Here are *your* beets. Aren't they pretty? Do you have Guthrie's silver?"

I question my own understanding of things when treated this way. It takes too much energy to stay aloft under a constant barrage of condescension. I place the beets in my basket. "Thank you."

My body is fit, my foot almost healed, but my mind and heart are so tired. Perhaps I am lower after all. Look at me. Running around dressed in men's clothes and looking for something that doesn't exist. I kick at a rock on the path on the way home. It stays in the ground, solid and unmoving. The cream stones, rocks and dust aren't cobblestones, but they are just as solid and cold and unfeeling. Stone. The Sirbahn aren't clever; a clever person never needs to tell you they are, it simply shows in their actions. The Sirbahn are just the same as the other villagers—fearful. Valuing themselves only on their intelligence and ignoring the seed, they drown it with facts and notations and superiority. I weave my way along the path, dodging the groups of Sirbahn that gather to converse and use grandiose gestures to bring more attention to their latest accomplishments. Behind their cream masks they're terrified they might be unique, different, *lower.* They scramble to the top of their own mountains, constantly striving for better, higher, but are never content with the view.

And how am I any different to them? I'm yet to conquer my own fears and I'm terrified about where this quest is taking me. What if I *am* the Eariss? What if I'm so inadequate I cause more deaths than I already have? Do people write legends about *that* sort of thing? A new sensation stirs within me, and I groan as I walk towards Guthrie's home. I also fear *not* being the Eariss. What if I am evil, and worthless, and filth, and shouldn't even exist?

I fear Feeney.

I fear that he has been right all along.

A t Guthrie's door, I reach back into the basket and stroke life into the beets. They grow plump, their leaves crisp. My eyes adjust slowly to the dimness inside his house and I stand still and wait, not wanting to incur his wrath like I did the time I staggered in blindly and ruined his work. The darkness transforms into shapes I recognize, and the form of Guthrie bent over his table comes into view. Thomas's work lies under his hands.

"Remarkable. Remarkable," Guthrie mutters before he notices my presence and slides the parchments under a book.

I show Guthrie the basket. "The beets are lovely today."

"Beets aren't *lovely*. They're nutritious."

The tiredness spreads over me just like the waterfalls used to. "Yes, Guthrie. Beets are nutritious."

"Get me more ink."

"Yes, Guthrie."

Thomas is outside cleaning up after the donkey and raises a pitchfork when he sees me coming. "I've already saved you some." He nods in the direction of my small garden among the rocks. Guthrie said I could waste my time playing with rocks if I chose, and that's what I've done. Only I have nothing to show for my time but scratched and cut hands and a few scraggly but hardy herbs. The promise of one day having soil in my hands feeds my heart as much as any food might nourish my body.

Guthrie calls to Thomas from the doorway. "It seems...," he says, "that you have a certain aptitude." He waves us to the door with Thomas's parchment. "Naturally, I shall confirm my results with my peers, but should we deem you worthy, you would need to study with my relative. She has far more patience than I do. I have no doubts in her ability—only yours." Guthrie nods sharply at his own words and follows the pathway past the house and down to the village.

My arms reach around Thomas. "It seems you have aptitude, young Thomas."

I've never seen him smile brighter. "But Guthrie's relative?" he says. "I'll wager she's got warts."

"And a bony finger to poke you with, I'm sure."

⁕

When it's time for our evening meal, Guthrie sits heavily in his chair and speaks sternly to Thomas. "Eugenica has agreed to meet you in the library workshop in the morning. Do not be late. Do not waste her time nor her talent. Do not be foolish."

Thomas's face pales behind Guthrie's pointing finger.

"And you." Guthrie swings his finger towards me. "You go with him and make sure he gets there."

⁕

The path into the village isn't too warm this morning, but I'm flushed with heat. Thomas tugs down on the cream tunic that Guthrie tossed into the stable this morning and takes another measured breath. I want to tell him how handsome and clever he looks, but I don't want to distract him. The tunic and the ability to breathe seem to be using all his attention, so I touch his arm occasionally in support.

I slip into the shade along the narrower paths, the tall, cream-colored homes on either side of us blocking the brightness of the sun before the paths widen into streets that cater to cart travel and the general business of life in the center of Sirban. All the village streets converge into the open square that lies in front of the library and the now-damaged and blackened hall of records.

From the other side of the square, the library's wooden doors don't seem imposing. People move in and out of the doors carrying scrolls, parchment and books, sometimes arguing amongst each other. Closer though, the fine writing and diagrams on the doors seem to mock my lower status and hold a bright torch above my brown clothing. Thomas reaches to open the door and I place my hand on his arm. "Whatever happens," I whisper, "remember to be thankful."

Cooler air pushes against our faces and the smell of leather, wood dust and inks surround us. The library is large and dark with shelves that reach to its roof. People work on long tables, writing, sorting and binding, while in other areas people recline in plush seats, grouped into circles for conversation.

Thomas stands tall and approaches the first long table. "I am here for Eugenica," he says.

A sturdy man with a short gray beard tucks his book under his arm and takes in Thomas's attire before raising an eyebrow at my brown-ness.

He places his book on the table. "Yes. You're Guthrie's study. Follow me."

Thomas strides after the man and I scurry along behind, suddenly terrified that the Sirbahn might hiss at my status and throw me from the library. We approach a group of young people surrounding the conversation chairs.

"Eugenica?" the gray beard says through the crowd. "Your study has arrived."

The crowd of cream tunics and dresses opens like the petals of a flower and a hint of oleander caresses the air. Eugenica rises from her seat like she doesn't walk upon the earth, her ivory skin slides beneath hair that is as sleek and shiny as a Trothsman's horse.

"Oh, I am so thankful," Thomas rasps.

Eugenica extends her hand for Thomas to take. I imagine it as tender and soft as a horse's muzzle. Her eyes flow over each part of him. "Guthrie has told me how exceptional you are. I look forward to our time together." Even her voice is musical.

Where are her warts?

Where's her awful Star-cursed bony finger?

Thomas takes her hand and bows gently. Her eyes meet mine over Thomas's shoulder and she strokes her soft hands and twists at the thin red ribbons braided into her hair. I hide my hands under my tunic and rub at the rough cloth inside. Eugenica steps forward to stand beside Thomas and holds his upper arm as she introduces him to the other young Sirbahn. "Such bravery," she says. "He has even been deathly close to those brutish Trothsmen."

The young Sirbahn dutifully gasp and murmur, and Thomas chuckles self-consciously. I can't see his face, but I know a hint of pink will be rising on his neck.

She rubs her hand on his arm. It would be impossible for her to not notice the warmth of his skin and the shape of his arm through the sleeve. "Shall we move to my private study rooms?" she croons and directs the way with the flow of the soft fabric that drapes from her arms.

Thomas places his hand on the small of her back as Eugenica looks over her shoulder at me and smiles.

"Ew," she says, crinkling her petite nose. "What's that dreadful smell?"

I imagined it all. I'm sure I did. Feeney always said I imagined many things, and that my eyes told me lies.

What are you talking about now?

Crazy child, that didn't happen.

Must you always make everything about you?

Then he would tell me the truth and I would nod until it was true.

I nod as the Sirbahn direct me from the library, gesturing with their arms but being sure not to touch me. I nod my way back through the streets, past the shaded alleys and back to the stable.

The donkey stands patiently as I rub behind his ears and lean my forehead into his. "He will learn a great deal with her," I whisper. "More than we could ever imagine. We should be happy." I wipe my sleeves over my face and show it to the donkey. "See? Happy tears."

I spend the morning busying myself with any chore I can find and even some I create. It keeps the red ribbons from floating and twisting their way into my mind. The pot is almost empty, and I decide we need some kind of celebration. My basket swings beside me as I walk the path to the village.

"A new meal with fresh herbs, that's what we need," I call to Guthrie as he approaches.

"Why so cheery?"

I spin and walk backwards as I speak to him. "When Thomas returns we shall have a fresh meal and hear about his lessons."

"Get more oil of vitriol," he grunts, "and be careful with it this time."

How was I to know it would burn holes through wood? "Yes, Guthrie."

The vessel of Guthrie's oil wobbles as I put it on the table and I quickly catch it before it spills. Guthrie doesn't look up from his work; perhaps he didn't notice. Small bundles of herbs lay about his work table sorted into piles that only he would understand. His hands cover the pestle and it would look like he was grinding the herbs with his bare hands if not for the sound of it scratching on the bottom of the mortar.

"There weren't any herbs in the market today," I say, picking up a bunch of rosemary and inhaling its scent. I pick a spiny leaf and put it in my mouth. "These are fresh."

Guthrie nods and goes back to his grinding. "So they are."

"They don't feel warm and wilted like the herbs the traders sell."

"I'm sure they don't."

"Where did they come from? There's no plots here. My garden is lucky to grow a weed."

Guthrie waves his hand behind him to the door that opens to the cliff. "From the valley."

My heart bursts into life. "The valley? How do you get in there?"

"You don't."

"But you just said the herbs came from there."

"They do."

"Guthrie!"

He turns in his chair to face me, hands clenched on his thighs, the pestle standing like a bright green mushroom near his knee. I wait for the order.

"Get me a drink and something to eat, lower girl."

Will a simple cup of water, some food and my obedience be a worthy trade for information? The water spills as I pour into his cup and I mop it with my shirt before he sees. I hand him the cup and fumble with a small loaf of bread on the table. I try to cut it carefully, but my mind is too distracted. "The valley?"

"There's nothing of value down there."

The cheese flops onto the bread and I sprinkle some herbs from his table on top. "There's herbs, at least."

"Yes, the herbs. And a small kinship, apparently. Of the very low variety." He taps his temple and only stops when I place the bread in his hand.

"How do you know people live down there if there's no way in or out?"

"Oh, the pail has always been there." He nods in thanks at the bread. "They provide items we require from the forest for study and put it in a pail we hoist from the valley. It's always been done that way."

"So they grow the herbs and just give them to you?"

"Perhaps they think they're making an offering... it's not the first time we've been called gods." He chews for a while and then chuckles to himself. "Would you believe they leave instructions for what we should do with them?" I stretch a small smile across my face for him, and he tuts and pats my hand. "Oh, I know what this is about."

"You do?"

"You're in search of herbs in the hope they may make you clever. There's no other logical reason for you to go leaping to your death." He shoves the last of the bread in his mouth and chews and grunts his way through several thoughts. "No one lays claim to the valley or the land beyond it, so don't expect anyone to retrieve your body."

"So it's beyond the reach of the Hall?"

"Mmhm," he grunts as he makes his last swallow and taps his temple as he leans forward to address me. "This will prove their lower status even to you." He stands and walks towards the door. "They call it the hidden valley." I follow Guthrie outside and for the first time he appears to see the treetops. "It's hardly hiding, is it? Right there—"

"In plain view," I finish.

❦

The vegetables tumble into the pot and I add the remainder of Guthrie's herbs I gleaned from his work table. I can't wait to tell Thomas about the valley, and my mind swims with possibilities.

Beyond the reach of the Hall.

A life without the Hall and Trothsmen and disguises. What is the soil in the valley like? What vegetables will we grow there?

And shelter. Maybe we could build a stone cottage like Galen and Maeve's, or even something like the stable would do—but without the donkey, of course. And blue flowers like the ones that grew on the river bank, the ones I wove into Joss's hair; they could grow in a barrel, perhaps. But first we have to find a way in. A way in that won't kill us.

"Watch out!" Guthrie yells and pushes me away from the pot. "What do you think you're doing? Ruining perfectly good food, that's what you're doing." The smell of burning food reaches my nostrils and Guthrie takes a few stabs at the vegetables before thrusting the spoon into my hand. "Pay attention!"

I scrape hard and remove most of the charred vegetables that attached themselves to the pot, and Guthrie lights the candles as darkness sets in.

"Are we going to eat, then?" Guthrie demands.

He sits in front of an empty bowl and even though I've delayed serving the meal for as long as I can, I scoop vegetables into our bowls, leaving Thomas's empty. I take my seat, although I have no appetite. We eat in silence and my eyes keep wandering to Thomas's empty bowl. My stomach rolls, flipping as much as my mind does between wanting to know where he is and the safety of denial.

Guthrie attempts conversation about the day. "Well, he must be exhausted. After all, Eugenica is..."

I can't bring myself to offer him a response. Guthrie occasionally catches my eye and I stare at the table. Before the candle draws too low, I gather our bowls. "Thank you for the meal, Guthrie. Sleep well."

As I pass him he reaches out and gently takes my arm. His eyes are soft. I hold his stare for a moment and pull my arm away and draw it close to my body.

W hen Thomas lands next to me in the straw I so desperately want to tell him about the valley.

"Shh. I'm too tired."

He smells of leather, wood, inks—and oleander.

The next morning Thomas stretches in the straw beside me before taking me in his arms. Even with my head on his shoulder I can sense the smile on his face. The sun is almost up and all too soon he'll be in the library for morning study. Until then I can pretend he is mine alone.

"So how were your lessons?" I don't want to say her name.

"She's amazing," he says. "Her head is filled with incredible knowledge and she teaches so well."

"Did she mention anything about the records?"

"I'll ask her today."

What he means, of course, is that he forgot. I want to ask him why he returned after dark but I'm not sure my heart is that brave.

"And that's all they do all day? Talk?"

"And write and feel superior," he adds with a chuckle.

I imagine them sitting at their desks nodding at their books. If ropes were to appear and tie them to their chairs, I expect they would relax and welcome them rather than fight. "I wonder how you help free someone who is bound when they don't even acknowledge the ropes?"

Thomas rises to dress. "What is it about the Sirbahn that bothers you so much?"

"The Sirbahn are different. The people of Muscone and the Fercies identify with things outside of them. In Sirban, their identity covers the seed and encases it like a shell. They're terrified of who they are without their minds, and it drives them to reduce people to categories."

I sit up in the straw and think of life outside Sirban. "When they don't bother teaching the lowers, it creates a gap of mistrust and misunderstanding. The Sirbahn don't know how to communicate with the lowers and the lowers aren't taught to think for themselves. So when the Sirbahn's words confuse them, they get angry and fearful and attack the Sirbahn."

I throw some straw in the air. "And the Hall has the power again. Without even lifting a blade. I fear when the unrest arrives we will all see to our own destruction. They will just stand and watch and blame us for it all."

"You make it sound like the Sirbahn are wrong in seeking knowledge, but to use your mind is a good thing,"

"It is, but only when you are its master, and not the other way around."

He stands tall and tugs at his cream tunic. "I'd like to think I'm the master of my own mind."

"I'd like to think that too."

❦

Days pass and I dismiss Thomas's careless remarks as a result of his tiredness or my sensitivity to the amount of time he spends with Eugenica. He speaks of her often and involves himself in discussions with Guthrie over the evening meal. I'm proud of what he's accomplished; it must be that aptitude Guthrie mentioned. It must be so wonderfully consuming to have all you've wanted, right within reach. Even so, caution sways through my belly and sometimes I swear his whole life is turning cream before my eyes. I haven't told him what I discovered about the valley, but I decide to make plans. One sunny day I hear his footsteps arrive home from lessons and stop beside me at the edge of the cliff.

"What are you doing?"

I don't bother opening my eyes. "Listening to the valley."

"Listening to the valley?" He fails to stop his snort in time and I ignore it.

"If I explain, will you listen like you used to?"

"I still listen to you."

"I need you to understand. I need you to remember the lights and the bandits and Bez and the Tallefix."

He sits beside me. "I remember," he whispers.

"I'm going to find a way into the valley—"

"You can't. Eugenica says—" He stops himself and I take a deep breath and hold the tears behind my eyelids. Perhaps he is already too cream.

"I know I'm meant to get into the valley, and when I find my way, however that happens, I need you to remember that all is well."

"When you find your way? You can't go alone, Eugenica says—"

I reach across and take his hand and gently squeeze it. "I fear you're becoming Sirbahn. It might serve you better to stay here."

"Oh, you needn't fear that. I am my own mind." He pats me on the shoulder just like Guthrie does and stands as if suddenly remembering something. "But look at you, hair everywhere. Everyone speaks of your strange hair that uh, smells, and grows like it comes from two heads."

He reaches inside his shirt and pulls out a piece of brown cloth. "Look, Eugenica kindly made you a hood, see? Eugenica says it will make you more pleasing to be around."

"Eugenica made this for me?" I pass the cloth from hand to hand. I imagine she had to search high and low for something brown to use. "It's just like a small message, isn't it?" And Thomas nods.

Know your place. My stomach swirls in panic, as if I must decide this moment if I want to be cream or brown, worthy or unworthy of Thomas. I must choose anything but my unacceptable self and my awful hair. I resist the urge to crawl into a ball, but the blows still arrive in my mind. *Worthless! Filth!*

Thomas interrupts my panic. "She seems to be kind as well as clever."

"Hair from two heads!" I shout. "How much has my hair grown, Thomas?"

He stretches his fingers to show me how much of my hair is new and unaffected by the Tallefix's paint, then follows me as I run. His footsteps crunch into the stones behind me all the way to the stable, where I take the shears in my hand.

"No! wait—" he calls, but the shears easily free me from the weight of my hair. He watches open mouthed as I hack at my hair and it falls in clumps at my feet. He seems confused, wanting to approach as I cut, but not knowing exactly what to do, perhaps worried I might turn them on him—and I might. Even I'm unsure what I could do at this moment, as if I'm watching from outside my body, unable to calm the horror that rages through me and decides my actions for me. I keep cutting, feeling my way with my fingers until the longest smelly tresses have all gone. I don't even understand why I'm crying.

Thomas snatches the shears from my hands. "Here, let me get the last pieces. At least I can fix it up for you!" He pushes me to turn for him as he evens up my hair and throws the brown hood on the ground at my feet. "Looks like you'll have to wear it after all. Surely even *you* can guess what she's going to say about you now!" He storms out of the stable.

Even the donkey is disgusted by my behavior and walks out and leaves me alone. I lie in the straw and try to understand why one person would deliberately choose to harm another. Not by accident or misunderstanding, but to make a choice to cause more pain in a world that is already unbearably painful. No understanding arrives, but my mind wanders to an experiment Guthrie performed one afternoon with the pot and the fire.

He heated the water in the pot until it created steam and he collected the steam in another vessel above the pot. At the very top of the vessel was a flap that would release when the pressure of the steam became too much, and it sounded a sharp whistle like a frightened bird.

Perhaps these acts to cause harm were like the whistles of that frightened bird, relieving the pressure and the pain they feel inside. But for every whistle of the bird, another fire is lit under another pot and someone else carries the pain. Asking people to simply stop acting out of pain would only stifle their truth and add to the pressure inside the steam vessel. The answer lay in the dousing of the fire.

But how to douse a fire of pain? Not with retaliation and blame; defensiveness would only fan the flames and cause more fires.

To douse the fire, we must love the seed. Could someone from Muscone forgo their pots and learn they are loved simply for the seed they don't even acknowledge? What about the Fercies? Could they possibly consider themselves worthy without their mirrors? Is it too much to hope that they might one day hiss at the mirrors instead? And the Sirbahn? If love entered their lives they might build things up instead of tear them down. The fires need to stop, and if a fire can't be doused completely, then at least I could choose to stop spreading the smaller fires and fanning the flames of those already lit. I reach across the straw for the brown cloth and draw it to me.

Thomas isn't near the cliff or in the house. He must be with Guthrie in the village. I wrap Eugenica's hood about me and wait for them at the cliff's edge, watching over the treetops and wondering what I'll find on the other side. Who am I to ask Thomas to be anything other than he is, or even Eugenica, for that matter?

I can't demand others behave a certain way. The only actions I'm responsible for are my own. A bird bounces on a scraggly dry tree along the path and stops to sing his song for me.

"Have you come to cheer me?"

He sings his song again.

"Thank you. Here, come and sit with me while I wait."

The bird hops around, the twigs bouncing as he flits between them while he decides.

"Come along. Don't be shy."

He drops to the ground. The tabby cat pounces, but the bird escapes before I register what happened. Coldness pours over me. I don't want this power. I don't want this responsibility. If the only actions I'm responsible for are my own, I'll make sure they never involve anyone else! A few tufts of feathers pulled loose from their encounter remain, and the breeze pushes the feathers along the path and out of view.

※

T homas's boots are the next thing I see on the path and they bring me back to the cliff, the breeze and his return. He carries the goods into the house and joins me on the cliff's edge.

"Feeling better?"

"Much."

"I see you wear her hood."

"She's very kind."

Thomas looks back towards the house. "Do you think Guthrie relies on us too much now? We should prepare him if we are leaving—are we leaving?"

"I am. But I'd still like a copy of the song first."

"I can get it for you tomorrow."

I nod. "I imagine all you desire is here in this village. Would it be better for you to stay? Here . . . with Eugenica?"

Thomas sits beside me and takes my hand. "There's something you need to understa—"

Guthrie charges towards us with Thomas's satchel in his hands and slides onto his knees. "Run!" He thrusts the satchel at Thomas. "For the love of Stars, Run!"

Our scrambling feet flick small stones into the air and over the cliff's edge as the sound of horses' hooves reach us. A few moments ago, this was the path back from the market, not the only track that promises we might live. We dash through the outer paths of the village and run and weave among the wandering Sirbahn. We knock and bump them with no time for apologies. I don't look behind. It's horse's breath that warms my shoulders, I'm sure of it. The rock. That immovable rock in the path. Don't trip on it. I'd hate for my demise to set by something I already knew existed. The Sirbahn are slow; they're not used to dodging anything. Thank the Stars they stay still and shout, rather than get involved.

"What are you doing!"

"This shouldn't be happening!"

"Have some respect!"

"They've gone mad. It's Guthrie's fault."

Wonder what they'll shout at the Trothsmen following behind?

My lungs burn. The village rushes by in a blur of cream. If only I wasn't so brown! Their protests about rudeness fade against the booming orders shouted by the Trothsmen.

"Halt!"

You jest!

"Stop them!"

They won't get involved, you buffoon.

Thomas catches the edge of a market table with his hip and I leap the tumbling produce as it crashes to the ground. We leave a water carrier and his yoke spinning outside the Hall of Records, but make it through without any further damage. On the other side of the village, we race down a narrow path cut into the side of the cliff. Trees grow tall on one side of us and the cliff drops away on the other. We pass Guthrie's pail. The herbs. I follow Thomas's feet and slam into his back when he stops.

"Who makes a path that goes nowhere?" he puffs.

"The Sirbahn!"

Thomas looks over the edge. I hope he's not considering sliding down there. He stretches for a vine that hangs just out of reach and almost topples and drops the satchel so it doesn't pull him off balance. I lean my weight backwards and hold his arm as he reaches over the edge to grab the vine.

"Will it hold us?" I ask as he puts his full weight on to it and nods. He pulls me into him and we wrap our legs together. I squeeze him as tight as I can. My mind races with Guthrie's warnings about no one retrieving our bodies and about us never coming back.

Thomas looks down to me. "Trust?"

"Halt!" a Trothsman shouts above the din.

I nod, and we fall from the edge of the path.

The vine takes our weight as our feet leave the edge, then shudders before the branch above releases it and we free fall. I tense and shut my eyes, waiting for the ground, sure that my stomach is still somewhere above me on the cliff's edge. Thomas cries out as the vine jerks, captures our weight and swings us above the trees. We are so close to them I could extend my leg to feel the whip of small branches and touch the leaves, but at the height of our swing the vine breaks and flicks us into the treetops.

Falling.

Branches, bark, twigs.

Scratches, thumps, clawing.

Leaves. Grasp. Miss.

Groans and shouts.

When will the ground join us?

Us?

Where's Thomas? Do the grunts and cries come from me or him? The last branch catches me in my lower back, flips me over, and slams me onto my hands and knees. My kneecaps crack at the sudden stop against the exposed roots of the tree. I dare not move but I catch my breath and gather my thoughts. I'm on the ground. I hurt all over, my shoulder stings, there's blood in my mouth. I can breathe. I knead my hands forward through the leaves and dirt until I lie on my stomach. My cheek touches the moss of the forest floor and I gasp and feel solid again, like I'm absorbing every piece of moisture and life I was denied in Sirban. Home. I close my eyes to whisper words of thanks.

"Ashling?" Thomas's calls in the distance, not loud or pained or panicked, just a curious, conversational tone. "Are you well?"

I don't open my eyes. "I think so. A little pained, but fair. You?"

"Think I'm all right too."

"Good."

We both spend time in the quiet and catch our breath before I lift my head and see Thomas's legs about two trees away. I raise my belly and crawl towards him, wincing when my knees don't find soft moss or leaves under them. It looks like he has landed on his back. He smiles when I arrive and lay beside him.

"Think I had my breath knocked out of me, but all my bits are working," he says, moving his arms and legs a little, although grunting in pain. His hands have deep cuts from the vine.

"Well, as long as your bits are working," I say. "My ribs, back and knees hurt, but I don't think anything's broken."

I gaze into the canopy of trees above us. Thomas looks up as well, finds my hand and sighs resignedly. "Well, you said you wanted to get into this valley, and I did promise to take you beyond Sirban, didn't I?"

"Yes, you did."

We both attempt a small laugh, but it hurts.

"Trust," he says.

"Trust," I reply.

I n time, we get to our feet and tentatively check each other for injuries before slowly moving through the forest.

"So now that we're actually walking around like a pair of old idlers there's no one to see us," he says as he finds a stick for support.

The sound of water leads us to a small stream. Further down its reach, a tree has fallen and created a small pool. We undress slowly, helping each other to avoid further pain, and pile our clothes a safe distance from the stream. The cold water stings our cuts and tightens our aching muscles, but we adapt and soon relax in the water.

"I'm sorry you left everything behind," I say, as I remember him discarding the satchel on the path.

Thomas closes his eyes and shakes his head.

"You finally had everything you wanted, and now it's gone. I'm not sure you can get back up there."

"I already had everything I wanted."

"To lose it, after you worked so hard, the respect of the Sirbahn, your own desk. Do you think they'll ever forgive you?" I say as I slide across the water to him.

He sighs and twists at the short pieces of hair that grow near my temple. "I'm sure they will. Someday." We pat ourselves dry with our outer clothes, tenderly, as our bruises are starting to appear, and help each other to dress. Thomas looks deep in thought, so I raise my eyebrows, inviting him to speak.

"How do you think they found us?" he says.

I want to remind him how much Eugenica likes to gossip but instead say, "Well, the Tallefix knew where we were headed. Perhaps he's no longer addled."

Yes, Eugenica likes to gossip, and it seems I like to make assumptions as readily as Guthrie does.

We move carefully through the forest, leaning on sticks we collected from the forest floor. Any slips and trips tense already-sore muscles and make us miserable so this pace seems to be safe as well as productive. As Thomas says, "We don't know where we're going, so it doesn't matter how fast we get there." A grassy road appears in the forest and we stand at its edge and look both ways along its length.

"Two tracks," Thomas says, nodding towards the cart tracks in the grass.

The grass grows almost to my knees. "Can't be used that often." I step onto the road and look from one end to the other. "This way," I say to his shrugging form and move along the cart track, pushing the grass curtain away with my shins as I walk.

Cleared land appears between the trees and we sneak closer and take refuge behind some fallen logs and observe the workers who tend crops and animals in the fields. The fences are made of two wooden rails, more for boundary marking than protection. The cart road leads straight through the middle of the fields to the first rise and a large stone lodge. Overshadowing the lodge, a large tree points its lower branches towards the two lower lodges that lie almost in the fields themselves. People walk between the buildings and the field. Everyone looks busy.

Thomas blinks hard. "Are they wearing uniforms?"

"Looks like it." The women's head-covers and under-dresses are a light color and they wear a red smock while the men wear light farmer's shirts with a sash in the same color of red. "Should we go in?"

Thomas looks up. "Got to be easier entering through the threshold than the treetops," he grunts.

"This must be the kinship Guthrie was talking about." Nerves, fear and excitement tumble in a cascade between my chest and my belly.

"You didn't think to tell me about it before we jumped?"

"Would it have made any difference?"

Thomas is quiet for a while. "What do you know about it then?"

My eyes don't leave the fields. "Not much. They grow herbs. Guthrie thinks they're stupid."

"Nothing new there."

"Oh, and the other thing—the Hall has no jurisdiction here."

"Ah, I see, so you won't be needing my protection then?"

Protection. I'll need it more than ever. I take his chin and make sure I have his attention. "Thomas of Feldston, I need you. You mustn't leave me now." I kiss him. The bruising on my face hurts but I don't care. There's something beyond that threshold I must face, and the only thing I'm sure of is that I don't want to face it alone.

Two tall poles stand high on either side of the gate into the kinship. Across them, a large beam stretches from one side to the other. There are no inscriptions, no jewels and nothing shines. It simply acts as a threshold. Inside. Outside. Nothing more.

We watch it pass above us and gently make our way up the road to the main lodge. The workers stop in the fields when they see us, and they wave. Thomas shrugs and I wave back rather cautiously. I don't remember anyone ever waving to me before. More people gather to watch us from the landing at the front of the main lodge and a man and woman approach us and meet us halfway along the road. By the time they reach us they seem breathless with excitement, and they are so clean. We are dirty, sore and emotional.

"We're so glad you've made it." The young man pats Thomas on the back then quickly apologizes and gently rubs when Thomas winces.

She takes my hands, and hers feel soft and clean and pure.

"We've been waiting for you."

Waiting for us? How? Why? Before I can speak several more people arrive to fuss over us.

"Have you traveled far?"

"Are you well?" they ask.

We nod and begin to answer their questions, but they ask more before we can speak. A taller woman with a piece of dark hair escaping from her head-cover approaches and spreads her arms wide.

"Allow them breath," she tells the others and they step back as she extends her hand to us. "Welcome."

I shake her hand. "How did you know we were coming?"

"We're always happy to see travelers arrive safely. No one ever arrives here without being called."

Thomas gently takes my hand and squeezes. I heard it too. *Called.* She beckons us to follow her and we walk the road towards the main lodge as most of our greeters slowly disappear back to their work.

"We expect you're like the others and are here for information and teaching," she begins. "There's much to learn, if you are willing." Thomas's pace increases. His excitement must be overriding his pain. She stops where two paths lead from the main road to the lower lodges. "Above all," she says, "know that whatever you have faced on your journey here, you are safe now."

I feel like a warm blanket has been placed across my shoulders.

We have so many questions and we open our mouths, but she speaks again. "Let us prepare you for the evening meal. You can meet Brenn when your belly is full." A woman appears by my side and the young man that first met us on the road leads Thomas away from me. Intrigue and excitement taps in my chest, but the sensation of his hand gently releasing mine reminds me that for the first time since the straw house in Smoutlea, I am alone.

❧❦❧

It's dark inside the lodge and it takes a while for my eyes to adjust. The young woman walks ahead of me and gathers things from a small table.

"Welcome, I'm Abigayl," she says as she hands me some clothing. It's the same as the uniform she wears, a white dress and a red smock. The room is large and smells of sweet hay, probably coming from the pallet bed mattresses that line the long walls. Two fireplaces made of stone stand at each end of the lodge, guaranteeing enough warmth amongst all the bodies once winter arrives. The lodge seems filled with mats but Abigayl and I are the only ones here. The others must be going about their work. My fingers caress the rough weave of the working smock, yet it feels like the finest silk in my hand. Abigayl brings a bowl and pitcher and a cloth for me to wash and busies herself with small chores while I bathe. She is quite perceptive; I don't feel like talking.

The water has been oiled, and smells like fresh grass, new and promising. I shed Galen's clothes like old skin and they land with a thud onto the floor. Are they heavy from dirt or the weight of the fabric? I consider for a moment how they led me here. Wherever here is. Abigayl whisks them away so there is no sign of heaviness anywhere. The water in the pond soaked most of the dirt and grime from my body but I still make use of the scented water, cleaning myself again and paying attention to my hands and broken nails. Their hands were so lovely and pure. The dress truly feels like silk as it slips over my body, and I twist to tie the sides of the red smock at my sides.

Abigayl gestures towards a chair. "Please."

My hands run down the back of my dress as I prepare to sit, and I'm quietly pleased with myself that I have remembered a behavior so simple and elegant. Thomas has never seen me in a dress; would he still recognize me? Abigayl kneels with soft shoes in her hand and begins to tie them. I cringe with embarrassment then still myself. With my injuries I couldn't tie them anyway.

"Thank you," I say as she rises. She can't be much older than me, yet her face is kind, motherly. She runs her hand over my short hair and I feel a flush of shame and drop my eyes to the floor. I'm embarrassed about my behavior with those shears, yet she would assume my shame was from something different. I don't bother trying to explain.

"Here." She takes a head-covering and drapes it over my hair, knots it behind my neck, and it seems like my hair is long underneath it. "Like new again," she says. I stroke my hands over it from the top of my head to past my shoulders. Another costume for my safety.

"Thank you."

She leads me to my mat at the end of the lodge. From this corner I can watch the whole room. A small opening acts as a window above my bed. It might be a squeeze, but I'm sure I'd fit if I had to make an escape. The faint smells of cooking that I thought I imagined now come through the window undiluted. It must almost be time for their evening meal. There are many people here—do they sit around a campfire like Bez's family? Soft voices sing and I can't place where they're coming from or even if they're real. Harmonies blend and at times it doesn't even sound earthly. I jump at Abigayl's touch on my arm. She pretends she didn't notice and smiles warmly.

"We sing to announce the evening meal is ready." Her hand slides down my arm and finds my hand. "Come," she says, and leads me outside.

⁘⁙⁘

It's darker now. In the twilight, lines of uniformed people make their way along the paths to the highest lodge. A trail of men travel the path that leads from the fields and the other lodge, the one with the roof in need of repair and the one I last saw Thomas being led to. I scan the bodies, but everyone is dressed in farming clothes and they look the same in this light. One man in a light-colored shirt starts to jump around and wave his arms.

"Thomas!" I wave back. How can he manage all that movement when raising my arms still hurts?

Abigayl reaches out and pulls my hands beside me. "Hush!" she says.

The men around Thomas subdue him, and I fear we have somehow ruined their ritual. The queue winds its way to the largest lodge in the most orderly procession of hungry people I have ever seen. How did something as natural as eating become so regulated? Soon our lines meet at the wooden steps and large landing at the entrance to the high lodge.

Thomas looks so fresh and handsome. Did he get to bathe with the scented water too? He stares at me, confused and frustrated. I stare back, concerned he's not well, until I understand. He has only seen me wear the idler's costume.

"It's just a dress, Thomas," I whisper.

We follow our lines into the lodge, separating again into two long tables where we take our seats for the meal. Still no one speaks. There won't be any campfire dancing tonight.

A small gong sounds and everyone chants words about thankfulness and bounty. I find Thomas's eyes trained on mine from across the lodge.

The door is open if I need it.

An arm reaches in front of me and blocks the view of the door. A steaming bowl of stew and bread it sets down sends any thoughts of the door to oblivion. As I lean over and savor the smell, its heat rises and steams the tip of my nose. I wipe the moisture away before grasping at a spoon and marveling at the flavors in each spoonful.

The young women around me discuss their day. Some tend gardens and fields, others wash, clean and prepare work for others. They all speak of their chores with appreciation and admire each other's work. They also giggle and tell stories about someone they call 'the old crone.' My mouth is always full and I have nothing to add to the conversation anyway. I learn the kinship relies on no other to sustain itself. Occasionally I catch Thomas watching and we both smile. Although I miss talking to him as we eat, this meal is so intoxicating I'm sure we wouldn't be talking anyway.

A second bowl is served to me. "There's been a mistake. I've already eaten," I say.

"It's tradition," one says.

"For new arrivals," says another.

"We all know what it's like to travel with empty bellies."

I receive the second bowl with thanks, sure that I could eat another ten. Thomas revels in his second serving, and the men who sit beside him have set aside some of their portions for him too. I decide it's a beautiful tradition.

A second gong sounds and everyone around me chants and stands. I stand too and am about to follow the trail of people leading out of the lodge when Abigayl appears beside me and directs me out of the line.

"You're to see Brenn, remember?"

Yes. Brenn. The questions. Abigayl nods to the far end of the lodge. A large woman, wearing only white, enters a side room, her backside just making it through the small doorway.

"Wait outside her chamber until she calls for you." Abigayl nods in the direction of the chamber. "On your way, now. Don't make her wait."

The streams of red and white channel out the door of the high lodge behind me. I smooth the skirt in front of me as I walk towards Brenn's chamber and consider how our costumes alter how we face the world. My costume as the old idler allowed me to hide, but I can't imagine stooping in this dress; instead, it encourages me to stand tall. Thomas waits for me by her door, swiping at the flush that creeps up his neck. Has he prepared his questions for her? Will she know anything about the Eariss? Surely she would. That's why we've been led here. I move close to him and slip my hand around his waist and he stares at me so intently it makes me uncomfortable.

"Have I spilled something?" I whisper and start wiping my dress, berating myself for my clumsiness.

"No." He directs his words to the ground.

"Honestly, what is wrong with you?" I mumble. We are finally going to get our answers and he's acting like a complete dolt. The door opens and Brenn appears in its frame, her bosom taking up most of the view.

She graciously lowers her head below the low mantle. "Come, come," she says and steps back from the door. I follow Thomas through the door and nudge him, annoyed that he chooses to stop just inside the door.

Brenn's chamber is larger than I expected. The stone walls have been purposely built with alcoves that hold books and scrolls, stretching all the way to the shingled roof. Smaller alcoves cleverly built away from the parchment storage hold candles that light the room in an amber glow. Some carved chairs are scattered around the room, but as Brenn sits behind her desk, she gestures to the wooden bench in front of her. I touch Thomas's arm so he will stop craning his neck to see the parchments on her desk, and as we sit I take comfort that his thigh sits right next to mine.

Brenn clasps her hands together on the desk. "Welcome to the kinship. I trust your bellies are full."

We both thank her profusely for her welcome, telling her how delicious the meal was, and I make mention of the tradition of second helpings for travelers.

She nods as though she's heard these words many times before. "Now," she begins, "please explain what led both of you here."

Explain?

I don't know where to start. Thomas must be as startled by her question as I am because we both sit and stare, unmoving.

Brenn sighs gently. "There are no trick questions here," she says. "I ask this of all our travelers. Remember, you're safe now. She opens her arms for added emphasis and smiles.

Thomas nods to me and I offer her some examples of providence and guidance and tell her about my longing to travel to the valley, hoping she will choose to keep us. Brenn smiles and murmurs in the right places and although I feel heard, I'm cautious. I'm not ready to mention the Eariss. There's something about the way she keeps reminding us how safe we are, the way she wears white while the darkness hovers unseen in her chamber. I battle within myself as I talk, finding excuses for her behavior. Maybe it's actually the rich stew that is causing the uneasiness in my stomach. Soon I've thought about it so much that I've confused myself.

She smiles gently at me and turns to Thomas. Thankfully, he was listening and not lost in his thoughts as he doesn't mention lights and rainbows in his story, but talks about being an orphan and how our travels taught him to trust.

Brenn leans back from her desk. "I must say, you two are very interesting," she begins. "Most of our travelers arrive alone; it's not often that the Called will find each other along the way."

"The Called?" Thomas says. "Is that what we are?" He turns to me. "Ha! There's a name for our madness. A title, in fact."

And just like that, he breaks the tension and we all smile at his discovery.

Soon she leans forward again. "If you are here, it means you have been called by the Traditions themselves."

Thomas fumbles for my hand and squeezes it.

"The kinship is where you will learn about the Traditions and how to apply them to your lives." Brenn's hands close over each other as she begins her foundation speech. I appreciate her attempt at enthusiasm this late at night. "You are here to acquire a greater understanding and knowledge of your talents. We will teach, and you will play your part. You will be assigned a help position that will fill your mornings by working alongside the others. There is a mid-meal before afternoon lessons, then more duties before evening meal in the high lodge. When we all work together, the days go so much easier. After your lessons each day you are free to ask questions of your teachers and young man...." She points to our hands. "Release her hand; her fingers are purple."

Thomas apologizes, and I shake the feeling back into my hand.

Thomas shuffles on his seat. "You mention questions."

"Yes."

"Can I ask... I mean... I want to know . . .could you..."

Brenn seems to bask in his nervousness. "Yes?"

"What can you tell me about the Eariss?"

Brenn twitches and seems unprepared for his question. She coughs and gathers her thoughts. "First there are many things you should discover about the Traditions that are more pertinent to your calling." She nods slowly, as if agreeing with herself.

"It's just... while we traveled, we heard people speaking about it. I'm curious about what you know of it here."

"We know of it."

"And the legends?"

"Yes." Thomas waits for her to continue and when she realizes he's not going to give up she relents a little, seemingly agitated. "The Traditions teach of such a thing, but it is ancient and not seen anymore. So you needn't concern yourself with it."

"So it's connected to the Traditions in some way?" Brenn's eyes narrow as if she's sizing up an opponent, and Thomas attempts to clarify. "The legend, I mean."

Brenn's patience seems spent, but she maintains her dignity. "Let me guess, you've heard the songs and stories, fables even, of the ones who have rainbows in their eyes?" She tidies the parchments on her desk without care, flinging them around, and speaks in clipped sentences. "Challenging and disrupting. Wherever they appear." She stands up to further her point and looks down upon Thomas. "Put your mind at ease. I'm yet to meet one. I would suggest they only exist within the legends and songs. You would do best to study the Traditions only and leave that nonsense for the more feeble-minded."

"But—" Thomas blurts, and I cut him off before she gets so agitated she banishes us.

"Brenn, have you heard about the uprising in the East?"

She sits down and her shoulders relax. "No, we don't concern ourselves with things outside the valley. But that would explain the rising levels of fear and agitation in the travelers." She smooths the papers she bent in her savage tidying. "Yes, fear and change. Two tiny little things that hold an incredible amount of power."

"Very true," I say and she smiles at me and slowly blinks at Thomas, who is doing his best to present a pleasant demeanor and failing.

Brenn rises from behind her desk and we stand with her without thinking. She fits her fists into either side of her waist, expanding her presence to at least double its size. "You will be told your positions when the sun rises."

I bow my head. "Yes, Brenn."

"Thank you, Brenn." Thomas lowers his head towards her and is a little more convincing.

We cross the empty floor of the great lodge together without a word. Once outside the doors, Thomas pushes me over to the shadow of a large tree and holds me close.

"There's got to be something in all those old scrolls," he whispers near my shoulder.

"But the satchel—"

"I'll work something out," he promises before kissing me with such desperation it takes my breath away. I'm not looking forward to sleeping alone. He kisses my forehead. "Be safe."

"Always," I whisper as Brenn steps onto the landing outside the high lodge and douses the torch.

"On your way," she says into the darkness. And we obey.

❧⟡❧

The next morning I wave to Thomas from outside my sleeping lodge. He's with a group of men making their way to work at the boundary.

Abigayl launches herself at me and slams my arms to my side.

"Don't wave to him!" she hisses.

"Why?"

"You will look too eager."

"Eager?"

Abigayl looks around her then lowers her voice. "If she knows your heart leans towards him, she will send you to another."

"She?"

"Brenn."

"But there are couples here. I've seen them."

"At Brenn's insistence only."

"I see." I nod once, and then slip her a smile. "But I saw you yesterday. You smiled at—"

"I certainly did not!" Abigayl's face flushes faster than I've ever seen. "Keep your lies to yourself!"

Thomas' work party fades into the morning mist that lies in the lower fields and Abigayl steps into my line of vision. I close my eyes and only open them once I'm prepared to hear her next request. "You are not to speak with him. It's how it's always been done, and how it always *will* be done."

She takes my shoulders and turns me to face the other lower field. "The herb garden is in the corner of that field there." Abigayl points towards the early morning sun and I hold my hand up to block its light. The field slopes away from our lodge to an area with a small hut and squared gardens. Some girls pass behind us and giggle. When I turn my head to them she adds, "You'll be working with the crone."

"I see." My mind scrambles for something good to latch onto. No Thomas. My days wasted with an unstable mind. Furthest from the high lodge that holds the answers. I pull my lips into the most genuine smile I can muster. "I love working with the soil," I say.

Abigayl raises her eyebrows. "On your way then."

***

I follow the narrow sheep track through the field, only leaving its path as I draw near to the herb garden. Stone fences as high

as my waist protect it from grazing animals and a wooden gate a
little taller than the walls is latched by a loop of rope. Once inside
I loop the rope back over its stay and scan the beds and walkways
but there is no sign of the crone anywhere. Short branches stand
upright along the edge of the garden beds and dry sticks weave in
and out of them, making the whole garden look like a collection of
low baskets laid out on the ground. The walkways between have a
few stepping stones in them but are mostly earth and mud, framed
by flowers that drape over the edges.

As I make my way to the small hut built into the wall on the far
side of the garden, the crone appears from within. I had only seen
her eating alone at the very end of the table at the evening meal, and
even then, I only noticed the top of her head as she bowed her head
to eat. Up close she doesn't resemble the crazy and unpredictable
character the young women had laughed about. Her tanned face
isn't as withered as they'd described, and the wisps of hair that have
escaped her head-covering aren't white as snow but a soft shade of
gray. The crone startles when she sees me and my muscles twitch
in response. I step back. She smiles and uses her full length brown
apron to clean her hands, exhaling as if she has been holding her
breath forever.

"Ah," she says. "You're here."

"I am."

"You're what?" she asks with a gentle smile.

"Here," I answer.

"It's a good place to be," she says, and collects two baskets and
hands one to me.

The crone guides me through her garden, explaining in simple
terms which plants grow best where and why. She teaches me
about the tools we will use, giving small demonstrations. I receive
instruction on changes and seasons and some basic uses for the
most important herbs in the garden. The crone mentions that
some herbs will not grow here no matter how she tries, and she
gathers some in the forest outside the kinship. The part of the for-

est she points to isn't far from the boundary where I spot Thomas repairing fences with a group of men. He puts his hands behind him and arches backwards. We may have been running, tripping, falling and climbing trees, but our bodies aren't fit yet for days of work.

The crone sets me to work weeding around some herbs with small metal spoons she calls tillers and encourages me to gently break up the soil with small taps so the weeds are easier to remove. I stand to stretch my back and catch Thomas's eye with a large wave that he returns. The men don't try to stop him, so perhaps Abigayl is wrong. I'm still smiling when I join the crone close to the ground, but it drains away when I notice her watching me—again. I concentrate on breaking the soil around the plants in little taps, even continuing when she stops her work..

"Do you have a name?" she asks.

"Ashling."

"Yes, that's fitting. Quite fitting." She taps into the earth. "The dream."

I watch her as she taps and mutters to herself, hoping this is not the beginning of an episode of her madness. "Dream?"

"Your name means the dream, the vision. No one's mentioned that to you?"

I shake my head.

I weed, tap the ground and remove the grasses. Would it be rude to ask for her name? Surely I can't call her the crone. She moves about the herb garden gathering stalks and leaves into a basket while I move from patch to patch removing grasses. The morning is almost over when she stands above me with the basket in her hand.

"The garden has certainly got away from me." She taps my basket of weeds with her foot. "You have some hard work ahead of you." The crone reaches her hand to me and helps me to my feet. "Are you ready?"

"I'd like to think so."

The crone hands me the basket of herbs. "These need to go to the high lodge. We'll meet here again after lessons."

I nod, wipe the dirt from my smock and prepare to leave.

"Ashling?" she calls after me.

I stop and turn. "Yes?"

The crone smiles at me. "My name is Martha," she says.

Our afternoon lessons consist of Brenn telling us the ways of the Traditions, the force of love and that we all share the ability to feel it, hear it and respond to it. People here speak openly about the Traditions and no one hides. The others nod their heads and peace floods my body. No Trothsmen. No guards. No Hall.

The Mystery stirs within me to speak, and I close my eyes to listen and am knocked by the person next to me. I try again and they prod. They must think I'm sleeping. It seems the only acceptable time to connect to the Mystery is when the kinship allows it. If they allow it.

Everyone around me listens and nods, cramming their Traditions into the space that lies between mid-meal and after-lesson chores. I'm used to dropping into the Mystery's call whenever it arises. Perhaps I should discipline myself and learn to contain it. Brenn's voice drones in the background as I consider the impossibility of containing the Mystery, of placing it into a box that only opens when we demand something of it. But Brenn has studied the Traditions for years and surely knows better than me. *Arrogant and prideful! Who do you think you are?* I have so much to learn. I concentrate, copy the others and learn to nod in the right places.

After lessons, Martha leads me along the paths of the garden and tells me about each different bed and her procedures. Her respect and knowledge of each plant astounds me.

"Ah, the babes," she says, bending to tend some shoots. "You must nurse them for the first wheel of the seasons, then you receive your reward. Colors, fragrances, tastes, textures and even sounds—the bees and birds will come to visit." On cue, a robin swoops past and my eyes open. Instead of a simple garden, I see a wealth of information and layers of insight. It happens in an instant. Was all that beauty and information always there and I completely misunderstood its purpose?

Martha tilts her head to see my face. "You see it, don't you?" She smiles.

"I see it." The scent of the broken herbs seems to hover around me and I close my eyes and take a deep breath. The late afternoon sun holds enough warmth that I feel it on my skin. After life in the forest, even a huge lodge can feel stuffy. For just this moment, I can breathe.

Martha chuckles. "Come now," she calls from further along the path. "There's much to learn."

A patch of fern with delicate leaves fanned out like a fox's tail catches my eye and I stop to consider it. "I've only seen these in the forest." Martha comes closer to inspect the plant and I stand and look over the garden. "I do understand the need for this garden and how helpful it is to the kinship, but it feels boxed in. Contained."

Martha stares at me for the longest time. I've spoken out of turn. Will she send me away? Her eyes are strong. Serious. But not dangerous.

She gently holds my arm so as not to lose my attention. "You're right, this is not their true design. They're contained for now, but remember it's only when they're released that they do their work."

I nod, remembering how she uses the herbs for salves and teas and relieved she's not angry with me.

Once we've gathered what we need for the evening meal, we stand and stretch, releasing the tension from constant bending and being on our knees. Martha rubs at her knees and her face pinches.

"Let me hurry and take them," I say, lifting the basket. "Rest here for a while."

I welcome her embrace of thanks.

As I move away, she grips my hand. "The Eariss won't be contained, Ashling. It will have its way."

I pull my hand away. Martha smiles, her eyes gentle and understanding, but I'm confused. The singing from the high lodge reminds me I must hurry. I look at it, then back to her, and she shoos me to the lodge. I hold my arms over the basket in front of me as I run along the sheep track to the lodge, careful of where I put my feet, letting my thoughts come and go from my mind and fighting the smile that pushes from my lips.

※※※

Steam rises from the evening meal in front of me. This time I notice the vegetables and the flecks of herbs stirred in just before serving, released to do their work. I'm thankful for each mouthful, grateful for each moment. The girls around me eat and giggle about the crone and ask what madness we got up to today. I laugh with them and at my joy of understanding why we are here. I can't wait to tell Thomas. Thomas. He's devouring his meal. My tending plants seems weak against his work of carting lumber and digging holes for fence posts. He looks up at me and rolls his eyes; he must've been trying to attract my attention while I'd been laughing and inspecting the herbs in my meal. He directs his eyes between me and the tree outside, and I nod. Yes, I will meet him outside the lodge after the meal.

I pretend to have a problem with the hem of my smock as I leave the high lodge, and I move away from the torches that burn outside. When I'm sure no one watches me, I dash from the shadows to the tree. Thomas arrives at the same time and we both talk over each other before he embraces me in an awkward, half-hearted squeeze. Where has our easiness gone? We don't have much time.

"Are you well?" he asks.

I nod, about to tell him about Abigayl and the garden and Martha . . .

"Good," he says. "This place is perfect."

"What?"

"You're safe, you have food and shelter. You'll be protected until I return."

"Return? From where?"

"Brenn has asked me to return to Sirban. To establish trade for the kinship."

My heart aches with each beat and nothing makes sense. *He's leaving me?* I shake my head. "Trade? With Sirban? Why?"

"You know how the Sirbahn already use the kinship's herbs? Brenn has decided to trade there and needs me to oversee it."

"How will you—"

"There's a narrow track out of the valley that emerges in Guthrie's clearing. You know, where he showed us the stars. It's hidden behind the tree."

"Your satchel!"

"I have to report to Brenn regularly and return for lessons."

"So you're not really leaving then?"

"I could even continue my work in the library!"

"Yes. You could." I force myself to think of his satchel and his work, but my mind only conjures up red ribbon.

He checks around us, but no one seems to have noticed we're missing. "How are you finding your work here?"

"You'll never believe it. There's this old lady—"

"Ha! I heard you got put with the crone." He looks around again and kisses my forehead. "Keep your head down and be safe until I can get back and find what we need to know." He squeezes me again, so caught up in his future that he can't see the present, yet his happiness is so contagious I grin along with him.

"Please try to see me before you go," I say, but I don't even know if he heard me, and he disappears back into the trail of men while I stand in the dark and gather my thoughts.

The moon provides enough light for me to join the servers as they return from the high lodge and I'm able to scurry to my small corner mat without attracting any attention at all from the chattering women. Guthrie will see more of Thomas than I will. I feel like being selfish and impudent and I pull the blanket over my head and imagine telling him to stay here, but end up embarrassed about my pretend behavior even as it plays out in my head. I could never ask him to give up his lessons. Perhaps I could travel to Sirban with him? But Martha's voice in my mind holds me to the floor—I could never leave now. The red ribbon in my imagination circles around Thomas and Eugenica and draws them closer and I remember the stupid daydream I had at Guthrie's about us building a cottage in this valley. Frivolous nonsense.

I turn over on my mat. The girls are quieter now; they've mostly settled, and I concentrate on getting my tired body to relax. My mind jumps from scenario to scenario, making my body jittery again, and I try to rope it in with some deliberate thought.

Thoughts that don't involve red ribbons and the hollowness inside my chest.

I remember our conversation by the tree. Guthrie said the herbs had always been delivered with the pail, so why would Brenn be changing something that old and traditional? The path behind the tree, hidden in plain sight... I didn't understand what it was telling me then. We might have found it ourselves if Guthrie hadn't come along and needed us to move his contraption. And if that was the case, we would never have gone to Sirban... not that it helped us understand anything, anyway. What a waste of time. But then I think about Guthrie, and his offer to Thomas, the traders at the market, waiting by the cliff, and even that awful dryness that made me appreciate the forest more. And Eugenica. Thomas would not have met Eugenica. I would not have met Eugenica. What a notion to think that a leap into the valley would leave her behind. I take a deep, shuddering breath and try to imagine a future without Thomas in it. He did what he had to do, didn't he? Delivered me safely to the kinship where I can find out who I am. Shouldn't he be free to do what he wants? Even if it involves Eugenica and her smooth black hair, red ribbons and soft hands.

This time I think forwards, not about stupid cottages and flowers in barrels, but with curiosity. I roll to my back and watch the moonlight stream through the little hole I had thought of escaping through when I first arrived here. I'm safe from the Trothsmen here, and safety provides an interesting luxury; a dream about a future. My future. I'm intrigued. The whole world opens up before me and could lead anywhere. Will I create a story worthy of Thomas's telling? Perhaps I'll live here in safety forever, anonymous among the workers. But what about the legends and my stick army? I smile in the darkness. My silly stick army.

Maybe Brenn is right; it's all just nonsense.

The terror on the Tallefix's face appears like a ghost in my mind, the vegetables flourishing under my touch, the trees whispering. Scenes of wonder and fear flash into my mind, each with their own tale and impression. There *is* something within me. Then I remember the bird that I called to my side at Guthrie's and the feathers on the path. I had asked it to cheer me, and almost killed it. Hadn't I caused enough death already? How am I to make decisions for others? Some leader I am. I can't even make them for myself. Whatever this thing is, this Eariss, I will learn what I can for Thomas, but I will not call on its power again. I pull the blanket over my head and curl into a ball to hide from the moon and my thoughts.

✿

I wave from the herb garden as Thomas leaves under the threshold. I don't care that the others see. I can only imagine how excited he is. I wish him well and force myself to think of how close he is to grasping his dream, and I summon every good thought like a crowd of people that have gathered in my mind. I'm still annoyed when Eugenica pushes her way through my crowd. My waves continue even when he is out of view. I don't want him to turn around and find me not interested.

Eventually my arm rests. "How do you mourn something that was never really yours?" I say aloud.

"Ah, disappointment." Martha nods. "It sneaks in like a weasel and takes what isn't even there."

"I just thought we'd always be together. It's a bit presumptuous, isn't it?"

Martha nods in the direction of the threshold where I last saw Thomas. "So, are you bound?"

"Bound? No." I shake my head. "That sounds awful, is it a punishment?"

"The binding brings two souls together. Are your souls together?"

"I thought they were." The emptiness inside me feels like a cavern. "I'd still like to think so."

"But you've not been bound?"

"If it's some kind of tradition, then no."

"No, no, it's not tradition," she says, dropping to her knees and tapping into the soil. "It's ancient. Traditions have their own ways of interpreting the sacred."

"If it's ancient, and there are no records, how do you know if you should be bound?"

"Sparks, my dear, sparks."

I nod at her, but the only pictures in my mind are of the sparks that never quite escape the fire, extinguished before they even get a chance to live, and I decide that this binding thing doesn't sound like such a good idea after all.

Martha looks up from her digging. "And would he choose you?"

I pretend I don't hear her because I have no wish to know the answer.

❦

We work either side of a trellis of climbing beans, weeding and checking on their growth and tying the straggly limbs to their frame. The breeze brings us the scents of the violets that grow along the far side of the garden, and when the wind rests, the morning sun presses us with its warmth. There never seems to be a rush when we work together. We talk occasionally, but we're fine in the silence too. It's the same companionable silence I used to share with Thomas. It reminds me of our closeness, where we didn't need words to communicate, just a sense of trust and knowing. Through the gaps in the plants Martha's soft hands till the soil. They're weathered with age and hard work and I consider things that are soft but hard and how one force inevitably creates the other. I'd love to talk about that with Thomas, but he won't be returning for a week at least. I missed him when we first arrived; I missed not being able to spend time together, and now I will miss even that small amount of care. I close my eyes and imagine his arms around me and his skin, then remember Martha is there and that I might not be alone with my thoughts.

"How did you know I was thinking about the containment of the Eariss yesterday?"

She glances at me through the vines and shows no expression. Her hands continue with her work. "I know things ... as you know things."

I let her words sit with me for a while, fearful of a trap, but desperately curious for some answers. I feel like that fawn at the lake, timid but so thirsty I'm prepared to expose myself. I remember how I'd urged the fawn to run and hide, worried that it was so defenseless. Deep inside, I know the answers are right here, so close I could touch them, and my mouth dries and my heart beats in my throat and ears.

I hold soil in my hand and swipe it across my fingers with my thumb. "How do you know what I know?" I say to my hands, too afraid to look at her.

"We are similar," she says and she shrugs, "... yet also different."

"Like the Eariss?" I whisper to the vines and she nods. "But Brenn said she'd never seen one."

"Only because you knew to keep yourself hidden." I can't see her face, but I catch glimpses of her smile through the leaves.

"Well, yes, I did, but—"

Martha stands, wipes her hands on her apron and looks over the fields. I follow her to the stone fence and she points towards the boundary. "The moment you walked under that threshold . . ." she says, and releases another of her long-held breaths, "it was like I'd waited forever." Her smile reminds me of Thomas's sneaky 'glad you're here' statements; warmth surrounds my heart and I don't feel like running anymore, as if hearing the words over and over has dulled my fear of them.

"You waited for me?"

"For a long time."

"How did you know I was coming?"

"I knew to wait, and that's what I did. And we'll stay here until we're told otherwise."

"So you're the Eariss too?"

She shakes her head. "I'm not the one everyone holds their breath for. I'm not the one with the message."

Message?

If I had a message for anyone it would be to stop holding their breath. "Can you tell me what I need to know?"

"It's my understanding," she says, as she takes my hand and leads me towards her hut, "that's why you're here."

Martha leads me to the seat beside the barrel next to her hut. She dips the ladle into the barrel, pours a cup of water and hands it to me.

"You might not like what you hear," she says.

I brace myself. I've spent my life not liking what I hear, and even worse, having to pretend I enjoy it, so I doubt I'll be shocked. "I'm prepared," I say and steel myself, but find the barriers I used in the Hall to protect myself have softened in some places my amour doesn't even exist. There is no way to deflect her words.

"The Eariss is the bridge between the known and the unknown. The messenger. The one that will teach the new way." She leans over me and taps onto my constricting chest. "That stirring in your heart, that's the truth making itself known." She grabs my hand and holds it to my chest. "Feel it. Feel it stir and know every detail of its completion. It's the truth you seek. All this time it has sought you, and now it has found you."

My chest and throat are so choked with emotion I can't move, let alone respond. I know what she says is true, just like when Maeve spoke that night in her home. And just like when Maeve spoke, the water in the cup I hold trembles in my hand. Why is this truth so comforting and powerful and yet so terrible and horrifying all at the same time? Sensations of delight and terror move through each part of my body, swirling and diluting themselves in each other so that a strange equilibrium settles me, as though I have been painted an entirely different color on the inside of my skin. The color turns to sound and my body hums the songs of the trees and settles into the steady rhythm of my heartbeat. Martha's face stays above me, her knowing smile offering protection and comfort at the times I am sure the world doesn't exist anymore.

"I promise to tell you all I know," she whispers, "but only you can decide who you are."

The singing starts again in the high lodge. Martha looks to it then back to me.

"Breathe slow and deep to recover," she says as she rubs my upper arm. "Just a little taste is good for now. Here." She pulls me to my feet and takes my hand. "Let us walk to the lodge together."

She collects the baskets of finishing herbs and leads me to the high lodge, encouraging me by saying that I will soon feel myself again and that it's perfectly fine to be still and speechless. There's comfort in knowing she has been to the place where I was, and that comfort so fills my mind there is room for nothing else.

By the time we reach the high lodge, the fog throughout my body has lifted and I'm capable of conversing with the servers, although I still feel like I've had too much ale. All I want to do is get back to the garden with Martha, but first I must sit through the most tedious of Brenn's lessons.

Brenn concludes the lesson with an announcement. She has created new roles within the men's section. She asks us to think of them as our shepherds watching over us, checking on us. She calls them herders and tells us they will wander the property to keep us safe now that she is expecting more contact with the outside world. They're friendly enough; they're just other members of the kinship, but to me they are another set of eyes and ears to be wary of.

She parades some men in front of us. A leather strap crosses their body much like Thomas's satchel crossed his, only theirs is wider and we're told to use this distinction to see them in the fields and ask them for assistance. I am aware of myself enough now to know I am reacting to the sight and memory of a uniform. It doesn't stop my heart from beating, but at least it allows me to understand why it beats so hard and to have compassion for my reactions. The others smile and nod and seem pleased for Brenn's care. I have seen this game play out many times in council and I am already weary and my heart weighted. I consider the herder's wide leather sash again. The only difference between theirs and the guards' is there are no holders for their weapons. Yet.

❦

A herder's presence near the garden just as we have settled into our work doesn't surprise me. Martha works by the hut and can't see him. I smile and nod at him, then rise in greeting.

"Thank you for your care," I say and pull a trailing vine back inside the walls. It will be best if he thinks we are playing the game, then his reports of the garden will be favorable. If I am honest, I don't want his feet to step inside these walls. I want to keep them out for as long as I can. Martha said she would tell me all she knew, and we need to be alone for that. With her help, I will study the legends for Thomas and from that, work out whether I believe I am the Eariss or not. Once the herder is far enough away that it would take him a while to return, I head towards the hut and sidle next to Martha as though she is a friend with a secret.

"Tell me what they say about the Eariss."

"There are many names used to describe your work," she begins. "The legends call you the gift with eyes of rainbows who leaves peace and surety wherever you lay your head." Martha tilts her head to watch my composure, but I have none to offer her yet. "The Eariss is said to know the deepest secrets of men but would never use it against them. Likewise, the power of the Eariss is respected and never misused."

I bite my bottom lip. There's no point mentioning the bird. Martha probably knows about it already or at the very least senses my trepidation. I hang onto it like a thread, evidence I'm not the Eariss after all. "But this message. I don't have a message."

"You do, you just haven't heard it yourself yet."

"But why me? Why can't someone else be the Eariss?"

Martha chuckles. "I don't make those decisions. I only do what I am compelled to do." She points her tiller at me. "Like wait for you. And perhaps if one day you do what you're compelled to do, the world will be brighter for it."

"But you said 'if.' Does that mean I don't have to? I don't have to be the Eariss?"

"The decision is always yours."

Instead of my strength falling away, I feel it coming back to me, like the waves at Ferce Point. I get to make the decision. Somehow the idea of decision-making feels foreign, and I try to think back about whether I've actually made a decision before. I always seem to be reacting and running. Situations forced themselves upon me. There was no choice in the way we landed in the valley, or how we were carted into Sirban as Guthrie's wares. What an awful thought—to be simply tossed around. But at the same time, Martha says she's been waiting. Perhaps it's not being tossed around, it's being guided. And if I consider that I'm guided, by the Mystery, I suppose, then lying underneath all my overgrown fears and beliefs there must be a path. Did I decide to stay and join Maeve and Galen for a meal at their house, or was I forced...

I mean *guided* by hunger and convenience? The moment I stood and spoke in the Hall wasn't for my benefit; it wasn't even my decision, was it? The Hall. It must only be three moons since I left, but it feels like three lifetimes.

"If I'm a gift, why didn't they want me at the Hall?"

"Fear makes men do crazy things. Can you imagine how afraid they are of a legend that wields incredible power?"

My mind shows me Feeney, the lord and the elders all wrapped in robes, screaming in fear at their loss of power but still tightly holding the robes as if they would save them. The robes are so thick I can't see a way through them.

"Men will always seek to destroy what they do not understand, because what they do not understand they cannot control. Don't feel condemned because they couldn't see you. They are far too scared to see anything, and are using violence because they are completely blind. Your power is contained in you understanding who you are—and they must keep you from that at all costs."

"But the things they did. The things they made me do—"

"Your story, the one that brought you to this very moment, is unique. It does no good to hide it, embellish it or change it. Accept it, all of it, not just the parts that make you smile, the parts you enjoy talking about." She pulls at some leaves and spreads them across her hand in front of me. "Look at these herbs. If you dilute their strength, you won't receive all the power of their healing properties. You must take the whole of the plant, all that it offers, to be well. In the same way, you must take all of your life, channel its power. When you pick and choose and hold the whole back, no healing, or perhaps less healing, will occur."

"Healing?"

"You are the healer, and there is great agitation." She nods gently at me. "I know you feel it. We need the Eariss more than ever. You will touch raw wounds and they will hate you for it."

I don't feel very much like a healer, and I don't want to go around prodding wounds and causing people pain.

"Remember the power hidden in the herbs." She holds out a collection of different- shaped leaves, some old and dry, others fresh and new. "Take no care for the power's form, whether it is dirty, clean, large or small, accepted or shamed." She taps into my chest. "It remains here within you and is unchangeable. You can cover it, hide it, deny it and run from it, even drown it in the busyness of the Traditions. It remains there, unchangeable as the day you were born. It is your essence and your call. You must find it and take hold of it; it is your power."

I understand.

If only because the Mystery had used apple seeds to try and teach me the same message.

T he earth in the next section of the garden is almost ready for sowing. It's tender and crumbly and the small weeds release with ease, almost as if they were waiting their turn to be taken. Martha works next to me turning and preparing the soil, and I pluck several more weeds without any exertion. Is it my strength that makes this so easy? Or is it that the soil is ready to give the weeds up, and any power I have means nothing at all?

"Martha, what about my eyes? Thomas says lights appear from them."

"This is what the legends tell us."

"What are they for if I can't control them? If I can't use them?"

"This is where you're mistaken. They are a sign, not a power."

"A sign of what?"

"Times of injustice. When you fear there's nothing left of you, it's what remains. It speaks on your behalf."

"Times of injustice?" I think about the bandits, the attack, the peasant at the Hall. "Then why didn't this power arrive to save me at the Hall?"

Martha stops her work and draws a breath. Her hand holds mine as she speaks. "Because the Hall made you believe you *deserved* that treatment . . . ." She moves her hand to cup my face. " . . . To you . . . there was no injustice."

T homas comes and goes with the weeks that pass, bringing news of the outside world to the kinship and silver for Brenn. He seems more grown up each time I see him, more of a merchant, and each time a little bit more like a stranger. He wears the full cream clothes of the Sirbahn now, and this change would have more to do with his relationship with Guthrie and the library than anything to do with Brenn's ambitious trade. My heart leaps into my throat each time I see his cart approach, but Brenn now keeps as watchful an eye on Thomas's movements as I do, so I resign myself to my own studies.

From sunrise to the singing in the lodge Martha shares her knowledge about plants and herbs with me, and when there are no herders, she teaches me about the Eariss. I learn about teas, tinctures and poultices, and the loosening of tightened muscles that fight against their overuse. The fight and tension within me goes too, and even though I don't baulk as much at her words, something within me still needs convincing I'm the Eariss, as if there's some invisible line I can't step over.

The lessons Brenn teaches in the high lodge add to what I learned in the forest and continually feed me a light broth, but Martha's teachings nourish and fill me to the brim. Her words form a heartier meal for my soul, and I've never felt so hungry in my life. Lessons appear everywhere in her garden, the sky and the forest and she never misses an opportunity to show them to me. Just like the herbs and plants that grow strong within the walled garden, I grow too, and relieve Martha of some of her roles within the kinship, not just the delivery of the herbs to the main lodge but suggestions for their use, both culinary and medicinally.

"Ugh, you're so much nicer to deal with than the crone," they say.

And I smile towards them and think how much nicer the crone is to deal with than them.

⁕⁕⁕

"They need more sage," I call to Martha as I enter the walled garden. I turn full circle to loop the rope over the taller post of the gate, as it has become our custom to surreptitiously check for the presence of any herders before we are caught speaking out of turn. They're not usually around first thing in the morning, but we check all the time now.

"I'm down here." Martha's voice is hidden by some overgrown plants at the end of the garden and she rises as I move closer.

Plants crunch beneath my feet, crushed onto one of the few stones on the path, hidden under the overhang of stems and leaves on the path. I jump back, horrified at the crush of small flowers and stems running between the flagstones. "I'm sorry, I didn't see them."

"Never apologize for that," Martha says, coming towards me. "It's my favorite thing to do." Her foot lands with a stomp on top of the plants. "See? The more crushed they are, the stronger they grow."

"Isn't that a bit odd? That they get their strength from being stifled?"

Martha holds some crushed stems to her nose, then offers them to mine. They smell fresh and lively, as if they hold much more than you might expect from such a dainty-looking flower. "Chamomyle," she says, wagging them in front of me like she does with her finger when making a point. "Their sweetness only releases when under pressure too." She points with the broken stems to this overgrown section of the garden. "I let it grow wild to remind me not all things can be tamed and will spread where you least expect it." She plucks several of the white flower heads and beckons me to follow her to the hut. "And," she says as she walks, "it makes a nice tea too. Which reminds me . . . "

Martha collects a wooden box from her hut and adds the flower heads to it then comes closer to me and opens its hinged lid. Different smells come out to tantalize, intrigue and assault me. Inside, it is split into many squared compartments, each filled with dried herbs ready for her wishes. Some are recognizable straight away, others are already ground into powders or chopped into smaller leaves.

"These ones here." She taps one section of the box, and the tiny seeds inside it bounce around on the crushed powder as if they'd been only half ground. "Flax. Brenn has a brew made fresh for her in the high lodge each morning, and then you must be sure she has access to her pot."

I scrunch up my face. I hope Brenn doesn't make Martha wait around to empty the pot too.

"Yes, she's a stubborn one." Martha chuckles. "It seems she can't let anything go."

I smile, not sure if I'm amused by her jest or her feeble attempt at nastiness; she doesn't do nasty very well at all.

Martha hands me the box. "From thence, you shall make the tea for Brenn," she says, and my smile disappears. "Oh, and add a bit of sweetness; it helps with her demeanor."

Martha walks back into the overgrown garden and I know that deep inside that heart of hers she is giggling at me and my new dilemma.

I call after her, "While I steep her tea shall I make one for you too?"

"Thank you, but no, I don't drink tea here."

I walk through the garden and move my hands around the large box, trying to find the best grip, and stop short. I turn and speak to the tops of the taller plants in the distance that rustle above Martha's hands. "What's the ark?"

"Ark?"

"Ark of Eariss? Thomas and I were hoping to find it."

"Where did you hear of this ark?"

"There was an attack—the guards mentioned it—perhaps it has some answers?"

Martha emerges from within the plants, her smile warm, her hands brushing on her apron. "Oh, my dear child, it's not the Ark of the Eariss you need to search for, it's *Arco Eariss*—and it's your name. You are the arch they speak of. The bridge. You live with a foot in each world." Even from that distance I feel her study my face. "Do you see it now?" she asks.

My mind replays how I told Thomas about the ark and how desperately I wanted to find it so it would take the Eariss away from me. Right now, if some magical ark appeared I'm not sure whether I would be happy to release my hold on the legend. Martha waits for my answer, but I don't have one. I unloop the gate and walk my path to the high lodge.

⚘

After Brenn's tea, I walk the sheep track and discard the tension from the high lodge on my way to the garden. I feel relief as I move closer to its walls, as if it reaches out to me before I even step inside. As safe as I have ever felt inside Thomas's arms.

Martha must have watched me turn my full circle because she exclaims, "Ah, my little warrior," as I loop the gate closed.

Stick armies come to mind and I chuckle at her absurdity. "I'm a warrior now?"

"Here, here," she beckons me to her with enthusiasm. "I have a lesson for you. One you are sure to understand." Once I am closer to her she slides her arm through mine and points upwards. The clouds above us are mottled and lay like dirty linen stretched across the sky. In the distance a deeper gray begins its spread towards us. The air is still, but the wind will soon be here. We watch their slow movement in silence together as the sheets of clouds blend and position themselves. A refreshing and gentle breeze brushes past us, a forerunner of the experience to come, and I shiver even though it is not cold.

"The rain will be good for the garden," I say as I watch the clouds. "It's part of the turning wheel you told me about."

"And what happens when you deny a turn of the wheel?"

"Nothing is balanced. Everything gets ill."

"I want you to imagine a magical garden," she begins. "One much larger than ours."

I nod so she knows I am listening.

"In the center of the garden lives a huge aloe. Its leaves spread thick and wide. Around it, and in fact under it, the other herbs and flowers are dry and dusty for lack of rain. Some get used to the dryness, some dare to complain, but the aloe declares everything is as it should be. Because the aloe is so old and strong, and courageous, beautiful and magnificent without rain, they believe it contains the secrets to help them overcome their desperation and weakness. What they don't understand is the aloe is desperate for rain too. The aloe brags about how its power keeps the terrifying storms away, how it keeps the garden safe. The dry and dusty plants speak only of how the bright sunshine is good for the garden and remind each other to be grateful to live in such a wonderful place."

She squeezes my arm in hers. "But you, you are like a raincloud that the aloe can never keep away. When you rain, you will wash away the dust and the filth that stops them from seeing who they are. They need the rain, they need the rainstorm, they're just scared of it."

I squeeze her arm in return. "Martha, you make me laugh," I say, but my giggle is filled with nerves. "So now I'm a warrior raincloud?"

Martha releases my arm, hurt that I have dismissed her lesson. "You will stand as a warrior. And there will be unstable weather, and I dare say, there will be a storm."

I wake unsure of myself and toss and turn on my mat in the half light, pictures of gardens and storms in my head.

Ah, my little warrior.

By the Stars, her brain's befuddled her. I'm no more a warrior than Feeney has a tender heart. My only battle strategy consists of silence, running and hiding. I doubt any of those things will win any wars. I turn again on my mat and surrender any possibility of returning to sleep as Martha's words run through my mind again.

"Ah yes, but warriors are made of courage. They step beyond their fear for what they know to be true and worth the fight. They come in all sizes and forms; you don't have to be physically present in the battle to be a warrior in the midst of it."

Wide-eyed, I shake my head in defiance.

I don't want to be a warrior at all. *Ever.*

I wish Thomas was here. I'd ask him if he thought I was a warrior. I might even get an answer out of him once he'd stopped laughing. The thought of his laugh stretches a smile across my lips that disappears almost as quickly as it came. He wouldn't be my ally; he'd side with Martha and be of no help at all. The morning outside brightens with each passing moment and I tilt my head to watch it lighten the hole in the wall above me.

Thomas is expected in the kinship today with news and wares.

And would he choose you?

Martha's words come back to me like a rebuke. The Mystery has apprenticed him straight into the arms of another. One with status and beauty and a heart that is far more stable than mine. I roll my body away from the light and pull the blanket over my head and curled form. Why would he want to be bound to me anyway? Who'd want to be bound to all this pain and these ridiculous delusions? All I have to offer him is an uncertain future and an unproven ability to turn into a warrior at short notice.

Shrieks slice through the quiet of the morning air and all the women of the lodge are on their feet. I follow their panicked dressing.

A girl bursts through the door and flattens her back against the wall. "It's Abigayl!" she tells the worried women.

Some gasp, some nod, but no one moves as Abigayl's cries continue outside. I move towards the door still tying the sides of my smock, but the women block me.

One shakes her head. "You can't go out there."

"Doesn't she need our help?" I hear more voices outside, jeering, accusing.

"No, she *needs* us to stay in here."

Abigayl's cries soften to sobs and the women stand firm, creating a wall around me.

"She hasn't been here long enough to see a cleansing," one whispers.

Cleansing?

One of the older women steps inside the circle and pats my shoulder. "It's obvious that Abigayl wasn't truly called, otherwise Brenn wouldn't have called for the cleansing."

"The what?"

"The kinship must be kept true," she says, but the only thing obvious is that these are not her own words. "When those who would deceive us are found, their treachery must be publicly displayed."

Abigayl's sobs are softer now. "What are they doing to her?"

"She will be unclothed and bound so there is nowhere for her deceit to hide, and then cleansed with waters to help her on her new path. In a silent ritual; she will be shown the importance of being true to the kinship. That truthfulness secures her place here."

"Why aren't we out there with her?"

"She wouldn't want us to see her in her shame. It's the kindest thing to do."

The women nod, desperate for me to believe their honorable tale.

"I see."

My words of acceptance release them from their circle around me but several stay at the door. Like the others, I return to tidy my pallet bed, but once there, I scrunch the blanket to my eyes and I try not to think of Abigayl, stripped naked and doused with cold water, shunned and expelled from the kinship to fend for herself in the valley.

⚜

The gate loops closed and I'm thankful to be back in the garden after lessons in the high lodge. The walls that protect the younger plants from the wind also block the cooling breezes on warm days like today and I tend to some weaker seedlings. Then I check on the mint, deciding which plants I'll harvest later in the day.

When Thomas's cart rolls under the threshold, my heart fills as if someone had poured a bucket of water into it. I hadn't even noticed it was empty. His face turns towards the garden and I know he sees me. It's painful not acknowledging each other with happy waves like we used to, but we've learned to not draw Brenn's attention. We have more chance of finding time together if she is not watching out for us and demanding duties that keep us apart the entire time he is here.

Brenn watches from the high lodge as the cart bows and scrapes towards her, bringing silver and prestige. Thomas will leave with the kinship's produce early the next morning, but not before Brenn has exhausted him with her thirst for attention and information. Herders meet the cart in front of the high lodge, unhitch the donkey and force him into a nearby field. Thomas's form hesitates and draws a deep breath before he follows Brenn into the lodge.

Later in the afternoon, I make an early delivery to the kitchen and pull vegetables from the basket, laying them on the table for the cook. The extra vegetables I harvested hide neatly under my smock. The donkey is as pleased to see me and my vegetables as I am to see him, but Thomas is nowhere to be seen. She will be keeping him until evening meal, I'm sure.

"And that means," I whisper to the donkey, "we might only get the tiniest of time together." I pinch my fingers together so the donkey can see how minuscule it will be. "Somewhere between after the evening meal and when the herders find us."

❧⟐☙

T homas sits next to Brenn at the high table. He forces a smile and nods when she talks to him, which is every moment she doesn't have a spoon in her mouth. How miserable to be an honored guest at a tasteless meal. His smile stretches and falls in time with the rising of her spoon and his sadness is palpable. He has the strange status of being an outsider now. He's kin, but not quite. Similar, I suppose, to how Martha explained me having a foot in both worlds. We're a lodge apart yet we sigh in unison. If he's treated as an outsider here among his kin, how do the Sirbahn view him? Brenn requires him to frequently leave their mountaintop, and because of this, they'd never consider him Sirbahn. We both have no home. Having no home means we have freedom. But free is the last thing I feel right now. We make eye contact and agree to meet at the tree.

At the second gong the kinship stands and we chant in thanks for our meal. The herders now stand at the door and guide us back to our lodges after meals. I delay my departure by speaking with a server about herbs and follow her back to the kitchen. From there I escape through the door when she turns her back and make my way to the tree. I almost leap into Thomas's arms.

"Come," he whispers and takes my hand, crouching down and leading me away into the dark.

The fields that rise behind the high lodge have recently been harvested and stubble rises and falls in uneven patches where the scythe has been swung. I can't imagine trying to harvest on a slope. We lay together under the night sky, the smell of freshly cut stalks and disturbed earth scenting the moment as if it was anointed with the finest oils. Below us, the torchlight outside the high lodge shows the shadows of the herders mingling and talking but it won't be long before they notice we are missing. Perhaps it's because we both have one foot in two worlds that we're also prepared to split this moment into two, kissing and comforting each other while we talk at the same time. If it was daylight I'm sure Thomas would be taking notes and I wouldn't be offended.

He begins with the questions he always asks of me first. "Are you well? Are you safe?"

"I am."

"I've started on your book."

"You have? You mean *your* book."

"'No, it's yours. Guthrie even lectured me on its frivolity—I had to tell him I was writing about legends but other than that, he leaves me mostly in peace."

I smile, thankful I wasn't there for the lecture.

"Is your Martha well?"

I pull away from him. It feels awkward to be discussing Martha while we kiss but I push the thought away. We don't have the luxury of time for awkwardness. "Yes, she is. She's training me to teach the nurses."

"The ones Brenn sends out to the villages?"

"In outbreaks and illnesses. Martha teaches me about the herbs when the herders are around, but when we are alone, she teaches me about the Eariss."

Thomas stops kissing me. "Will she talk to me?"

"I can ask her, but we'll have to watch for herders."

"Speaking of herders . . . "

The torches that stand around the high lodge splinter and move in groups away from the lodge. We have been missed. I follow Thomas through the dark, crouched low as before, until we arrive on the far side of the high lodge and take refuge behind his cart as a group of herders appear.

"Well met, gentlemen," Thomas calls to them as he moves towards the donkey in the field. "What a fine night we have. Will you join me in tending to my ass? You may kiss it if you prefer."

Silence. *Oh Stars, Thomas. No!*

The quiet night rings with the guffaws of the herders. Rather than take offense they join in his jest with their own humorous quips, and Thomas makes sure to laugh heartily and round them up like a shepherd with some well-placed back slaps that lead them further away from the cart. My lodge is only a short distance away. I can make it in a quick sprint. Something hanging from the cart catches my eye and I rub the small favor between my fingers. It's been tied carefully to the reins so it remains in his sight. A red ribbon to remind him of home. I remind myself it is tied to the cart—perhaps the cart is all she's laying claim to.

❧⁂☙

I n the garden the next morning, my heart leaps into my throat when I turn and see Thomas standing at the gate, his satchel stretched across his chest as I remembered it on our travels. I step towards him.

"No," he says without moving in the slightest. "We are watched. I turned a herder away too. Told him I was picking fresh herbs for my return to Sirban and I wouldn't require his help."

I place my bodyweight on the other foot so I might gently look past him. Brenn stands at the high lodge, watching.

"Will Martha speak with me?" he asks.

Martha barges past me and unloops the gate. "Of course she will, young scribe."

I'm still rooted to the spot as she takes him by the arm and barges past again, this time with Thomas lifting his hands into a shrug.

Martha leads him to an open part of the garden, a place where she knows Brenn can easily observe them, and they crouch down and pretend to harvest the herbs that I collect on their behalf.

"I've heard you are an exceptional teacher," Thomas begins.

"Enough talk. Did you bring parchment?"

"Well, ah, yes," Thomas replies, reaching into his satchel. He produces burnt sticks for marking the paper.

"Good," she says. "In this garden we call the lessons from the high lodge, the things we believe that don't really cost us anything, the roots of the plant. The lessons of the Eariss are like the leaves and flowers of the herbs that provide evidence and healing." Martha tilts her head to look at his marks. "Are you writing this down?"

"Yes, yes. All of it." Thomas nods.

She seems satisfied but frowns before she continues. "As the summers passed, the kinship placed more and more emphasis on the roots, less on the leaves. It did make the plant stronger, and it stood tall, but so very, very rigid. Brenn created new rules and inserted them in the root structure and soon there was no movement at all. You know what doesn't work with rigidity and limits?"

Thomas simply shakes his head.

"Leaves, my dear scribe, leaves."

They both stop and face me and I hurriedly return to harvesting as Martha continues. "When the roots become intertwined and tangled they end up strangling the plant. Then there is no hope for the leaves."

Thomas gently holds a spray in his hand. "Why don't the roots like the leaves? Surely in these herbs the leaves are like the crowning glory and give it life and beauty?"

"The roots of a broken plant don't like the attention given to leaves. They demand all power be given to them. The leaves are in the light, the roots are hidden and controlling. Every village is now like a broken plant with its identity too close to the roots. They won't let leaves flourish even though the leaves provide the nourishment for the roots."

Thomas continues writing as I approach them, hiding the basket of herbs against my body. He speaks to me with the strongest conviction I have heard. "You were right to remain hidden, your place to unfurl isn't here. Everywhere we go is tangled in its own importance. Especially here. This place is root bound."

Martha raises her hands in the air and laughs.

Thomas takes notes and I kneel next to him and gently touch his hand as he writes. He's so proud of himself, and my heart swells with all he has learned and in many ways for what I have learned too. We're still working together, even if we are apart. Martha waits for him to finish and pushes our hands together, enveloping them in hers and squeezing them so tight I swear I feel the hum of the trees between them. Thomas stands, and for Brenn's benefit bows to Martha and to me. He takes the basket from my hands and he is gone again.

My knees ache like they've fused shut into this position as I kneel to tend a small patch of marigolds that have sprouted near the side of Martha's hut. Her voice drones in the background and if I try hard enough I can ignore her just like I do with the other buzzing and annoying insects on this warm day.

I screw my nose up against the marigold's scent. The heat releases its perfume into the air and straight into my nostrils.

Perspiration slides down my temple. This weed won't loosen itself from the soil.

I understand she's trying to fill my head with knowledge, but I'm terrified of what lays ahead.

I can't be the Eariss if I'm scared of myself, can I?

Let go, you stupid weed!

The sound of a passing bee covers Martha's nattering.

These marigolds stink. How can Eshnae have spoken of them as though they were dear to her?

Stars, my knees ache, and this heat, I can't breathe. I try to draw air into my lungs but I can't seem to catch my breath.

"Look what I've done to you." That's what Eshnae said.

A wave of heat forces the marigold's essence into my body.

I groan as I tug on the weed. What had I done to *her*?

Martha's voice drones above the bugs and the thumping in my chest sounds through my body. Bile creeps up my throat and my ears become muffled, deafened by the heat and the sound of my heart.

How am I supposed to calm the unrest if I can't even calm my own heart?

Still she natters. Perspiration drips and my heart thumps into my throat as if it's in a race with the bile.

"Are you listening to me?" she demands.

I leap to my feet, my growl drowning out the pain that smashes through my stretched-out knees. "Enough rabble, Martha!" I force myself to ignore the pained look on her face. "I don't want to be your bridge or your leaf or your storm or your anything! Hold that wretched tongue of yours!"

I flee from Martha and the garden and have barely left the safety of its walls when I run straight into a herder who takes me by my upper arms. His fingers dig into my flesh and I raise my arms up between his, just as Thomas had taught me, and smash them down, releasing his grip on me. "Don't!" I shout into his face. A silent moment passes. We are both so dumbfounded by my behavior that we stare at each other until I remember to run and he remembers to make a poor attempt to catch me. As if sent by the Mystery itself, Thomas's cart rolls under the threshold. My feet fly across the field towards him, the grasses beneath my feet rush past in a blur of swirling greens and I ignore any stumbles and twists of my feet.

The run across the field draws all the air from my lungs and I stop just short of the road, drained and gasping but calmer, knowing his presence will comfort me. My chest heaves and I frown as Thomas takes Eugenica's hand and helps her down from the cart. Eugenica tilts her head as she sees me, pulls a ribbon from her hair and smiles as she ties it to his wrist and leads him away. My chest crushes me like a large weight has been thrown on top of it and I fight myself for air, taking a gulp just as Thomas turns and calls out to me, "I tried to warn you, believe me. I tried to get a message to you but—"

"What are you talking about?"

Then the carts arrive, one after the other. I can't believe what I am seeing.

There is nothing around me. The sensation of exposure and nakedness so overwhelm me that I hug my arms around and over my body, hoping to find some kind of shield somewhere. My legs seem to act of their own accord, following the pattern they know well, and run back through the field. Martha meets me along the way, having trotted down through the field after me.

"She lets the outsiders in now?" I shout at her as I approach.

"Look how your smock and headdress covers you. You are still safe."

"Nothing is safe! It's all gone!" I shout as I get closer, my gaze fixed on the forest on the other side of the field. "No safety, no Thomas, there's no place for me here. There's nothing to hang on to!"

Martha grabs my arm as I pass and pulls me off balance. "And that is it!" she shouts for emphasis. "Who are you when there *is* nothing? Tell me that?"

I wrench my arm away from her, unable to tell her anything.

"The answer," she calls as I run, "can only come from you."

I'm shocked and scared and vulnerable and hurt and—running.

⁂

M y run slows once I'm hidden under the canopy of the forest. Even the cooler air helps calm my thoughts and I make plans to find a quiet place to sit, a tranquil place where I might soothe myself enough to call on the Mystery. I trip on a root and land face first in the dirt. I don't even complain. It's where I stay.

I stay with my cheek pressed against the mud and wet leaves that stick to my face as thoughts pass in and out of my mind. There's only a slight breeze on the forest floor, but sweet smells of decaying wood mix with fresher air that hints of a blossom somewhere in the distance, and my thoughts continue to pass through my mind just like the scents pass through on the wind. Light splashes onto my eyes as branches above me move and, apart from the occasional squint in response, my body barely moves, as heavy as the earth beneath it and breathing in the same rhythm. It's only when I have surrendered to this moment that the Mystery speaks.

It's time to grow past this reaction.

I know.

What do you want to do?

Be brave.

How do you imagine you'd do that?

Stop running...but I'm so scared.

Of what?

I don't even know anymore.

Seems you have a choice.

Run or stand.

You can run blindly through a forest, you can stand to walk through fire. Either way, I am there.

At some point I've got to stop running.

True. Only you can decide when that will be.

It will be today.

Go back when you are ready. And I will go with you.

❦

I enter the walled garden in time to begin gathering the herbs for the mid meal. My basket waits for me on its stool beside the gate. Below it are the jars we keep close to the herbs when making syrups and tinctures. The many carts are still in the lower field. I'll pick more to cover for our visitors. Martha stops her work for a moment when she hears me enter but doesn't turn. My basket is lined with herbs when she finally speaks.

"My heart is glad," she says as she works. "See? You're braver than you think."

I'm still not quite myself, and I don't respond.

"Shall we talk?" she asks

"Later, dear Martha."

"Of course."

M artha assures me for the hundredth time that my head-covering is fine and that my uniform protects me as we walk the sheep track to the high lodge for mid meal and lessons. As we enter the lodge I seek out the herder I yelled at this morning with hopes that a sincere apology might avoid any further repercussions.

"Please forgive me for my behavior and for speaking to you so terribly this morning."

He winks and pinches my cheek between his thumb and finger, shaking it so hard it hurts. "Come see me if you need an escape. Can't imagine you get much fun with that stupid old crone watching over you." My body shivers from the point of his touch right through to my feet.

The high lodge feels like it's filled with outsiders even though they're outnumbered by those in uniform. I'd already expected Brenn's announcement about no lessons after the meal. Her sales of the valley's produce have increased her appetite for silver and the outsiders are invited to experience what the kinship can offer. Naturally, we are required to provide the entertainment.

Brenn stands at the high table, the outsiders seated beside her, as she boasts about the Sirbahn's use of her medicinal herbs and how the kinship's nurses can provide the best knowledge and care. Brenn's nurses don't necessarily have to be well trained; they do know some basic healing methods, but it's more common for people to be almost dead before a nurse is called. I expect they're hired to provide comfort in final days more than for healing or nursing skills.

The nurses stand in rows as men with portly bellies and sacks of silver tied to their belts make arrangements with Brenn for their services. Others gather around Thomas and discuss business and orders for herbs and other produce from the kinship. I manage to avoid all contact with him and slip away with Martha to walk the sheep track as soon as we can.

"I'm not sure I can face him ever again," I say.

"He searched for you among the crowd. You didn't see it?"

"He wears her ribbon."

"You said she placed it on his wrist. He didn't ask for it."

"If it's as you say, he could always take it off and return it to her. Can't you see that she is everything I am not?"

Martha nods. "I can. I'm sure he does too. But there are other things to see here too. Do you not see the position Brenn has him in? That young scribe's intention has only even been for your safety. You being here. Brenn keeps you safe, and if that means he must keep the wealthy of Sirban happy for Brenn's sake, be sure that he will do it."

I ponder her words. I've only ever reacted to Eugenica's behavior, not his. I reacted to being alone in the field, to being exposed, found out. Betrayed. I think about the fear robes I told Thomas about. I've been hiding myself under them again. I shake my head. "I seem to spend more time going backwards than forwards, Martha."

"You were scared and you rushed backwards. You know backwards, it's comforting. We can always find excuses to go backwards when we're afraid of going forwards."

I unloop the garden gate and hold it open for Martha to enter. "Does this ever end, this backwards and forwards?"

"Backwards and forwards is like a saw through a branch, but it's the only way to cut the dead wood free. You'll become more skilled at it—your muscles will grow stronger against the fear and you'll find being honest with yourself sharpens the saw and makes the lopping easier. Having less defenses, like the tough bark of stubbornness, doesn't make it any less painful." She tilts her head as she thinks. "But maybe it passes quicker."

The thought of a saw blade makes my body tense. Why does everything have to involve so much pain and losing things? Hope being wrenched away from us whenever it dares to lift its head? I think back to the Hall—the same nothingness I felt in the field was present when the cobblestones turned to blood and my hands start feverishly rubbing on my smock. They heat up to burning and only stop when Martha walks to me, takes them one by one and places them on the basket in front of me.

"Tell me about the marigolds," she says as she leads me through the garden. "Your backward journey started before Thomas arrived."

"I had a friend once. I think she was what you might call a friend." My memories of Eshnae when I was a young child return and I can't help the smile on my face. "She loved marigolds."

"Is that why you planted the marigolds next to my hut?"

"I didn't plant them. I thought you did."

Martha shrugs. "Things sometimes arrive in the garden unannounced... but not unneeded."

"I behaved badly," I say and sit on the ground, pulling at the heads of the herbs I've collected.

"Toward your friend?"

"Yes, but it's a secret."

"And why is it a secret?"

"Because I'm sure you wouldn't think much of me if you knew what I did."

"It seems the marigolds know your secret, and they still bloomed for you."

Further down the path the little marigolds bounce in the breeze under the weight of their orange heads. In my chest the secret threatens to bloom whether I want it to or not. I close my eyes, thinking if I don't see her reaction it won't hurt as much to tell her. "The secret is . . . my friend . . . I killed her."

Silence. I dare to open my eyes. Martha stares at me, stunned. *She'll banish me from the garden! What have I done?*

Martha rises and wipes her hand on her apron and sighs deeply. "Oh dear," she says. "We need tea." She doesn't even look back as she makes her way to the hut.

"But you don't drink tea," I call after her.

"Today," she calls to the sky, "today, I will make an exception."

❧

T he cup Martha hands me is hot to the touch and I push my hands closer into it.

Burn!

After a while I don't even feel its heat anymore. The inside of Martha's hut contains bunches of dried herbs that hang around her small mat, a table for her work and some tools. My dark mood is grateful there's only a small window for the light to enter. Before I sit, I move the stool she gestured for me to sit on away from the window. Martha sits on her mat and places her cup of steaming chamomyle tea onto the stone floor.

"Tell me about your friend. She had a name?"

"Eshnae."

"Lovely."

I can smell those disgusting marigolds wafting through the open door. "I killed her."

"How did you manage that?"

"I behaved badly and she was punished for my error."

"I see. Was that your intention?"

"Never! But I should have known better. It happened often enough."

"It wasn't your hands that ended her life?"

I shake my head. "But I caused them to be laid on her."

Martha rises from her mat and runs her hand across my shoulder as she passes. "No, you didn't."

I turn on the stool to follow her. I thought I was being clear. How could she not understand my words? "If I had behaved correctly, she would be alive this moment."

"Lies!" She turns on me so quickly my body jumps on the stool. "If those hands had not touched her, she would be alive this moment!"

I frown, trying to make sense of her statement. "No." I shake my head. "It was my fault, if I—"

"Watch this." Martha pours tea from her cup onto the stone floor. A pool of dark shadow spreads where the liquid soaks into the flagstone at her feet. "Whose hand tipped that cup of tea?"

"Yours."

"Now ask me to tip it again."

I raise an eyebrow and she nods encouragement. I shrug. "Tip your tea onto the floor, Martha."

Martha's hand begins to tip the tea but stops just as the liquid reaches the rim of the cup. She sloshes the tea back into the cup and watches my face as she *almost* tips it again, then exaggerates her moves, pretends to toss it over my head, passes it behind her back and holds it close to my face as she leans over me. "Whose hand controls this cup?" she asks me.

"Yours."

"And whose mind controls this hand?"

"Yours."

"Are you sure *you* don't? Because that is exactly what you're suggesting when you declare that you caused another's behavior."

My mouth opens to speak but no sound comes out. I can understand what she's saying, and the next moment I can't. The old thought feels familiar. Then it all makes sense, then it doesn't. It feels like the backwards and forwards motion of the saw blade again.

"Stay and finish your tea," Martha says as she pats my shoulder. "I'm going back to the garden."

<hr />

Before long, I join Martha in the garden and she lifts her head from a row of radishes as I come closer. "Does your mouth work now?" she says.

I smile. "Yes, it does, Martha."

"Good," she says. "You will need to use it more."

"I will?"

"Those thoughts you have. The ones that run loose all over your mind, causing you pain— how do you know if they need correction if you don't let others know what you're thinking?"

"My thoughts are my own. They keep me safe." My mantra from the Hall returns and I feel bound in chains.

Martha gazes over the garden and pats my arm. "In a safe place, your thoughts can be tended. The healthy ones can bloom and the weeds can be pulled."

I look over the garden too. The row of beans stand tall against their trellis and the rosemary that grew after much coaxing is almost as high as the stone wall. In the other direction, gourd vines balance along their section of the wall like performers on a wire. Their wide leaves bounce in the wind and I catch a glimpse of a herder on the sheep track but refuse to let the thought of him tarnish my moment. This is my safe place. What a dramatic difference from the Hall. There must be safe places everywhere.

"How do I know when a place is safe for me?"

"You'll feel it."

I already know about feelings and people and places, such as when Brenn's not happy and how the herders have grown to feel entitled to take whatever and whomever they please. I feel the Mystery when it flows through my body and teaches me things I can't even begin to explain, even to Martha. I feel happiest when I see Thomas, and grateful when I'm with Martha. I don't remember feeling much at the Hall, but when I think about my feelings they bob like fallen leaves floating on a river, dipping up and down on the ripples. If I think about them for too long, the river becomes deep and dark. When my feelings drop into the darkness I force them back up to the yellow leaves on the surface. Something keeps drawing me to the depths of the river and each time it takes more of my energy to keep my mind on the leaves and my heart feels like it is cold and sinking.

A shout makes me jump.

"Crone!" The herder unloops the gate and enters the garden. "Brenn wants the outsiders to have tea. Now."

I stand between him and Martha. "I'll collect what Brenn requires and take it to her immediately."

The herder smiles. It's the same man that pinched me earlier. He follows me to Martha's hut and watches as I collect the large wooden box from the shelf. I turn to find him upon me and I step back against the wall and brace myself for another pinch, but instead of grabbing my cheek he strokes my face with his hand and lets it fall over my arm and down to my waist. I shiver and my stomach turns.

He leans in to me as he takes the box in his hands. "I'll take this up to the high lodge, and the servers can make her tea. You stay right here," he says. "Right here so I know where to find you."

I force a smile onto my trembling lips. "Here," I say opening the lid. "These herbs here will make you . . . healthy." I know they're only supposed to be for Brenn, but I direct his attention to the little square of half-crushed seeds.

He chuckles and nudges me off balance. "Like 'em strong, do you?"

I'm not sure how to answer his question so I make sure he knows which is the best tea to create a moment he will be unlikely to forget. The tiny seeds bounce on top of the half-crushed flax as I point it out.

"I'll be sure to make extra." He winks at me as he leaves the hut and stomps his way out of the garden.

Martha kneels over some herbs near the hut and I stand next to her form and watch the awful man striding his way along the sheep track.

"Oh Stars, Martha," I say and bring my hand to my mouth. "What have I done?"

There is silence for the shortest moment before Martha cackles like a chicken and rolls into the garden holding her sides as she laughs.

"You heard what I told him?" I join her on the ground as tears stream down her cheeks and our laughter bounces around within the walls of the garden. We end up lying side by side in a bed of herbs watching the clouds pass in the sky and chuckling the last of our humor away.

Once we are composed again my worries return. "Won't he return once he's feeling better? By late morning tomorrow, I expect."

Martha pats my hand. "But we won't be here in the morning."

"We won't?"

She moves her head side to side among the herbs. "We'll be in the forest."

W e must look unearthly—two dark robed figures gliding our way through the early morning mist. At the boundary, Martha hands me her sack of tools and provisions as she slides through the rails of the kinship's fence line. I almost drop it as I pass it back to her, before I choose to drop the baskets I carry to be more observant of the sack.

"Do you always travel to the forest this early?" I ask her.

"When I gather in the forest, I am usually gone for the day. It just so happens that our gather coincides with a convenient time to be away from the kinship." She smiles at the memory we created and lifts the sack to her shoulder and walks away from me as I crawl through the fence. "Besides," she calls back to me, "there are lessons waiting for you here."

Light mist hangs like a blanket across the forest floor. It looks solid from the distance but once we are inside its embrace it's barely noticeable. We gather, thanking the trees as we collect bark from their branches. Martha explains their use and collection times according to the seasons and the turn of the wheel. The recent rain has made the floor damp and fills the air with the scent of the pine needles that bow under our feet.

"I think a fire is in order," Martha says as we enter a clearing.

Without the time constraints of the kinship we slow and take our time to collect the kindling and prepare the fire. While the needles steep in the hot water I roll a small log closer to the fire for my seat. Martha sits on a rock that protrudes near the clearing. The morning is still cool and I look forward to the warmth of the tea. Martha takes another cup from the bag she carries.

"Another exception?" I ask.

"I'm always happy to drink with you."

While we wait, Martha tells me about the things we'll be looking for as we further venture into the forest. She describes plants I've never seen with strange names like bitter poisonpie and wooded hen.

I point to a plant growing nearby. "The wooded hen is this fungus that grows from the side of the tree like a serving platter?"

"Isn't it marvelous?" she says. "That the trees would give us food that tastes like chicken?"

"And this little sweet thing?" I ask, pointing to the red toadstool poking through the damp needles at the base of the tree behind me.

"Ah, that's namatia. They don't last long, good for pain in small doses, but otherworldly in strong concentrations."

"And people know of its . . . qualities?"

She nods slowly. "It seems people are always more knowledgeable about how to cause harm and destroy than how to use that knowledge to heal."

I reach behind me to collect it.

"No. We have no need for that one in the kinship. Leave it to be."

Leave it to be. Exactly what everything in the forest does. It just is. I take a moment to draw breath and close my eyes, the crispness of the morning still cold in my nostrils. I wonder if I could talk Martha into staying here forever.

"I think I shall have another cup before we move on," she says.

"Then I will too."

Martha pours the water into my cup. "Are you ready for more lessons?"

The oil from the needles spreads over my tongue. "Yes," I say and tilt my face to the sky and watch the pines spread out above me. "All the things you know are fascinating,"

"And you'll know them too if you listen."

I know what she says is true. I need to try and hear the song again. I close my eyes to listen.

"Are you ready for more lessons?"

I smile but I don't open my eyes. "You've already asked me, Martha. I said yes."

"There are lessons that contain knowledge for all. Sometimes there are lessons that are orchestrated just for you ... If you are ready to accept them."

I open my eyes. Martha sits on her rock, comfortable and relaxed yet she watches my face for some kind of reaction. What am I supposed to be doing? I look around me; maybe there's a plant somewhere I missed. I half laugh. "I don't know what I'm—"

And then I see him.

A young gray wolf sits a short distance away, half his body hidden by the strong base of the pine tree he peers from. He's curious but afraid. Brave and unsure all at once. I smile at him and he pads his feet into the pine needles.

"Should he join us?" Martha whispers.

My heart thumps in my chest and a band tightens around my gut. I watch him through the sting and blur of my tears as the morning breeze cools their tracks down my cheeks.

"You understand your lesson?"

Did I miss the lesson of the bird's trust in me? Do I have to trust myself again? Do I trust the Mystery? Can I trust the Mystery? Can

I trust myself? I tremble a nod that spills more tears from my eyes. He lifts his head to watch me.

"He waits for his invitation." She reminds me so softly that I could have mistaken her words for the breeze. It's every lesson about trust in one. I feel the air slide in and out of my body as I concentrate on my breath, fearful my body has forgotten how to breathe.

Martha senses my reluctance. "Decisions and vows made in the past need not rule the ones we make now. It's fear that distorts what is in plain view."

He sits now, perfectly content to wait this moment out with me. He breathes with me. Eager, compassionate and waiting as the saw blade moves within me. I draw a deep breath and close my eyes as I exhale. When I open them again he still stares into them. With love, I offer him a smile and a message.

Will you join us?

Martha releases another of her long breaths as he comes to sit beside me. My hands long to feel his coat but I don't dare touch him without permission. He slips his head under my hand; he longs for my touch as much as I long for his. I step out of the moment and observe the scene: a crone, and a girl sipping tea around a small fire, with a wolf as an invited guest. The trees embrace us, join our conversations and hum in a vibration that calms the air and can be felt by all of us. This simple moment is perfect. Each of us know and acknowledge the presence and power of the Mystery.

❦

The wolf walks beside me as I gather, watching as I slice into sections of tree-borne mushrooms, and sits to wait for me while I collect leaves from higher plants. The scent of the pine needles permeates everything around me and although I'm tempted to reach out and touch the namatia, whenever I see their sweet little red heads poking through the needles, I remain dutiful to Martha's warning and leave them be. The wolf's ears prick to something in the forest, and after he nudges my thigh with his body, I wish him well.

"Thank you and farewell," I say as he disappears into a thicket.

Martha gathers plants a few trees away from me, talking softly to them and thanking them as she collects what she needs. I sigh in complete safety and contentedness. This scene is something I could never have imagined if I had a lifetime for every star in the sky. The branches high above me look like friends reaching out to each other, or perhaps fingers interlocking. To speak without having to stop and consider every consequence before I open my mouth is a new kind of freedom and it's intoxicating.

"By the Stars, I never imagined my life like this," I say, still taken with the branches above me.

"How did you imagine it?"

"I don't know, the Hall wasn't a place for imagination." I try to think back to what I expected of my life, but the only things that consumed my thoughts were survival. I rub my hand down the side of a pine, the cracks in its bark as wide as my fingers. "I suppose I dreamed of a life free of the Hall. I'd make a life where I could forget who I was there. Be someone brand new. Someone more balanced, someone without any link to the Hall at all."

"So now you're free, and you'll create a new person?'

"Yes, I suppose I will."

"I see," Martha says as she moves between the trees, watching the ground for signs of her next plant to collect. "And will you love this new version of yourself?"

I think about how brave and sure and clever she'd be, and smile. "I'm sure I will."

"And will you only love this imaginary person, the one without your past?" Martha's voice is firm and I frown, unsure of how to answer. She walks towards me. "This imaginary being with a different life to the one you have lived, the one without any pain—" she scoffs at me. "She's not even real!" Martha drops her basket, takes my hands and leads me away from the tree, extends my arms and gestures for me to spin as if she invites me to dance. "Would you look at yourself?" she asks as I turn slowly. "Look at this fair and wondrous creature before you, the one with the scars and the memories. She's so much more deserving of your love than some imaginary person and their perfect life could ever be." I stop moving. It's true. Martha continues. "She survived to tell the tale. There's celebration in that. Won't you let her celebrate instead of demanding that she be like your imaginary perfect friend? Don't silence her."

It was easier to blame the Hall for silencing me and, in many ways, they had. But Martha's words made me feel like I was betraying myself by wishing my past away. I'd always thought I was observant, but part of me was missing and I'd never even noticed as it slipped away.

"I feel like I've broken my own heart," I say to her. "Is that even possible?"

"Hearts are very strong. They hold dreams for the longest time and yes, they break. But some are imprisoned, which is far worse."

"Something can imprison a heart?"

Martha nods. "Wraps it so tightly in chains its truth can barely beat."

My chest crushes just like the imprisoned heart Martha speaks of, beating but unable to give life, unable to flow. "What is this weapon?"

"You know it well. It's silence."

Martha leaves me with my thoughts and collects her basket, moving between the trees, engaging them in low conversation. My feet stay planted where she left me, as much a part of the soil as the trees around me. Can silence really cause more damage than an actual event? Is it strong enough to destroy? Silence means someone's truth is not heard. It makes their pain insignificant. And every time they are forced to silence they are taught, in little increments, just how insignificant they are. *Filth!* Feeney's voice and the sound of the chains break into my thoughts just as Martha speaks.

"Never, ever blame your heart for what it needed to do to keep you alive. When it's too painful to feel, we run and hide in our heads." She shrugs as though it's the most natural thing in the world. "It takes time to gather all the pieces of ourselves we left behind in our flight. But we must feel to move forward."

Feel to move forward. I remember blindly feeling my way through the forest when I escaped the Hall. Maybe this is similar. Why is it always backwards and forwards? Why is it always pain?

"It will hurt, won't it?" I ask.

"Think of it as a fence of brambles you must force yourself through to reach a lush field." She stops her gathering and offers me a gentle smile. "Keep your eyes on the field."

"You sound like you know the power of this fence intimately."

"Not nearly as well as I know the power of the field."

M artha seems satisfied with our collection from each loca-
tion in the forest, and we stop to sort the plants and bark,
separating them into piles on large pieces of cloth from the sack.
We roll them, some gently, some snugly, to protect them for their
journey to the kinship. I place the last bundle of rolled cloth into
the sack and lift it to my shoulder and follow Martha into a deep
ravine. The earth here feels looser under my feet, as though it
breaks apart as I tread on it even though it is saturated with icy
water that occasionally seeps its way into my shoes. The plants
and leaves here aren't nearly as green as those above us, but they
are wider and more distinct in their purpose. Martha takes care to
explain the intricacies of collecting the sticky sap of one and how
to avoid the stinging barbs of another.

"Listen," she says, closing her eyes.

With my eyes closed, the trees above us still sound as rhythmic
as the waves at Ferce Point. Small drafts of cold air wind their way
through the ravine, brushing past to cool me but not enough to

wish I was anywhere else. Large birds call from the woods above us, smaller ones titter nearby among the bushes. Insects buzz, grasses rustle and water trickles its way somewhere through the ravine and now that I stand still, finds its way into my shoes. But beyond the sounds, even beyond the silence that lives behind them, I hear a call.

"There's something I've not told anyone before. You might help me understand it," I say, opening my eyes.

Martha holds her hands out for the sack, takes it onto her shoulder and gestures for me to guide us through the ferns and out of the ravine. "I might," she says.

"Before, when you were talking about silent hearts. There's so many of them." I glance over my shoulder. Martha watches where she places her feet, but she nods. "And I can feel them. I try not to. They float to me on the breeze, and they call to me. What am I to do?"

"Answer them."

"How do I do that?"

"You need to feel."

I scramble up the last embankment and take the sack from Martha. "I already know how to do that," I say and take her hand to steady her climb. We've talked about how I'll feel safe places in the garden, I feel things for Thomas and I feel things for Martha, and just like a huge wave the cold sensation of that dark river deepens inside me and swirls and drags me into its depths. There's no way I can summon the bobbing leaves at the surface now. Can Martha feel the coldness and how it's dragging me further away?

She releases my hand, drops the sack to the ground and gently takes my lower arms. "No, I mean really feel. Deeply. And to know your feelings are acceptable, to never again tell yourself *I shouldn't feel this way.*"

The cold river now flows like ice fingers that scrape across my belly as it passes, deep and quiet. So incredibly, darkly deep. My arms reach behind me for a log I recollect is somewhere nearby, and it supports me as I squeeze myself tightly, hoping to stop the pain and cold from shattering my body.

Martha's hand rests on my shoulder and she kisses the top of my head. "All that continual surrender kept you alive, but you've forgotten how to feel."

The river swirls around me and through me like it's about to sweep me away. I squeeze tighter against the pain and a groan escapes my lips.

"It's the only way you'll discover your truth and what you should do."

"What do you mean?"

"If you don't allow yourself to feel, how will you know your heart, your truth? Surely that message you carry must come from your heart?"

She helps guide me as I slide from the log to lie on the earth. "And what you have to say to us is acceptable. Your feelings are acceptable." Martha sits beside me on the leaves and leans into my legs. "Consider what you see, what you feel and what you hear. Your reactions to these things are yours alone. No one can tell you how you should feel." She pats my legs and coughs. "And stop trying to find excuses for why or what you believe is wrong and what they believe is right."

I smile even though I still clutch at my body.

Martha rises. "Stay here as long as you need, but go slowly, the process will last a lifetime. Always listening, always feeling. When you don't feel, you don't have joy, and then you don't really live."

I open my eyes. "I thought joy was just being happy," I say as she makes her way into the clearing.

Martha's face tilts to the sky and she turns in a slow circle with her arms outstretched, as if she was pulling everything in around her. "Joy," she says, "is standing in the presence of the Mystery and being so complete, you don't even *need* happiness."

"Ah, how perfect!" It's much later when Martha calls me over to a patch of herbs at the base of a large tree. She points out its dark leaves and the particular formation of the taller spikes that hold little purple flowers. "How wonderful that the Mystery provides the best herbs for this annoying cough right when it's time for tea."

"More tea?" I laugh.

"Let me teach you to harvest it first, it's quite particular. It's not commonly found here. And then we'll set the large pot up to steep some bark." Martha coughs again. "Last time I was ill, this flower cured all. This and time in the clearing. See over there near the pond? How the sun breaks through the leaves? Sunlight on my skin and fresh tea. Healed in no time."

I rub her back and she coughs again. "I must say I'm worried about your chest, Martha."

"Don't be. All is well." She pats at my hand. "I'll get the pot, you gather some kindling."

Even the quietness of gathering the kindling stirs the deep river of my emotions, but this time I don't get swept away. I watch the cold river pass by as if I'm standing on the bank. I know I'll need to dive deep into it again, to clear away the unfamiliarity of its coldness but I remind myself it's my decision. When and where I enter its waters are my choice now. The river and its depth are mine.

We create a larger fire and set a pot over it to steep the bark, make tea, and enjoy a break from our gathering and constant bending. Martha finds a soft patch of grass where the sunlight streams through the canopy, raises her skirts up to her thighs and removes her smock to allow the sun to work on her skin. She glows so brightly on the green I wonder if the glow is from her or the sunlight.

A short distance away I lift my skirts too, but only to soak my feet in the pond next to the clearing. I ease them into the cool water, but my movement still makes the nearby lily pads bob up and down. The straps of green on the far side of the pond, ready to burst into blue flowers at their appointed time, bend and tap their fingers into the water as the ripples reach them. The grass clearing reaches right to the edge of the pond, trees overhang the other side making the dappled sunlight look like blotches of yellow on the brown water. Just the right size for some quiet bathing on a warm day.

Martha rolls to her belly, caressing the loose dirt around her, picking it up by the handful and letting it crumble through her fingers with admiration. I roll over too, and lift my feet from the water, its droplets run down my lower legs towards my knees. She smiles when she notices me watching her.

"My body has served me well. It's been fed by the land, nurtured by the sun, cleansed by its waters. When the time comes for me to go, I will leave this earthly body behind as a gift to the earth to use. It's the way it always has been and the way it always will be."

"Martha, I wish you wouldn't speak of sadness in such a beautiful place." I pick up a dried reed and start picking at it with my fingernail.

"Death's not sad, it just is, and it's beautiful. It's simply part of the wheel."

I don't think I've ever known a beautiful death. To me, death has always been a form of currency, and life something always taken, never given. The idea that death could be beautiful hovers in my mind like a bee hovers above a flower, not knowing where to set itself down.

"Of course it's perfectly natural to mourn when we lose something," Martha continues, "whether the death of a loved one or the death of a dream or an even an idea or a plan, because they have attached to our heart, and been a part of us. Of course it hurts to release them."

I think about the gorge and that wet robe that clung so tightly to the rocks at the bottom and I imagine that I would do the same—stubbornly refuse to let go no matter how much the river rushed at me.

"Want to know what the secret is?" she asks. "Only rely on what doesn't change. The unchangeable."

"So I'm not to rely on Thomas—or you?"

"When you rely on something, or someone, it brings fear that you might lose it. Reliance and fear. They come as a pair, like swans. You can't have one without the other."

My stomach flips. Why is she always right? I do rely on Thomas and paired with that, just like swans, is my fear of losing him.

Voices singing the announcement of the evening meal reach us inside the forest. We both look up from the last of our harvesting to acknowledge the song but don't make any effort to rush our return.

*   *   *

Twilight settles over the kinship as I unloop the gate and help Martha through with her sack.

"Leave it there," I say. "I'll come back for it. You've carried enough today."

I carry the heavier baskets through to her hut and go out of my way to stomp on the chamomyle as I pass. Martha chuckles as her feet tap and crunch behind me on the stones so much that she must be doing a jig. Her laugh then disintegrates into a cough that leaves her gasping for air and I rush to her side.

*   *   *

Days pass, and Martha's cough is no better and no worse. She rests in her hut while I eat my evening meal alone in the high lodge. I smile pleasantly at all, even to the herder who offered to rush the tea box to Brenn's guests. He squints his eyes at me, unsure of my role in the incident he recently endured, and I'm pleased to see that his bravado has decreased along with his bodily fluids. I hide a small smile behind some bread and look forward to telling Martha about his composure.

A strange heaviness sits in the room like a thick cloud. People around me eat and talk but it's like they're wading through their lives.

Fatigue. That's what's in the air.

Brenn's latest ruse takes more than it gives, and no matter how many times she explains it I can't nod along with the others. Perhaps there's some wisdom in her plan and I will nod eventually, but for now I watch from the outside.

The kinship field workers, actually all the workers, must now labor harder with less food.

"Half a bowl to benefit all," Brenn tells us from the high table. "Smiles show forth your gratitude."

The faces of my kin grow gaunt before my eyes. What exactly should they save their greatest happiness for? That their grain is held in Muscone's shiniest pots, their nurses parade in Ferce Point or that they grow weak while their medicinal herbs are sent to impress the Sirbahn? Herders now ensure that each worker meets Brenn's quota. How does this honor the Traditions? How does this prepare the called? Brenn's explanation frustrates me more than soothes me.

"It's only understandable that the outsiders should see where their wares and services originate," she explains, heaping praise on the workers for the quality of their produce that generates higher prices. "Be proud of our fine accomplishments, let us put them on show for all to see." And what a show it is. The Tallefix would be proud.

Instead of repairing the roofs of the lodges, she builds guests houses using the finest materials. The price of this finery goes beyond silver and leaves the kinship children hungry.

"It's only right," Brenn suggests, "that outsiders pay me for the use of the guest houses." The houses where the furniture shines, beauty surrounds the guests and they receive attentive and healthy care. Brenn incorporates a private study of the Traditions with her guests and extols the virtues of what the Traditions can provide for *their* benefit.

Along with the guests, news of life outside the valley and the disruption the unrest is causing reaches us. The old ways continue to fall apart, and the lack of control causes the Hall to tighten its grip on village life, containing the unrest by forbidding travel. Rumors that Feeney now forces guards to serve out their full terms by holding their families hostage causes a knife to twist in my stomach. I buckle over, and I don't remember it hurting so much, but perhaps I'm no longer used to it.

It's not often I step into Brenn's chamber. The last time I was here was with Thomas. My mouth pinches into a one-sided smile—we were happy and excited then. I was surprised when Brenn agreed to my suggestion of a meeting. She'd raised an eyebrow at me so I blurted out that I had some new ideas for the kinship and now I'm standing here before her, unsure of anything. My mouth is dry, and my hands fumble along the edge of her desk. I try to cough to clear my throat of its constriction. Brenn sits with her hands clasped on her desk waiting, a sour expression on her face.

"Thank you for granting me an audience, dear Brenn. I understand you yourself have become very popular . . . along with the kinship."

She acknowledges my praise with a nod formed by the slight tilt of her head.

"I wanted to raise a concern, well, more like . . . ." I try to think of what Brenn wants to hear so she won't dismiss me. " . . . increasing the efficiency of the kinship."

Brenn looks intrigued and gestures for me to take a seat.

I can't begin by telling her about the rumors that detail the cost of tailoring our uniforms, so I try another path to the subject. "As you might be aware, kin work with broken implements, and the seed supply is down." Brenn shuffles in her seat and I rush my words. "The nurses and those representing the kinship look wonderful in their new uniforms but—" Ugh. Why did I say 'but'; I may as well have struck her with a stick. ". . . wouldn't the little silver you have be better used to prepare the workers for the upcoming season, or finding a better way to—?"

Brenn stands up. "Is your sole intention to insult this kinship?" Her voice is so loud everyone in the high lodge must be able to hear her. "The uniforms show the Tradition's prosperity. How else will people know we are favored?" She takes her stance, hands on her hips, her wings spread wide. My shoulders tense as I battle the urge to curl into a ball.

I try again, this time appealing to her sense of compassion and her strong relationship with village dignitaries. "Thomas has spoken with Guthrie. If we plant the new seed now, we will have enough food for everyone. We won't have to listen to the children cry; surely this is what the Traditions tell us?"

"Who do you think you are?"

I try to use the Traditions to explain, but she dismisses my squeaky voice sharply, talking about rules and introduced regulations and I don't even understand how they fit into our conversation. All I know is what I see and what I feel. Brenn has an opportunity to make life easier for her workers and to feed the crying children. Instead of solving the problem, she chooses to blame them. Dismissed from her presence, I tremble as I duck under the low mantle, not from fear, but amazement that I stood.

⁕

A few days later I pick up my basket and head to the gate. "I think I'll take these up early," I say to Martha.

"He's here then?"

I smile. She didn't even have to see or hear Thomas's cart to know why I'm eager to take the produce to the high lodge. I'd hoped we might get a chance to speak, but now that he's in Brenn's chamber I wonder if I'll see him at all. Brenn's voice rises behind her door and all the workers in the high lodge dart about like mice.

"You represent the kinship in Sirban. You will wear this uniform!" she bellows. "How are they to know where the goodness comes from?"

"But the Sirbahn will not respect me dressed like this. I need to wear the cream clothes!"

My mouth drops open—he's never raised his voice to her before and I'm fearful and excited at the same time. I scurry away like the others, not wanting to be in her sight when she opens the door. I head out the main doors and into the fields. Thomas is right. He knows the Sirbahn better than she, and still she will not listen.

I wander into the lowest field below the garden when Thomas approaches behind me, trotting to catch up.

"Are you safe? Are you well?"

I nod to both.

"What has happened to this place? It's now got more rules than one of Guthrie's formulas!" He puffs to catch his breath.

I shrug. "It was probably here all along, but we just didn't see it. And it's been made more obvious by the outsiders."

"It's like Brenn sees something and wants it, and she interprets the Traditions so no one can question her." Thomas turns to look to the high lodge. Brenn stands guard over the fields with her hands on her hips. "There's no time to write about the Eariss when all I'm doing is tallying profits for Brenn." Thomas paces, fuming at the kinship's injustice. "You have no idea how I need to be near you, and . . . " he shouts to the sky," . . . how exactly does a uniform show what's inside someone's heart?"

He takes my hand and leads me further away from the high lodge and Brenn's presence on its landing. "I just this minute told Brenn

I'll train another to take my place in Sirban and that I am eager to return here to study." He laughs one of his loud chuckles. "Her eyes lit up thinking her library a school, but I just need a way to come back to you."

"A school? How can you expect to be honored if you're not truthful? Aren't you being untruthful?"

"How am I untruthful?"

"You told her you wanted to study the Traditions."

"That might be what she heard . . . But I'm returning to study the Eariss. I'm returning to study *you*."

He takes my hand as if to lead me somewhere, but just as quickly realizes there's nowhere to go in the open field and he lets it go. "You need to understand something. I spend each night writing about you, thinking about you, desperate to get back here. The desperation only ends in your presence. Do you know what that feels like? To be away from something you know is just . . . right?"

He doesn't see my nod, his eyes shut in the concentration of a life-or-death decision. He opens them and speaks again "I don't even care if you choose to shoot me with rainbows. May I be the one who looks into your eyes every day of my life?"

His face is hopeful, and I smile, my mind filled with shooting him with rainbows. His hand reaches for mine and a white flash jumps between them like lightning. Its force throws him backwards and he lands on his backside. I stagger backwards but still stand. I offer him my hand but he's unsure whether to take it or not and I laugh at him. Martha cackles in the distance.

Thomas climbs to his feet and we try again, holding our palms up to each other but staying a few strides apart. A large white spark leaps from his hand to mine. We both jump back in shock and almost fall over laughing.

This is nothing like the timid sparks from the Tallefix's fire that tried to escape, but a forceful power that will not be disrespected or dismissed. We can now hold our palms up to each other, still a distance apart, while a thin crackle of light jumps between them.

I'm stunned and can't take my eyes from our hands or the line that runs between them. "Have you heard about—"

"Binding?"

I nod, not that I think he's watching my head. "Have you always known about it?"

"Eugenica told me about it but I didn't understand it until now. Ritual and fairy tales to her; she talks a lot but has no idea." He moves his hand higher and lower and watches the thin line move with him as he steps closer. "She was more interested in the property rights it gave someone. But this is . . . "

I don't even know what word he could come up with to describe it, but I still nod.

"Will you?" he begins, "I mean, would you . . . do you want to?"

"Should we?"

Seemingly convinced it is safe, he picks me up and laughs. Martha chuckles from within the walled garden and smiles with us, wiping her hands on her apron, and Brenn turns on her heels and strides into the high lodge. Her hatred and disgust pound like a wave into the field and I fight my instinct to hide. Will daring to be happy bring death into my life? For this moment, I push it aside. For this moment, I don't care. I let the happiness bubble up within me and fan itself out through my chest and into every cavity of my body. I enjoy the sensation and the energy and lightness it brings to me for the first time. I take Martha's advice and I feel it and revel in its goodness.

⁂

Moonlight is never harsh, even at its brightest. The small twigs that have made their way to the forest floor don't snap under our feet but bend to accommodate us and allow us to pass without obstacle. Martha sets the torch she carries among the boulders in the clearing and even though it seems washed of color it still feels warm and welcoming. Recent rain adds dampness to the air and softness to the ground, and a distant stream guides trickling water into the pond. Martha tends to her bowls, removing them from her sack and arranging them here and there, and after some time passes, I pace from one side of the clearing to the other.

What if he didn't mean it?

What if he's changed his mind?

What if he doesn't turn up at all?

Martha looks up from her preparations. "Remember he had to wait until dark to sneak away from Sirban. He will come." Her words don't soothe me, and she adds, "Let me finish here, and we'll make a garland for your hair."

I draw a deep breath and relax. "No." I smile. "He'll just rake them out." Thomas has never asked me to be something I am not. He's a piece of the Mystery I can hold.

"Are you sure Brenn won't interfere?" I ask as I pace again.

"After seeing those sparks? I think she'd be scared to."

Thomas emerges through the trees in a bundle of nervous energy that bounces around between us before cycling its way through excitement, happiness, love and joy. I smile to myself; joy is here too. He's not wearing the cream clothes from Sirban nor the uniform of the kinship, but the clothes he met me in. The ones he wore while we traveled together. Martha notices too, and removes the kinship's smock from my body, leaving me in my light under-dress. For now, this is all I have to offer as I join him in our affiliation only to each other.

"Are we ready?" she asks us.

Nerves tumble through my body as she asks us to sit on the earth on either side of a large flat boulder that creates a small table between us. She stands and leans over us and the nerves flutter and melt away. I know I am safe. But even with Martha's earlier guidance, I feel unprepared. Small. Martha begins and asks us to confirm this is truly what we want.

I want this. "Yes," I say.

Thomas dips his chin once. "Yes."

"This is about trust," Martha says.

Thomas smiles. "Last time we trusted we were beaten black and blue by tree branches on our way into the valley, remember? Surely this won't cause us too much injury."

He smiles broadly at me and the nerves roll in my stomach again . . . and Martha says nothing.

"The human soul longs to be adored and cherished."
Martha's voice travels around the entire clearing even though she is right beside us at the flat boulder. "But to be truly cherished, a soul must be discoverable, open and vulnerable. The binding creates its own presence, a bond that requires protection and tending. You must remain open, guarding each other's souls and championing them." Martha kneels and takes our upper arms. "Never forget how delicate a soul in your keeping is and how privileged you are to hold it. The moment you forget that, the moment you don't offer the respect it deserves, the power of your binding loses its intensity." She nods with her eyebrows raised, we nod in return.

"Understood," Thomas says.

Martha rummages inside her sack. "There are many lessons for us to learn, and you two have the privilege of learning them together." She brings out smaller bowls and places them on the edge of the boulder. "Some lessons we learn in what we call good times, other lessons we learn in what we call bad times. But don't be fooled, they're neither good or bad, they just are, and they are a gift to you." Alongside the bowls she adds fine ribbons of leather knotted together and adjusts her torch so the light falls best on our hands. "All circumstances, whether brought about by your actions or arriving like a gust of wind, are gifts. All lessons. This binding forms all kinds of connections. Your connection with each other, connections with those around you, and connection with the Mystery."

She gestures for our hands and we each stretch an arm across the boulder, our elbows resting on the stone. Martha takes our wrists and aligns our hands, fingers and palms together. Small sparks arc from our fingertips and Martha jumps and smiles. They aren't strong sparks, just gentle humming ones. Not unlike the hum of the trees, and the song I tried so hard to hear. The song plays in our hands and I listen as it travels up my arm and into my body.

Martha sings too, but her song is slow and respectful, in a language I've never heard. She pulls a long and wide strip of leather from her sack and lays it across the crease of my bent elbow, arranging it so that each end stays in contact with the boulder, and then does the same for Thomas. The placement of the leather brings the sensation of the waterfall pouring on my head again, this time it is sacred waters, smooth and deep, and so incredibly still. Thomas's wide eyes are fixed on mine; he feels it too.

Martha's song is finished. But she keeps the solemnity in her voice. "Your first connection is with the rock. This is the source of your stability."

She hovers over our joined hands and my body feels so heavy I can barely move. I don't want to take my eyes off Thomas. Our hands stay in my vision, but I'm merging with the rock, as if all I am is a motionless hand and head. I grab at the edge of the boulder with my free hand so as not to disappear completely.

Martha separates our first fingers and places cool, rich earth between them and then squeezes them together again. Taking the

ribbon leather, she begins to bind our first fingers together. I feel
her place the beginning of her strip, first up and over our fingers, and then around. She winds snugly, but not uncomfortably.
Again, she sings an ancient melody, this one lighter and shorter,
which relieves me of some of my heaviness. As she binds our fingers she speaks of the richness of the earth, and how our survival
depends on its bounty; she speaks of its dust, its barrenness, the
mud, how the earth allows us to mold it for use in building shelter,
how its ways must always be respected. Everything she mentions I
see, even though my eyes are wide open. I see the mud, I see the
dust and barrenness, I see lush growth in rich soil.

She finishes binding.

"May you be each other's grounding stability and growth."

She patiently waits for us to remember our part in this ritual and
then coughs as a reminder. Thomas's face comes back into focus,
our hands in front of us and his free hand clutching the edge of
the boulder, his knuckles as white as mine. My mind races for the
promises I've practiced and they arrive in my mouth at the same
time that Thomas finds his voice. With one finger bound we look
into each other's eyes and promise together.

"This I will remind your soul, do not judge the gifts that are given.
Welcome the unchangeable and grow alongside me.
In the midst, I will remind you of love.
Your soul is safe with mine."

Satisfied, Martha separates our second fingers and drips cool
water between them. Thomas and I have not broken our gaze,
and the boulder doesn't feel like a barrier anymore, the song of
our hands continues to hum. Martha continues with her song as
she lays the ribbon up and over our fingers and begins to bind.
"Water is essential for life, just as love is essential for the soul. Water
can cleanse and cool, but be mindful, it also arrives in floods and
torrents and can be destructive. It is a force that demands respect.
Water will freeze you when cold and burn you when hot. This is
its nature, and this is unchangeable."

She finishes binding our second fingers. "May you be each other's refreshment and sustenance."

"This I will remind your soul, do not judge the gifts that are given.
Welcome the unchangeable and grow alongside me.
In the midst, I will remind you of love.
Your soul is safe with mine."

Thomas's eyes speak straight into my soul without using words. I've left the rock behind and am only a soul, treasured by him alone. His face contains the same faraway look I must wear, seeing the visions as Martha speaks. My eyes see his body yet I'm speaking to his soul and all that he is. He is not his body just as I am not mine. Everything is clouded and dreamlike. Could we be souls? Could we have left all behind? We might fly away, but Martha pulls our third fingers apart and waves a feather over them. Does she sing? I can't hear her. Perhaps her song is as light as the feather she holds. She speaks of the privilege of the air that fills our bodies, and I see eagles as she speaks of the winds that carry the seasons to us. She speaks also of harsh winds and smoke and explains we can no more wish them away than the rock that is before us. Our third fingers are bound. "May you be each other's breath of air in the changing seasons of your life."

"This I will remind your soul, do not judge the gifts that are given.
Welcome the unchangeable and grow alongside me.
In the midst, I will remind you of love.
Your soul is safe with mine."

Air? Air? I'm still flying with the eagles, and even though I know my hand is just before me, I'm soaring and looking down on the boulder. I circle from above, descending as Martha carefully pulls apart our fourth fingers and drops a strip of glowing embers from her torch between our fingers and squeezes them closed! The pain screeches through my finger as it envelops my hand and claws its way up my arm, drawing panic towards my heart.

Martha begins her fervent chant as I struggle to deal with the shock. Thomas is reeling but we can't move as we are bound. We quickly discover the answer is within ourselves. Looking into each other's eyes we find the strength to endure the shock and enough balance to allow us to continue. Martha has finished her chanting song and begins to bind our fourth finger, up and over and then around.

She keeps her eyes on our fingers. "Pain has a way of bringing the reality of this world back to us, doesn't it?"

We refuse to take our eyes from each other, occasionally wincing in pain as she continues to bind our fingers.

"Fire warms us but can also destroy us," she says. "It has an appetite like no other, yet it provides us with light and it purifies and seals. Its beauty and its danger and its power are altogether vicious, but you have found the answer to its pain within yourselves. This is one of the hardest lessons to learn, that the answer to your pain is never without."

Martha finishes binding our tender fourth fingers. "May you be each other's light in the darkness."

My teeth are clenched as we recite our part,

"This I will remind your soul, do not judge the gifts that are given.
Welcome the unchangeable and grow alongside me.
In the midst, I will remind you of love.
Your soul is safe with mine."

My teeth are no longer clenched when we finish, and I am found again.

Martha takes a deep breath as she hovers over our bound fingers and prepares a new ribbon of leather for the next binding. I look into Thomas's eyes and find that rather than wonder what on earth could be next, I am confident that whatever it might be, we will endure it together. I know already my soul is safe with him, and he must know now too—that his soul is just as safe with me.

I'm disappointed that I flinch when Martha gently prizes our thumbs apart and rubs them with a little sand and then lets them return to each other only to separate them again to paint them with mud. Thomas and I continue to search for each other's bravery and barely notice her collection of items. She brings her torch and blows smoke over our thumbs, then rummages in the ashes of her torch but mercifully only smears black ash on them. Finally, she pours a bowl of water over them.

She begins an ancient song, one that is brave and strong and measured, as she begins to bind our thumbs—up and over and around. I close my eyes to hear her song and even though I don't understand the words, I understand the song. It is a song that has been sung for thousands of summers. It's a song of thanks. Warmth touches my exposed thumb and curiosity opens my eyes to catch Martha's tears washing our thumbs in accompaniment. When our thumbs are bound, she speaks.

"There is no element on this earth that can adequately describe the nature of light."

Martha uses the last of the leather ribbon to weave our fingers together. Backwards and forwards as if working a loom, she binds them closer together.

"For life is not just earth, sand and mud. Life is not just water, steam, ice or even tears. Life contains far more than the passions of fire and heat or the regrets of ashes. More than wind or flight and the dispersal of seeds. Life is so much more than the immovable rock and unchangeable elements. Yet with light, they all make the one. Light is soft and harsh, and refracts to make a rainbow, its nature and essence unbeaten. Above all, remember that darkness can never diminish the light."

As she weaves, our fingers pull together to create the one. I feel the heaviness of the rock, the height of my eagle's flight, the warmth of her tears, the courage of Thomas, the pain of the ember. I feel the dust storms and the floods. I smell the sage and heat up with fire. I share in all the Mystery has given to me, and I want to share it with others. When she has woven all our elements together, Martha begins to bind our hands. We had relied on our elements through the binding, so when our palms touch again emotion floods my body and I cry.

I'm not sad; I can feel Thomas's heart. Can he feel mine? I want him to know I'm not sad, but I can't stop the tears. It's as if all the tears I didn't share in the Hall are being taken in this softness. The protection around my heart has broken down and Thomas and his heart are allowed in. I am vulnerable, but I am not afraid. His heart offers me courage I didn't know I had. He is not taking anything away from me, he is adding to me.

When we traveled together we slept comfortably among the roots of the trees, so we're not bothered when Martha tells us we must sleep our first night bound in their arms. We are used to adapting our bodies to what will work amongst their roots. But our night is uncomfortable being tied together in such a way that we can't even fall asleep or perform basic functions without consideration for the welfare of the other. Being bound means we must first respect and honor that our two hearts beat simultaneously and whatever one does will affect the other. We find an acceptable position in facing each other and try to rest.

Thomas lifts our big leather entwined hand up to admire it. "You know what I'm thinking?"

"What?"

"That when we unwind all of this in the morning, ripping that burn apart on our fingers is going to hurt less than leaving you for Sirban."

I don't even want to think about the morning yet. A tiny light flashes beyond our bear-like joined hand. "Is that Guthrie's Always star?"

Thomas moves his head closer to mine to see the light through the treetops. "I believe it is. But right now, I'd believe anything."

My eyes always seem to be watching the threshold. Martha has taken to scolding me, I do it so often. I've convinced myself that Brenn must be disapproving of every person Thomas suggests as his replacement in Sirban, and all this does is create a sullen mood in me.

Martha's illness refuses to improve. Any undue exertion causes her to cough, and the pace of our days are much slower. She assures me it's fine to lower the consumption of her tea to make the herbs last until we can get back to the forest, but I think the extra work demands are wearing her body out quicker than the tea can replace her energy.

Rather than rush back from the high lodge after the mid meal, we stroll along the sheep track with our empty baskets and shake off the heaviness of life in the kinship. Although we're not happy to see a herder on the sheep track, we still offer him a smile as he passes. In the distance a patch of white flashes in the garden's open gate.

Open gate!

"I can't imagine the sheep have learned to unlatch the gate, can you?" I pass my empty basket to Martha and run.

Martha stands outside the gate as I shove the last of the sheep, an old ewe that won't budge, through it. I could have asked the ewe to move, but it seemed easier to force her through.

Martha secures the gate behind her. "I hope the shepherds weren't watching; they'll take you from me to help round up their flocks." She smiles as she returns the baskets to the hut. "Did you notice how easy it was to guide the sheep when they were moving, and how much energy it took to push the old ewe out because she stayed still?"

I hadn't thought about it, but anything would be easier than trying to get that old ewe to move.

"Whenever you see sheep I want you to remember this moment and this lesson. It's much easier to guide your life when it's fluid and moving. When you get stuck and become rigid, it takes so much more energy to get on the move again. Whether it's to change your path or simply change your mind."

The sheep didn't do too much damage—they helped themselves to some of the juiciest plants and hadn't eaten too much of anything that might cause them harm. I tidy the pots along the edges of the garden beds. Thank the Stars they didn't have enough time find you! Small seedlings grow out of the little clay pots lining the basket weave of the herb garden. I pick up one of the pots and gently touch the new leaves that are destined for a garden in Sirban. A garden in Sirban? The whole idea seems too ridiculous for words. How will these tender shoots weather the storm of their lives that is almost upon them? Perhaps they'll grow strong and adapt.

I hold it higher and watch the color of the leaves brighten in the sunshine. "In the forest they'd be sheltered and shaded by larger trees and plants but what we're doing here is unnatural. Taking them out and making them perform in gardens and rows for our convenience."

"Anything removed from its natural cycle must be compensated. How often do we get broken and smashed by the wider world when we step out before our time, or force ourselves into something?"

"This is about trust again, isn't it?"

"And impatience, thinking we know the better time." She ponders for a moment and then adds, "and some who like to say they're patient when really it's an excuse to cover their fear."

"And that would keep them still like the sheep. And harder to move. So how will I know which one I am if I can be fearful and impatient about moving forward and fearful of staying still?"

"No one can tell you that but yourself." She stops her work to look at me. "It's a difficult and painful process to be honest with yourself, but once you learn to be compassionate and accepting of who you are, it becomes easier to see the tricks you play on yourself."

The tricks I play on myself. Martha is so patient with me as I swing between confidence and horror about my future. She celebrates my wins and gently coaxes me back by her side when I'm unsure and falter. She keeps reminding me that once I know something, I can't unknow it. But there's knowing with your head and knowing with your heart. And the bridge between the two is belief.

Thomas and Martha tell me I am the Eariss and it's true that wondrous events happen around me. My mind might know and understand I'm meant to be the Eariss, but I also know I don't believe it. Can't believe it. It's as if I'm listening to someone describing the taste and texture of a crisp apple without ever having tasted one myself. And how do I get to taste that apple? Do I bite into thin air and expect the apple of belief to meet me there, or do I wait for it to appear magically within me and bite it once I know it truly exists?

For now, I listen and learn while my heart stays surrounded by a fog. I apply Martha's lessons to my mind and imagine their truth might trickle to my heart. Maybe the answer isn't found in knowing who I am, but in accepting who I am. Allowing who I am.

I pick up another small pot. This shoot grows at an odd angle and I try to help it, guide it on its way. It's too weak to stand on its own and needs the protection of the walled garden. I'm sure it can't wait to grow tall and strong, but for now it will wait and be patient for its time. I look beyond the shoot and Martha catches me watching the threshold again.

"He said he had work to complete. It must be important to him or he wouldn't stay away. You do understand that, don't you?"

I nod and return the pot to its sheltered position.

"He will come. The winding road of your patience will still get you there—and there's better scenery," she says, coughing at her jest. "Tell me what lesson that cow in the field there has for you."

The cow pulls the grass from the field, takes a few more steps and pulls again. Occasionally something catches her attention but she concentrates on the grass and moves again to a better patch.

Martha wipes her brow with her apron. "Have you noticed the animals don't complain that it's warm? They just go about their business. They might notice it's hot, but they have no need to label it as good or bad, it just is. They are wiser than us, they don't fight what is. The stream doesn't complain there is a rock in the way, it just goes around it. Flow with life and don't bother wasting your energy making judgments about things you can't alter."

"Like trying to stop the wind."

"Life itself doesn't rush us; it's only when our thoughts demand it be a certain way that the sense of rush is created. We blame our lives when the culprit is really our thoughts."

I'd created my own stress by deciding that Thomas should have finished with Sirban by now. But he wasn't. I was concentrating on what it wasn't, rather than what it is and letting it be.

T he tea-drinking herder comes through the gate and wanders the garden. I do my best to ignore his presence, thinking that somehow if I don't acknowledge him he won't acknowledge me. Like all the herders, his uniform provides him with a sense of superiority, it somehow cloaks his soul in anonymity and makes him invisible to blame or reproach. Along with his sense of camaraderie, this uniform has wiped away any sense of restraint. He knows he can do as he pleases with no consequences. I stand to gather some beans from the higher trellis, and as I pick, I watch Brenn on the landing of the high lodge as she surveys the fields and her workers. She only moves her fists away from her hips to point or call orders.

Martha's ideas about going with the flow of life seems better than Brenn's and her constant striving to be the best. It's exhausting—all this constant improvement that only forces judgment about each other's growth and potential. Inspiration, led by the Mystery, removes any feelings of missing out on something better. But still, we work harder, eat less to accommodate impressing those outside the kinship, and the sour expression on Brenn's face never changes.

"You. Crone." The herder pushes his boot into Martha's thigh as she kneels on the ground. "Make sure Brenn has all the rosemary she wants with her evening meal."

I don't know how much more our spindly little bushes can give.

"Of course." Martha smiles at him and coughs as he turns and leaves the garden.

My teeth grind. I'm not sure whether I'm angry at the way he spoke to her or angry that she allowed him to speak to her in that tone. I find the last of the herbs for her cough in the hut and make her some tea. The frustration has almost left me as I approach her, and I hope she can't hear it in my voice. "Doesn't it bother you that they call you names and treat you badly?"

"People can call you by whatever name they like, but what matters most is what you call yourself, because that is who you will become."

I nod and go back to my work, taking my place next to her as I weed among the lemon balm. I still don't think he should have spoken to her in that way.

She stabs her trowel into the dirt beside me. "What you believe about yourself," she says, "is what you will become!" Her face is flushed, her chest moves as though she is suppressing a cough. "Do you understand?" Martha stares at me with such force I feel rebuked.

"Yes," I say with my chin on my chest. "I understand."

The exertion overwhelms Martha and releases itself into a coughing fit that leaves her gasping for air. I help her to her feet and lead her to her hut, making her comfortable on her pallet. I use some wooden boxes to prop her mat up so she can recline and breathe a little easier.

"I'll go to the forest and gather the purple flowers. I remember where they are."

Martha carefully draws breath. "It will be safer for you if you seek her permission to leave first."

I stop, stunned, as if a rope holds me back. Martha coughs again and raises her eyebrows at me.

How can I speak when all I've done is be beaten down for opening my mouth? When the very act of saying anything causes my heart to die inside of me from fear and disgust and self-loathing. "I'm not strong enough. Look what happened last time. She made life harder and increased the quotas."

Martha draws another gentle, measured breath. "Then you will know it is not your outer strength that you rely on when you do speak."

"When I do speak? You mean there's no way out of this?"

She smiles and whispers, "Not if you have a need to grow into yourself and not be owned by your past."

A gain I find myself sitting in Brenn's chamber. I try not to be distracted by the sounds of the servers hurrying to prepare for the evening meal. I concentrate on breathing smoothly, but my breath staggers around as unreliably as a herder on strong ale. Why she agreed to another meeting I don't know; I'm simply grateful she did. This time I hope I'll be precise, persuasive and less judgmental. I stand as she enters and she acknowledges my presence with a strange little grunt that makes me think she'd forgotten I'd be here. Too bad.

She lands in her seat and gets settled but stops suddenly and stares at my hand. I frown before realizing she watches my binding scar. I clench my hand to hide it. It is mine.

"Martha is unwell," I say

"Yes, I have heard."

"I wish to ask permission to gather herbs in the forest."

She leans back in her chair. "Why now? Don't you normally gather on the waning moon?"

"There is a particular herb helpful to Martha's condition that I would like to gather there, then also treat her with sunshine—"

"No, we follow the Traditions closely in time of illness." I open my mouth, but she continues. "Her best chance of recovery is in a darkened room." Brenn stands and pulls a book from her shelves and turns to a previously marked page. "Here. A room of night and only water to wash away ills. I wrote it myself."

"Respectfully, dear Brenn, your book is just your ideas, just as Thomas's book is his ideas."

"Well, we've always followed the Traditions. The procedures are recorded in this book, and they've not let us down. As you are well aware."

"Perhaps this once we could try a different way—"

"This is how it's always been done."

"Could you at least acknowledge that if we—"

"Who do you think you are? Are you suggesting you know more about this topic than I do?"

Yes! my head screams. "No," I say.

"I will not acknowledge ignorance!" Brenn's voice is shrill and as she lifts her hands to her hips and down again she seems like a bird in flight. "The Traditions of the kinship go back hundreds of years; they will not be altered. This discussion is over!"

It most certainly is. And I've failed again.

As I reach the door she clears her throat and squawks, "Stay away from the garden, you will now work the main field." I don't turn to face her, merely nod so she knows I have heard her, and I bend in a forced bow as I leave her room. Brenn's squawking attracted the attention of everyone in the high lodge seated for their meal. Every face watches me as I take my place alone at the end of a long table. If Thomas was here . . . No. I stop myself from wishing he was here. I should learn to rely on myself and my own judgment.

The servers work quickly, placing half-filled bowls in front of all the workers while I wonder if I could have handled my meeting with Brenn better. I scrunch my face in shame. Look how quickly

I'd returned to who I was at the Hall. Brenn may as well have been Feeney or the lord screaming orders at me. But at least this time I found a voice to speak back to her—even if it did no good at all. That same sensation from the Hall creeps across me; the fear that I have spoken and the world is about to end. How foolish to think I have grown and changed here and yet in an instant, one without a threat of violence, merely a raised voice, I find myself as weak and feeble as if I was within the stones of Brennyn Hall. *It's just a habit of your behavior,* I hear Martha explain in my mind. *You can't change it if you can't see it.* How quickly those familiar behaviors return! The server slops my bowl in front of me and some of my food spills out the side and onto the table. I sigh. Contempt is to be expected when you choose to irritate Brenn with your ignorance.

I straighten my back. I have grown. *I know who I am!*

I don't bother fighting my shoulders when they slump. *No I don't.*

The workers' heads bob up and down like chickens at a feeder as they eat their meal. This is exactly where she wants us. Uniformed and obedient and unquestioning. I have simply moved from one Hall to another. Chanting and singing the same words over and over until they lose all meaning and joy is the same as wandering powerful passageways that lead nowhere—and just as impotent.

The Mystery always asks me to dismiss the things that the kinship now tells me to favor. There is nothing different here than in the streets of Muscone, Ferce Point or Sirban. If the kinship isn't safe, where should the called go? The broken? Will their spirits be crushed, heated by guilt and poured into molds of kinship expectations? How are their gifts to be released if they only become uniformed keepers of the Traditions and of Feeney's book of shame? Brenn complains about waste when there is so much potential wasted here in this room.

I curl up on my mat and wait for the others in the sleeping lodge to calm and settle for sleep, for their breathing to become more rhythmic. It won't be long now. When it does, I leave the lodge and make my way through the darkened fields to Martha's hut. The night is still, but not at all cold.

My hand stays on the unhooked latch of the gate for the longest time. Martha coughs quietly inside the hut, and a herder stretches in his sleep on a mat that lies across her doorway. I watch and I wait and I think, but there's no way to get into the hut without disturbing the snoring barrier between us. I hold my breath and slowly unloop the rope from the gatepost. I don't even step inside the garden but kneel down to reach around the garden wall and roll one jar of vinegar and one jar of honey towards me. Once they are safely nestled in the grass beside me, I re-loop the gate, lift a jar under each arm and sneak my way along the garden wall and out into the open field where I can finally break into a run towards the forest.

Powerless. That's how I feel. My jaw squeezes my teeth together. If Martha wants me to feel things, then this is how I feel.

I lug the jars through the forest, resting them on my hips as I walk. I'll be fine as long as I don't trip. I should have brought a third jar to put her syrup into but instead I'll make a larger and more potent batch inside the honey jar. I'll make sure I stuff extra hyssop into the half-filled honey jar before I shake it up with the vinegar inside. Martha always prefers honey to vinegar anyway.

I mean to sigh but it escapes my mouth as a grunt. Powerless. How can I solve the problem if I don't have the tools?

How can I gather herbs if I can't get into the forest?

How can I feed her syrup if a herder lies across my path?

I stop walking, right there in the middle of the forest, caught up in a thought that seems to require all my attention. The tools in the fields, the broken ones, they keep us dependent, powerless and exhausted. The Hall demanded I solve impossible problems and punished me no matter what answer I chose. Is it really any wonder

I surrendered? I was powerless. As I begin to walk again, a question rises up inside me. I don't know if it comes from the Mystery, from Martha, or if it's something I imagine Thomas would say. It doesn't really matter who asks because the question still sits there waiting for an answer I cannot give.

If you find the tools you seek, will you be brave enough to use them?

⚜

I work in the field alone the next day, tilling with a broken hoe that bounces as I work, using twice as much energy to perform half the task. Some men heighten the fences and place reeds of sharp blackthorn in the gaps to stop the people that now camp outside the kinship from coming in. The blackthorn tree produces the dye for our smocks, creating our identity and telling a story to anyone watching. I think its jagged thorns in the fence does exactly the same thing. The campers haven't asked for anything, just a sense of protection that being in the valley and close to the kinship brings from the unrest. I watch them set up their camps and remember how thankful Thomas and I were when we found the valley, to breathe at last. I imagine their hearts relaxing and I wonder how many of them will be finally be sleeping a deep, restful and fearless sleep tonight.

I'm thankful no one goes out of their way to talk to me during mealtimes and after lessons, and I spend more time glancing at Martha's hut than I do on watching the threshold. I managed to sneak her the jar of syrup with her meal, but other than delivering it to her under the watch of the herder we have had no time to talk. I surprised myself with how firm I was with the herder.

"Why is she being guarded?" I demanded.

"She's not. I'm only here to help if she calls out."

"I could easily do that."

"Brenn asked that I take care of this."

This? Martha is a *this?*

Martha interrupted. "Don't worry too much about what they are doing. Focus on what you are doing."

I let my mind wander wherever it wants to go as I work and try to stay calm amongst the jumble of happiness, worry and disappointment that flows between my heart and my head. It's not until the next morning I begin to notice no one going out of their way to greet me. No one smiles at me, and it's not because they're solemn—they're friendly enough with each other. Any discussion is clipped and as shrill as Brenn's voice. It feels like the dress being pulled so tight by Eshnae that I can't breathe.

The herder strolls from the herb garden along the sheep track on his way to the high lodge, and I sneak into the hut and fall beside Martha's mat and rest my face to her hand. How I've missed her. We share silence for a while as she strokes my face and hair. I know she has felt my tears with her hands.

"I have been shunned," I admit in a whisper.

I am surprised that she attempts a chuckle. "And what will you do about it?"

"I don't know."

"Yes, you do," she says. "You just need some time to see it."

I understand. She's spoken many times about the conflict between the head and the heart. And that it's the silence that becomes the translator. Her hands continue to stroke my hair and I wait for her to say something that will fill me with hope. "They'll be safe with you, all of them. The Eariss is a mirror. They'll see themselves in you."

Confused, I sit up and reach for her jar of syrup, open the cork and sniff inside. It can't have fermented by now. "Like the Fercies?" I say, still trying to make sense of what she said. I don't even own a mirror.

The door bangs open and the tea-drinking herder points to the jar in my hand. "What's that? And why are you here?"

I stand. "I was bringing her some herbs and checking she's been taking her syrup."

Martha chimes in with a smile, "Feeling better already, and it's only been a day."

"Get back to the fields before Brenn sees you," he says and widens his stance to fill the doorway.

Before Brenn sees you. Is he being helpful or controlling? I bow and show him the jar in my hand before placing it on the flagstones. "Make sure she always has this by her mat where she can reach it and help her to stay upright as it loosens the phlegm." He watches closely and listens as I draw closer to the door. "It's best for the kinship that she recovers; she has much knowledge."

I slide between the herder and the door frame, its wooden edge scraping deep into my back, and I turn my face away from his leaning presence. "This place'll be yours," he breathes, "...once she's gone."

J ust before the mid meal the herder leaves the walled garden
with a basket of herbs destined for the high lodge. The herbs
stick out at odd angles from the basket and roots with clumps
of earth on them bounce with the pace of his walk. The kitchen
mustn't have told him they only need the leaves, not the whole
plant. The eagerness to impress Brenn at her harvest meal takes
away from the grateful celebration it's supposed to be, and everyone seems preoccupied with their own strategies. Including me.

From his path along the sheep track, the herder nods to me in
the lower field and even though I return his nod, this particular
behavior only reminds me I'm still not sure of his character. As I
understand it, this signal means he will pretend he hasn't noticed I
am nearby when he leaves and that I may visit Martha without fear.
Is he friend or foe? Perhaps he doesn't even know that himself.

In only a few days Martha's cough has almost disappeared.
Within a few more days she'll be back in the garden and we'll
figure out how to deal with Brenn and this strange herder with

the confusing behavior, the one whose return I watch for from the open door of the hut as I tend to Martha. I know that on his return when he is halfway down the track I have time to say my goodbyes and be beyond the wall before he gets too close to it, and to me.

"Is he kind to you?" I ask her as I watch him disappear behind the sleeping lodges in the distance.

"As kind as you expect a herder to be."

I fill her pitchers with water and tidy her hut while she talks about the thoughts she's had during the day with no one to share them with. "There's something I must tell you," she says. "There's a riddle in your life you need to understand,"

I giggle at her. "Won't it cease to be a riddle if I understand it?"

She pats the side of her mat. "Stop being a dolt and come here and listen. Quickly."

I check for the herder once more and take my place beside her bed.

"So here is your riddle. It's that your call may cost you everything you desire, but also deliver all you desire at the same time."

I nod and rub my hand down her arm. She's lost a little weight, but she'll be well soon. I've already decided that I'll share my half bowl with her and have spent my time in the fields imagining my answers to her protests. I don't understand her riddle, but I don't really care.

"I don't know what I'd do without you," I say and kiss her forehead.

She waves me away with her hand. "You don't need me. All the answers are already here." She points to my chest, then tilts her head slightly. "You're not imagining those answers that rise up inside you, you know—is that what you need to hear? Someone else's words to make you stand taller? You stand tall from within, not without." She shakes her head. "I can't teach you the things you can only learn from yourself."

But she's taught me so much already. I'm stronger, more solid, as if the parts of me that had disintegrated to dust were somehow transforming themselves into something tangible and reforming a part of me that was strong. Strong and real.

I shake out the blanket that's been rolled behind her back and she coughs again, a rattling, productive cough, before she settles into her upright position.

"Don't fuss, all is well," she says, and I release my unconscious frown. An air of excitement fills her dark hut, an anticipation of something wonderful. She must feel it too and rubs her hands together. "So close. I will see you come into your fullness. I will see you bloom."

She makes me smile. I imagine myself blooming like a flower with a million petals that needed to know where they belonged first, and how she's like a gardener that coaxes each one out one by one. I look around her little hut and think about how magnificent this woman is, how wise, how comforting. She belongs in the greatest Halls of Lewtshire, not some dingy stone hut in a field. "Do you ever worry about your choice, dear Martha? You could have done something grand."

"I did. I waited for you."

Martha nods towards the door. I've forgotten to check for the herder. "He's coming," I say and slip through the door, but I'm not quick enough through the garden and I meet him by the gate. His demeanor is rough, sour. Perhaps Brenn has had words with him. I know the agitation she brings on all too well. Has she discovered that he lets me visit Martha? Has he taken punishment on my behalf?

"Get to the harvest meal."

"I could stay here and you could go if you prefer," I suggest.

"Go!"

My skin prickles with tension. The herder's face sets like stone and a crashing wave of fear washes my previous excitement away. What waits for me in the high lodge? My heart thumps so hard in my chest it hurts to draw breath, so I stand and stare at him. I don't know what to do.

So I smile and I obey.

And a knife twists in my gut.

The settings inside the high lodge are the same, nothing seems out of the ordinary and I take my solitary place at the end of the long table. During the harvest meal, Brenn doesn't follow the Traditions that require a ritual of gratitude and wellness but chooses instead to explain how our rest times will be shortened and staggered to increase the kinship's yield. The others agree, wishing to see the kinship become as productive and wealthy and beautiful as any other village. Even if the kinship was never meant to operate as a village.

She places fear in their hearts by railing about the uprising and imminent destruction if the kin don't adhere to her words. Suspicion builds among everyone and particularly any new travelers that Brenn allows through her fortified gates.

"Perhaps they should be turned out," some whisper. "Perhaps they are part of the uprising, sent to destroy us, our crops and our tradition."

When we first arrived, there was simply a threshold. Now there is a gate guarded by herders. Protecting the Traditions according to Brenn. When I'm in the fields I often watch the camps outside the fences. Brenn says they're not called, not chosen, so they can't share in the kinship's bounty. Instead they forage in the forest for their food. For now, they are safe. Just like me. How long will it be before the Trothsmen find their way into the valley? Thomas always says 'people talk' and it won't be long until they find the path behind the tree. And the unrest will find its way into the valley. Then it won't matter whether anyone is from Muscone, Ferce Point, Sirban or from the kinship. There will be no more difference. Doesn't Brenn see that? We are all no different. What will matter is how we treat each other. Why can't we start treating each other well now instead of grasping onto the old ways that just don't work anymore? Attacking each other in fear instead of understanding the fear.

Powerless. That's how I feel. Like I'm watching a wild river wash away everything I ever understood. Fear controls the behavior of people all through the land, and now the kinship and through the valley. Martha said fear makes men do crazy things, and I think back to Guthrie's steam machine and the spot fires of fear we fan in each other when we let fear have a foothold. When we react instead of respond. I watch a vision of the whole land being swallowed up by a fear robe that squeezes all hope from within it and paralyzes those with the power to make any changes. Martha always spoke about power. I don't have any power. I am useless and hopeless. Unable to speak and now shunned. The kin continue eating and talking among themselves and the heaviness of my thoughts cover me so completely I don't want to move at all.

I close my eyes and go in search of the Mystery. I imagine myself fighting through thick vines to find its stillness and finally there it is. It waits to soothe me, balance and calm me. I breathe deeply and try to relax amidst the surrounding noise of the high lodge.

As my heartbeat stills and aches begin to leave my body, the Mystery asks me a question.

If you find the tools you seek, will you be brave enough to use them?

A shove to my shoulder pushes me off balance and the smiling face of a young herder appears beside me on the bench. His grin is as cheeky as Thomas's and his friendliness melts away the annoyance I first felt. Other faces around us smile at our antics and I welcome a sense of belonging that I didn't even know I had missed until this moment. He nudges me again, chuckling as if he's about to share a story in jest. If only he knew how much I need my spirits lifted right now. I laugh too, eager and ready to join his lightheartedness.

"Yes?" I ask and return his smile.

"Your crone's dead."

M artha's hut is cold.

As if when she left the earth she took all warmth with her. Nothing moves. Nothing sounds except for the small puffs of breath that stagger from my mouth now that I have stopped running.

She looks sweet in her sleep, content even. She lies flat on her mat, her arm draping loosely to the side so her knuckles almost touch the floor. I drop to my knees on the flagstones and slide under her arm, bending it so her hand rests on my head. It's still warm enough for hope to momentarily stir in my chest before it silently slips away and joins her under the blanket covering her body. I cling to this moment and the last of her warmth, scared that moving away from her will make this moment true. And so I hold my hand on hers and I somehow manage to breathe in and out, in and out, with a million stone petals weighing on my chest until her hand is cold.

Her hand feels thick and silent, but I still hold it as I rise to sit by the mat. I press her hand between my palms and carefully match our fingers together. The tops of her fingers stand tall above mine and dirt and dust track their way through her fingerprints like tiny pathways. Nothing at all like the clean hands I admired when we first arrived, yet these are the purest I'd ever known. Voices in the fields distract me and I'm grateful no one will disturb us until sunrise when they'll come to collect her body for the pyre.

The water in the bucket isn't too cold. It releases the same scent I bathed in when I arrived each time it ripples and swishes under the cloth in my hand. It's fresh and clean and washed my previous life away from me for life in the kinship. Now I gladly use the same water to clean the kinship from Martha. To wash every trace of this place and its treatment of her from her skin. My voice breaks even though I only speak to her in whispers.

"Thank you," I say. "Thank you for waiting."

My fingers rake her hair and I thread her beloved chamomyle through its locks. "I don't know any lullabies, Martha...." But I sing my sweetest version of the crown of fire song that Eshnae taught me. The extra chamomyle I kept aside scrunches in my hands and pushes its fragrance through the air before I close her hands around it and kiss her forehead. As her shroud folds around her and I tuck and cover her body, my arms feel as heavy as rocks, and I fight against my back as it tries to push me to the ground. I sit alongside her shrouded body and the heaviness of her loss presses against my need to breathe. Each breath becoming a fence I need to clear to survive. In and out, in and out.

"Yes," I whisper to her shroud. "I know what I need to do. I will go, and I will feel."

***

T he forest welcomes me as I fall to my knees in grief, humming louder than I have ever heard before, thousands of arms reaching towards me. Holding and supporting me through the aches and tears that threaten to rip my chest apart, big enough to swallow me whole. Their song continues, rising and falling with the waves of pain, vibrating through me like a swarm of bees and finally drawing the most unbearable pain away from me like a poultice. The heaviest pain comes relentlessly like the waves at Ferce Point, battering me again and again until the sharpest points are worn down and made bearable by sharing each crash with the Mystery. I keep my body flat to the earth, as close to my beloved safety as I can manage. The earth absorbs my tears and eventually replaces despair with tender and raw acceptance.

I wander the forest and collect some of Martha's favorite plants and remember her lessons. Another wave of grief reminds me of when I thought Thomas had fallen from the cliff and how this time, even through the pain, I am peaceful. This grief is not of anger and fear, but thankfulness, gratefulness and acceptance. The sun is beginning to set as I head back, my basket filled with remembrances of Martha. The day should provide me with enough light to stop in the herb garden and add some fragrances to my final gift to her.

❧❦❧

The quietness of the sheep track splinters the closer I get to the high lodge. The evening meal has finished and the herders channel people to their sleeping lodges. The shadows do well to hide me until the commotion passes and the lodge empties. I creep inside to a quiet corner table and light my candle. Should I empty my basket, lay my collection out for ease? No, I'll draw from it as I create and keep its contents close to my heart.

Although I'm alone now, I might be disturbed at any time. Brenn still wanders the lodges and herders make checks when people are missing—although I don't expect they'll bother checking for me tonight. My eyes close and grief washes over me again, my tears quietly escaping in thanks for the life that loved me and understood me. A soul who answered her own call by attending to mine. The thoughts in my head come and go, and pictures appear in my mind as I remember her lessons and her laugh. I reach into the basket for the ivy and begin to weave.

The ivy winds around itself as I gently guide it to create a circle, and thoughts of her love comfort me. I weave in some sweet alder and bluebells and thank her for loyalty. The fresh and sweet scent of the melissa sweeps some of the pain away and reminds me of warm days, and a smile stretches my lips and catches some of my tears. Among the intricacies of the weaving, leaves and stems crush and release their oils. A small gasp jolts my body; the leaves of hawthorn and the petals of a wild rose are for me. The Mystery hums softly inside me and I smile again. My heart is supported and intimately known by something greater than the whole kinship. I am alone in my grief, but I am not alone.

The completed wreath rests on my fingers and the dull ache behind my eyes threatens to stab into my head. My palms slide along the table, sweeping any leftover stems and leaves into the basket, freezing in place when I hear footsteps enter the lodge.

Please don't be Brenn.

Please don't be Brenn with some ridiculous notion of sorrow.

I don't know what I might say. I don't know what I might do.

I don't want conversation. I don't want anything. I want to be left alone. I wonder if she'd consider it punishable not to speak to her in the dark when you're not even supposed to be there. I blow out the candle, but the moonlight still makes the shadows visible. The footsteps move closer and I inhale through my teeth, ready to pretend all is well. Thomas glances at the wreath in my hand, my swollen eyes and now trembling lip. I open my mouth to tell him about the wreath but no words come out, only a wail.

He scoops me into his arms. "I must be back in Sirban by morning."

Is it ungrateful to reject a beautiful day? The sky will continue to be blue, the breeze just as freshening and the grass just as green whether I acknowledge them or not. Martha would say every day is beautiful, it's only our thoughts that make it so. Is it a waste then, or perhaps some kind of ruin, to send a pyre's smoke into a clear sky? I imagine the sky is so vast it will just absorb Martha's memory into its own, and her ashes will return to the earth she loved.

I'm yet to see the beautiful death that Martha described as she tumbled soil through her fingers. A group of kin gather close to the fence line in the lower field and watch the final preparations for the ceremony. The herder from Martha's hut watches me intently. How convenient for him that I am now alone. They mingle amongst themselves, but I keep myself separate. In a few strides I could be with them, in a few strides I could *be* them. It's more comfortable here to the side of their group. Alone.

There is no beautiful death. Death is still currency.

Brenn dutifully performs the ceremony according to her beloved Traditions, occasionally stopping to sigh with disinterest. My hands clench onto the side seams of my smock, but what would I prefer? That outsiders were here and Brenn perform an act of sorrow and remorse? In some small way she *is* being truthful, and as swiftly as a breeze brushes past us, the truth being here in this field with us suddenly seems very important.

Now that the men have built her pyre high enough, those present follow the Traditions and add their final branches to the heap before its lighting. Some place the sticks with respect, some toss them, eager to return to their days activities. I will mourn their crone. The one who chose to treat them respectfully no matter how they treated her. The Mystery was here, right before their eyes, and they didn't see it—they ridiculed it and called it names.

Thank you, Martha. My stick drops between two larger branches and disappears within the pile. I hold the wreath close to my chest and step back to watch the lighting as the others walk back to their duties. What am I meant to do now? The stone wall of the garden draws a dark gray line across the field behind me. Apart from the plants that wait for me to tend them, there's nothing for me here.

The fire takes hold on the pyre, heat flashes on my face like strong rays of the sun, but I don't look away.

Am I even strong enough to do anything on my own?

There's no Hall here, there's no forest, no Thomas, no Martha, nothing.

And who are you when there is nothing? Tell me that! Martha's voice sounds in my head and the heat of the fire flashes at my face.

But I don't know what I'm doing. Who will teach me?

Who do I ask for answers now?

An answer as familiar as Martha's words rises within me, as familiar as the Mystery's.

Me. I have the answers; all I have to do is listen. Why was I so blind before? Moments in time flash in my mind and fit together like a puzzle, glued together by Eshnae's words.

". . . the world waits for you to see, this world needs you to see."

A cool breeze pushes into my face as my mind shows me the door opened wide—all I need to do is step through it. The wreath passes gently through the flames and I'm overwhelmed with gratitude for Martha and for this moment. The heat releases the oils from the wreath and burns them away like the ash of incense. I draw a deep breath and hold it then let it move away from me as surely as my past has already done.

It's easier to flow than fight against the river. I'm tired of fighting this river, the one Maeve called my life. As I drop my defenses against it, stop fighting the flow, everything slows almost to a stop and then I gain a new momentum. It's barely recognizable at first, a faint movement in my chest that builds in intensity and spins and turns like a wheel on fire, spinning so fast that it threatens to spin from its axle. The energy is so deep within me there's no escape from its excitement, its drive and its passion. Faster and faster it spins, as though I am about to be overtaken by its motion and splinter all over this field.

I run to the herb garden and leap the wall. I rip and tear at the white flower heads, pulling them from the ground by the roots. I gather bundles, as much as I can carry, and I stand before her pyre and twist and squeeze and break the stems until all of their life is released.

Then I throw them.

I cover Martha's pyre with a sacrifice of every piece of crushed chamomyle I can find.

They burn with her, twisting and releasing until they have nothing left to give. My lungs sting with both smoke and the freshest of air as my hands lean on my knees and I puff in exhilaration and happiness and the strangest sense of freedom and lightness. The workers in the fields stand and watch, two girls murmur with their heads together, another man scratches his head, but most look towards the high lodge. Brenn watches from the landing, her wings out in a silhouette of contempt as she stares at me from her perch. My usual response would be to shrink, to curl in a ball and pretend I didn't exist, to make apologies, become invisible. But my body does something strange.

Boldness floods my veins, my feet find their strength in the soil, my spine lengthens and my chin lifts towards Brenn.

Who do I think I am?

I'm in a place beyond thought now.

This time I know.

I am the Eariss.

A Note from the Author

Thanks for reading *Crown of Fire*. I hope you enjoyed Ashling's story and that you'll continue to follow her journey through the Awenmell Series.

❦

I truly appreciate the feedback I get from my readers. If you enjoy my work, please consider leaving a review at your store of purchase and on review websites such as Goodreads.

Reviews not only help other readers find books they might enjoy, they can be instrumental in a book's success.

❦

You can also share your Awenmell experience with friends and on social media. I love it when my friends recommend books to me, don't you? #awenmell #crownoffire

ACKNOWLEDGEMENTS

It's easy to think of writers as solitary beings, hidden away tapping on keyboards at all hours of the day and night. And while this image is mostly true, it's the support that writers receive when they emerge from their creative sanctuary that makes all the difference. The 'team' that waits on the outside to encourage, wipe tears away, and listen to ramblings, is the mainstay of any creative endeavor. Simply put, without an author's team, books just don't get written.

I've been blessed with an incredible support network of friends and family who freely gave their time to help bring the Awenmell Series to life.

The early team; Michelle Capper, Sarah Patterson, and Joanne Smith, who read initial drafts and always rescued me when I feared I would drown in self-doubt. Thank you. I'm deeply grateful for your insights, but mostly for your enthusiasm. Your excitement kept me at the keyboard more than you will know.

Love and thanks to those who joined the team later in the process, Amy and Anthony Deamon, Ashlynn O'Brien, and Lynda Pedder. Your 'fresh eyes' helped prepare this book for the wider world.

❦

Big-hearted thanks to the talented professionals who brought Crown of Fire to life.

To the amazing Lauren Sapala, thank you for understanding my process, and using your content editing skills to make the story shine.

A big thank you to Rebecca Hendry for polishing Crown of Fire to a sparkle with your copy-edit.

Many thanks to Heather Musingo for her inspired art work and cover design, and to Ali Strachan for her copywriting expertise.

And finally, to my beloved Stewart, who has not for one minute expressed any doubt in this project, nor that I could accomplish it. I'm so glad I get to do life with you. Thank you.

About the Author

Lisa King is a international award winning author and amateur nature photographer who lives near Brisbane, Australia. When she's not writing, you can find her hiking though lush rainforests, and exploring the wide open spaces of the Scenic Rim, taking notes for her novels and capturing the diverse and complex ecosystems where she feels most at home.

Lisa loves to transport readers to worlds where the heroes have everyday struggles, flaws and inner conflicts, and the natural world is part of the nurturing and healing process. As an advocate for education and empathy for trauma survivors, Lisa hopes her books will encourage readers on their own healing paths.

You can connect with Lisa on social media @lisakingauthor and join her readers circle at www.lisakingauthor.com

ALSO BY LISA KING

AWENMELL SERIES

Crown of Fire - Awenmell Series : Book One

Rise - Awenmell Series : Book Two

AWENMELL CHARACTER SERIES

Magic Man - Awenmell Characters 1

Eshnae - Awenmell Characters 2

STANDALONES

Dandelion Wishes – The Untold Story of Coral Maxwell-King

www.ingramcontent.com/pod-product-compliance
Lightning Source LLC
Chambersburg PA
CBHW030340120726
47901CB00007B/1850